Death Wore Black

Bill Redding

Death Wore Black

Bill Redding

Wexford Press

Death Wore Black

By Bill Redding

Wexford Press
2401 Haight Avenue
Eldersburg MD 21784

Library of Congress Control Number: 2010936786

Paperback ISBN: 978-1-60019-102-2

Casebound ISBN: 978-1-60019-202-9

Printed and bound in The United States of America

DEDICATION

God has blessed me with an angel, my beautiful wife, Ann, without whom I would decay into dust—without whom naught would I pen.

Prologue

Pulaski, A Suburb of Milwaukee

1966

Seated behind a two-way mirror, with a camera in his lap, the detective watched men and boys use the men's room facilities. *A disgusting assignment,* he thought, *but it was easier than working the peace march on this hot and humid Saturday morning.* The washroom, in the Pulaski Public Library, was enlarged and renovated in 1958. In response to some molestation allegations, a two-way mirror was installed in the men's washroom. The surveillance side of the mirror was in a small, musty, storage room without air-conditioning. The only cool air in the room came from a small fan near the door. When he took a drag on his cigarette, he had to face away from the mirror so the glow would be hidden from the washroom side of the mirror. Suddenly two boys walked in, talking, evidentially friends. They used the urinals and left.

For the next hour, there were intermittent users of the washroom mostly grammar school boys.

A man with black pants, black shoes, and a black windbreaker entered the first stall.

The detective picked up the telephone receiver, dialed and waited until there was an answer. "It's me," he whispered. He listened for a few moments. "Yeah, I know it's a disgusting assignment." After another few seconds of listening, he said, " it beats working the street with all those stupid calls and those stupid students and their demonstrations—like today. And don't forget all that goddam paperwork." He moved his coffee from the center of the desk, then swung his feet up onto the desk crossing his ankles. He took a cigarette from his pack, and said " Yeah, see you later."

Twenty minutes passed while Black Pants remained in the first stall, but the door was now ajar about an inch. Maybe another pervert, the detective thought, as he adjusted his camera on the desk. He had captured two perps last Saturday. One was a sixteen-year old he turned over to the youth division—not much paper work and no court. The second was the middle-aged owner of a local sporting goods store. The detective gave him a pass, and the perp gave him a brand new Remington shotgun. *Great, working alone didn't have to bother splitting any take with a partner* , he thought. Black Pants was the only one in the washroom when a pimply-faced teenager came in and went directly up to the wash basin under the mirror. The boy leaned closer to the mirror. The detective held his cigarette down low. *Don't get any closer,* the detective thought, *or you might be able to see me.*

Suddenly the first stall door opened. The boy turned his head. The detective couldn't hear the whispered conversation. The boy turned and shook his head—no. Black Pants opened the stall door a little wider, inaudibly speaking to the boy. The boy turned again, then turned then slowly walked over to the first stall. The detective had to stand at the far right end of the mirror in order to see into Black Pants stall. From this oblique angle, he was able to see Black Pants raise himself as the boy approached him. From this angle, he could only see the right rear side of the boy. It appeared that Black Pants was reaching for the boy's crotch. At that moment the detective saw Black Pants face, he snapped the picture—not realizing that when he stood to obtain that advantageous angle, the chair he'd been sitting in rolled to a position directly behind him. He turned to go after Black Pants he bumped the chair causing it to roll against a metal cabinet sounding a loud noise. He fumbled in the dark and struggled to the storage room door.

He ran down a short hallway, which intersected with the hallway from the bathroom. He saw Black Pants rounding the corner into the library proper, then out the front door. *Damn, he's fast,* the detective thought as he ran out the front door. He saw Black Pants far ahead disappear into the crowd of war protestors.

Run, asshole, I got your picture, I'll find you!

1

THE PRIEST COULDN'T ASK JACK FOR A BLOND, BLUE-EYED BOY. They were too hard to find in this Slavic parish. A knock on the door interrupted the priest's thoughts. "Come in," the priest raised his voice in response to the knock. The study door opened a bit, and Jack Hamlin stuck his head inside.

"Hello, Father. Ah, someone here to meet you."

"Come in, come in." Jack's thin frame slid through the doorway followed by a young boy. "This is David Merriman, Father. He's in the eighth grade here at St. Mike's and is..."

The priest smiled warmly and set down his fountain pen. "I know who he is. David has assisted me at mass, haven't you, son?" The priest stood and brushed a wrinkle from his black suit coat. "Thank you, Jack. You can go now."

Jack nodded and backed out the door, closing it softly behind him.

The priest walked around the mahogany leather-topped desk. He allowed David time to absorb the opulent study of St. Michael's rectory. The boy stared wide-eyed at the floor-to-ceiling shelves stuffed with musty, faded books, the windows covered by red velvet draperies and a well-worn oriental rug over parquet floors. To the lower-middle-class boys of St. Mike's congregation, the rectory looked very grand, indeed.

The priest waited while David felt its full impact.

"Here, David, have a seat." As the priest gestured toward the cracked leather couch, he remembered the first time he saw the boy in the sacristy. David Merriman was a blond, blue-eyed cherub, an angel, a pure white lamb, and a perfect candidate. Again Jack Hamlin had done very well.

"Son," he began, settling in next to the child, "one of my duties is to advise and instruct boys interested in the priesthood. Jack tells me you may be interested in serving God." He sat with his back against the couch and his right arm resting along the top of the couch behind David.

"Well, sort of." David pivoted in his seat, moving his thigh away from contact with the priest. "Jack, he asked me what I thought. Like, would I like to be one? I said, you know, maybe. However, it was really Jack's idea. Guess every boy once in a while wonders what it'd be like to be a priest, and all."

"Yes, but Jack recognizes something special in you. He does not bring every boy in here to talk with me."

"Yes, Father . . ."

"Do you like being an altar boy? Assisting?"

"Oh, yes, Father. And helping with the paper drive. My dad and me, we've collected newspapers from all over the neighborhood."

He saw the corners of the boy's mouth tip up with a smile—a beautiful smile over even, pearl like teeth, glistening with saliva. Images of his own youth surged through his mind, memories of himself and his own father.

The study suddenly seemed stuffy, and with shaking hands he loosened his Roman collar, prying imaginary fingers from his throat, allowing air to quell his anxiety. He held his breath, then took deep, and measured inhalations, wanting to control the rapid beat of his heart.

"It may surprise you to hear this, boy," he said with a heartiness he didn't feel, "but I wasn't sure myself at first. Most priests aren't sure in the beginning. You have me to help you, to advise you."

The boy's large, round eyes avoided those of the priest. "Consider me a representative of God on earth. Remember the Twenty-third Psalm? I am as your shepherd, and you are my lamb." *And what a beautiful lamb,* he thought. "You've read that psalm?"

"Of course, Father." Uncertainty rippled across his face. "But I never memorized it. It was never an assignment."

The priest leaned forward and picked up a plastic-laminated card from the coffee table in front of them. As he sat back, his knee rested against David's knee. The boy had no room to withdraw. "Here, this is a gift for you."

David took the card and looked at it. "The Twenty-third Psalm."

"You must love the shepherd and trust the shepherd. I am your shepherd, my sweet little lamb."

David glanced at his watch. It was child's jewelry, with a bright plastic band and a multicolored face. "I have baseball prac..."

"Let me see it a moment." Reaching to retrieve the card, he engulfed the child's hand in the motion, letting his fingers slowly slide along David's. He held his breath again, this time relishing the excitement. "So many wonderful phrases in this psalm. 'He maketh me to lie down in green pastures.' Don't you like the idea of lying down in cool, green grass?"

"Yes, Father."

The priest's arm slid down from along the back of the couch to David's shoulders.

Again the boy looked at his watch. "I'd better go. Before practice I have to finish today's paper pickup."

The rejection infuriated the priest. Was this child too young to appreciate the honor of spending time with the priest? "David, you are very special to me, to the Church. I'm very fond of you. Certain levels or spheres of relationships are acceptable to God, and they are offered only to those who have been chosen to carry on His work."

"Me chosen?" David moved to the edge of the couch.

"But you were sent to me because you expressed a desire for the priesthood." He layered a smile over his frustration. "You're an excellent altar boy. You have most of the attributes necessary for acceptance to the seminary."

"Thank you, Father."

"Other areas may still be a little weak, but we'll work on those. I will help you, David. You and I can work on them together. Do you want to get a higher education and better your lot?"

The priest looked down at David's hands, crossed on his lap. They were scratched, with dirt under the uneven nails. However, the skin was fair, translucent, and the fingers long and elegant.

"No one in my family has gone on after high school. I'd like college, I guess. Jack says it's the best. But I don't know if my dad has the money. Probably I'll just go to work, like my brother and sister done."

The priest moved closer to the boy. "Now, David, money is no problem to the Church. You must trust me. I am the shepherd."

"Yes, Father."

He took both of David's hands in his left hand, not moving them from David's lap. "Trust me, David. Trust God."

"Yes, Father."

"David. I want you to memorize the twenty-third Psalm. We'll discuss it next time."

The boy looked up at him and smiled. "Yes, Father."

"Friday, you come to me for confession. I'll be in church on Friday afternoon. And let us not discuss our meetings and discussions about the priesthood with anyone—not even your parents—until you're sure what you are going to do. Understand?"

"Yes, Father."

"Are you sure?"

"Yes, Father."

The priest smiled with anticipation.

2

SERGEANT CASIMIR "SLAT" SCZLATSKI LOOKED DOWN AT THE CORPSE of Sam Tyrone, a man he'd known for years, the man who had changed the course of his life. The father figure who had made him smile and laugh; who had been his first father image; who had freed him from the orphanage; who had found him a family, and who had led him into police work. Sam was in his underwear, and the blue-steel revolver was still in his right hand. It appeared as though he'd been sitting on the side of the bed, then fell backward when the bullet lodged in his brain. Coagulated blood hardened along the right cheek and red speckles fanned across the white pillowcase.

Slat looked around the room with its old dresser, ancient wooden chair, bed, and tan metal wardrobe. His gaze stopped at Jenny who stood next to the foot of the bed—her sympathetic eyes appraising him. Grief and guilt twisted around his guts, but he couldn't vent the sorrow— there, then. Beside Jenny in the miserable cubicle were her partner, Detective Homer Braun, two uniformed patrol officers, and a police photographer

"Thirty fucking years a cop, and he has to do himself," Homer said in disgust. "Why the fuck do so many cops kill themselves?"

"Don't know, man." Slat shook his head. "You and Jenny handle the paper on this. I've got to get out of here."

"Sam have any family?" Jenny asked, sketching in her notebook.

Slat stopped in the doorway. "Nah. His parents long dead. He and Maisie divorced twenty, twenty-five years ago. Never had kids."

"Probably the closest person to him was his old partner, Ernie Pope," Homer suggested over his shoulder from the drawer he had started searching.

One of the uniformed men shook his head. "Sam and Ernie haven't gotten along in years, since they both left the detective bureau."

"Who found him?" Slat asked.

"Landlady." Homer opened another drawer. "She comes up to his room every morning to clean. Never heard the shot. She was at St. Mike's last night, playing bingo until eleven. I figure it happened before she got home. She says he had no company before she left at six-thirty, and no one else was in the house."

"Okay. Wrap it up. I'll go see the chief and let him know."

Slat's shift went into action, and he fled down the stairs. Halfway down he nearly collided with Father Julius, who was ascending the steps two at a time. "Hi, Father."

"Slat." Father Julius was the unofficial chaplain for the city of Pulaski. "Heard it's Sam Tyrone."

"Yeah."

"Sorry, Slat. I know what he meant to you. Natural causes?"

Slat shook his head.

"Suicide?"

"Appears."

"Oh, no. Religion?"

"Not really, Father."

"Never saw him in church." Father Julius looked up the stairway. Grim resignation darkened his earnest, clean-shaven face.

"Top of the stairs, Father."

As Father Julius hurried past, Slat combed his fingers through his thick, coarse brown hair. At thirty-eight, he had only a trace of gray, while Father Julius, a couple of years older, was all silver. *Father Julius,* Slat thought, *always here when you need him.*

As Slat stepped out onto the wooden front porch, a woman called his name. He looked up into the lens of a camera, then into the attractive face of a tall, shapely woman in a conservative suit.

"I'm Cheri Duncan, Sergeant. Are you in charge here?"

"At the moment," he answered, and kept walking toward his squad. "Milwaukee paper?"

Her long legs matched him stride for stride. "No, I'm with the *Pulaski Press.*"

He barked a laugh. "My sympathies." He got into his squad, slammed the door, and drove away. Slat glanced into his rearview mirror and saw Cheri Duncan standing next to the curb. "Pain in the ass," he said aloud.

* * *

Father Patrick Daley, eager to see his best friend, Tony Tattaglia, from their seminary days at Mundelein, had arrived at the Billy Mitchell Airport an hour early. Father Daley made special arrangements for the Vatican jet to park at Poole Tractor Company's private hangar on the west side of the main terminal.

It had been no surprise to Father Daley when his wild, carefree friend got kicked out of the seminary; but he still couldn't understand how Tony Tattaglia had made it through law school, then ended up in Rome, working as an anti-terrorist agent and negotiator for the Pope.

It was ironic, Patrick thought as he rode to the hangar, that a man who couldn't make it into the priesthood would be assisting the Milwaukee archdiocese with an errant priest. Patrick was also surprised; the archdiocese had never requested the Vatican's aid before—they simply transferred the priest to another parish or, in the case of an alcoholic, someplace to dry out.

However, new rules were in force now. Media publicity prompted discreet removal of the errant from the country. And that was what Tony was paid to do. With Father Daley's help, he would find the pedophile and take him to Rome—with or without his cooperation.

The jet rolled to a stop outside the hangar, and Father Daley, recognizing the tall man with black, curly hair and dark brown eyes, hurried toward it.

"Patty, me boy!" Tony cried out, imitating an Irish brogue.

"Tony, it's good to see you!" Father Daley said. They embraced and thumped each other on the back.

"How long has it been?"

"Twenty-two years." He didn't remember Tony's shoulders being so broad or his skin so dark.

"Wish it hadn't been so long, my friend," Tony said, standing back and grinning.

"And I wish we were not reuniting for this reason," Patrick said, taking his arm and guiding him toward the exit. "But we will do whatever is necessary, eh?"

* * *

As Slat drove across town toward the chief's house, he couldn't get Sam Tyrone out of his mind. When he was thirteen, Sam had spent time with Slat at a Milwaukee orphanage and found him a foster home with the Monkarian family. Hagop Monkarian, Sam's partner in the city's Detective Bureau, had been a terrific guy, and his wife, in Slat's opinion, had been an angel. The Monkarians even had a son, Armen, six months older than Slat. He had never been so happy in his young life and devoted himself to pleasing them. His gratitude to Sam had never paled.

Slat and Armen did everything together. Instead of joining a neighborhood gang like the other boys, they worked out with weights at a nearby gym. After high school, they joined the army together.

A few years later, while Slat and Armen were in Vietnam, a drunk driver killed their parents. Because Slat had never been legally adopted, he couldn't go home for the funeral. Returning to Milwaukee turned into an obsession for him. Months later, when his tour of duty was up, he left immediately for the States, while Armen re-enlisted.

Slat arrived home—only there was no home. Nobody was waiting for him. He found nothing but his foster parents' gravesites and un- abating loneliness—until he remembered Sam Tyrone. The older man had moved from Milwaukee to the smaller city of Pulaski, where he had joined the police department. He talked Slat into joining it, too, instead of Milwaukee's.

Hot tears burned Slat's eyes as he thought about all the other suicides in the department. Ten years ago one of the guys blew his brains out a week before retirement. Two others blew themselves away a year or two after retirement. He'd heard of many more instances, but he had known those three personally. And now Sam. Policemen killed themselves so often, suicide was known as "taking the Smith and Wesson cure."

But it had to be more than the pressures of the job, Slat thought as he turned north on Lincolnwood Avenue. All four men were divorced. None had kids, or their kids had little to do with them. The only real family they had were the other cops.

Slat parked in front of the chief's house, a modest bungalow on a quiet street. He found himself clutching the steering wheel tightly. He loosened his grip and reached to lock the passenger door when he saw his eyes in the rearview mirror. He gasped. Those blue eyes couldn't be his— they seemed too frightened. *My God,* he thought, *I have those things in common with those four suicides.* He sat back in the seat. "Get a hold of yourself, buddy," he said as he opened the car door. "You don't have to be alone. You could have Jenny or Theresa."

Slat walked up the cement walk to the yellow-brick house. Chief Martin Turski opened the door before Slat could knock. "Glad you made it so soon," Turski said.

Slat had never seen the chief in casual clothes. He looked almost ridiculous in them, as if his knitted shirt and chino trousers were a Halloween getup. In a suit the chief appeared to have no neck on his squat, square-shouldered body. Seeing him now in a polo shirt, Slat saw that Turski, in fact, had no neck. The chief was not quite fifty years old, but he looked tired, years older.

Slat followed him to a book-lined den, where the chief closed the door behind them and pointed with his knotty-knuckled, huge hand to an overstuffed chair. "Was it suicide?"

"Yes, sir." Slat lowered himself into the chair. "Seems that way."

The chief seated himself across the glass-topped coffee table. "Makes sense."

Slat was startled. "Sir?"

"Before we discuss Sam Tyrone, I want you to know that even though we haven't talked privately since I became chief in Pulaski, I am very well aware of who Casimir Sczlatski is."

Slat couldn't remember that the time someone used his first name.

"I try to know all my people."

Slat began to feel a little uncomfortable, not knowing what to expect.

Turski laughed. "Relax, Sergeant. I'm not going to pull any bones out of your closet and rattle them in front of your nose. You've been on the force for about fifteen years. Spent time in all divisions. Received several commendations—forgot exactly how many. You have the highest felony arrest record of anyone in the history of the department. And before you were appointed to sergeant, you were skipped over on four other sergeants' promotional lists. I assume that was internal politics."

Slat felt his face turning crimson. "Don't know, Chief. They told me I wasn't a team player."

"Love to fish, and you're single. I get it all correct?"

"Not quite. I'm divorced—ten years now."

"I see. Well, anyway . . . Tyrone was under secret investigation by the state's attorney general's office for accepting gambling payoffs. No hard evidence, just rumors. He was scheduled to be interviewed by the investigators Monday morning."

Slat felt the room tilt. He didn't know if now was a good time to tell the chief that Sam had been like an uncle to him. "Sir, why would they be conducting an investigation now? Payoffs can't be hidden from a street detective. Besides, nobody pays attention to gambling. Look at the clubs, even the churches! If any cop asked for a payoff on gambling, he'd be laughed off his beat!"

Chief Turski moved to the edge of his seat, and Slat could feel the man's narrowed eyes taking his measure. "A little passionate about the subject, aren't we, Sergeant?"

"Sorry, sir. I...I knew Sam when I was a kid. We had fun together."

"My sympathies, then," the chief said. "Didn't mean to put you in a compromising position." The single lamp off to the side cast shadows, exaggerating the man's furrowed face, small protruding ears, and pug nose.

"Thank you, sir. Our relationship dwindled over the last ten years or so. Sam was a loner. Just sort of withdrew from me. I'm feeling guilty, I guess, I wasn't there for him when he needed someone. But it won't affect my police responsibilities."

"No, I'm sure it won't. In fact, your connection with Sam convinces me you're the right man for the job."

"What job, sir?"

"Understand, Sergeant, that all this is off the record. I requested the investigation when I accepted this position, and nothing may turn up. It's like a new president of a firm who calls for an audit of the company's assets and liabilities. Let's call it an 'integrity audit.' When the investigation ended, the only policeman they had a tip on was Sam Tyrone."

"Sir." Slat thought the chief, a former Chicago district commander, was being a little paranoid. "If Sam was involved in payoffs, it had to have been many years ago. There have been no payoffs or any corruption since you've been here. Take my word for it, sir."

"That's good to hear, of course, but . . . Let's keep all this confidential. Tyrone wasn't proven guilty, so we'll let him rest with a clean record as a career law-enforcement officer. I'm telling you this because I want *you* to be absolutely sure what we have is a suicide, not a homicide."

"Yes, sir." As miserable as Slat had felt because of Sam's apparent suicide, now he felt even worse as he considered the possibility that his friend might have been murdered.

"Incidentally." The chief stood, indicating the meeting was over. "How was your vacation?" Slat stood. "Fine, sir. Spent most of the month fishing and just plain relaxing. Got back this morning."

"Glad to have you back. Sorry it was with such a sad occasion."

"Thank you, sir." Slat hesitated a moment. "The *Pulaski Press* was at the scene. Didn't know what to say. They'll be looking for you in the morning."

"So what else is new?" The chief smiled, but it didn't reach his eyes.

* * *

As his trusted sergeant drove down the street, Turski watched out the window. He knew by the book he should have brought this investigation to the attention of Slat's supervisor, Lieutenant Leon Lovemore. But he didn't trust Lovemore. He was too ambitious. Besides, Lovemore had been a detective during the time of the payoffs.

He knew all about Sam Tyrone and Casimir Sczlatski and felt particularly gratified Slat had brought it up voluntarily. Slat had been a troublemaker at the institution, and Sam had taught the kid how to play basketball, then got him a home. *Sam probably would have taken Slat into his own household,* Turski thought now, *but there was the racial thing.* Sam was black.

Feeling satisfied with how the meeting had gone, Chief Martin Turski reached into his pocket and reread a memorandum he'd brought home from work.

MEMORANDUM

City of Pulaski

To: Mayor

From: Alderman Archie Dunn,

Chairman, Finance Committee

Re: Hiring of females.

During the short period of time Chief Turski has headed the police department, he has hired five women as police officers.

We are too small a city to test whether or not women can handle this type of work.

These experiments should be left to the large cities. I suggest you advise Chief Turski that we discontinue this practice.

Archie Dunn had been snapping at his heels ever since he took over the police department, and every memo Dunn sent, he sent a copy to the mayor. Turski chuckled, knowing the mayor would never pay attention to Dunn's barking. The alderman had wanted to be chosen as police chief but come in second, behind Turski. It was as clear a case of sour grapes as Turski had ever seen.

3

SLAT WALKED THROUGH THE FRONT ENTRANCE TO THE DETECTIVE BUREAU, then passed through the citizens' service counter and the swinging gate into the restricted area. His people were already working. Hazy sunlight slanted through dusty windows as he strode between the two rows of eight desks to his glass-enclosed office, called the "glass cage," at the far end of the room. The desks, chairs, and file cabinets were painted dull gray. He shared his office with the other shifts detective sergeants. As soon as Slat sat down and lit a cigarette, Homer and Jenny came in. "The guys weren't surprised about Sam," Homer said, slouching into one of the chairs across from Slat's desk. "He'd been unhappy for years."

"Had his hands tested for powder residue–waiting for the report. Then we can wrap it up," Jenny told him, as she waved the floating cigarette smoke away from her face. "You ought to quit that."

"Talked to his old partner yet, Slat?" Homer asked.

"No. Called his house, Elinor said that Ernie's at the lake with no phone." Slat put the cigarette out. "I'll run up there and see him." Slat flipped through the report. "Did Sam leave a note?"

"Nothing," Jenny said. Slat felt as if he'd been punched. Not even a good-bye or explanation. Most suicide victims left a note. Maybe Turski's suspicion of a homicide was right.

"Probably Sam's way of saying fuck you all." Homer shrugged. "There's a new reporter from the Pulaski piss paper who asked me about you as we were leaving Sam's. She said you wouldn't give her the time of day."

"She'll have to talk to the chief," Slat said.

"She did," Jenny said. "But she said she wants to talk to you."

"She's got a nice ass," Homer said.

"She can get her information by reading the Milwaukee papers," Slat said. Jenny and Homer laughed.

"Her boss and the Pulaski paper do nothing but shit on us," Homer complained. "And then they have the balls to expect cooperation."

"Anything else?" Slat asked. "I'd like to get going—it's a long ride to Fox Lake." Homer shook his head. "Nah."

"Anything I can do? Slat . . ."

"Thanks, Jenny," he said. "I'm fine."

* * *

"If you're here to see me, I'm shoving off this pier in five minutes." Ernie's voice echoed around the green-framed, blue waters of Fox Lake. "Grab a rod off the porch, and we're outta here." Slat had parked his car next to Ernie's pickup truck, alongside the big log-and-stone cabin. "Gotta talk to you," Slat hollered. "Brought my own gear."

"You wouldn't be here if it was good news," Ernie called back. Slat slammed his trunk closed, then walked to the pier, handed his rod, reel, and tackle box to Ernie, and climbed into the small boat. Slat laughed at the stubble pointing askew off Ernie's pointed chin. "You haven't shaved since you retired. Between the beard and your being so damned skinny, you look like an old hippie." Ernie grinned and rubbed his chin. "And I love it. No polishing shoes either. Even if I step in dog shit, I won't clean my shoes–buy another pair."

"Sounds great."

"And I hope it gets better. I retired a week ago, on my fiftieth birthday, after twenty-eight years. Elinor and I put the house in Pulaski up for sale. I'm ready for a total change—Florida in the winters, then back here for summer and fall. Until the house sells, Elinor'll stay there, and I'll be up here as much as possible, soaking up the sweet perfume of retirement." Sixty seconds later the thirty-five-horse engine was pushing them across Fox Lake. Slat was sitting on the forward seat, his back to Ernie. "You get the word about Sam?" Slat asked over the noise of the engine.

"What word?"

"Blew himself away two days ago." Slat didn't turn around. Ernie slowed the outboard. "Funeral?"

"This morning." After a few minutes of silence, Ernie said, "Guess I'll cast a few for him." Ernie's sidearm cast carried the lure out to meet the water. "Suicide for sure?"

"Looks like it."

"Figures. But you didn't drive all the way from Pulaski just to tell me that and fish." A breeze passed Ernie before it reached Slat. He wrinkled his nose. Ernie smelled as if he hadn't taken a bath since he retired. Reluctantly, Slat swiveled in his chair and faced the man.

"There were rumors about Sam. Thought I ought to check them out, to set the record straight." While waiting for a reply, Slat looked at Ernie's cabin. Besides that and the house in Pulaski, Ernie had a nice fishing boat, a couple of grown kids working in Milwaukee, and grandchildren. Nevertheless, Ernie had a wonderful wife. *He had a lot to look forward to,* Slat thought. People loved him. Ernie would have no reason to take "the cure." *What do I have?* Slat wondered, then pulled himself from his morose thoughts. "Are you sure there're fish in this lake?"

"Naw. That's why we've got hamburger in the 'fridge for dinner tonight." Ernie cast his line and talked about the old days. Slat personally knew a few of the old-timers Ernie mentioned. Some he hadn't heard about, and others he recognized as names from ancient rosters. He listened patiently, letting Ernie work his way around to talking about Sam. After three hours of fishing and reminiscing, Ernie finally opened up.

"Sam and I were good friends back then—as good as a white and colored could be in a city like Pulaski and a department like ours. He got some cases from me, but never did anything about them except a lot of whitewash. That's when we drifted apart. We had coffee once in a while through the years, but our friendship was never the same."

"What cases?"

"A homicide case around nineteen seventy. Two black gamblers—Stu Watson and Tiny Jackson, they were assassinated against a basement wall, shot from behind. A real execution." The smooth whine of the Mitchell reel was the only noise for a moment. "I heard about that case. Didn't the guy who did it die in prison?"

"So some people say. Got my doubts."

"Was Sam on the take?"

"Never saw him take a nickel." Ernie cast too hard, and the plug slapped against the water four feet from the boat. "Back then we made only five grand a year. Sam bought a new Lincoln or Caddy every other year. He wore two hundred dollar suits and wore this big diamond ring on his pinkie." Slat swatted a mosquito on the back of his neck. "Maybe his folks—"

"Bullshit," Ernie interrupted. "You know as well as I that his folks were dirt farmers from Mississippi. His dough came from gambling, Slat. There was lots of it. Some numbers, card games, tables, horses, dogs . . . Sam was in charge of gambling investigations, so we couldn't make a raid without his okay. You'd give him a tip, and he said he'd take care of it. There were a dozen regular locations, six separate organizations going. I believe Sam was getting a piece of the action from every one."

"Along with who else?" Ernie's round eyes stared a challenge into Slat's unblinking gaze. Then the man chuckled. "You remind me of myself, kid. To answer your question, don't know. Could guess, but I really don't know." Ernie looked away, far across the blue lake, while Slat said nothing. He knew he had to give Ernie plenty of line.

"During my years with the force, I always believed that crime didn't pay. For many people—small people—it didn't pay. For bigger people—you know the ones who made the big bucks—it paid plenty. Today I read about some of those crooked assholes I knew years ago. They're wealthy retirees now, in Arizona or California. It's all bullshit, Slat-ski. You think you'll change the world? Well, dream on, kid." Rather than anchor, they let a gentle current carry them across the lake. They cast their lures lazily, creating a pattern of concentric circles across the smooth water. Birds chirped, and the leaves spoke softly to the breeze.

"You can't operate a take without the okay of those directly above you." Slat wasn't asking.

"You'd have to prove that." Ernie snorted. "Good luck."

"Why were you transferred to patrol?"

"I'm not sure. It was after those assassinations I mentioned. I started the investigation. After I had completed the initial report and a few interviews, I got pulled from the case."

"Who got it then?"

"Sam Tyrone."

"Did Sam work on the homicides?"

"No, but a month later, Billy Boyd and his uncle Curly took over the entire gambling operation in the black neighborhoods. Curly Boyd combined all the separate gambling houses under his control. Remember, two bosses had been killed." He paused. "I always had a gut feeling that Sam was involved."

"You think Sam was taking payoffs from Billy Boyd?"

"Yeah, until Billy told Sam to scratch ass. Do you remember the race riots and the riots at the university? Well, when that was going on, no one paid much attention to the black gamblers who were killed. Everybody was too busy. Sam kept the case to himself for years . . . unsolved. To tell you the truth, I was glad when Turski transferred Sam out of the bureau."

"What do you know about Curly Boyd?"

"He operated gambling from the thirties to the sixties and ran liquor during Prohibition. He was the big cheese in those days. Hell of a nice guy—everybody liked him. He's dead now. He turned the reins over to Billy sometime after the assassinations." They changed lures.

"Could Sam have been getting any payoffs after the chief demoted him from detective?" Slat asked.

"Billy Boyd and Lincoln Pitford would have to answer that." Slat laughed. "Fat chance."

"Fat chance is right. My guess is that Sam didn't get a penny after his demotion."

"Who's Lincoln Pitford?" Slat asked.

"Billy Boyd's cousin, Curly's stepson—never adopted. Both boys worked for Curly back then. Pitford helped out with the gambling, but mainly he was a pimp. He handled Curly's prostitutes. That dwindled away soon after Curly died."

"I remember him now. I picked him up once for disorderly. A royal pain in the ass."

"That's the one," Ernie confirmed. "He sometimes operates one of Billy's houses. They're always fighting, then making up. You know I feel a little sorry for Pitford. It can't be easy being Billy's cousin."

"Why's that?"

"Pitford's older, but Billy was the brilliant kid. He could have been a doctor or lawyer. Instead, he became a gambling kingpin. Who said crime doesn't pay, eh, Slat-ski? Now Billy's in the real-estate business. Owns four or five of those strip shopping centers, a nightclub, and God only knows what else. A real lady's man. Divorced four or five times. Still runs gambling but never gets his hands dirty."

"You think Billy killed those gamblers?"

"Maybe. He had the motive. Always suspected him and Sam together. But considering the way Sam acted over the years, and now with his suicide, I'd guess it was probably just Sam." Ernie let his spinner bait sink to the bottom and did not bother to retrieve it. He stared across the lake toward some distant place. "Ever wonder, Slat-ski, why gambling is so much more prevalent in the black neighborhoods than the white?"

"Lieutenant Lovemore says it's because the blacks don't have country clubs with backroom betting. They don't have clubs like the Lions, Kiwanis, or Knights of Columbus with their games. Black Baptist churches don't allow illegal gambling like the Catholic churches do. So we don't touch black gambling."

"It's still against the law," Ernie pointed out. "And Lieutenant Lovemore's a cop." Slat's bait sank into the calm water.

"Yessir," Ernie said, stretching. "I guess things haven't changed much in the last twenty years."

* * *

Early the next morning Slat wiped the morning dew from his windshield. "Ernie, you're too young to retire and fish."

"I know. Elinor thinks I should work for Father Daley at the archdiocese for a few more years. I'm in charge of security there. Been part-time for years."

"Well, whatever you do, Ernie, I wish you luck." Slat shook hands with the older man, then got into the car and rolled down his window. "Thanks for all your help."

"Thanks for telling me about Sam, Slat." He shook his head sadly, then looked up and brightened. "Have a good trip. I'll be down in a few days." While driving back from Fox Lake, Slat felt disappointed. He'd hoped he'd learn something more definite about Sam, the gambling payoffs, and the assassinations. But Ernie had no proof, only suspicions. Slat had been a cop long enough to know that anything was possible. Still, he couldn't believe that Sam had been on the take. And no way could Sam have killed any gamblers. Ernie had to be wrong. The only persons alive with a motive in the twenty-year-old murders were Billy Boyd and, maybe, Lincoln Pitford. Slat committed himself to learn more about both men and, he hoped, clear Sam's memory at the same time.

4

WHEN DAWN MAZURSKI TOOK THE ENTRANCE EXAMINATION for the Pulaski Police Department, she had scored the highest of any candidate on the written test. After she had passed the physical-agility test ahead of most men but still ended up 103 on the list of applicants, she sued the city of Pulaski in federal court. The city settled the discrimination suit by hiring her, promising she'd be transferred to the Detective Bureau or youth section within twelve months.

Slat took a calming breath as he looked down at Mazurski's personnel file. He already had enough trouble with his staff. All of them complained because of the workload. Half needed to cry on his shoulder so they wouldn't go off the deep end. Now this female with a chip on her shoulder comes along, dropped on him cold first thing this morning.

He sat back in his chair and looked across the desk at her. Officer Mazurski stood in a military at-ease stance, her hands clasped behind her back. He had seen her around the police station and on the street, in the sexless blue police uniform. Now, dressed in a gray business suit on her first day in the Detective Bureau, she looked attractive—very attractive. "Sit down, please."

She sat on one of the four metal chairs under the glass window. Her back was rigidly straight, her knees tightly together.

"You've been in patrol a year."

"Yes, sir."

"It takes most cops five to ten years before they make it into the Detective Bureau."

Her eyes never left his face. "I don't care about most cops, Sergeant."

Slat looked back at the file, then stretched back in his chair. "Degree in Criminal Justice . . . "

"Straight A's," Dawn interrupted.

"Twelve credits toward your Masters."

"Yes. One day I'll get your job, then the lieutenant's job, and so, even if I have to file suit every few months around here to be treated fairly."

Slat pitched her folder onto his desk, then leaned back in his chair. He made eye contact and held it. "You're a bitter young lady."

His gaze did not intimidate her. "I've learned to be around here. Just want you to understand me up front. I'll do a good job for you, and I won't stand for being held back because I'm a woman of color, Sergeant."

"You can call me Slat. The rest of . . . "

"Sergeant'll do," Dawn interrupted again.

"Take a break while I figure out your assignment."

After Dawn left his office, Slat wondered what to do with her. Homer Braun's partner had quit, and Jenny was paired with him temporarily, while Mike Duffy was on vacation. Logically, Mazurski would be assigned to

Homer, but that would be like mixing fire with gasoline. Slat chuckled in spite of himself, thinking of Homer's reaction to Mazurski and vice versa. No, that would be impossible.

Stan Osinski and Odell Fowler had been working well for four years. Though they initially hated each other, they'd object vehemently now to being separated. Besides, if he put Braun with Osinski and Dawn with Odell, it would appear as if he was segregating his black detectives.

Jenny Herschel and Mike Duffy were another good match. If he put Dawn with Jenny, he'd be accused of isolating the two women.

The sharp ringing of the telephone jerked Slat from his deliberations. "Sergeant, patrol has a dead kid. Looks like a homicide. Room one-twelve at the Sunshine Motel."

Trailing his suit jacket in his left hand, Slat burst from his office into the Detective Bureau. Dawn Mazurski was standing in front of the bulletin board, reading departmental notices. "Come on, Dawn," he told her. "Got a homicide to check out. Good way to get your feet wet.

* * *

Father John Julius walked into the large rectory kitchen and headed toward the coffee maker. The carafe was empty.

"I'm making a new pot," Father Daley said from the sink.

"Pat! Didn't know you were here."

Patrick Daley was jacketless, but he had on his clerical shirt and Roman collar. "Thought I'd come early for the eleven o'clock mass, have a chance to sit down and relax for a few minutes." He carried a pitcher of water to the coffee maker, poured it into the reservoir, and flipped the switch to start the brewing. "I'm making it strong."

"Just how I like it." John glanced at his watch. Ten fifteen. "You ready for mass, or do you need some time alone?"

"Nope, all set," Pat answered. "Something on your mind?"

"Actually, yes. I-I'd like to speak with you in confidence."

Pat's watery green eyes widened slightly. "Confession?" he asked.

"Well, yes and no." He hesitated, watching the water spurt in a steaming shower into the coffee grounds. "I have a problem. Nothing new. Maybe there's no resolution. Might have to wrestle with it for the rest of my life."

"Come on. Let's go into the study." Patrick stood and led the way toward the study. John Julius, looking longingly back at the coffee, followed, then shut the door behind them.

Father Daley sat in plump earnestness at one end of the couch, and Father Julius sat at the other.

"What's the problem, John?"

Father Julius shifted in his seat and felt foolish. *Why,* he wondered, *does Pat's peace of mind come so easily to him, while I'm struggling every day of my life?* He glanced again at his colleague, with thinning red hair and receding hairline, a sprinkling of freckles over rosy, fat cheeks. Father Patrick Daley did not look like a sexual animal. Maybe that's the answer, John thought, then took a deep breath and looked again at his watch.

"It's the celibacy," he admitted. "I feel as if I've been asked to do something impossible, unnatural. I'm having trouble keeping my concentration—even during serious discussions—if I'm talking with someone . . . attractive to me. Sometimes I feel as if I'm going to fly apart and . . . "

"John." Father Daley's hands rested on his knees. When he took a deep breath, his shoulders came up. "At those moments you must scream at yourself to stop thinking the thoughts that lead you to no good."

"That doesn't help," John said miserably. "It's not just a mental thing, Pat. It's physical, too."

"You must pray, and pray, then pray some more."

"I've tried that, too. Hearing confessions . . . sometimes I get aroused listening to them." He felt his cheeks flame from embarrassment. "I've even encouraged people to be more descriptive. God, I'm so ashamed."

"You aren't alone, you know, John. Many priests battle similar demons."

"Pat, I've even thought about leaving the priesthood."

"We mustn't . . . - "

"It hasn't been serious," John said quickly. "But the thought has passed through my mind."

They were interrupted by a knock at the door. It opened, and Sister Catherine, the elderly nun who ran the rectory's household matters, peeked in. "Father Julius, the police department called. They need you— last rites for a homicide victim."

Both priests stood, and John moved toward the door.

"We can talk more about this later," Patrick offered.

"Yes," Father Julius said over his shoulder. "Thank you."

5

HOMER BRAUN STOOD NEXT TO THE BED AND WATCHED SOLEMNLY as Father Julius completed the last rites. The nude boy lay facedown. There was no blood, but the sight of a dead kid turned Homer's stomach anyway. Father Julius wasn't doing so well, either, he thought. The priest's face was drained of color.

Homer looked up as Slat and a beautiful woman with skin the color of something delicious to eat entered the dingy single-bed unit of the Sunshine Motel. Now, with two uniformed officers and the medical examiner, the room was crowded.

"Slat," Father Julius said, "I know this child. David Merriman. He's from my parish—an altar boy. His parents are going to be crushed."

"Father, would you . . . ?"

"Of course. I'll talk to the family with whomever you send."

While taking notes about the crime scene, Homer shifted his eyes from Slat to the woman. His gaze slid up her long, elegant body until they reached her face. She was staring back, and her eyes flashed defiantly at him. Then he recognized her. Dawn Mazurski, out of uniform. A detective? he thought with a sinking feeling. What a bitch.

"What've you got?" Slat asked the medical examiner.

"Minor anal bleeding and a petroleum-based lubricant. The boy was engaged in anal intercourse. No apparent trauma to the body. My preliminary guess is that he suffocated."

Homer pretended to write in his notebook, but out of the corner of his eyes he was looking at Mazurski. Ordinarily a horny cop would like a sharp looking broad for a partner, he admitted to himself. Except he'd heard that uniformed cops, including females, didn't like her because she had an attitude.

"Those are probably semen stains on the inside of his left thigh," the examiner continued, pointing to a spot with his pencil. "We'll analyze it at the lab."

"What about personal property?" Slat looked at Homer.

Homer said nothing.

"Braun! Personal property," Slat repeated.

"Uh, yeah, Sarge. Just this shirt, shorts, socks, shoes, and wallet, lying on the floor at the foot of the bed. No money."

"It's your case, Homer," Slat said.

"No problem. I'll handle it. Be an easy one . . ." His voice trailed off. "Maybe." He looked with pleading eyes at Slat, then tucked his notebook under his left armpit and put his palms together in prayer. No, he mouthed, shaking his head. Please, no.

Slat stifled a grin. "Dawn Mazurski," he said, "Meet your new partner, Homer Braun. I'm going back to headquarters. Homer, Dawn will ride with you."

While Dawn was talking with the medical examiner, Homer followed Slat into the parking lot. "This is temporary, right, Slat?"

"Probably. She was dropped on me this morning."

"Now, I'll take that one for a partner," Homer offered. The *Pulaski Press* car had pulled up in front of the motel, and the leggy Cheri Duncan was headed their way.

"They're like leeches, those reporters," Slat said. "I'm getting out of here. Don't you say anything. Go back to work."

"Sergeant Sczlatski!"

Slat ignored the woman as he opened his squad door.

"I don't bite, Sergeant." She laughed good-naturedly, with the confidence of a woman who's known all her life how pretty she is and how far her looks have gotten her. Her teeth were white and even, and her chestnut hair glowed in the sunlight as she leaned against the fender. "May I get a statement from you? We've gotten word of a possible homicide."

"Talk to your informant, then."

"Sergeant, I'm just trying to do my job."

"Talk to Lieutenant Lovemore." He cut her off by slamming the door, starting the engine, and putting the squad car into gear.

* * *

Tony Tattaglia and Father Patrick Daley sat in the dark sedan parked a half block behind a detective's car. They had discreetly followed the detective from the Sunshine Motel to a line of humble row houses on the South Side of Pulaski—a white, working-class neighborhood with children and laundry lines everywhere. Every once in a while, a spot of color brightened the street—a window box with geraniums, a new paint job on a house. Otherwise, it was a drab, lusterless place.

The men watched as Father Julius, Homer Braun, and a woman climbed the steps to a wooden porch and knocked on the front door.

"Why didn't you call me sooner?" Tony demanded. "I hate rushing."

"I had mass," Patrick Daley explained. "Called as soon as I could."

The front door opened, and the three visitors were ushered inside.

"Women in macho cop roles," Tony mused. "That's kind of a turn on."

"You haven't changed a bit, have you?"

"Don't think I could handle spending eight-hour shifts with a nice-looking woman in a police car," Tony said. "Is the priest always with these cops?"

"Yes. He's the department chaplain."

"When will I meet Archbishop Coughlin?" Tony asked.

"Whenever he can fit us into his schedule."

Father Daley, as an archdiocesan priest, fulfilled some of his priestly obligations at St. Michael's. His first assignment after ordination was to a failing parish in a deteriorating neighborhood. Within eighteen months, he had brought it out of debt and was immediately recognized as a pecuniary wunderkind. Archbishop Coughlin promoted him to financial secretary for the entire archdiocese, and that role included internal affairs and security. As a result, he was serving as liaison between the archbishop and the Vatican representative.

"When do we grab the priest? And is the evidence sufficient?"

"Soon as we get the word from the archbishop. We don't question the archbishop."

"It had better be soon. I want to be back in Rome by the day after tomorrow."

"What will happen to Father Julius?" Patrick asked quietly.

"Are you concerned for his soul?" Tony asked.

Patrick looked indignant. "I've worked with the man for years. I know he's in spiritual pain."

"He'll probably be reassigned to a monastery in Upper Slobovia."

From Tony's tone, Patrick knew his old friend was not interested in discussing Father John Julius' ultimate fate. He sank down in the seat and watched the house down the block.

* * *

After notifying the deceased boy's parents, then dropping Father Julius off at his car, Homer and Dawn returned to the motel. They located the front-desk clerk, a college student named Jack Hamlin, bent over a physics textbook in the lobby.

"Do I have to go into the police station?" he asked. "I really have a lot of studying to do."

"Not if we can get a private place to talk here," Homer told him.

Dawn followed Hamlin and Homer into a private office behind the lobby's counter. Hamlin sat at the desk, while Homer and Dawn hovered over him.

"Who owns the motel?" Homer began, taking out his notepad.

"The Sunshine Property Management Corporation."

"Their address?" Homer asked.

"Seventy-six hundred Dodge Avenue."

"Your address?"

"I'm a permanent resident here at the motel. I work in exchange for my room."

"How old are you?"

"Twenty."

Homer turned to Dawn. "You want to take some notes?" he asked testily.

She quickly dug her notepad out of her purse.

"What hours do you work?" Homer asked.

"Three-thirty to eleven-thirty."

"Were you in your apartment before the body was found?"

"Only for about five minutes. I attend the University of Wisconsin in Milwaukee. Got back here from school about three-twenty."

"You married?"

Hamlin laughed, then abruptly stopped. "No."

"Ever been arrested?"

"Yeah. Once. For drunk driving."

Homer moved to sit on the edge of the desk and stared down at Hamlin. "Was room one-twelve locked?"

"Far as I know it was, but I wasn't here."

"Where's the room key?"

"Still in the pigeonhole."

"When you arrived to work, were any guests registered in the motel?"

"None."

"No one had checked into that room?"

"A couple came in at twenty to four. They found the kid in there."

"Patrol got a statement from the couple. The door was locked. No signs of forced entry." Dawn held up the report.

"The housekeeper would have been the last to close the door," Hamlin told them.

They got the name of the housekeeper from Hamlin.

"Ever seen that boy before?"

"He looked familiar. I think he goes to the same church I do."

"Which church?" Dawn asked.

"St. Michael's," Hamlin answered.

Dawn shuddered as she remembered St. Michaels—an imposing, white-stoned church that covered one side of an entire city block. The two- story, white-brick grammar school engulfed the other side. Dawn had spent nine miserable years there, starting with kindergarten. Beside the school was its playground, where she had been beaten up fairly regularly and called nigger. Before she was eight years old, Dawn had learned her lessons about survival and how to fight back.

Across the alley from the church were the convent and the rectory, separated by a courtyard and flower garden. Covered parking stalls had recently been built behind the rectory. While she had been in uniform patrol, Dawn had driven down that alley, occasionally recognizing a nun who had been a teacher. . .

"We pride ourselves on having an integrated school, Mrs. Mazurski," one of those nuns had told her mother after a particularly brutal attack had broken Dawn's collarbone. "There aren't many colored children in this city. Dawn must stop being an instigator. We don't want the white children to get a bad impression of a colored child . . . "

"Her father is Polish," Mrs. Mazurski had interrupted.

"Yes. I understand," the Irish nun had replied.

But nobody had ever understood, Dawn thought. They still didn't. . . .

"What hours do the housekeepers work?" Homer's question brought Dawn back to the present.

"Seven in the morning to three in the afternoon."

They thanked Jack Hamlin and left.

* * *

Jenny opened the door and walked into the "glass cage," as the sergeants' office was called. She held a report. "Slat," she said, her tone gentle, "the powder tests show that Sam fired the weapon. The burns on his temple show the weapon was about an inch away when he fired it."

"Damn it!" Slat rubbed the furrows on his cheeks.

"Hey, why so uptight?"

"I'm not uptight!" Slat threw the papers in his hand onto the desk.

Jenny, wide-eyed, stared at him.

"Okay, okay," he said. "Sorry. Guess I am a little stressed out. Here, sit down."

"The guys are always saying I don't smile," she said. "But I think I smile more than you. You gotta . . . "

"Yeah, I know. I think about it at times. Smiling's on my Christmas wish list." He pushed himself back into his chair. "Guess it stayed with me from the orphanage. I was afraid that if I smiled, they'd think I was happy and keep me there. I smiled only when couples came to look at me." Slat stared past Jenny. "I wanted someone to like me, to take me home with them. I wanted . . . ah, never mind." He straighten himself up and forced a smile. "A few jokes tonight at Ski's, and we'll all be smiling, right?" He nodded at the papers in her hand. "What've you got?"

"We found another bullet in the mattress. He must have test fired the gun before he shot himself. I think we'll leave it as a suicide and close the case. All right?"

"What choice do we have?" Slat asked. "It all adds up to a suicide." He blew out a long breath. "Yeah, Jenny, go ahead and close it."

He knew she wanted an invitation to stay and talk, but he didn't extend one. After she had left the office, Slat returned to his preoccupation with the old gambling assassinations and the role Sam might have played in them. He knew Ernie was wrong about Sam. Even partners who work together for many years can make mistakes about each other's character. After all the hours Sam had spent with Slat in the orphanage, all the special attention he'd paid to him, Slat owed Sam a clean reputation and a peaceful rest.

Before Chief Turski arrived in Pulaski, there had been other sloppy homicide investigations. After Turski appointed Slat to the Detective Bureau, Slat had pulled thirty years of unsolved homicide cases from the dusty vault and stuffed the dog-eared file folders into a cardboard box next to his file cabinet. He had intended to go through each and every one, no matter how long it took.

Whoever had murdered the gamblers in the early seventies might still be involved in gambling. Slat planned to interview gambling kingpin Billy Boyd and small-time gambler Lincoln Pitford. First he'd have to run a complete background check on both. Before he did anything, he'd have to pore over the reports on the assassination.

Slat sat back in his chair and spun around to face his file cabinet. The dusty cardboard box sat on the floor next to the end cabinet. He took the top off. With a sinking feeling in the pit of his stomach, he realized that all the unsolved homicide cases, including the assassination of the black gamblers, were gone.

6

HOMER BRAUN PUSHED OPEN THE DOOR TO THE DETECTIVE BUREAU. A sense of purpose gave strength to his arms. Today, Saturday, he thought, Slat will change his mind and assign Detective Bitch Mazurski to another partner. Dawn and he were scheduled to begin interviewing David Merriman's schoolmates within a few hours. If the two detectives were still matched for that, chances were he'd be stuck with her for the entire investigation. He glanced toward her desk. Miss Goody Two Shoes was already working. Homer was pretty sure he'd quit the force or strangle her before they found the kid's murderer.

"Morning!" Homer called out. His colleagues muttered their response from behind their gray metal desks.

"Homer." Slat was standing in the doorway to his glass cage. He held file folders in both hands. "You and Dawn stay with this Merriman homicide. I understand from Dawn that you have several of David's schoolmates to interview."

"Yeah," Homer said, all hope gone. "I figure about ten of them." He sank down into his worn swivel chair.

"Keep me posted."

"Yeah, Sarge." Homer spun his chair, eyes following Slat. He decided to give it one more try. Please, Slat . . . "Anything else?"

Slat hesitated a moment. "No. That's it."

"Come on," Homer said to Dawn. "We'll make our calls later. Let's get some breakfast."

"I ate breakfast before I came to work," she responded loftily, and loudly enough for all to hear.

"Fine. I'll go without you. Here." He tossed the Merriman file on her desk. "You set up the appointments, I'll interview the motel housekeeper."

* * *

Mrs. Hatter was a thin, black woman with contrasting strands of white hair entwined with black hair. She had finished cleaning room 112 at 2:30 on the afternoon David Merriman was murdered but had seen nothing suspicious. Homer and the medical examiner had narrowed the time of the crime to between 2:30 and 3:40. Mrs. Hatter was very sure that she had closed the door to each room securely and that each door locked automatically.

Someone had to have entered that motel room with a key, unless it had been left open on purpose, Homer thought. Alternatively, the perpetrator could have tried doorknobs until he found an open door. Homer decided to check every motel door to make sure they were all locked. They were. He called in to the station and reported his finding to his partner.

"I called the parents of those ten kids," Dawn said. "They're all scheduled for this afternoon."

"Good. Be right in." He hung up the phone. "Smart-ass broad."

As Homer was driving back to the station, the radio dispatcher broadcasted, "Unit four-oh-one and any units near Seventy-six fifty-four Asbury. Prowler on the second floor. Woman home alone on the first."

Homer picked up his mike. "Twenty-four responding from five blocks away." As he approached Asbury Street, he heard another unit sign off in front.

A marked squad car showed up in the alley with Homer. "Watch that corner of the house," Homer said to the officer. "I'll go around front." The officer nodded acknowledgment.

Two men in uniform were at the front of the two-story frame house. One stayed at the corner of the house; Homer and the other officer, a veteran named Paul Chalmers, entered the front door after an agitated, elderly wisp of a lady let them in.

"Upstairs!" she quavered through bony fingers covering her mouth.

"Shhhh," Homer whispered. "We don't want to announce ourselves. Which room?"

"The room above the parlor. I heard a crash. He must have broken in through the window." The woman was shaking with fear. "Don't be scared, ma'am. You've got Pulaski's finest with you now. We'll catch the guy." Homer followed Paul up the stairs.

"Homer," Chalmers whispered over his shoulder. "I hear something."

"Oh, my God! the woman wailed. She was following them.

"Lady," Homer whispered, "does anybody else live here?"

"No. Not since Walter died."

At that moment, another officer entered the front door. "Hey, you guys," he whispered foyer, "the screen above the porch is ripped open."

"Watch that window in case he plans to go out the same way," Homer said.

"I think we got a live one here," Homer whispered to Paul as they thread across the carpeted second-floor hallway. The door to their targeted room was shut.

At the sound of a loud crash from inside the room, both Homer and Paul jumped and drew their weapons. Paul stepped to one side of the door. Homer took the other side. They heard rummaging inside the bedroom. Homer turned the doorknob and pushed the door open. His weapon was at the ready.

A cat screeched and ran across the bedroom and into an open closet, and a small squirrel fled out the window.

"A cat!" he sputtered. "And a squirrel!"

Paul burst out laughing. "Looks like the screen has a rusted hole. The squirrel must have . . . "

He did not notice the lady behind them.

"Stallone! My poor kitty Stallone." The old woman, rushing into the room, bumped into Homer, who was placing his snub-nosed .38 into its hip holster. The gun discharged.

The woman screamed. Paul jumped.

"Son of a bitch!" Homer screamed. "My fucking foot! My fucking foot!"

They all looked down. There was a hole in the top of Homer's right shoe. Paul ran to the window. "Get an ambulance!" he shouted.

"All for a fucking squirrel!" Homer shouted, hopping from the pain.

"Sit back, Homer." Paul guided him to the bed. "Ma'am, you'll have to excuse his language. He's in pain."

* * *

"How about a purple heart?" Slat suggested to the police gathered in St. Luke's Hospital Emergency Room. They guffawed, while Homer, lying on a cot, glared at them.

"The tavern won't be the same without you," Jenny teased. "Mama's will have to close down."

"You know, Homer," offered Father Julius, squeezing out a rare smile, "if you spent more time in church, these little accidents might not happen to you."

"I'm thankful it wasn't worse," Chief Turski said. "But going to such extremes just to . . . "

"Chief, don't listen to those guys," Homer said. "Swear I didn't do it on purpose."

After Chief Turski and Father Julius excused themselves, Homer leaned up on his elbows. "Slat, I know I do some crazy things, but I'd never shoot myself just to get out of being partners with . . . "

"Hey," Slat said, suppressing a grin, "that never would have occurred to me. I know you're a little odd, Homer, but you're a pretty good cop. Gotta go now. I'll drop by your house tomorrow and see if you need anything."

After Slat said good-bye to the other officers, he walked out onto the emergency-room vehicle ramp, where he saw Cheri Duncan taking notes while talking to the chief. Slat nodded to Turski but didn't acknowledge the reporter's presence.

When Cheri saw Slat, however, she quickly closed her notebook and thanked the chief for the interview. In moments she was at Slat's side. "The chief is very nice," she crooned. "Too bad some of his subordinates aren't. Why are you so—so difficult?"

Slat stopped at his squad door. "Miss Duncan, you're new here, so allow me to educate you about police-newspaper relations. For years the *Pulaski*

Press has misquoted police officers, victims, and politicians—with the rare exception of Councilman Archie Dunn, who, for some reason unknown to yours truly, has been deified. Your paper has consistently printed lies and false innuendoes. Finally, your publisher, the illustrious Matthew Baker, just plain doesn't like the police."

Cheri's cheeks flamed with color. "Don't blame me for the editorials, Sergeant. I don't write them."

"It's not just the editorials." He got into the squad and slammed the door, then told her through the window, "Try reading the Milwaukee papers. Somehow their reporters always seem to get things right."

Before he backed out of the parking stall, he thought he heard her hiss, "Asshole."

* * *

Tony Tattaglia walked from the emergency room to the hospital parking lot. He slid behind the steering wheel of his dark sedan. The car rocked as the big man made himself comfortable.

"The cops were behind some curtains," he told Patrick Daley.

"Father Julius, too?" Father Daley slouched low in the passenger seat.

"Yeah, evidently a cop has been injured."

"If Father Julius was with them, it must be serious."

"Wish we didn't have to wait so long. The blond detective was with them. You know, she reminds me of someone."

"Tony, will you stay focused on Father Julius?"

"I am, Pat. But since we've been watching him, he's done nothing suspicious. I have to get back to Rome. When will the archbishop see me? Why the delay?"

"The archbishop wants to be sure our information is more than just speculation. John Julius spends too much time with young boys. My sources say he and David Merriman—the murdered child—were very close."

"You should have separated truth from appearances before you contacted the Vatican," Tony said testily. "Can't you call the . . . "

"No. I have to wait for the archbishop to get back to me."

As rain began to fall, Tony thought that the weather matched his mood. Being stuck in this dingy, backwater town without a decent restaurant or hotel was getting on his nerves. Moreover, his old friend had been less than effective in getting things done with the archbishop. "You know, Pat, you don't have to stay with me. I can follow Julius myself."

"No, that's all right. Who knows when I'll ever see you again? Besides, I expect that we'll get the go-ahead from the archbishop to nab him anytime now."

7

MEMORANDUM

City of Pulaski

To: Mayor

From: Alderman Archie Dunn,

Chairman, Finance Committee

Re: Day-Care Center

I received a memo from Chief Turski requesting we conduct a feasibility study for a day-care center for city employees because of the number of single parents (females).

I think it's time you had a talk with Chief Turski about the conservative philosophies of this city. We are not in the baby-sitting business.

After leaving the hospital and returning to the Detective Bureau, Slat asked Detective Stan Osinski to step into the glass cage. Stan, in his late fifties, was the oldest detective on the force, and Slat respected the man for his level head and decisive thinking. Called the "bull dick," he had a stable family life and a manner with Slat that balanced somewhere between fatherly—he had more than twenty years on the sergeant—and respectful. Slat could ask Stan's advice without confusing their roles in the bureau.

Now that Homer was out of commission, Slat had thought about the best way to pair off Dawn Mazurski, but he hadn't come to a satisfactory decision. He explained the situation to Stan and knew that Osinski would help him select the best path.

Stan settled in one of the gray, hardback metal chairs and listened intently. His pale blue eyes never left Slat's face. "She can't be left alone on the Merriman homicide," Stan said at last. "You shouldn't take her off it, though—not because she's a woman or because she's new. It wouldn't be fair to her."

"I agree."

"Put Herschel and Mazurski together until Duffy gets back from vacation," Stan suggested.

"I've thought of that. But if I team up Jenny and Dawn, I'll catch shit from all sides for putting two women together." "You don't have time to worry about what people think," Stan responded. "Besides, nobody in power is going to give you problems about the women."

"Except Archie Dunn."

Stan snorted with derision. "Fuck Archie Dunn. He's such a woman hater, no one'll listen to him, especially the chief. The Merriman homicide would be a good case for those broads to get their feet wet."

Slat realized the bull dick was right. It might be tough on the women to handle the murder of a child, but they might be more sensitive and less intimidating than men when it came to interviewing children and dealing with Mr. and Mrs. Merriman. The parents were devastated.

"Thanks, Stan," Slat said. "How's your family?"

"Number one, Slat," Stan said. "Always number one. You should think about giving it a try—wife and kids. Really helps to keep things in perspective, if you know what I mean. And another thing, while I've got your attention. You're gonna end up in the funny farm if you don't lighten up. Joke a little, smile once in a while." Stan stood and punched Slat on the arm. "And quit those stinking cigarettes."

"I'll try."

"Sure." Stan grabbed the pack from Slat's shirt pocket and threw them in the wastebasket. "First step." Slat watched Stan return to his desk. He'd never commit suicide, Slat knew, thinking of Sam and worrying about himself. Stan had love and support and would probably live to be a hundred. Slat closed his eyes and envisioned himself as he usually pictured Stan—at home, in the backyard, grilling kielbasa on a barbecue. A small, dark-haired boy heaved a basketball at a net hung over the garage door, way too high for him . . . a bright-eyed little girl in pink overalls drew a hopscotch pattern on the sidewalk leading to the back door. Then his wife would come out the door. She'd be carrying a tray of paper plates and plastic cups, mustard and slaw.

The vision vanished. He couldn't see her face. Jenny, with her long blond hair? Or Theresa, with her dark, saucy curls? *Naw,* Slat thought. *Theresa's good for a laugh and a lay, but nothing more serious. Or will I end up like Sam,* he wondered, *alone, in a stinking room, with a bullet in my brain?*

Slat looked up and studied the back of Jenny's head as she sat at her desk. Several months before, he had driven her home from Ski's Inn and gone up to her apartment. They were both inebriated and lusting to make love, but good sense had intervened. They hadn't allowed themselves to get into that situation again.

Slat watched as Jenny pushed back her chair, stood, and walked gracefully to retrieve a file from the bottom drawer of a file cabinet. The weight of her shoulder holster tugged at her loose-fitting blouse and accentuated one breast. She was wearing jeans, and as she squatted in front of the file cabinet, his eyes followed the curve of her buttocks, thighs, and legs. As usual, she was deep in concentration, and her expression was intense. The crew tried hard to get her to smile and laugh. They were successful only after their shift was over, and everyone was relaxing at Ski's Inn. Whatever Jenny Herschel's inner demons were, she was a good cop. When she smiled, though, her perfect white teeth sparkled, and her green eyes shone.

He had to tell her about teaming up with Dawn. He couldn't wait for her to be in a good mood.

Slat opened his glass door. "Jenny, would you step into my office, please?"

8

JENNY HERSCHEL NEVER WANTED TO BE A TRAILBLAZER for women's rights. She just wanted to be a cop—like her dad. After she quit teaching elementary school she joined the Eagleton Illinois Police Department, her husband divorced her. He said he didn't want to sleep with a cop; he wanted to sleep with a woman.

Jenny was the only female on the force, but no one gave her special treatment. That was how she wanted it. She was her father's daughter, and all the cops knew and liked her dad. Soon she earned their respect through her own actions. Then she fell in love with one of the guys on her shift, and they got engaged. Shortly after that, he was blown away in front of her, and Jenny checked into a psychiatric hospital for a month. After her release, she left Illinois and planned to return to teaching. But police work was in her blood, and within a couple of years she ended up on the Pulaski Police Department. If there hadn't been other women on the force, she wouldn't have taken the job.

After Chief Martin Turski took charge, he met individually with everyone in the department. During their conference, he asked Jenny if she would like to be transferred to the Detective Bureau. She was thrilled and surprised.

"What about seniority, sir? About sixty officers are senior to me."

"Seniority is not the sole criterion. Transfers will be based on performance and needs. We need two or three women in the Detective Bureau. Many victims in Pulaski are women."

"I don't want to be a pioneer," she insisted.

"I'll keep that in mind, Herschel," he responded.

The chief attended all roll calls and explained his reasons for assigning women to all sections. A month later, a veteran female officer was the first transferred to the Detective Bureau. Two weeks later, Jenny joined her. A year later, the other woman detective resigned, and Jenny became the only female on Slat's shift until the transfer of Dawn Mazurski.

Conceptually Jenny was glad for Dawn's presence. But the newcomer's reputation for defensiveness preceded her, and Dawn's haughty behavior proved that assessment correct. Jenny had made no attempt to welcome or befriend her new colleague. No doubt being teamed with Homer was a nightmare, but with his being out of commission, Dawn would get someone else.

As Jenny walked into the glass cage, Slat looked down at his desk. "Something wrong?" she asked.

"I need your help." He sat back and looked up at her.

"Sure," she said. "What?"

"I'm teaming you and Dawn . . . "

"What?"

"Temporarily. Until Duffy gets back."

"Give her to Fowler or Osinski."

"Why break Fowler and Osinski up? You and your partner Duffy will only be apart for the three weeks he'll be on vacation. It's only logical."

"Let her work alone. And me, too."

"She's too new to the crew. Besides, she's got that homicide to handle. She needs help."

"Come on, Slat," Jenny groaned.

"That's it, Jenny. No more discussion."

"Yes, sir."

Slat walked her to the door and called Dawn into his office. Jenny stalked to her desk and sat down hard in her chair. *Damn Homer for shooting himself* , she thought. She and Dawn would be the center of attention. The first chance the media had, they'd focus on the female team. It was pioneer time again. That meant no errors.

When Jenny had been transferred to the Detective Bureau, many uniformed men felt she hadn't paid her dues in uniform. They were backed by Archie Dunn, who was still bitter about losing the position of police chief to Turski. After a while, the officers got over it, although Dunn had not. With Dawn's being transferred ahead of several men into the Detective Bureau, all those old wounds would open up again.

Well, she thought, watching Dawn through the window to Slat's office, Mike will be back in three weeks. I can handle her for that short of a time.

Mazurski approached her desk, which was right behind Jenny's. She didn't look happy. "The sergeant told me we'll be working together," she said to Jenny. "I've typed up the Merriman homicide reports, including interviews with the victim's ten schoolmates. Here, take a look."

"Thanks," Jenny said, taking the folders. "After I finish reading them, we'll decide what to do next." As she scanned the reports, her fury cooled. Dawn had written good reports and asked the school kids the right questions. Maybe it wouldn't be so bad, after all.

Jenny spun her chair and looked at her new partner. What a beautiful woman, she thought, surprised she hadn't noticed that before now. "Which medical examiner handled the case?" "There are a few details I'd like to get."

"Schroeder."

Jenny called Craig Schroeder at the Milwaukee County Medical Examiner's office and asked him for specifics that Dawn, as a rookie detective, would not know were omitted. She took notes as he gave her the information she wanted.

"He suffocated," Craig told Jenny, "but we cannot say it was done at the scene. Besides the semen in his anal passage, all else is speculation. The offender could have accidentally held the victim's head in a pillow during prolonged excitement before and during ejaculation. There were no marks to indicate a fight or struggle. That's about it."

"Any drugs?"

"No preliminary indication. When I get the finals I'll call you."

After they hung up, Jenny told Dawn what Shroeder had said.

"Everybody tells us what a perfect kid David was. How can a perfect kid have such an imperfect ending?" Dawn mused.

Jenny intentionally tried to elicit some opinion from Dawn. "Maybe the kid was a homosexual."

Dawn just shrugged.

"Come on we've got more work to do at the motel."

* * *

Dawn and Jenny interviewed the four permanent Sunshine Motel tenants and verified their alibis. Afterwards, they sat in their detective car in the parking lot. "What about the desk clerk, Jack Hamlin?" Jenny asked.

"He was at school." Dawn flipped through her notebook. "He attends college in Milwaukee. His first class is at nine in the morning, and his last class is over at about three."

"Did you check with the school?"

"Yes. The teaching assistant for Hamlin's last class checked the attendance sheet. He was present. And it takes him about twenty-five minutes to drive here from school."

"What about the day clerk?"

"We need to talk to her." The women walked back to the motel and found Ruby Elwood folding towels in the steaming motel laundry room.

"Miz Detectives," the clerk said sadly, "you know we have so much crime, robberies, and damage to our motel."

"Yes, ma'am," Jenny said as she wiped her sweating forehead.

"Miz Swanson, my boss, she told us always to write down license numbers. Vandals and thieves, you know."

Jenny's mind locked in. "Ma'am, we'd love license numbers."

"Well," Ruby said, "in the early afternoon I was in the office behind the desk. I look out the window and see this new-looking black car just facing out the driveway of the rear lot. Maybe it just backed in to turn around and went back the way it come in. You know, trucks always block one end." Ruby fumbled through her apron pockets. "Anywise, I wrote down the license number because we had no tenants in."

"About what time did you see the car?" Jenny asked.

She handed the scrap of paper to Jenny. "I'm not sure. Maybe one or two in the afternoon."

"Did you see anyone in the car?" Dawn asked.

"No." Ruby pointed a long finger out the fogged window. "The sun was shining off the windows."

"Which way did the car go?" Jenny felt that familiar pump of excitement, realizing they might have a good lead.

"To the left."

"Thank you, ma'am," Jenny said.

* * *

On the way back to the parking lot, Jenny turned to Dawn. "No sign of forced entry, right?"

"Right."

"Then we've got to find out who has a key to that motel room. If Ruby is telling the truth and there were no tenants, then someone must have let himself inside."

9

LIEUTENANT LEON LOVEMORE, Sergeant Casimir Sczlatski's immediate supervisor, was placed in charge of the Detective Bureau, the Narcotics Section, and the Gang Crimes section because he was good, not because he was black. His race did, however, give him an advantage in this city of black-dominated street crime. As Slat sat quietly, waiting for Lovemore to finish approving a requisition form, he looked around and wondered how his supervisor managed to keep his office and desk so neat and organized. Nothing was out of place- not even a stray paper clip. Lovemore's fastidiousness extended to his person. The big man's suits were always clean and crisp; his shirts bleached to a glaring whiteness, his conservative ties knotted according to the laws of geometry. The lieutenant signed the last line, then placed the form carefully in his out basket and looked up.

"What can I do for you, Sczlatski?" Normally, Slat laid it on the line with Lovemore. Now, because the chief didn't trust the lieutenant with the knowledge about the attorney general's investigation, neither would Slat. "Sir, I had some files in my office before my vacation. I can't seem to locate them, and I was wondering if they came across your desk by mistake."

"You mean those old homicide cases?"

"Yes, Sir. Those are the ones." Lovemore folded his big arms across his barrel chest. Slat noticed that the lieutenant had had a manicure. "Sczlatski, I've got those cases." Lovemore nodded toward the file cabinet behind him. "I examined the cases to see if they warrant your attention. I don't think they do. I'm sure you feel the same way." Lovemore pushed his chair back and challenged Slat with his eyes. Slat hid his irritation. "Lieutenant, homicide..."

"If you want me to be blunt, Sczlatski," Lovemore interrupted. "I don't want you wasting the bureau's time with those old cases."

"Why do you have such a hard-on for me?" Slat stood.

"Me?" Lovemore widened his eyes." A hard-on for you? Come on, Sczlatski. I've got a division to run. It's strictly a business decision."

"Yeah, sure, Lieutenant." Disgusted, Slat turned to leave. Lovemore jumped up and raised his voice. "Do you want to know, Sczlatski? You really want to know?"

"Yeah." Slat turned back and stood his ground.

"It's you. I recommended two other people for the detective sergeant's job. If you were black instead of white and Polish like the chief, I wonder if you would have gotten the promotion.

"Sorry you feel that way, Lieutenant, but you're wrong. I got the job because I deserve it."

"Each to his own opinion, Sczlatski. Just do your work. And if you want to investigate any case that's more than a year old, I want a justification report on my desk before you or any of your squad starts it...That's an order."

"Yes, Sir." Slat said with a hint of sarcasm.

"And another thing, Sczlatski." Lovemore evidently caught the sarcasm. "Quit sending the *Pulaski Press* reporter to see me all the time. As detective sergeant, you handle the press unless I say otherwise. If every one of my sergeants sent the reporters to me, all I'd be doing is talking to the fucking press."

* * *

Slat, drumming his pencil eraser against the desk as he tried to make a decision, stared out of his glass cage. He watched Fowler and Osinski pound their keyboards. Their industriousness made his uncertainty even more aggravating.

"Should I call her?" he said aloud only because his office door was closed., "I should have called her right after her divorce and not waited. How long? Six months? I shouldn't have waited until I needed something." He stood and paced around his desk. Slat wanted the most recent financial information on Billy Boyd, and Theresa Farmer, who worked at the Pulaski Credit Bureau, could get it for him. She'd done plenty of favors for him in the past. But with a hot- blooded woman like Theresa, one thing always led to another—and he wasn't sure how involved he wanted to get right now. He sat down, picked up the phone, and changed his mind, set the receiver down. He glanced at Fowler and Osinski for a few more moments. "What the hell've I got to lose? If she's pissed, she's pissed. If she's not..." He shrugged and lit a cigarette. He got her number from his disk drawer and dialed it. The phone ran, she answered.

"Theresa? It's Slat."

"I've been divorced six months now, lover boy, and I'm horny, " she purred. He laughed. "You're too much," he said appreciatively. "Here I thought you'd be angry' cuz I hadn't called."

"I'd be pissed at anyone but you, honey. But if I was waiting for anyone else, I'd probably wouldn't be so goddamed horny."

"Theresa, the reason I called . . . "

"Oh, hell, Slat. I thought this was a social call. Don't you want to see me?"

"Sure, Theresa. But . . . "

"If you want one of these extracurricular credit checks, you'll find it under my pillow tonight, Sczlatski."

"I do. but I can't go through regular police channels on this one."

"Don't want Lovemore to see your requests on the monthly credit bureau printout?"

"You'll get me the information?" Slat asked. He was met with silence.

"C'mon, Theresa...."

"Tonight, at my place. I'll have your Augsburger and your pilaf."

"You never forget."

"That's not all I remember, Sczlatski. I'm going to make you do every kinky there is, some you know, some I'll teach you, maybe know. See you tonight." She hung up, and for a second the telephone receiver sizzled in his hand. Why not pick up the information at Theresa's apartment tonight? he asked himself. It had been weeks—or months—since he had been with a woman. He coped by working long hours and going to bed half-drunk. Now the image of Theresa's voluptuous body flashed in his mind. She had been great— no, superb—the last time they made love. Every muscle in his body felt as if it had been separated from its bones fiber by fiber. Besides, he liked to wash Armenian pilaf down with Augsburger beer.

* * *

Sunlight seeped, through the slats of the mini blinds into the room, he watched her get out of bed and walk across the room. Her lush nudity stimulated him. She turned and looked down at him, then brushed her thick, dark hair back from her face with both hands. She smiled as dimples framed sensuous, full lips.

"You want that information now, Sczlatski?"

"What information?" he mumbled.

"About William Jackson Boyd."

"Oh, yeah. Him. Later. Come here, baby. It's still early."

10

AS THE JET APPROACHED THE BILLY MITCHELL International Airport outside Milwaukee, Billy Boyd wondered why his attorney, Soft Sound, called him back home early from Florida.

"Almost there, man," Billy said to his bodyguard.

"Yeah, Boss, I'm awake." Billy had two trusted bodyguards, the six-foot, seven-inch, three- hundred-pound muscular Mountain Top and the tough, wiry Popper. Mountain Top's size was a great intimidator.

"Popper going to meet us?"

"Yeah, Boss."

Billy had few requests of his protectors. One was to defend him so he'd never have to wear a firearm again. The other was that Mountain Top and Popper never wear white clothing. Billy dressed only in white. He had searched shops for the latest fashions in men's garments. His white silk shirts were offset by his neckties, which had to be white except for small decorative sprinklings of gold snowflakes or gold stars. A special designer made them to order at a price high enough to stroke Billy's ego.

His cars were all white. Every year he bought a new Lincoln Continental and a new Cadillac. His Mercedes and Rolls were kept at his condo in Longboat Key, Florida.

Gold chains, bracelets, and rings adorned his body. Billy would have looked good without them. He was six-foot, three-inches tall and weighed 195 pounds. The time he spent in the weight room kept his fifty-one-year-old body looking twenty years younger.

The passing flight attendant smiled at him. Women, he thought. I can't get rid of them. His ex-wives still came around, except for Lillie, the mother of his four children—the only woman he had ever loved.

After the plane landed at Mitchell, Popper met Billy and Mountain Top at the gate. When Billy was safely locked inside his stretch white Caddy with its bulletproof, dark-tinted windows, his bodyguards retrieved the luggage. While he waited for them to return, he wondered again why Soft Sound needed to see him. Business was better than ever, so it couldn't be creditors. Archie Dunn was in his pocket, so it couldn't be political problems. It's probably Lincoln causing some shit, he thought.

He stared glumly out the window. An unkempt black child on a fenderless bicycle weaved in and out of the airport traffic. Billy shook his head, thinking about his own childhood and how different his life could have been without the benefit of his good luck and intelligence. Now he had more money than any other black man did in Milwaukee.

Billy's father had been fatally shot in a card game before Billy was born. His mother polished toilets until she got a job as a maid at the Allerton mansion. Mrs. Allerton hired Billy full-time every summer to pull weeds and cut the grass. On weekends during the school year, he polished the silver and ran errands on his own fenderless bicycle. Lincoln Pitford, his older step-cousin, worked next door at the Smith mansion with his mother.

The pink and pretty Allerton sisters were a couple of years older than Billy. They'd look at him and giggle behind their hands. One day the older one said, "Billy, is a colored boy's thing longer than a white boy's?"

Shocked and embarrassed, he didn't respond. He told his mama, and, fearful of losing her job, she forbade him to talk to those girls. Today he owned the old Allerton mansion.

At sixteen, Lincoln and Billy were running numbers for Curly. The pay was good, but Billy wanted more. He made extra money at night, playing cards, until Curly hired him as a doorman at one of the gambling houses. A few months later, Billy ran the game at that house. While Billy worked endlessly, Lincoln slid by, doing the minimum. He spent his salary, then spent what salary he hadn't earned yet. And he hasn't changed a bit, Billy thought, disgusted.

The sound of the limousine's trunk swinging up startled Billy from his thoughts. He listened to the thump of the luggage being loaded. Then the car interior lights came on as Mountain Top joined him in the back seat.

"Soft Sound's office?" Popper asked from the front seat.

"Yeah," Billy said, and watched the cityscape pass by, so dark and old when compared to Florida's.

When Uncle Curly semi-retired, he split his gambling and prostitution businesses between Billy and Lincoln in exchange for fifty percent of the gross. Even though Billy had to pay for the overhead of the three gambling houses from his share, he was happy that Lincoln chose the prostitution business.

Billy had known that Curly was making payoffs to the police. One day Curly introduced Billy to Sam Tyrone by saying, "I want you to meet your guardian angel. Every week you give Sam fifteen hundred dollars in an envelope—five hundred a week for each place. Understand?"

From that moment, Billy hated Sam Tyrone—a corrupt black cop leeching off his own people.

"We're here, Boss." Mountain Top roused Billy from his reverie.

Sanford G. Washington, nicknamed Soft Sound, had a twelfth- floor office in the First Federal Building on Orrington Avenue. The secretary ushered Billy and Mountain Top into Soft Sound's office, while Popper stayed in the reception area.

"Billy! Billy!" Soft Sound screeched. "Top! Top!" The skinny little man with a pronounced Adam's apple and large, horned-rimmed glasses jumped up to greet them.

Soft Sound was one of the few people who could make Mountain Top smile. "Screeching Shit, we should'a named you in the old days."

"Soft Shit would do him better." Billy laughed.

Soft Sound chuckled, used to the good-humored ribbing. He had been friends with these men since they were children. The trust and affection they felt for one another were shared with no other business associates. "Billy, Top, sit down."

"Don't tell me it's about Pitford again. . . ." Billy began.

"Pitford's not why I called you, but we can deal with him first if you want," the lawyer said.

"Oh, shit," Billy moaned, putting his head back and covering his eyes.

"He makes too much noise," Soft Sound said. "He puts the bad mouth on you—not just around the hood but all over town. Of course, as Curly's stepson, he has some rights."

"Fuck him," Billy said angrily. "Do I have to put up with his shit the rest of my days?"

"I've told you a hundred times, man," Soft Sound said with elaborate patience, "give him more action. That'll shut him up."

Billy looked at Mountain Top. "What do you think?"

"Give it to him, Boss," the bodyguard said. "I can make a deal with him. He gets the action from you, but he agrees to shut his mouth. Otherwise I'll shut it for him."

"You'll still get your rent," Soft Sound pointed out, "maybe a little reduced."

"That fucker is the biggest pain in the ass." Billy sat and stewed for a few moments while the other men watched him. Billy had worked ceaselessly to build up the gambling houses, and Lincoln had allowed the prostitution ring to fall apart. Then he had come crying to Billy, needing money, needing a job, needing help out of trouble, needing . . . "All right, all right. Give him three houses. The smallest three."

Mountain Top grinned. "I'll take care of it, Boss."

Soft Sound visibly relaxed. "Now that that's settled, let's get back to why I called you in. Over at the police department there's a cop, Detective Sergeant Casimir Slat-ski. Know him?"

"Slat. Yeah, I know him. He's been around for years. Never bothered anybody on the West Side." That meant the black neighborhood. "You, Top?"

"Never bothered me." Mountain Top sank onto the cushions on the couch.

"Why do you want to know?" Billy asked.

"He's been asking questions about you, trying to run down your holdings."

Mountain Top was no longer smiling, but Billy waved off any concern. "I don't know why the cops would bother. The tax people go through my records every year."

Soft Sound concurred. "It didn't bother me much, either. All I have to do is call Leon Lovemore and holler harassment. But it came back to me that Slat-ski was also asking about Stu Jackson and Tiny Watson."

Silence. They all knew those names—the two gambling bosses who were blown away twenty years before. Billy remembered how the whole mess had started. . . .

He had been sitting at his desk at his largest gambling house. As his uncle Curly had requested, $1500 a week was going to Sam Tyrone in exchange for the cops looking the other way. Then, one day, Uncle Curly called Billy to a meeting. Sam was there.

"Billy," Curly had said, "there's too much competition with three other gambling operations on the street, sucking up the roll money. Sam and I talked to them about forming a consortium. The only one who agreed to consolidate is your friend Mountain Top, and his house is the smallest. The other two—Watson and Jackson—told Sam to fuck off."

"What're you going to do?" Billy had asked.

"I want you, Sam, and Mountain Top to lean on those two bastards until they come in with us."

Then Sam Tyrone had left. Curly told his nephew that the new partnership would yield a higher gross and that he'd be willing to drop his share of the profits from a half to a fifth.

"I'll be happy with a twenty-percent pension. I'm going into full retirement. It's your business now, Billy. I'm proud of you, boy."

That had been the happiest day of his young life. But over the next few weeks, in spite of the strongarm tactics, Jackson and Watson refused to yield. Their stubbornness resulted in their death, and from that day, Billy and Mountain Top took control of all black gambling in Pulaski. The police investigation into the homicides was inconclusive.

After the takeover, Sam Tyrone demanded $3,000 a week. Billy told him it would stay at $1,500. Then one day Sam and another detective came to the house to threaten Billy, but he didn't scare. He had been preparing for this eventuality because he had hated Sam Tyrone from day one. First, Billy had founded the Sunshine Property Management Corporation and laundered his gambling profits through that very successful, legitimate business. Second, he had inherited Curly's political power with the black aldermen, and his own efforts resulted in alliances with several white alderman. Billy Boyd no longer needed Sam Tyrone. He threw the detectives out of the house and canceled the payoffs entirely.

* * *

Detective Jenny Herschel slipped her revolver into her shoulder holster, shoved her notebook into her shoulder bag, and then led the way down the stairs from the Detective Bureau.

She was concerned that the motel key to room 112 might have been recently cut. The motel day clerk had said that the manager, whose office was at the Sunshine Property Management Corporation office, handled key replacements. Jenny decided that she and Dawn would check to see who had access to the motel keys, reread all the reports, and make a line-item checklist of leads to follow. She wanted to be overly conscientious. Any mistake—no matter how insignificant—by two women detectives would be magnified.

She also wanted to try to loosen Dawn up. The investigation would progress more smoothly and effectively if Dawn were more conversant. Many a crime were solved while the partners brainstormed. Jenny had enjoyed the luxury of easy discussions with Mike Duffy. She didn't have that with Dawn.

"We're stopping for breakfast or coffee," Jenny told her after they got into the detective car.

"I don't drink coffee," Dawn responded after sliding into the passenger side. "And I already ate."

"Well, I eat breakfast on the job, and I drink coffee on the job," Jenny said from between clenched teeth. "So you're coming with me."

Dawn didn't respond. She sat upright, her short skirt pulled tight above her crossed knees. Her hazel eyes stared straight ahead.

"We're partners," Jenny said, her anger building. "We work together physically and mentally." She spun the steering wheel as she turned the squad around a corner. "You can't plan your moves in the office. You can't think imaginatively in the office. People interrupt, phones ring. We've got to do it together in a coffee shop. Or sit on a park bench together."

After noticing she was speeding, Jenny quickly braked. "Most officers won't admit that they don't want to work with their partner. But you can bet your ass I will. I've got a job to do, and I'm going to do it with or without you. If you're going to be an unpleasant leash around my neck, then good-bye, Dawn Mazurski. So make up your mind—are we are going for coffee or not?"

Dawn, her gaze riveted out the window, didn't respond.

The hell with her, Jenny thought, pulling the car into the parking lot that separated Mama's Restaurant from Ski's Inn. She'll come across as a partner, or she'll go. A sudden realization swept over her, and she felt different. Jenny had always been with a senior partner. She had been the student, the receiver of advice, the listener, and the recipient of orders. Now, for the first time, it was the reverse. To Jenny's surprise, she felt confident and tough—and she liked the feeling.

Without a backward glance, Jenny walked into Mama's Restaurant. Dawn followed. A blue-speckled counter bordered one wall, and six booths lined the opposite wall. In the center were twelve round tables with calico cloths. The gray-headed Italian grandmother who spoke broken English and knew all her customers by their first name was a first-rate cook of Polish cuisine.

"This is Dawn, Mama." Jenny straddled a counter stool.

"Breakfast for you?" Mama asked Dawn after she took Jenny's order of coffee and a bagel.

"Iced tea," said Dawn as she, too, straddled a stool.

Jenny pulled out her notebook and reviewed aloud what information they had. Dawn, hesitant but businesslike, contributed a couple of good ideas. Jenny was pleased. It was a start.

* * *

The Sunshine Property Management Corporation could never be accused of racial discrimination. Though blacks were the predominate employees,

Billy Boyd hired whites, Orientals, and Hispanics. His rental-property manager and occasional escort was Ericka Swanson, a very tall, extremely attractive blond of Swedish ancestry. She was his type. It was well-known that Billy's wife, Lillie, had been a lovely blond—one of the most popular girls in their high school. She was a legend in Pulaski. It had taken guts—or incredible stupidity—for her to defy her parents by breaking up with Archie Dunn, the football team captain and student council president, then eventually marrying a young black man.

Jenny introduced herself to the statuesque manager, then asked if any keys for room 112 had been lost or missing recently. As Miss Swanson pulled open a file drawer labeled Motel, Jenny eyed the woman's short Lycra skirt and tight pullover blouse. *Ericka,* she thought, *is dressed to attract men—certain types of men.* She glanced at Dawn. Her skirt was short, also, but she looked stylish.

Ericka reviewed a file folder, then looked up and said, "I can't answer your questions without Mr. Boyd's permission."

"What's the big deal?" Jenny said congenially. "We're only asking about missing keys."

"Miss Swanson," Dawn said. "We're conducting a homicide investigation. We certainly would appreciate your cooperation."

Jenny glanced in surprise at Dawn. *She's coming around. Will wonders never cease?* "That's right, Miss Swanson. I'm sure Mr. Boyd would expect you to cooperate fully with the police."

"And I will," Ericka said tersely, "after he's told me to do so."

"When can we see Mr. Boyd?" Dawn asked.

Miss Swanson turned her attention to an appointment book. "I'm afraid his schedule is booked today...and tomorrow."

"May we have his home phone or address?" Dawn asked.

"I can't . . ."

"Of course not," Jenny said, disgusted. "Forget it."

On their way to the car Jenny said, "Don't you know where Billy Boyd lives? I thought all cops knew that."

"No."

"One of the mansions on Sheridan Road. You know the ones you can't see from the road?" Jenny buckled her seat belt in place. "We're going to find him. You're not going to believe his house. Get out the drool bucket. It's gorgeous."

11

JENNY STOPPED THE CAR NEXT TO THE INTERCOM in the brick wall by the ten-foot-high iron gate.

"A black man lives here?" Dawn asked, incredulous.

"Yes. It's a real rags-to-riches story, if you can ignore how he made his dough."

After identifying themselves, the gate swung open, and Jenny drove the squad car a few hundred yards down the driveway, past a pond, flower gardens, and several towering oaks. She parked under a stone- canopied driveway.

"I hope it's okay to park here," Dawn said.

"Hey, we're the law. We can park anywhere," Jenny told her.

Dawn followed Jenny up the half-dozen cement steps to the front door, which was opened by a tiny black woman before the detectives could knock.

"Please wait here," the housekeeper said in a small voice. "I'll tell Mr. Boyd you want to see him."

Dawn looked around. Everything was oak, shined to a deep, rich polish: the floor, doors, stairway, and paneling. A carved oriental rug in maroon, navy, and cream graced the floor. Deep gold damask draperies covered the windows and pooled on the floor. Massive furniture lined the walls, and an enormous mirror with cut-glass flowers hung between two doors that led to elegantly decorated rooms. Dawn caught a glimpse of herself in the mirror. She was wide-eyed and gaping. She snapped her mouth shut and tried to look more nonchalant.

After the housekeeper returned, Dawn and Jenny followed her through the house and out a rear door to a glass-enclosed swimming pool. Dawn's eyes adjusted to the sunlight. There, in front of her, was a man patting himself dry with a towel. She sucked in her breath at the sight of his magnificent bronzed body. Embarrassed, she hoped Jenny hadn't heard her.

Her gaze traveled to his face. His features were as pleasing as his body—symmetrical, fine, balanced. So this was Billy Boyd.

"I'd ask you to join me in the pool, but I know you're both working. May I offer you ladies a soft drink?"

"No, thank you," Dawn and Jenny chimed.

"What can I do for you today?" he asked.

Jenny explained the reason for their visit.

"I'm sorry you were inconvenienced," Billy said, draping the towel around his neck and down his chest. "My employees are expected to follow my company's policies. I'm sure you both understand, having your own department's protocol to contend with. I'll call Ericka and have her get you the information you want."

He pressed a single button on his pool phone. Dawn's eyes followed the distinctive lines of his chest muscles, the flat belly, the— she looked up and found him watching her. She flushed.

"Ericka, are any keys missing for one-twelve?" he asked. "Not in the past three years? Okay, thank you. Hold on a minute." He looked at Jenny. "Anything else?"

She shook her head.

"Okay, Ericka, that's all. Thanks." He hung up the phone and looked at Dawn. "Is there anything else you need?"

Feeling the heat of his gaze, she shook her head stupidly.

"Nothing," Jenny answered for her. "Thank you. You've been very cooperative. We'll find our way out."

"Anytime," he said after them.

As the detectives walked quickly through the house, Jenny playfully bumped into Dawn. "He sure was eyeballing you."

"I-I didn't notice."

Jenny chuckled. "Yeah, yeah. Don't be embarrassed—he's a very handsome man." They went down the front steps and to the squad. Jenny, grinning wickedly, pointed at the windshield. "See? No parking ticket. Okay, let's track down that car seen behind the motel—or have you had enough excitement for the day?"

Dawn didn't know what to make of Jenny. The woman had been so resentful when they first were paired. Now she was relaxed, a tease. Not knowing how to interpret her partner's changeable behavior, Dawn did not respond to Jenny's jokes. She pulled her notepad out of her purse. "The car's license checked to Raymond Tee in Milwaukee. Nothing on him in either our criminal or traffic records or with NCIC." Dawn was referring to the National Crime Information Center in Washington, DC.

During the drive to Milwaukee, Dawn thought about Billy Boyd. She knew very little about him. Although she was a woman of color, having inherited her complexion from her Jamaican mother, her father was a white Pole, so she had not grown up in Pulaski's black community. As a result, gossip about the West Side's native sons was unknown to her.

She'd heard talk among the cops that Billy had made his original wealth from illegal gambling. For some inexplicable reason, she felt proud of him for that—for creating opportunity where none existed. He, like her, had fought the white system and won. How tough had his battle been against the white odds? As tough as hers? Had he suffered as much as she had because of prejudice? Did he hate the whites and their closed system as much as she did? Dawn wanted to find out the answers to those questions and hoped that, as a result, she might learn to understand herself.

* * *

When Jenny found South Twenty-seventh Street in Milwaukee, she drove slowly around the block while she and Dawn checked in vain for Raymond Tee's dark sedan. Jenny parked the squad near a two-story, four- flat brick apartment building. Drizzle fell on the empty, desolate street.

"The license number checked to this address," Dawn confirmed.

"The guy was probably just turning around behind the motel," Jenny said, wanting to go home.

It had been a long day. The phone conversation with Tee's landlord had yielded nothing. The man wanted to help, but he didn't know what his tenant did for a living or whether he was married or single. Tee always paid three months' rent in advance with a money order. There was no lease. And no, he didn't have anything with Tee's signature. He had seen Tee once, when he rented the place two years before. He remembered a middle-aged man.

They checked for Tee's vehicle in the garage behind the building. It was not there. The drizzle turned to rain as they scurried into the building's vestibule. They found an R. Tee listed on a brass mailbox. They rang his apartment, but no one responded.

"Let's check with the neighbors, then go home," Jenny said. "You take the one upstairs, and I'll get the two downstairs."

They talked to all three neighbors. No information. *Time to call it a day,*Jenny thought. *Thank God.* She and Dawn walked in silence to the squad car. Neither spoke until they approached the turnoff for Pulaski. The windshield wipers slapped a rhythm that was soothing, hypnotic. *That bed is going to feel mighty good tonight,* she thought.

"You all right?" Dawn asked. "Want me to drive?"

"No, thanks. I'm fine. Just thinking. The two downstairs couples said he's never home days," Jenny said, just to keep awake. "Sometimes at night they can hear him but don't recall ever having seen him."

"Same with the one upstairs," Dawn said. "Odd that none of the neighbors ever see him."

"He probably comes and goes only at night," Jenny said through a yawn. "Let's come back tomorrow night if Slat'll okay the overtime. We're probably wasting our time. My guess is that Raymond Tee was just turning his car around behind the motel because the alley was blocked."

"Maybe," Dawn said grimly. "But what was he doing in that alley in the first place?"

* * *

The next night Jenny sandwiched their unmarked squad car on the street between two parked cars a half block from Tee's apartment.

Dawn made herself comfortable in the passenger seat. She stole a sideways glance at Jenny. The woman had been thawing, that was for sure, and

Dawn wanted to make some move toward friendship. “Ever been married?” she blurted out, then felt embarrassed.

“Yeah,” Jenny said, surprised. “Once. But it didn’t last long. There was another guy I would have married.”

“He didn’t ask?” This second question came out easier.

“No, he died,” Jenny said quietly.

Dawn turned toward Jenny. “Oh, God! I’m so sorry!”

“That’s okay. It was a long time ago. How about you?”

“No. I’ve never even been engaged. Hell, I’ve never gone steady with a guy.”

“Don’t you care for guys?”

Dawn turned toward her window. “Sure I do. I just can’t seem to find a good one who likes me, too. It’s harder for women of color. The men . . .” She shrugged. “I know someone *you* like. . . .”

“Who?” Jenny rolled down her window, allowing cooler air into the car.

“The sergeant.” Dawn lowered the volume of the police radio, so the noise wouldn’t carry.

“Slat?” Jenny asked, incredulous.

“Yes, Slat. Don’t bullshit me, girl. You’d love to climb in his drawers. I see how you look at him.”

“Not me. He’s just a great guy.”

“Great, my ass. You don’t fool me.”

Jenny looked at Dawn, and they both laughed. A barrier of newness between the women dissolved. As they watched the apartment- building’s entrance, they talked the night away. Finally the sky lightened with a false dawn.

Dawn stretched, arching her back. “No Raymond Tee,” she said, yawning. “We’d better head back to Pulaski. I guess we wasted the night on this stakeout.”

“I don’t think our time was wasted,” Jenny told her. “We had a good time.” “Yeah.” Dawn smiled warmly. “We sure did.”

* * *

A few hours later, after going home to shower and change, Dawn and Jenny met at Mama’s, to sort through a list of former employees of the Sunshine Motel.

“We’ve got thirteen males. About half are maintenance, and half are desk clerks.” Jenny buttered her bagel. “We’ve got dates of birth and addresses.”

“Two are dead,” Dawn said. “That bagel smells good. Maybe . . . yeah, I’ll take one.” She called her order to Mama.

“Okay, so that leaves eleven.” Jenny blew on her steaming coffee before risking a sip.

“Nine of the eleven have arrest records, mostly minor. Two have a record for sex crimes. One is in jail, and the other lives here in town.”

With a satisfied look Mama placed the toasted bagel in front of Dawn. "Thanks, Mama."

"Who?" Jenny asked.

"Roger S. Cooper. I pulled some old arrest reports. He's a thirty-eight-year-old homosexual, possibly unemployed."

"Why did he leave the motel?"

"Fired after being arrested for taking indecent liberties with a twelve-year-old boy."

Jenny whistled low. "Guess we check out Roger." Jenny remembered the name and the man. Homer Braun had arrested Cooper a few months before for soliciting the detective in Centennial Park. He'd grabbed Homer's crotch, and it had taken poor Homer a month to live down the ribbing from the other officers.

* * *

An hour later, Jenny and Dawn were riding the elevator to the third-floor in one of Pulaski's newest and most fashionable apartment buildings. Jenny rang the doorbell, which chimed, and Roger Cooper opened the door.

Dawn held up her police badge. "I'm Detective Mazurski, and this is Detective Herschel."

They stepped inside as Roger moved back, extending his arm in a gesture of entry. They followed him into a well-furnished living room. The white walls were adorned with colorful abstract prints. Off-white shag rugs the same color as the modern leather sofa and love seat covered the parquet wooden floors.

After some small talk about the apartment, Jenny got to the point. "Mr. Cooper, you used to work at the Sunshine Motel. Where have you been working since?"

"I am on unemployment," he answered crisply.

"Why did you leave there?" Jenny asked.

"They let me go."

"Why did they let you go?"

"Recession."

"Yes," Jenny said. "I'm sure."

"Well," he drawled, "there was a minor disagreement over my life-style."

"Roger, did you ever have any reason to take keys from or have keys made from the Sunshine Motel?" Jenny asked.

"Absolutely not!" He placed both hands on his hips.

"Are you sure about that?" Jenny asked.

"Of course I'm sure!" Roger abruptly sat on the couch and wiped the dampness from his forehead.

"Would you take a polygraph test to verify that?" Jenny asked.

"Yes!" He stood and stuck his hands in his pockets. "I have nothing to hide."

"Did you know a young boy was found dead in the motel?" Jenny asked.

"I read something about it in the newspaper." He slowly walked to the other side of the room and lowered himself into a chair. Both women pivoted as he changed position. Roger looked at his hands, before sitting on them.

Jenny felt as if she were in control. It was a new high for her. Whenever she worked with her regular partner, Mike was always the one in charge. His interrogation style was direct, and because of his imposing physique, he usually got answers. Mike relinquished control to Jenny only when they interviewed female victims or young children.

She watched beads of sweat slide down Roger Cooper's forehead. Dawn, wide-eyed, stared back and forth from Jenny to Cooper.

"That child was murdered last Friday afternoon." Jenny walked closer and stood over him. "Where were you last Friday, Roger?"

"I don't—yes! I was at the park." He cleared his throat. "I think."

"Would anyone remember seeing you?" Jenny fired the question. She had to hit him again and again until he went to his knees.

"I don't know," he whined, covering his mouth. "Wait! There must be. I have lots of friends."

"Their names?"

Roger gave three first names.

"Last names?" Jenny asked.

"I can't remember." He sank deeper into the chair, crossed his legs at the knees, and folded his arms protectively across his chest. "You're making me nervous."

"Roger, we'll be back tomorrow. We want last names, addresses, and phone numbers. You need an alibi. Understand?"

Roger burst out crying. "Yes," he wailed.

The women let themselves out while he blubbered.

"You sure had him squirming," Dawn said as they waited for the elevator. "I like the way you interrogated him."

"Thanks." Jenny looked at Dawn and smiled. "Who shall we put the fear of God into next?"

Dawn checked her notes, then looked up, surprised. "Father Julius is next. He's in charge of the altar boys."

12

"It was one of the most difficult funerals I've ever officiated at." Father Julius closed his eyes and leaned his silvery head back on his chair. "What worse grief is there than to bury a child? I'll tell you—to bury a youngster who has been defiled by a sexual deviant! Murdered! Ah, Lord, that poor family! As for Mr. Merriman—well, there is no comforting him. Won't even talk to me. God in heaven, preserve us!"

Jenny, seated on a couch next to Dawn in the St. Michael's rectory study, thought it best not to interrupt what might be an inner reaching for grace from the Almighty.

At last Father Julius looked up. "You ladies Catholic?"

Jenny noticed that he refrained from addressing them as police officers or detectives, though he'd worked with her at times when she was in uniformed patrol.

"I was baptized Catholic," she answered.

His brown eyes frowned, as he said, "In other words, you have fallen away from the Church?"

Jenny wished she had never responded to his question. She had broken a rule by placing herself on the defensive, but as a child in parochial grade school, she had been conditioned always to answer a priest's questions and do as he said. He was all-powerful, God's representative on earth. Even the nuns, who carried much authority, deferred to the priests.

"I'm agnostic," Dawn said.

Jenny suppressed a grin, realizing that, in her way, Dawn was defending her by attracting Father Julius' attention on to herself.

"Maybe sometime we could—" the priest began.

"Sir," Dawn interrupted, "we understand that the Merriman boy was active at St. Mike's. We have to know what he did here and whom he may have been close to."

"I'm not sure." Father Julius' reply was curt. "I can tell you that the boy was a good Catholic. Helped with masses, vigils, weddings, funerals, and baptisms. He was involved in this year's paper drive."

"Who did he work with?" Dawn asked. "Who's in charge of the paper drive?"

"The church council. You'll have to talk to its chairman, Alderman Archie Dunn."

* * *

While Dawn and Jenny were talking to Father Julius, Tony Tattaglia and Father Patrick Daley were parked down the street from the rectory.

"So Father Julius is permanently assigned to St. Michael's," Tony said.

"Yes."

"Are you familiar with this parish?"

"Yes," Patrick answered. "I help out here with mass and confessions at least once a week."

They were still keeping an eye on the priest and his activities. Tony felt tense. If Daley had an informant, then the police had their sources, too, and would be closing in on Julius. The point of the game was to spirit the errant priest out of town before the bad publicity hit the papers and before the local law-enforcement and justice systems got him. But Tony still hadn't seen Archbishop Coughlin, and Patrick couldn't arrange the appointment, in spite of what was getting to be a desperate situation. Pedophiles couldn't control themselves. Other children would suffer—or die. But until the archbishop told him to move, Tony couldn't do a thing.

His voice was low, distant. "That detective reminds me of — yeah! That's it! Looks like a girl I worked with at a summer camp."

"Which one?" Father Daley asked.

"The one in Michigan."

"No. Which woman?"

"The blond."

"Tony, what are you talking about?"

"I was nineteen. I took a summer job at a camp for orphans near Iron Mountain, Michigan. You had to go back to Chicago to help your dad."

Father Daley nodded.

"I remember it as if it was yesterday," Tony went on. "A man can forget some women in between, but never the first or the last."

"Hah! Bet you don't remember the name of the first."

The challenge was met with a long pause. "I'll think of it; don't rush me. Anyway, the rigors of the seminary were over. I had three months of light work, fun, and relaxation. I was assigned to work as a swimming instructor. I was also in charge of a cabin of sixteen kids, seven- to ten-year-olds. And, of course, I would assist with morning mass."

"Was it co-ed?"

"Yeah, in a separate-but-equal way. After the first month at camp, the female swimming instructor injured her ankle, so they had me also instruct the girls." Tony was talking with his head back and his eyes closed.

"All this time goes by, and you still remember," Patrick said. "No wonder you didn't make it through the seminary."

"Of course, I remember! Lost my virginity to her."

"I'd thank you for not telling me more," Patrick told him.

Tony grinned, thinking back to that great summer. He couldn't remember her name. She had been a counselor and a canoe instructor and sent him sidelong glances during the evening swim hour set aside for counselors. Whenever Tony surfaced after a dive, she'd be smiling at him. She'd wait until he was looking her way, then she'd climb onto the diving raft, bending so her suit top would expose most of her....

"Breasts."

"What did you say?" Father Daley asked.

"Nothing." Tony closed his eyes and again escaped to the past . . ..

For three weeks, she kept smiling, teasing, and tormenting him. He had enjoyed seeing those breasts. Actually, it was the enjoyment that bothered him. He'd fold his hands in prayer at night, trying to avoid fondling himself. *Dear Jesus,* he'd pray, *keep my mind from straying to thoughts of the flesh. Help me, dear Jesus. Mother of God give me the strength.*

However, halfway through the Our Father, her breasts would enter his mind. He'd forget where he was and would have to start over.

In confession on Saturday he'd confess to impure thoughts, but he never got specific. Therefore, the priest thought little of it; most young men had such thoughts. If he'd said that he had impure thoughts about one of the counselors at the camp, he'd have been transferred immediately.

As the lifeguard assigned to the evening swim, he couldn't leave his post on the diving raft until all of the swimmers were ashore. One particular Friday evening, the counselors were walking up the path toward their cabins. He climbed up to the high dive to take one last look around, then checked the tag board on the end of the pier. If all tags were gone, then all swimmers were in.

On this evening, one lone orange tag dangled from the board. He looked around. The blond was waving at him and treading water about fifty feet beyond the raft.

"Time's up," he called, his voice cracking. He cleared his throat. "You'll have to go in."

"Not unless you can catch me."

"Please!" he shouted. "Time's up!" He glanced toward shore for help, but no one was around. He didn't know what to do.

"Come get me!" she shouted, and swam toward the center of the lake.

"Jesus help me." Again he looked toward the shore, then jumped in and, as the sun set, swam toward the girl. When he got to within a few feet of her, she dove under the surface. He stopped, treading water, and waited.

She surfaced behind him and tapped him on the shoulder.

He turned. She was a foot away, topless, and laughing at him. She spewed water into his face. Through the clear water he saw her small breasts with large, protruding nipples. As she moved closer, there was an explosion in his trunks . . ..

"Tony! Tony!" Father Daley brought him back to the present. "Pay attention."

"Yeah," Tony said dreamily. "I wonder whatever happened to that girl."

"I certainly don't know," Father Daley said, his frown fixed on the rectory's front door.

Tony closed his eyes and tried to recapture the feelings from that special summer. During the remaining month at camp, they had made love almost every night. In between the lovemaking, guilt assailed him. He prayed, but images of her fine, athletic body would surface, blanketing the guilt. He was afraid to go to confession. Not until after he dropped out of the seminary did his guilt subside—somewhat?

When he left the seminary, he went to Loyola University Law School in Chicago. There, he met several Jesuit priests and thought about becoming a Jesuit. The vow of celibacy changed his mind. So he compromised by working for the Church as an attorney.

Time and events led Tony into secret work for the Vatican. He learned things about the Catholic Church structure that only a handful of people knew.

Father Daley moved in the seat. "Hey! They're leaving."

They watched as the female detectives walked from the rectory to their unmarked squad.

Tony turned the key in the ignition and the car wouldn't start.

"C'mon," Father Daley said with a tone of sarcasm, "Can't you start a car?"

"Damn engine flooded."

"They are out of sight now. Nice going."

13

FATHER JULIUS WENT TO THE WINDOW and peeked between the draperies. He watched the detectives drive away.

"Oh, my Lord," he moaned. "Why do You test me? Please ease my burdens so I solve my own problems and control my own desires. I cannot deal with all this."

He sank into his chair, picked up the phone, and punched a number. "Archie? This is Father Julius. Sorry to bother you at work, but I was just interviewed by those two female detectives."

"What'd they want?" the alderman asked.

"Matter of that Merriman boy. The department should have sent a male detective under such sexually sensitive circumstances. I suggest you advise the police department to separate these women, so they'd each be under the protective arm of a male detective."

"They should be at home under the care of a husband," Archie growled. "I'll talk to the mayor. Turski is too liberal."

The priest was beginning to feel heartened. "I respect Chief Turski," he said carefully, knowing how Archie felt about the man, "but he doesn't realize that traditional values are deeply inbred in this community. Female detectives are almost as radical a concept as female priests."

"Father, I'll handle the matter."

"One of them, that dark one, was wearing a skirt absolutely inappropriate to the responsibilities of her position. It was much too short."

"They won't bother you again, Father. I promise."

"Thank you, Archie, I knew I could count on you."

* * *

With only half his mind on his morning tasks, Detective Slat forced himself through his duties. The furrows on his cheeks sank deeper as he frowned. He figured there had to be useful information in Ernie's old report about the assassinations: birth dates, friends, and relatives of the deceased gamblers. But all of those old homicide cases were now in the locked office of Lieutenant Lovemore.

Preoccupied, he moved from desk to desk, up one side of the long detective office, then down the other, distributing reports to his crew.

"Whoa! Slat!" Stan Osinski fanned out the reports handed to him. "Herschel's been working this one."

"Oh, sorry." Slat took the file back and placed it on Jenny's desk with the same hand he was holding a cigarette.

"You're dropping ashes on my desk, Sergeant." She brushed them to the floor with the papers he'd handed her.

"Wait, Sarge." Odell Fowler sifted through the reports Slat had handed him. "This is Jenny's, too."

Slat took it but remained deep in thought. If he wanted to understand Sam Tyrone's suicide, he'd have to start with the assassinations, where the principles in the investigation were linked.

Lovemore refused to release the files Slat needed. He could go to the chief, but Lovemore would go nuts. Going over the head of a supervisor was almost as bad as failing to back up a partner. *Had Lovemore been involved in the payoffs?* Slat wondered for what seemed like the hundredth time.

After assigning cases to his teams, Slat walked out into the hallway and toward the water cooler. Somehow, he had to get his hands on those files . . .. The door to Lovemore's office was open. He glanced inside; the room was empty. Slat hurried back into his office and dialed Lovemore's extension.

The one secretary for four of the administrative offices on the second floor answered.

"This is Slat," he told her. "Is Lovemore available?"

"No, he had to run over to City Hall. Said he'd be back by nine-thirty. I'll tell him you called."

"Never mind. I'll catch him later."

The moon-shaped clock on the wall showed 9:15. Slat hurried into the hallway, walked to the water cooler, and stalled for time. As soon as the hall emptied, Slat slipped into Lovemore's office and pulled at the handle to the top drawer of the three-tiered file cabinets. It was locked. The plunger lock was depressed on the other two file cabinets.

"Any calls for me?"

Slat heard Lovemore's voice in the hallway. Shit! The sergeant grabbed a handful of papers from the In Basket on Lovemore's desk and affected a nonchalant posture as he fanned the reports.

"Slat. He said he'd contact you later, Lieutenant."

Just then Lovemore stopped short on the threshold to his office. "What can I do for you, Sczlatski?"

"Last week's activity reports have an error," Slat lied.

"They're not there." Lovemore took a ring of keys from his briefcase, unlocked the center file drawer, and then extracted the form from a file folder. "I already forwarded the original to the Records Bureau, so you better correct it, too."

"Thanks." Slat took the report and made his escape.

* * *

"Mary Lou?" Slat called, leaning on the Record Bureau window.

The clerk came around the corner in her wheelchair.

Slat smiled. The chair was decorated with colorful plastic streamers, and an ever-changing selection of signs hung from the backrest.

"Hi, Slat! What can I do you for?"

"Would you please get me the original of last week's Detective Bureau activity report? I've got to make a correction."

"Sure, honey. Have you been behaving yourself?"

"Too old not to."

She laughed, then narrowed her eyes at him. "You look thin! You need a good woman to fatten you up."

"If I ever settle down, it'll be with you, Mary Lou. By the way, honey, who's pulling clerk duty tonight?"

"Hazel has the four-to-twelve shift. Then I have to double back from midnight to eight."

"Hey, how about dinner tonight?"

Her eyes sparkled. "Sure. I love going out to dinner with young boys. It'll have to be a quickie, though. I have to get some sleep between shifts."

"A quickie, eh? What kind of a guy do you think I am?"

She laughed, and color flooded her cheeks.

MEMORANDUM
City of Pulaski
Office of the Mayor

To: Chief Turski

Re: Detective Bureau

It has come to my attention that two unseasoned female detectives have been assigned to a highly sensitive homicide investigation.

I recommended you reevaluate this use of personnel.

The large, knobby-knuckled hands of Chief Martin Turski slowly crushed the memo into a ball, then pitched it into a wastebasket across the office.

14

THE FOLLOWING DAY, DAWN AND JENNY MET to interview suspect Roger Cooper about his alibi on the day of the murder. At his apartment, Cooper had a guest. A tall, handsome man with a flowing blond mustache who blocked the women's access into the apartment.

"Detectives, I'm Elliott Samuelson. I'm an attorney representing Roger Cooper. I have affidavits here from three witnesses attesting to his whereabouts during the afternoon in question." Samuelson handed the documents to Jenny.

She read through them. "Are these three witnesses all homosexuals?" She immediately knew that she had made a mistake.

Samuelson looked at her in triumph. "May I see your badge, please?"

Dutifully she displayed it for him, and Samuelson scribbled her badge number on his yellow legal pad. "I didn't inquire about their sexual persuasion," the attorney said coolly as he wrote. "Just as I'm not inquiring about yours."

Roger puffed out his thin chest. "And we prefer to be called gays, not homosexuals. Right, Elliott?"

Samuelson did not respond. Instead he smirked at Jenny. "You're in big trouble, Detective."

* * *

*

From his office window at the Sunshine Management Corporation, his thumbs hooked in his white vest pockets, Billy Boyd stared at the bright, new day.

"Damn," he muttered, realizing that he'd forgotten to call Archie Dunn.

When Billy needed a political favor, he didn't go to a black alderman, nor did he go to the two representatives from the upper-class ward where he lived. Instead he called Archibald Dunn. Billy had known Archie for thirty-five years. When Billy was a teenager, his black gang fought with Archie Dunn's Irish gang. He shook his head and chuckled. He and Archie had given each other fat lips and black eyes more than once. Those were the days before kids were armed with guns and hopped up on crack cocaine, when you could blow off some steam and have a good time without killing someone.

Billy had known Archie's father, too—Archibald Dunn, Senior, had owned and operated Archie's Tavern on the South Side. He occasionally laid off a few horse bets with Billy's uncle whenever the heat was on the Irish. That man was a son of a bitch if there ever was one, Billy remembered. He wouldn't serve a black man in his tavern—in fact, if one came in for a drink, the old man would chase him out with a baseball bat— but he'd place his bets with a black man, no problem.

Archie answered Billy's call on the first ring. "Archie, Billy. How're ya doin', man?"

"Ho, Billy! Long time no see! Everything's good. How are you?"

"Busy, man. Too busy. Don't know how you stick everything into your schedule like you do. How's your Kiwanis group doin'?"

"Fine, Billy. You coming to our annual pancake breakfast this Sunday?"

"Aw, man, Can't this Sunday. But I'll take a hundred dollars' worth of tickets." Billy grabbed a pen from its holder and wrote a note. "I'll have a check sent to your office."

"Thanks, Billy. What can I do for you?"

"Archie, I'm getting complaints from some brothers on the West Side that a detective sergeant Sczlatski has reopened an unsolved murder case from 1970. The guy I think was the shooter died in prison a long time ago. Anyway, my people want me to complain to the West Side alderman. Well, man, you know those black aldermen . . . .

" Billy laughed " . . . they'd raise hell from the floor of the city council, and you guys don't need that type of publicity while the mayor's trying to attract new business here."

"None of us needs that kind of bullshit. I'll take care of it, Billy."

"By the way, I'm dealing with a couple of Chicagoians who are looking for about thirty-thousand square feet to relocate a light industrial plant."

"Hey, we gotta talk more about this."

MEMORANDUM
City of Pulaski
Office of the Mayor

To: Chief Turski

Re: Firearms Training

Embarrassing jokes and innuendoes have reached city officials about the officer who shot himself in the foot.

Please ensure this office that proper firearms training is being conducted.

Chief Turski's secretary, Ellen, handed the memo back to him. She shook her head sympathetically.

"Is this a joke?" Ellen asked. "You just requested more firearms training."

He looked at her in disgust. "And last week the city council turned down my request for more money for practice ammunition."

He took a deep breath. "Anything about it in the morning paper, Ellen?"

"Nothing in the Milwaukee papers," she said evasively. The chief did not look good to her. Dark circles rimmed his eyes, and he looked as if he had lost weight.

"What about the local paper?"

"A cartoon," she replied reluctantly, "showing officers shooting themselves in the foot. They had bull's-eyes painted on their shoes."

"How about the editorial?"

"Condemning women police officers as partners, alongside a drawing of women in uniformed miniskirts, capturing a criminal who was ogling their legs and forgot to run away."

15

"I KNOW A LOT ABOUT PULASKI,"Jenny told Homer Braun, Odell Fowler, and Stan Osinski. "But never realized there was such a huge gay population."

The detectives were sitting around their usual table at Ski's Inn. The tavern was located in the Polish neighborhood, where mass was said in Polish at the Catholic Church across the street. Mama's Restaurant, Krakowski's Butcher Shop, Kwasnieski's Grocery Store, Stan's Pool Hall, and other shops served the ethnic community. In order to be with their own, the foreign born and first-generation Polish chose to live in cramped frame houses built at the turn of the century. It was a stable, relatively crime-free area. Ski's Inn had occupied its present location since 1910. Ski, a retired Pulaski police officer now in his fifties, was a third-generation innkeeper. He could afford to move to a nicer neighborhood but would never leave the apartment just upstairs. It had belonged to his parents and grandparents. Chances were good that when his son grew up, he would also live there.

Detective Odell Fowler pushed his gold-rimmed glasses up on his nose, then filled his friends' mugs from the sweating pitcher. Drinking, if not their favorite pastime, was certainly their most absorbing one. Stan, sitting at a right angle to the table, his feet propped up on another chair, was the only shot-and-beer man in the police department. Everyone else enjoyed unadulterated "brew-skis."

"Pulaski's got more than its share of queers," Homer grumbled. Since shooting himself in the foot, he'd been on sick leave and devoting himself to opening and closing the tavern.

"You should know," Stan said distastefully, "since you keep that homosexual file in your desk. If you ever leave that folder out where I can get it, I'm going to burn the son of a bitch. You should spend your time looking for criminals and leave those people alone."

"Hey!" Homer said indignantly. "Those files are the result of years of extensive sociological research."

Odell was trying to read the sports page. He raised his head just long enough to say, "Bullshit," then returned to the scoreboard.

"Homer, the only research *you* do is with your dick," Stan growled. He fired down a shot, then yelled to Ski to bring him another.

"The perp probably picked the kid up at the park and took him to the motel," Homer continued.

"Hell." Stan lifted the shot glass between his thumb and forefinger. "Their suspect used to work at the motel. He probably had a key and used it himself or gave it to one of his friends."

Odell noticed Homer staring moodily into his mug. "Aw, Homer's sad. You miss Dawn?'

Homer cringed. "If I never work with another woman the rest of my life, that'll be fine."

"Homer, you crab ass." Stan laughed. "Take a Midol and shut up."

"Aw! Fuck you guys!" Homer hobbled on his crutches to the bathroom. On the way back, he stopped at the bar and made a phone call.

* * *

Jenny watched Homer go out the front door. *He was leaving Ski's early,* she thought. He never left the tavern early unless he had a woman somewhere. She reached for the half-empty pitcher and wished she had an important reason—a man, a lover—to leave Ski's. Her eyes slid toward one of the empty chairs that circled their table. It was Slat's chair, and no one else ever sat in it. They were always expecting him to arrive. But he'd said that he had to work tonight. Disappointment tugged at her even as she glanced at the door, hopeful he might come in anyway.

She'd leave Ski's early for Slat. Frequently their eyes met in the bar's dimness or at work. They always seemed to say the same thing. Yes, Jenny, there could be something between us. But no, Jenny, we work together.

Last year, she remembered, Slat had dated a detective. When Slat ended their relationship, the woman had quit the force. Her resignation had been a loss for the bureau; she'd been a good cop. Slat had felt terrible about her decision and made it clear he wouldn't risk that happening again.

* * *

It was just after midnight when Slat, hoping he wouldn't be seen, entered the police station.

"Don't want you to worry about this, Mary Lou," Slat said as she let him into the Records Bureau. "If I get caught, I'll say I sneaked in and took the keys while you were in the john."

"Not to worry, hon. No one'll find out." He followed her into the supervisor's office. This week's poster on her wheelchair read, What Other People Think of You Is None of Your Business. She retrieved a ring of keys and handed them to him. "A copy of every file cabinet key is kept on this."

"Thanks, Mary Lou." Slat bent and kissed her on the cheek, then hurried down the hall to Lovemore's office.

He slid a credit card between the door and the doorframe, and the door opened. Quietly he entered, then methodically tried the keys in the first file cabinet. The key worked, but those drawers did not hold the homicide files.

He opened the middle file cabinet, found the homicide files in the bottom drawer, and quickly scanned the tabs until he located the files on the two gamblers' murders. Unclipping the detective's working copies from the originals, he kept the copies. If Lovemore realized the copies were missing, Slat would say he forgot he had them in his briefcase.

He shut the bottom drawer, locked the file cabinet, and returned the key ring to Mary Lou.

"You owe me, Slat," Mary Lou said as he kissed her again on the cheek.

16

SERGEANT GORDY MACBELL, THE THIRTY-YEAR-OLD SUPERVISOR of the 6:00 PM to 2:00 A.M. Tactical Unit, responded to Homer Braun's phone call. He met Homer in the parking lot between Mama's Restaurant and Ski's Inn. Homer maneuvered through the gravel parking lot to Gordy's squad car then slid his crutches into the back seat.

"Hey, man, what's going down?" Gordy asked.

"Gordy, we have to do Jenny a favor," Homer told him. "You know the case?"

"The kid in the motel?"

"Yeah. Jenny's got a suspect, but one of those faggot lawyers is claiming Cooper up, and three park queers are giving him alibis. You know how they stick together—no pun intended." They both laughed. "If we can get a couple of faggots up tight on a bust, they might come up with some info on Cooper and his alibis."

"What can I do?" Gordy asked.

"Rouse them tonight. How many guys you got working?"

"Six."

"Great. Let's go."

"Homer, you're on crutches . . . in case you haven't noticed. Aren't you on sick leave?"

"Don't worry about me, pal. Let's do it."

Homer drove back to the station with Gordy, who put four of his six men, himself included, in plain clothes. Then they proceeded to Centennial Park, to the area known to be frequented by gay men. The police divided into three teams of two cops, with Gordy and Homer on one team. The remaining two uniformed men parked a block away in a marked prisoner van, ready to roll when summoned to transport the accused.

Homer planned to stroll through the darkened park, with Gordy as a backup. That would be a good balance, he figured, with his being incapacitated and Gordy being a marathon runner. Knowing he'd never live down another injury, Homer carefully placed the points of his crutches in the darkness.

The police cruised under trees and between bushes. Gays usually roamed a sparsely wooded meadow and made their contacts near small trees not far from the central parking lot. Aldermen consistently denied budget requests from the Park Department to place lights in the parking areas and along the hiking paths.

As Homer hobbled along, he saw the brightly glowing ends of cigarettes some gays used as signals. "I should call this the lightning- buggers brigade," he muttered to himself, struggling on the soft grass toward a slender middle-aged man.

"Oh, you hurt your foot? Poor fellow."

"Yes," lisped Homer, playing a part he loved.

"Maybe I can help it feel better." The man knelt and patted the cast with one hand. His other hand swiftly felt its way up Homer's leg.

"Pheeet!" Homer whistled for Gordy as he reached for the man. Because of his crutches, Homer lost his balance and fell forward, sliding over the man's back and landing with his face in the grass. His mouth was full of dirt and leaves.

"Oh, you poor man," the fellow said while trying to scramble out from under Homer. "You shouldn't get so excited so quickly."

"Fuck you!" Homer said, spitting debris. He heard the sound of Gordy's approaching footsteps.

But as Gordy reached down to help Homer up, the gay man struck him on the back. "He's mine, you bastard! Go away! I saw him first!" he shouted, and took a swing at Gordy's face.

"Get that asshole!" Homer hollered, managing to raise himself on his hands and knees.

Gordy, grabbing the man, identified himself as police officers.

"Don't hurt me," the man pleaded.

"Shut your fucking mouth!" Homer found his crutches and balanced himself.

"Oooh, you're so tough. I like that." He man said running his tongue over his lips.

"I said shut up, asshole!"

"Relax, Homer. I got him." He led the man toward the parking lot.

"Homer? Your name is Homer?" The man twisted in the belt hold Gordy had on him. "I love that name."

"Shut up!" Homer shouted while trying to keep up with Gordy and the prisoner. "I'll beat your fucking ass!"

"Let me help Homer with his crutches," the prisoner offered.

"Gordy, slow down. I want to pound lumps on that asshole."

They arrived at the prisoner van. The other two teams stood ready with prisoners. "You guys are slow," the driver joked.

After locking their prisoner in the van, Gordy and Homer headed back into the park. Again, Gordy followed Homer.

"Fucking faggot," Homer grumbled under his breath, and headed for another red cigarette glow, centered between two large clumps of bushes. As he hobbled closer to the bushes, the lit cigarette flew toward him, end over end through the air.

"Hey, you faggot motherfucker," someone shouted from the darkness. "Gimme your fucking wallet before I bust your fucking balls."

Three big teenagers emerged from the darkness and strode toward him. Homer dropped one crutch, grabbed the bottom end of the other crutch to use as a weapon, and spread his legs for balance.

"Pheeet," he whistled, then shouted, "I'm a cop! You're under arrest, you shit pile."

"Yeah, right," one of them said, waving a knife menacingly.

The boys kept coming. Homer swung his crutch at them. The crutch hit the boy with the knife, but another assailant grabbed Homer from behind. The third yanked the crutch from Homer's grip, swung it around, and hit Homer hard over the head. He pitched forward onto his knees. Stars burst before his eyes.

"Freeze! Police!" Gordy shouted.

The boys disappeared into the blackness.

"Help me up, Gordy. Shit! My head's killing me." He reached up to feel the back of his head. His hand came away wet and sticky.

Gordy stuck his weapon in its holster. "Oh, shit, Homer. You got blood all over your face. Come on, I'll get you to the hospital."

* * *

Father Julius, the police department's chaplain, stopped short at the anger in Slat's voice. The sergeant and his detective were on the other side of the curtain in the emergency room.

"For chrissakes, Homer! You weren't supposed to be working." Slat was furious. "You're on sick leave!"

"Seventeen stitches, and they couldn't freeze it," Homer moaned. "Can you imagine their running a sewing needle in your scalp while you're awake?"

"That should teach you a lesson," Slat said without sympathy.

As he was waiting to visit Homer, Father Julius noticed Chief Turski arrive at the hospital.

"Hello, Father!"

"Good evening, Chief. Visiting Detective Braun?"

A disgusted noise escaped Turski's throat as he came to a stop. "Yes."

"Chief, I've received complaints over the years from homosexuals regarding treatment from your officers." They both stepped aside as a tall man in a dark suit exited the emergency room. "I've never brought the matter to any official's attention. I generally counsel the victim."

"Wish you'd bring it to my attention from now on, Father."

The priest nodded agreement. "Wish I had. Detective Braun's name has been mentioned several times as being intimidating and insulting toward homosexuals. I'd appreciate your looking into it."

"You can count on it, Father. Thank you for bringing it to my attention. In fact, I can think of no more appropriate time than the present, can you?"

"No. I can't."

Turski opened his mouth, then shut it, as if reconsidering. Then he went ahead anyway. "I'm interested, Father, in your concern for homosexuals. The Church hasn't looked with any favor—"

"The Church should love and accept all of God's children," Julius said flatly.

"You're right, of course. Good-bye, then."

Julius nodded good-bye. *Weaknesses of the flesh and weaknesses of the mind,* Father Julius thought. *Which is easier to live with? Which is easier to suppress? Both are really problems of the soul. Please help me, Lord.* Father Julius blessed himself, then followed Turski back into the hospital.

"I didn't see those women detectives," Tony said as he slid into the driver's side of their car in the hospital parking lot.

"So what? It's Julius we're concerned with," Father Daley told him.

"Did you call Rome?" Tony asked.

"Yeah. Monsignor Popodowski said we could stay here a few more days."

"Hmph. That's a surprise. Your archbishop must have clout. But I can't understand this waiting. If he wants him apprehended, then let me have at him before he hurts another kid—if he is the murderer."

"Why are you complaining?" Father Daley asked. "You're paid well. Your expenses are covered, and your assignments are usually interesting and glamorous."

"Following an errant isn't interesting or glamorous, Patrick."

"No, of course not," he said edgily. "But how often are you given these cases?"

"Between rarely and never," Tony growled. "More often I'm mediating between governments and terrorists. That's what I'm trained for, and that's what I'm good at. And why are you so angry with me all of a sudden? You've got a good life."

"Yes, yes," he said. "It's everything I've worked for. But I believe in what you're doing, too. Priests who fall victim to temptation— be it wine or women or little boys—must be taken out of circulation until their problems are rectified."

"This is garbage work. It's kidnapping, Patrick."

"It's not!" Father Daley said hotly. "It's an involuntary transfer for the overall good of the Church!"

* * *

The morning after pilfering the files from Lovemore's office, Slat opened his dust-covered office windows. The smell of bacon and coffee from the firemen's kitchen exhaust next door drifted through the air.

He usually arrived at work early to review the reports from the night before and prepare assignments for his detectives. He decided that today, immediately after he got his detectives out one the streets, he'd review the files he took from Lovemore.

An hour later, after his three teams had seated themselves at their desks like sleepy cows bumping around into their stanchions, Slat began handing out cases.

Suddenly, Lieutenant Lovemore, bald head glistening, slammed open the front door of the Detective Bureau. "Sczlatski! Chief's office!"

"Be there in a minute. I'm assigning cases."

"Now!" Lovemore said from between clenched teeth.

Slat handed the files to his senior detective. "Stan, hand these out, would you?"

Slat and Lovemore left. "What kind of fucking shit you got me into now, Sczlatski?" Lovemore hissed out the side of his mouth as they hurried down the long hall.

"What do you mean?" Slat asked.

"Can you recall a time when you and I have been called to the chief's office and I haven't been surprised by some shit you've stepped into? If I don't know what's happening, I sound like a dumb asshole."

Ellen waved them into Turski's office.

The sight of the chief in uniform momentarily distracted slat. Turski, with his squat, wide body, homely pug-nosed face, and protruding ears, didn't fit the police executive image. He sat leaning forward, elbows braced on his desk, and looked at them with sincere eyes. His entwined knobby hands reminded Slat of the shell of a snapping turtle.

"Lieutenant. Sergeant. Have a seat."

As a matter of courtesy, Slat let Lovemore choose a chair first.

"Men, what's the story on some twenty-year-old murders? I got a call this morning about some questions being asked."

"Since Sergeant Sczlatski is closer to that investigation," Lovemore said, "so I'll let him explain it to you, Chief."

Slat was caught off guard. He had Turski's sanction to look into these cases but had been cautioned not to let Lovemore know about it. Was this meeting a ruse to keep Lovemore in the dark? He wondered. Slat also wondered who had complained to Turski. He decided to tell the truth and proceed with caution. He'd assess any changes of expression on the chief's face and govern himself appropriately.

"According to Ernie Pope—the original investigator, now retired—a homicide investigation of two black gambling bosses in nineteen- seventy was never completed. While checking into the suicide of Ernie's old partner, Officer Sam Tyrone, I thought that I might clear any doubts of complicity the department may have had in those murders. So I looked into information about the principals in that case.

I know these are old cases, sir," he continued, "but none of us wants a murderer getting away with it. I've been working this case on my days off and after working hours."

"Chief," Lovemore said, "as you know, the sergeant has an extremely busy workload. I agree that those old cases should be tied up, but we don't have the time during normal working hours. Besides our normal personnel shortage, we have some other time-consuming homicides."

Slat had cause to wonder yet again why Lovemore was so resistant to his working those cases. He didn't want to say in front of Lovemore that he suspected Sam Tyrone was involved in the assassinations. The lieutenant had been in the Detective Bureau back then, and must have heard rumors.

"I can understand the frustration you both feel," the chief said. "There isn't much overtime money available, and if we don't pay overtime, we'll have a complaint from the union. I suggest that you not extend this investigation too much on overtime. Do a little during your working hours and submit overtime requests for at least half your time."

Slat tightened his jaw to stifle a grin. All that work burglarizing Lovemore's office was for nothing.

"Chief, we are right on the line with our overtime," Lovemore pointed out.

"But I'm assuming that we have no idea how much time these old cases will require." The chief sighed. "I have to go to the Finance Committee for some line-item adjustments. I'll make a special request for four thousand, strictly for homicide investigation overtime. If I'm lucky, I'll get half.

"Lieutenant, with your excellent presentation ability, would you prepare the justification on paper? You can present it with me at the Finance Committee meeting Wednesday at four." As the chief stood, his grotesque hands separated. "Thank you, gentlemen."

"Sczlatski," Lovemore complained as they walked back down the hallway, "you not only cause me more fucking grief than anybody on this job, now it's more work. You better get me a time estimate on that case." He walked into his office, then came right back out into the hall. "Today, Sczlatski! Today!"

* * *

The morning after the fiasco while trying to interview Roger Cooper, Jenny pulled the squad car into a visitor parking space next to the guard cage at the Poole Tractor Company's main entrance.

The white-haired security guard eyed the two detectives, then shook his head in disapproval. Jenny grinned. She was wearing form- fitting slacks. Dawn had on a miniskirt and tight sweater. The guard waved them begrudgingly through the gate.

"Why'd he shake his head?" Dawn asked.

"Our clothing. He probably thinks we should be wearing bloomers and a bustle. He's a former cop. So's the guy we're going to see- -Archibald Dunn, Junior." Jenny followed the arrow under the sign that read Elevator. "What a name. Archie. Ugh."

"Archie's better than Junior," Dawn remarked.

"He's a middle manager here, an alderman, and the parish council president at St. Michael's. He's single, good-looking, and was a football star at Pulaski High."

"He's too old for me." Dawn pressed the elevator button. "Why don't you take him?"

"Way before my time," Jenny retorted. "Be prepared for a rough time. When Turski was appointed chief, he was chosen instead of Archie Dunn. Dunn thought he had the votes of enough commissioners, but he lost by one."

Dawn clucked her tongue in mock sympathy. "So Dunn lost to an out-of-town Polack."

"Enough to piss off a homegrown Irishman big time."

On the third floor, they were directed down a corridor to a door labeled Purchasing. Inside, a secretary directed them to Dunn's office. Through the windowed door they saw him standing behind a desk laden with stacks of papers. The man was youthful looking, with his red hair graying at the temples, startlingly blue eyes, and dapper red mustache.

"Not bad," Jenny said. "Could the report have the wrong date of birth?" She knocked on the door.

"Come in. Come in." Dunn's tone was unfriendly. "I'm a busy man, too busy for this. What do you want?"

"Police, Mr. Dunn."

"I know who you are."

"We'd like a word with you about David Merriman." Jenny put her badge back into her shoulder bag. "The boy murdered last week."

"I went to the funeral. Listen, ladies, I'm an alderman. If you want to take up my time, then let it be as an alderman, not here at Poole." Dunn sounded as though he were scolding some minor employee.

"Sorry," Jenny said sweetly. "You tell us when. Tonight after work? Of course, then we'll be on overtime. Naturally, if the chairman of the city's Finance Committee okays O-T for a couple of detectives, then . . . "

Dunn sighed. "All right. Just make it quick."

"Father Julius suggested we talk to you," Jenny said, "because David Merriman worked for you on St. Michael's paper drive."

"I don't run the drive. A volunteer directs the kids on the pickups."

"Who's the volunteer?" Dawn asked.

"Jack Hamlin."

"Jack Hamlin?" the women echoed in unison and exchanged glances.

Dunn nodded.

"That's all," Jenny said, then she smiled. "Quick enough for you?"

"What a bastard," Dawn murmured once she and Jenny were out of earshot of Dunn's office. "Wonder if he's gay. Every man we talk to ogles us a little. He hardly looked at us."

"Yeah," Jenny said. "I wonder. Now we have to talk to Jack Hamlin."

17

THE DETECTIVE BUREAU WAS EMPTY, so Slat grabbed the report on the assassinations and began reading. According to the police file, Stu Jackson and Tiny Watson had been shot at the same time with a .38 caliber weapon in Watson's basement. Slat read the report several times; he was surprised and impressed by the extraordinary number of details Ernie Pope had included. Slat hadn't thought the grungy old guy had it in him. Ernie hadn't had the case pulled from him because of malfeasance, that was for sure.

Stu Jackson had told the last person to see him alive that he was going to Tiny's house for a meeting.

The last person to see Tiny Watson alive was his cousin Willie Patton. During Ernie's first interview with Patton, he didn't say much. In the margin, Ernie had penciled in BS.FU, which meant that Ernie didn't believe the alibi Willie had provided. The FU meant he planned to conduct more follow-ups on Willie Patton.

Slat scanned the pages but found no follow-up—probably because the case had been taken away. Any additional light Willie might have thrown on the case had died with him in prison.

Ernie had also interviewed Billy Boyd, who had been at a family party at his uncle Curly's home. His presence there had been corroborated.

On the back of one of the reports, Slat found columns of Ernie's scribbling. He could make out a scratching that read "To Interview." Several initials had check marks after them. Slat referenced all those initials but one set—M. T. Slat couldn't plug M. T. into any page on the homicide report.

The office remained quiet, so Slat called Ernie.

"Hey, Ernie, you been back fishing on the lake?"

"Yeah. And without you bugging me, I been getting my limit."

"That's because you don't shave that ugly chin of yours."

"Your ass. What do you want, Slat?"

"On the old homicide report, there's this initial M. T."

"That was Mountain Top," Ernie said. "Can't remember his real name. Never forget that huge son of a bitch. I never talked to him about the assassinations. He was always out of town whenever I went looking for him, and before he came back, the case was taken from me. He's Billy Boyd's right-hand man and has been around as long as I can remember. But I want to warn you, Slat," Ernie said. "Mountain Top has this super macho image around his friends and associates. If you plan to talk to him you'll have to catch him alone."

The Records Bureau showed no arrests. The Drug Unit supervisor said neither Mountain Top nor anyone in the Boyd organization had any involvement in drugs. Reports from the state and FBI disclosed nothing while a check of old records in the vault disclosed entries for gambling and battery. Mountain Top was clean, but where, but where had he been during the murders? Slat would have to interview Mountain Top and find out.

* * *

A clerk dropped some mail onto Slat's desk. One thick envelope was from the Pulaski Credit Bureau. Slat knew that would be from Theresa. He opened the credit report and read it. Sylvester Eugene Jefferson, also known as Mountain Top, owned the Mountain Detective Agency at 7600 Dodge Avenue, the same building as the Sunshine Property-Management Corporation. Sixty-five percent of the agency's business came from credit checks and investigations for Sunshine Property-Management Corporation. The rest was a guard service. Also, the agency handled some private detective work. That meant Mountain Top could legally carry a gun.

According to the file, Mountain Top lived on Sheridan Road in Billy's mansion.

18

AFTER WORK, SLAT PARKED UNDER THE MIGHTY ELMS along Sheridan Road near the entrance to Billy Boyd's mansion and waited for Billy to leave. After an hour of chain smoking, he saw Boyd's white Lincoln pull out of the driveway. Because of the darkness, Slat had no idea whether or not Mountain Top was inside the car.

In five seconds the Lincoln was out of sight down the winding road, and Slat drove through the long, scrolled-iron gates before they closed. As he entered the driveway he was blinded the oncoming headlights. Both cars screeched to a stop, their bumpers inches apart.

"Hey, man, get that motherfucking pile a shit outta my way!"

Slat leaned out the window to see Mountain Top pulling his three hundred pounds of muscle from a black Cadillac.

"Sylvester, its Sergeant Sczlatski. Pulaski Police." Slat quickly stepped from his car and leaned over his open driver's door. Having been called Sylvester, Mountain Top would know that Slat had done some checking on him. "I'd like to talk to you."

"You and I ain't got shit to talk about, man."

"Mountain Top," Slat said, "let's talk. I only need a minute."

Mountain Top stomped toward Slat. "I wouldn't be seen in the same shit house as you."

Slat stepped from behind the door. "I want to know where you were the night Watson and Jackson were killed."

Mountain Top stumbled a moment, then continued his charge up to Slat. His blacksmith-forged arms rested on disproportionately small hips. "Fuck you. How the fuck am I supposed to remember where the fuck I was twenty years ago? Get that fucking car outta my way. Cop or no fucking cop, I'll break your fucking ass. You're on the boss's property. And you ain't got no warrant."

Just then flashing headlights bore down on both of them. The white Lincoln skidded to a stop behind Slat's car, and two car doors slammed. Billy, silhouetted by the headlights' glare, approached, followed by a wiry man with bug eyes.

Mountain Top walked over to his boss and pointed angrily toward Slat. "This motherfucker's putting some shit on me about them old shootings."

Billy's white teeth flashed a big, congenial smile. "Slat-ski, you harassing us poor old colored folk?"

"Cut the bullshit, Billy. We've reopened the Watson and Jackson cases."

"Don't go blowing no shit up my ass," Billy said, a sudden hard edge to his voice. "You're on my property without a warrant, and you're violating my employee's civil rights by not allowing him to leave his residence."

"Yeah! Get the fuck out of my way," Mountain Top said as he turned back toward his car.

"Have it your way, Sylvester," Slat said.

Billy turned back and, looking at Mountain Top barked a laugh.

"Sylvester? Did he call you Sylvester?"

"Forget it, man!" Mountain Top was enraged.

"You had an alibi for the night of those murders, Billy, but Mountain Top didn't," Slat told him loudly enough for the huge man to hear. "Both of you had motives. If I can't get any cooperation here, I just might be able to get a grand jury to decide what to do." No matter how tough Mountain Top was, Slat knew he'd worry about the possibility of an indictment.

Slat also knew that no sane district attorney would take that case to a grand jury. Mountain Top would probably name a couple of alibi witnesses who would be dead. Then the defense attorney would ask what type of criminal investigation lets the police wait until all the defense witnesses are dead before they proceed with an indictment.

* * *

Dawn had felt the prejudice and hatred emanating from Archie Dunn in palpable waves when Jenny had interviewed him at the Poole Tractor Company. Emotions she had felt as a child, beaten in the playground at St. Michael's, and newer feelings, coursing just under the surface from the discrimination she had suffered at the police department, had threatened to overwhelm her in Dunn's small office.

To Dawn, the alderman was the personification of all that was wrong with Pulaski—the city that had hurt her, and that she might, in turn, be able to hurt, to satisfy her quest for revenge. Archie Dunn, she decided, had to be the guilty one in the Merriman homicide. And if he was, she would get him.

Jenny typed the reports, and Dawn checked the records bureau on Archie Dunn. She found one entry: Applicant, Pulaski Police Department, 1960.

Meanwhile, Dawn called the Pulaski Credit Bureau and used the special police department account number to learn that Dunn owned his own home in Pulaski. He had worked at Poole for nineteen years. He owned one automobile, and his credit was excellent.

Dawn returned to the Detective Bureau, sat in the chair next to Stan Osinski's desk, crossed her legs, and exposed a few extra inches of thigh. She had been advised to ask an old-timer if there was some information she couldn't find in the records. She didn't want to really talk to Stan Osinski, but because of her hatred for Archie Dunn, she'd make an exception.

Stan wore a cautious look on his square, clean-shaven face. “You want something, young lady?”

“The Merriman case. The kid worked the paper drive for Archie Dunn. I'm trying to check Dunn out.”

Stan cleared some papers off his desk. “Kid, I've known Archie Dunn for thirty years. I used to punch his lights out when we were kids.”

“Is he a friend?” Dawn asked.

“No. The most we've said to each other during those years was hi, even when he was a cop here. Did you know that?”

“I found a record of his being an applicant.”

“Applicant? He must have been a cop for close to ten years, about half in this Detective Bureau.”

“Why'd he leave?”

“He couldn't get along with the bosses and a lot of the guys on the job. Even today he don't like the brass or the cops. Now he runs this city. Except he's still frustrated because when he tries to run the police or fire departments, he deals with men with—oh, you know.”

“Yeah, balls.” Dawn didn't blink.

Stan grinned appreciatively, and his posture relaxed. “Yeah. That's it. So he doesn't like us. When he applied for the chief's job, three of the police and fire commissioners voted against him. Since then, two have resigned from the commission because of political pressure. In other words, don't frig with Archie Dunn. He's a vindictive son of a bitch, and he'll get you.”

“Is he gay?”

He laughed. “Now how would I know that? But I don't think so. Archie Dunn has double-crossed so many people over the years that if he was gay, somebody would have dropped a dime on him. In high school he had all the good-looking girls on his arm. He was the class stud.”

“What can you tell me about the years since he left the police department?”

“Nothing. I see him on the golf course and in the taverns, but he's always with men—usually politicians.” He fell silent, and his eyebrows came together. “Come to think about it, never with a woman.”

* * *

MEMORANDUM
City of Pulaski

From: A. Dunn, Chairman, Finance Committee

To: Chief Turski

RE: Overtime

At last night's meeting of the Finance Committee, two items regarding the police department were on the agenda.

1) A request by Lt. Leon Lovemore on your behalf for overtime monies to investigate old homicides was denied by a vote of the committee.

2) A discussion about clothing allowances for detectives was placed on the agenda for the next budget hearing. The committee is considering dropping such a benefit for detectives. A defense by the police department for maintaining a clothing allowance for detectives would be a dress-code policy for detectives acceptable by this committee.

Chief Turski stared at the memo. *Why don't they let me run the police department. Why did they hire me?*

* * *

Back in his office, Slat began reading the reports turned in by his crew. Reviewing the files was difficult because he couldn't keep his mind off the old homicides and Sam.

Because Mountain Top had not cooperated, Slat decided to resort to old-fashioned detective legwork, asking questions and hoping for a break.

Shortly after the murders, relatives or friends of the suspects or victims might have been afraid to talk. The intervening years might have loosened their tongues. Slat decided to find a relative or friend of Stu Jackson's and Tiny Watson's.

He set the day's reports aside and started checking old records. He learned that Jackson's wife, Maybelline, was still living in their home on Leland Avenue. First he'd stop by Ernie's place and get some background and ideas.

* * *

Elinor Pope, a wide-eyed beauty with white, translucent skin, ushered Slat into the yellow, two-story, frame house, then into the pine- paneled kitchen.

"This is a terrific place, Elinor," he told her. "You've got a real eye for decorating."

She flushed with pleasure. "Why don't you get married, Slat, and we'll sell it to you?"

"It's almost tempting," he told her, then sat happily at the kitchen table as Elinor called to Ernie, then set two cups of coffee in front of Slat.

"If you weren't married to Ernie, I'd marry you and get the house in the bargain."

"Are you trying to steal my woman?" Ernie demanded as he came in the back door. "Jesus! Can't I trust anyone nowadays?"

Elinor's color rose higher. She kissed Ernie on the cheek, then put her hands on her hips and faced Slat. "He hasn't shaven since he retired," she complained. "I'm hoping Father Daley says something to him about that beard. Can you image a security officer at the archdiocese walking around with a face like that?"

"You love the tickle, woman," Ernie said, pulling her close.

"Oh, you!" She freed herself and hurried out the kitchen door.

Slat settled back in the vinyl chair. "Elinor sure keeps a nice house." He peered into the dining room, with its beautifully polished mahogany dining set.

"Yeah, especially since the real estate people are bringing people through. So what's happening, boy? You want to go back to the lake and fish?"

"The old shootings, Ernie. Read your reports. Mountain Top won't talk. He won't even give me an alibi. And it's hard to push for one- -we'd look stupid. So I'm going to pass on him for a while. I'm going to talk to Stu Jackson's wife now."

Ernie shook his head. "Salting an old wound, eh, Slat? You know, even after all these years, she's still known as Stu Jackson's widow."

* * *

After Slat walked up the steps of the bungalow and rang the doorbell, the door was immediately opened. "Mrs. Jackson, thank you for seeing me."

"Not at all. Please come inside." She was a heavyset woman with very dark skin. He watched her swaying, careful step as they went into the house.

"Coffee, Sergeant?" A tray with a crystal bowl full of little sugar cubes and a small crystal pitcher of cream was already on a French provincial table in the living room, surrounded by two flowered chairs and a sofa. Lithographs shared the walls with a cherry wood buffet and two lace-curtained windows. "Yes, please. This place is beautiful, Mrs. Jackson."

"Thank you, Sergeant."

Sixty-one-year-old Maybelline Jackson led the choir at the Tabernacle Baptist Church, and Slat understood why. Her voice was so pleasant. He took a sip raised his cup, looked into her eyes, and said, "This is delicious coffee!"

"I put cinnamon in the grounds."

"Wonderful." He took another sip. "Murder is a crime in which the file is always kept open. We're re-opening the investigation into the murder of your husband."

"I should ask you why the police department has waited all these years. However, I suppose it doesn't really matter. Whoever killed my husband, I have long ago forgiven with thousands of prayers. If our society cannot find and punish, then God will."

"Mrs. Jackson . . . .

"

"Please call me May, and I'll call you Slat."

He wondered how she knew his nickname. He wouldn't underestimate this woman. "May. The night your husband was killed—what do you remember?"

"Stuart had just came home for dinner. We had ham hocks and cabbage. Before he'd finished his meal, the phone rang. He came back to the table and said he had to meet Tiny immediately. I presumed it was gambling problems. He had seemed worried that week. He left for Tiny's, and that was the last I saw him alive. God rest his soul."

"Who called?"

"He didn't say." May refilled Slat's cup.

"In the week preceding your husband's death, did he talk about anyone to you?"

"No, no one."

"What about his competition? The Boyds, Mountain Top, and Tiny Watson?"

"They weren't really competition, Slat. They were all friends, you see. They'd grown up together. Mountain Top and Tiny were unmarried. Billy's wife, Lillie, and I were best friends." The peaceful smile that dominated her face suddenly vanished. "Until Stu and Tiny were killed, of course."

"Why not...ah...friends after?"

Slat slipped his hand under his suit coat and felt the pack of cigarettes in his shirt pocket. Empty. Damn, he thought, coffee and cigarettes go great together. Then he remembered leaving the pack on the seat of the squad.

"I'm sure you know that Curly got greedy and decided to take over all the boys' businesses. Tiny and Stu didn't want to join with him. Then they were murdered. I know in my heart neither Billy nor Mountain Top did that terrible thing. And I can't imagine Curly doing that, either. But I've prayed for them all in case I'm wrong."

She refilled Slat's cup again. "But Lillie seemed to think differently. She never said a thing, but I know that woman. She suspected her husband. She stopped visiting with me. Then, soon after, she divorced Billy. Haven't seen her in fifteen years. She moved to Tennessee— Memphis, I think—and took their children with her."

May took a sip of coffee from the dainty cup. "Her eldest, William Junior, is here working for his father. I've seen him on the street. A fine-looking young man. He has his mother's blue eyes. He told me that Lillie never remarried. And that she's a churchgoing woman."

May stared out the window. She seemed to have found an unhappy moment somewhere in time. Then her smile returned, and she wiped tears from her shining black eyes. He sat quietly, unmoving, until she turned back to him.

"What about Curly Boyd's wife?" Slat asked.

"Oh, she's been dead many years, God rest her soul. Another good woman."

"Was there anyone else who was close to Stu who may be around today?"

She thought for a few moments. "Just Mountain Top."

19

JACK HAMLIN, THE YOUNG DESK CLERK from the Sunshine Motel, had an alibi for the time of David Merriman's death; he was in class at the university. Then Jenny thought about the enormous first-year classes she had taken in college. Sometimes, as many as three hundred students packed the lecture halls, and the professors never took attendance. So Dawn and Jenny drove to the University of Wisconsin campus in Milwaukee and located the professor of Hamlin's last class.

Dr. Baxley checked his attendance book at their request. "Jack called in that day for his assignment," he said. "See this T? It means 'telephoned in.' An A—see this one, here, means attended. It's my policy to credit students if they at least call in for their assignment. It's my own personal coding scheme," he added with a touch of pride.

As Jenny and Dawn drove back to the station, they discussed what to do. Both agreed that Hamlin had seemed nervous when they talked to him at the motel office and decided to call him in for questioning in the small interrogation room where others could watch through the two-way mirror.

* * *

Bam! Jack jumped as the door slammed open against the wall as Jenny followed Dawn into the room. Already Jenny felt sweaty and tired from watching him through the mirror.

"Why did you lie to us?" Jenny said and straddled a metal chair, backwards.

Hamlin started crying.

"Knock it off and tell us about not going to school that day."

He cried harder and pulled a rosary out of his pocket. He closed his eyes and prayed, the words rushing from his mouth.

"Put that away!" Dawn said.

Hamlin jammed the rosary back into his pocket. He looked desperate, Jenny thought, as if his body might explode into vapor, sucked out through the vents of the tiny room. His shirt, brow and cheeks were soaked with perspiration, and his hair stood out at odd angles. He had picked at his pimples.

As Dawn brushed her blond hair out of her face and behind her shoulders, she stared at the suspect and wondered what to do next. He flicked a glance at her, but then looked quickly away. A low moan escaped his lips, it then grew into a wail.

Sensing they were close to a confession, Jenny turned the tape recorder on and nodded to Dawn, who took a small card from her notebook and read Hamlin his rights

"Do you understand those rights?"

Hamlin cried louder.

"Shut up and listen!" Jenny ordered.

Hamlin sobbed louder.

"Do you understand those rights?" Jenny asked.

He cried louder.

"Do you?" Jenny hollered.

"Yes!" he sobbed, tears and saliva rolling down his face.

"Will you talk to us?" Jenny asked.

"Yes."

"Why did you kill David Merriman?"

"It was an accident. We—I didn't mean to. Oh, God forgive me." He rubbed his wet face.

"Tell me what happened, Jack," Jenny said softly.

"We—uh, David and I got to be good friends. And David and uh— well, he came by my room in the motel. We were doing—you know—and he said he didn't want to because it hurt."

Hamlin's chest began to heave, so the women waited quietly until he had caught his breath. Dawn reached for the wastebasket in case he threw up. Finally his breathing returned to normal.

"So we—I held him there, and he passed out. He didn't wake up. Oh, God, I checked for a pulse. There was none. So we—so I didn't want him in my room. I got a laundry cart, put him under some towels, and wheeled him down to room one-twelve. I had a master key."

"Jack, you keep saying 'we.' Was someone else with you?" Jenny asked.

"No! Please don't ask me any more . . . "

Although a sign reading Interrogation in Progress was posted outside the door, someone was knocking.

"Who is it?" Jenny demanded, annoyed at the interruption.

"Me. Slat."

She opened the door and looked up at her boss, who filled the doorway. He crooked his finger, and she followed him into the corridor, closing the door behind her.

"Hamlin's lawyer is here, demanding to see the kid. Have you advised him of his rights?"

"Yes. And he said he understood them."

"Get anything?"

Jenny smiled triumphantly. "A partial confession."

"Well, I think you'd better tell him again about his right to an attorney, then let him know his attorney is here. If the court learns that a lawyer came and we didn't advise Hamlin, you might lose what you have."

"Okay." Jenny stepped back into the room. "Jack, your attorney is here. You have the right to consult with him before we continue."

"Yes! Yes! I want to talk to him!"

That was the last time Jack Hamlin talked to the police.

* * *

The next morning, Slat burst from his office. "Dawn," he said, "come with me. The chief wants both of us in his office."

Dawn got up from her desk. She had been preparing the report about Hamlin's involvement in the Merriman murder. The sergeant did not look happy.

"Do you know what's going on?" she asked as she rushed to keep pace with Slat's long strides. She had never been called to the chief's office.

"One of those goddam politicians bitching about something you did."

Dawn's palms dampen and her heart race. What had she done wrong? She had merely executed the search warrant on Jack Hamlin's apartment, but had turned up nothing.

As they walked into the chief's outer office, his secretary jumped up. "I'll tell him you're here."

Slat held up his hand and shook his head. Sounds of shouting came through the closed door.

"They've been going at each other for ten minutes," Ellen said.

"Maybe you were a suspect, Dunn!" Turski yelled. "You knew the victim!"

Archie Dunn, Dawn's stomach tightened.

"Checking my credit history?" Archie Dunn hollered.

"That's routine!"

"And Father Julius is as upset with her as . . . "

"I don't care about what you or Father Julius think. Her evaluations are excellent. She's a fine police officer, and before I'll transfer her, you two will have to fire me! And I'm damn serious! If either one of you interferes with that young lady, you'll have to climb over me to do it! Now I have work to do!"

Archie Dunn and the mayor stormed out of the chief's office. Neither acknowledged Slat or Dawn.

After a brief hesitation, Ellen went into the chief's office and announced the visitors.

"Send them in."

"I'll bring you some water."

"Thank you."

Slat stepped back, allowing Dawn to go first. She could see the chief was upset. His knobby hands shook as he wiped his craggy face with a handkerchief. He pointed to the two chairs in front of his desk.

"Sir," Slat said. "Should we come back later?"

"No." His secretary brought a glass of water, and he paused to drain it. "Now, then. I do read copies of all major reports. You considered Archie Dunn a potential suspect in the Merriman homicide?"

"Yes, sir," Dawn began, "because . . . "

"Yes answers my question, Detective. That's all I want to know. I have faith in your ability. You don't have to explain yourself or your rationale. You both may go back to work."

"Sir, is there anything . . . "

"Nothing, Sergeant." The chief stood, and his officers rose, too. Before Slat and Dawn exited the chief's office, he said, "Another thing."

They stopped and looked back.

"If I were younger, I'd be proud to work on your team."

The chief turned his back and stared out the window behind his desk. Slat began walking, but Dawn didn't leave. She stood transfixed, looking at the chief's back. Slat paused, then gently took her by the arm and led her out of Turski's office.

"Never, ever, in my whole life has anyone spoken up for me like that," she said as they walked back to the detective bureau. No one, not even her parents had been able to stand up to the petty dictators of her school and the city.

Dawn felt overwhelming warmth for Chief Turski. She felt pain for his pain. He had defended her against Archie Dunn, the mayor, Father Julius, and Pulaski. For the first time in her life, she felt protected, safe. She vowed she'd make Chief Turski proud that he had hired her and made her a detective. She'd do whatever she could to help him in the fight against Pulaski.

* * *

". . . and that's all since my last confession, Father," the young woman whispered through the grated confessional window.

He never heard her sins. "Say five Our Fathers, and five Hail Marys. Go in peace." The priest closed the sliding window door at his left and slid the right sliding door one open for the next confession.

Both priests at St. George were sick with the flu, so he was called in to say both morning masses and hear the afternoon confessions of the seventh and eighth graders. Unable to focus on his duties he gave everybody five Our Fathers and five Hail Marys regardless of the severity of the sin. He couldn't stop thinking about the phone call from Jack Hamlin . . ..

"Jack, under penalty of hell, you must never mention my name."

"Yes, Father," Jack had said.

"The church will get you out of this. Eternal damnation, Jack." He had tried to impress upon Jack the importance of keeping his identity secret from the police.

Now a youngster's voice interrupted his thoughts. "Father? What shall I do for penance?"

"Oh! Say five Our Fathers and five Hail Marys." He'd lost count of the number of confessions he'd heard. Not that it made any difference.

Jack had been good at recruiting young boys for him. *What would he do for boys now?* he wondered. *God forgive me!* He placed his face in his hands. *There's a chance of being exposed,* he thought, *and I'm finding boys for my sick pleasure.*

Lord God, dear Jesus, help Jack to trust me, he prayed. *Lord, I am Your servant. Do not let Jack expose me.*

He pulled a handkerchief from his pocket to wipe the perspiration from his face. The confessional booth was confining, he thought, confining like prison, confining like hell.

"I masturbate about three or four times a day because of those thoughts"

The statement woke the priest from his thoughts. "Is that every day, my son?"

"Yes, Father. I can't help it. Whenever I look at a girl or think about one, I, well, it's just there."

"What's there?" the priest asked.

"Well, you know." The child hesitated. "It's long."

"Your penis?"

"Yes, Father. But I can't help it."

"When that happens, my son, you should pray. Fold your hands in prayer."

"I've tried that, Father. It doesn't go away. Not unless I make it go away."

"You masturbate it away?"

"Yes, Father. I'm so sorry."

A slow smile spread across the priest's face. "My son, you are an unusual boy. You are different. Very sinful. Very, very sinful."

"Other boys aren't like me?" the boy asked.

"No, my son. Most other boys aren't that sinful. You are in need of special attention, special counseling."

"Yes, Father," he murmured.

"You are very important to me." The priest felt the familiar warmth spread across his groin. "And to the Church, and to the Lord." The priest felt the excitement of his own arousal. "I'm going to see that you get help. Are you the last one in line?"

"There are two boys behind me, Father."

"Wait for me in the last pew. Tell nobody about this. You don't want your classmates or your parents to know about this excessive self-abuse—the unrestrained masturbation."

"No! No! Father."

* * *

After hearing the last two confessions, the priest waited until the church was empty, then he left the confessional and walked toward the last pew. He saw the boy—a handsome young boy with wide golden eyes and light brown hair, looking at him as he walked toward the back of the church.

The priest stopped. "Come with me, my son."

The boy stood, and the priest took him by the hand. "I will show you my special counseling place, my child." He placed his arm around the youngster's shoulders as they walked out the back door of the church.

* * *

That evening, while walking with Jenny into Ski's Inn, Dawn wiped sweat from her forehead. She'd always felt too threatened to go into the hangout. The place had its regulars, and she had always been an outsider, no matter where she went. The patrons at Ski's would look at her and know she didn't belong.

She followed Jenny through the door. The smell of beer and cigarette smoke sickened her. They weaved their way toward a round table. The crew she worked with sat there, and as she glanced around the dim interior, she recognized other faces. The main difference between Ski's and work was the clothing—no uniforms—but the faces were all the same.

"Here's our girls!" bellowed Stan Osinski. He was wearing an old Wisconsin State Fair '68 T-shirt, the short sleeves tautly stretched around his huge biceps.

Several patrons applauded; some shouted accolades.

"Hey, Jenny, you're grinning for a change," called Homer, whose head and foot were still bandaged.

Jenny's grin expanded as her eyes slid to Slat, who stood, cleared his throat dramatically, then read from a Milwaukee newspaper: "'Two female detectives assigned as partners solve a homicide in a matter of days.'" He flashed a grin. "The TV stations and papers are carrying the news. And a writer from Time Magazine called the station for interviews."

"The Pulaski piss paper mentions the case," Stan said. "But it doesn't give the detectives' names."

Recognizing the obvious pride of the men for her and Jenny, Dawn was still apprehensive.

"Come on, partner," Jenny placed her hand on Dawn's back to guide her to the table.

"You came here on an unusual night, Dawn," Slat said. "The only time anyone laughs in here is when someone tells a joke."

"Or when Braun falls on his ass," Jenny said, chuckling, as Homer hobbled to the bar.

"Sit down," Stan told Dawn. He grabbed Homer's chair and swung it around for her.

Dawn felt out of her element and in awe of the environment. She had never been to a tavern socially—only on a police call. Taverns were always the enclaves of the other side—the drunks, the bikers, and the fighters.

"Hey, where the fuck is my chair?" Homer placed a full pitcher of beer on the table.

"Watch your garbage mouth," Odell Fowler said.

Slat stood and raised his beer mug. "Here's to Dawn and Jenny, for a great job."

"Hurray! Way to go!" The shouts came from all sides in the smoke-filled room.

"Good cops!" Homer hollered. "I trained 'em both."

"You couldn't train a baby to shit in his diapers," Stan said and hurled popcorn at Homer.

"Meant to ask you earlier," Jenny turned to Slat. "Where did that lawyer come from for Hamlin?"

His eyes widened in surprise. "I assumed you two had let him make a call."

He glanced at Dawn, and she shook her head. She noticed that Jenny and Slat were sitting close to each other.

"Then I've got no idea," Slat said. "And the lawyer didn't say."

"We picked Hamlin up at the motel," Jenny continued. "He made two phone calls—one to Sunshine Management for them to send a clerk to relieve him. During the second call, I heard him say, 'Yes, Father' once."

Slat shrugged. "Julius, probably. Same church, you know. Sunshine must have called a lawyer for him."

Dawn leaned forward. "I'm still bugged by what Hamlin said in his statement. He kept saying 'we.'"

"He must have meant the Merriman kid," Slat said.

Ski brought another pitcher of beer.

"That guy sent it over." He pointed at a man sitting alone in a far booth. "Anyone know who he is?" Stan asked, filling their mugs.

The officers peered into the darkness, but it was impossible to make out their benefactor's face. Instead they lifted their mugs to him in salute.

"You know, at night I hear these loud noises that wake me up," Homer said to Stan.

"Do you feel better after you hear those noises?"

"Yeah."

"Then it's gas," Stan told him.

"Who's the good-looking broad with the long legs at the bar?" Homer turned his chair for a better perspective. "She sure sits a mean bar stool. Think I'll go introduce myself."

"Forget it," Jenny said. "She's the reporter with the Pulaski piss paper—the one who interviewed Dawn and me. Cheri something or other."

Homer wore a look of disgust and turned his chair back toward the table. "The hell with her then. But she keeps glancing over here at me."

"It's not you," Odell said. "It's Slat she's looking at."

After a couple hours of listening to jokes and greeting coworkers, Dawn was exhausted. "I have to get some sleep."

"You want a lift home, kid?" Stan asked.

Dawn smiled. "Thanks, but no. A breath of night air, and I'll make it fine."

* * *

After Dawn left, the rest slowly drifted off, leaving Jenny and Slat alone. Rarely were they the last to leave. Never had she had so much to drink. However, tonight was a celebration.

Jenny looked at Slat as he drained his mug. She watched his strong profile as he tilted his head back. He needed a shave, she noticed. As he took the mug from his mouth, the light caught the wetness of his lips. His eyes looked into hers, and, embarrassed, she looked away.

"Getting late," he said.

"Yeah, guess so."

She stood, pushing her chair back. She felt dizzy and stumbled back into the chair. Slat jumped up and grabbed her so she wouldn't fall. They both laughed.

"I'd better drive you home."

"No, I'm okay. Just tired." She had dreamed about his taking her home every night, home to a place they shared.

"It's been a long day." He was behind her, holding her shoulders. "But I'm taking you home."

"Yeah," she said.

Arm in arm they said goodnight to the giant bartender, who winked at Slat as a knowing look.

The night felt cool and refreshing on her face as the car sped along the evening thoroughfares. She peeked at Slat while his attention was on the road. She wanted to let Slat know how she felt about him and see if he cared about her She wanted to know if he cared about her, too. They drove in silence along Dempster Street toward Jenny's apartment.

The rules. The system. Why does it have to be this way? she thought, miserable. He felt something for her; she knew he did. But was it love?

He glanced at her eyes for a fraction of a second. She knew he wanted her, that he would make love to her tonight, unless the rules got in the way.

He parked in front of her building. "Here we are."

They both hesitated. After a few seconds, he climbed out, walked around the car, and opened her door. "I'll see you to your door."

Jenny smiled softly. He had made the first move. That was all she wanted. Slat held her arm as they walked into the four-flat vestibule and to her first-floor apartment. How easy it would be, she thought, leaning against him, to give herself to him and begin their new life together.

After fumbling with her keys and opening the door, she started into the apartment. She turned and held her hands out to him. He shook his head, and the world crashed down around her.

"Just being polite," she said lightly, recovering. "Cup a coffee, maybe?"

"Jenny, I—well, you know how it is," he said with regret. "We have to work tomorrow. Work together."

She didn't care. Not knowing if or when this opportunity would come again, she reached up and wrapped her arms round his neck. She raised her mouth to his, and his lips, warm and full, crushed hers. He held her tightly, and she knew that her dream would come true. She rubbed herself against him, glorying in the feeling of what was to be.

Then he pushed himself away. "It won't work, Jenny. As much as we want it to, we can't let it happen." He turned and walked down the stairs. He stopped at a safe distance and looked at her. "Sorry. More sorry than you could ever know."

20

DRINKING AT SKI'S LEFT DAWN WITH A HEADACHEshe didn't need for the morning headlines: "Minority Rights Association Files Suit against Pulaski Police."

Every detective in the bureau was reading the newspapers. Named in the lawsuit besides the chief of police and the mayor were Homer and Gordy, for their group arrests of homosexuals in the park, and Dawn and Jenny, for violating the rights of Roger Cooper. Elliott Samuelson, Esquire, had filed the suits.

"Ten million dollars," Stan Osinski said, then gave a low whistle. "Hope the city has that much insurance."

"Samuelson'll probably win the case," Odell Fowler said. "This article says Pulaski has a history of violating the rights of minorities."

Homer, leaning on his crutches, shouldered the Detective Bureau door open. "The boss called me in," he announced to his coworkers. "Must need my expertise. Guess I'm irreplaceable." He moved aside and held the door for the tall, attractive woman behind him.

Ski's last night. At the bar."

"Sure, I remember you very well." He looked her up and down. "What can I do for you?"

"I'm Cheri Duncan with the *Pulaski Press* , and I'd like to talk to somebody about the lawsuit. Maybe you could . . . "

"No! No!" Homer backed away. "When it comes to the press, I keep my mouth zipped. You got to talk to the sergeant."

"Sergeant Sczlatski, behind that window?" she asked. "Would you tell him I'd like to talk to him?"

Homer picked up a phone at the counter and dialed Slat's extension.

"Boss, this pretty thing wants to speak to you." They watched as Slat looked through his office window. A couple of seconds later Homer replaced the phone on its carriage. "He says you've got to talk to Lieutenant Lovemore."

"Thanks, Detective, but e lieutenant sent me in here."

"Homer's the name," he said. "Let's have coffee sometime, when I'm off these things." He raised his crutches.

"Maybe. We'll see." She said doubtfully, then turned and left the office.

Odell continued to read aloud. "The president of the Minority Rights Association is demanding a meeting with the chief and mayor about police harassment."

"Hey, Fowler, you're a black man. Are you a member of the Minority Rights Association?"

The crew laughed. They all knew the MRA was a gay rights organization.

"Kiss my ass." Odell handed his paper to Dawn.

"Homer, your stupid antics make us all look bad," Stan said. "All people have rights. If you can't learn to respect them, you ought to get into another line of work."

Gordy Mac Bell walked into the bureau. "Hey, everybody!"

"What're you doing here?" Homer asked. "Aren't you off duty?"

"Yeah. Slat called me in."

The sergeant walked out of his glass cage and pointed. "Homer, Gordy, Dawn, Jenny, come with me," he said. "The chief wants to talk to us."

No one spoke as they walked the long corridor to the chief's office. Officers they passed on the way gave them a wide berth and looks of sympathy or approbation.

Ellen escorted them into the chief's office. Turski told them to sit down, and stood until the women were seated. There were only four chairs in the room, so Slat chose to stand.

"Ladies, gentlemen," the chief began, "I'm sure that you had good intentions in the pursuits of your cases involving gays as witnesses. But it is our job to protect all people, regardless of their lifestyle. Because your statements about this matter were honest and affirmed the allegations, I've recommended that the city attorney settle the case out of court. And I expect you to exercise discretion in the future and, of course, not to pass judgment. You must understand the difference between life-style and perversion. Pedophiles and homosexuals are two very different things."

An uncomfortable silence ensued as the chief looked at each officer in turn. Homer was about to say something, but Slat shot him a warning look.

"Any questions?" the chief asked.

After a pause, Slat said, "I've talked to them all, and I think I can sum up their feelings, Chief. They are sorry for having placed you and the department in a bad position."

"Apology accepted." Turski rubbed his hands together, and his somber expression lifted. "Now that that's over, you can get back to your usual good work." He stood. "Slat stay for a moment."

The others left, and the chief asked, "Sergeant, what kind of discipline do you recommend?"

"Nothing for Mazurski. She didn't make the comment. The others should work on a few of their days off—we can't afford suspensions."

"Fine. Take care of it."

* * *

Back in his office, Slat ordered Homer into the glass cage.

"That went pretty well." Homer said happily. "It ain't going to change my style any."

Slat felt like beating Homer with one of his crutches. Even the bandage on the man's head tilted at a cocky angle. "One more goddamn incident like that, Braun, and you can go back to patrol—if you still have a job."

Homer's eyes widened. He didn't reply.

"You treat everybody equally! Everybody! Understand?"

"Yes, sir."

"Then get out of here. And don't come back until you're off sick leave."

* * *

A few minutes after Homer left the cage, Stan walked in, carrying a foam cup of water. He handed it to Slat. "You okay, Boss?"

Slat chuckled, realizing that he was still fuming from his brief time with Homer. "Yeah, Stan, thanks. But I don't know if I should drink this or pour it over my steaming head." He lifted the cup in a toast to his friend, then drained it. "Thank you. You know, I wonder if I should spend more time with these detectives. Did they go off half-cocked because they were insufficiently supervised? If I'd been on top of things, maybe they wouldn't have had those problems with the gays."

"Boss, they're adults and should've known better. Did Turski mention anything to you about that?"

"Naw. It's all me, Stan."

"Then you're doing fine. Otherwise the chief would've taken you off the Watson-Jackson homicides."

"Of course I haven't heard from Lovemore about this yet."

"Lovemore has to answer to Turski. Do what you believe in. Continue your investigation of those old homicides. Billy and Mountain Top had the motive: money and control of Pulaski's West Side gambling. Time proved that motive right because Billy is now a millionaire." Stan stood to leave. "And one more thing. Relax. Smile once in a while."

Slat blew out a long breath. "Thank you, Stan. This job is tough, but it would be a lot harder without you."

The white-haired bull dick waved off the compliment. He picked up the empty cup and went back to his desk.

* * *

Later that morning, Slat checked volumes in the Records Bureau. He couldn't find a person alive who was related to Tiny Watson. Watson was a dead-end.

Slat wanted to talk to Lillie Boyd, but he didn't want to tip his hand to anybody close to Billy. According to Maybelline Jackson, Billy's first wife had moved to Memphis, but a check with the Memphis telephone company and police department turned up no Lillie, Lillian, or L. Boyd in the area.

Back in his office, Slat called May. "Would you do me a favor? I have Junior's phone number. Would you call him and ask for Lillie's address? I'd like to talk to her."

"Of course, Slat," the woman replied. "I'd like to write her anyway."

"May, don't mention me to Junior. Okay?"

"I understand."

May called back with the news. Nine months before, Lillie moved to a trailer court in Bradenton, Florida.

* * *

Slat knew he'd be putting the chief on a political hot seat if he requested money for a round-trip plane ticket to Florida. Maybe he'd spare everyone a lot of trouble by spending a couple of days on the Gulf Coast. He had two days off and nothing to do. And he had enough money to cover expenses.

From Tampa International Airport, he took a cab over the Sunshine Skyway Bridge, across the entrance to Tampa Bay, through the city of Palmetto, then over the Manatee River and into Bradenton.

At six in the evening the cab pulled in front of a double-wide trailer with a tiny, neat lawn bordered with white stones. A husky, gray- templed black man of about sixty came to the door.

"I'm looking for Mrs. Lillian Boyd." Slat pulled out his badge. "I'm Detective Sergeant Sczlatski from Pulaski, Wisconsin."

The man knitted his brow. "Have a seat here on the lanai, I'll tell her you're here."

21

MEMORANDUM
City of Pulaski

From: A. Dunn, Chairman, Finance Committee

To: Chief Turski

RE: Disciplinary Action

The city attorney has informed me that the city should settle the suit filed by the Minority Rights Association.

Please inform this office the length of suspensions or demotions you will be giving the police officers involved.

Chief Turski scribbled a note across the bottom of the memo: "Mayor, the matter has been taken care of."

MEMORANDUM
City of Pulaski
Office of the Mayor

To: Chief Turski

Re: Potential Civil Rights Problem

It has come to the attention of city officials and this office that Detective Sergeant Casimir Sczlatski has been harassing black citizens and community leaders about a twenty-year-old murder case.

We have built many bridges with our black community and don't want city employees damaging them--not to mention the fact that you yourself have decried the present crime rate as too overwhelming to maintain consistent enforcement.

The chief trashed the memo. Nobody would tell him how to manage the police department. A pain burned in his gut, and Martin Turski reached for the brown prescription bottle of Tagamet. The job was getting to him. He knew it, his wife knew it, and his secretary knew it. The stress had trashed his appetite, and he'd been plagued with something his internist called EMA–early morning awakenings. He'd have no problem going to sleep, but at one or two o'clock he was wide awake. Three hours' sleep were not enough to get him through his day.

His wife and the internist had talked to him about seeing a psychotherapist. But in a small town like Pulaski, that was impossible. Someone who'd recognize him was sure to see him on the way in or out of the office, then sure as hell the mayor or Dunn would find out about it. He'd be dead in the water. No, he'd just have to deal as best he could.

* * *

Lillian Boyd stopped her motorized wheelchair by the edge of the pond, then tossed croutons into the water. Mallards and the shy, delicate marsh hens, with their chartreuse legs and feet, swam toward their supper. The serenity of the moment captured her, as it had so often, and lifted her over the years of hardship and illness to the excitement of her high school days. She had been Pulaski's golden girl then, with the future shining bright before her.

Lillie Andressen had dated many of the handsome Pulaski High School basketball, baseball, and football players. The peak of her youth was her junior prom. She had been elected queen, and people predicted that she would be the only girl in the school's history to be queen two years in a row. The king, her escort, was Archie Dunn. So athletic, so handsome, he had swept her off her feet when they danced to "Paper Roses" and "Candy Kisses."

She had saved herself for Archie Dunn. Other boys had tried to take her virginity, but that prize meant everything to her. Her mother had taught her that it was a gift to give that special someone, who would treasure it. That evening, after the junior prom, she and Archie made love in the back seat of his Chevy. She gave her prized possession to the boy she adored. It was okay they weren't married yet. Everyone knew that they would get married after graduation and have Pulaski's most beautiful children.

The following night the boys traditionally partied and drank at Freedom Beach, below the cliffs of Centennial Park along Lake Michigan. Lillie knew where they would be, and she and the other cheerleaders and pom- pom girls decided to spy on their boyfriends.

The girls walked along the dark beach and used the boys' bonfire as their guide. Giggling, they hid behind shrubs and watched the boys, who were laughing, drinking beer, and singing. The girls were preparing to holler "police!" then run away.

Lillie squinted at the boys' firelit faces, looking for her Archie. She did not see him and began to worry. Then, finally, she saw him emerge from the darkness. Relief washed over her until she realized that he was with two girls—girls who had the reputation of putting out for all the boys at school.

"Who drew number six?" Archie hollered.

Somebody called back, "Jerry's next. How was it, Arch?"

He laughed. "A lot better'n Lillie," he shouted. "It's nice to screw someone who knows what she's doing for a change."

Lillie jumped and ran back down the beach toward the parking lot. Her friends cried out to her, but she ignored them. With tears blurring her vision, she sped away in her car.

After driving aimlessly and crying for an hour, she pulled into a drive-in restaurant near Mitchell Airport. As she turned into a parking stall, she misjudged the distance and bumped into a car parked in the next space. She immediately stopped, dropped her head to the steering wheel, and bawled. Her father was going to kill her.

"Hey, it's only a car!" a deep voice said. "And you can hardly see the dent. Come on, it isn't that bad."

She took a deep breath, wiped her red, swollen eyes, and looked up at a smiling, handsome young, black man who introduced himself as Billy Boyd.

Lillie never went back to school. She didn't want to see Archie again, and she didn't want to face the scorn of the community that had once placed her on a pinnacle. The white youth of Pulaski either ostracized the blacks or fought with them. They did not date and fall in love with them.

The month she turned eighteen she married Billy Boyd and moved to the city's West Side. Her parents never spoke with her again, even after their first grandchild, Billy Junior, was born. Her life took on a new meaning, and three more babies joined the family over the next five years. She made friends in her new community, and Billy gave her plenty of money. But nothing could replace his love and attention, which became scarce as his position in the black community grew.

Then came the day of the shootings. After Stu and Tiny were murdered, some of Lillie's black friends looked at her with suspicion and distrust. Both victims had been well liked on the West Side. They'd grown up there and had strong family ties. Curly's strong-arm tactics, meanwhile, had won him no friends in the community, and Billy's huge success engendered envy among the legions of the less fortunate. Lillie was left with no one.

After her divorce from Billy, she escaped to Memphis with her children. They weren't accepted in the white community, so she settled again among the blacks. She met a fine man who had become her lover and friend, although they never married.

After her children were grown, she retired to Florida. Her four wonderful children and her two beautiful grandchildren visited her often and brought solace to her life.

"Lillie?" Her companion, Bob, propelled her from the past. "There's a man from Pulaski to see you."

She looked down. The crouton box was empty.

"Do you know who he is?"

"I've never met him before," he said vaguely. "I'll give you privacy."

She turned her electric wheelchair and drove to the trailer. *A gentlemen from Pulaski calling on me. Had he been at the junior prom?*

* * *

Slat was amazed to meet a beautiful blond woman with deep-set blue eyes. "I-I'm Detective Sergeant Sczlatski from Pulaski, Wisconsin."

She slumped for a second into her walker. "You're going to tell me someone has died." Her companion helped her into an easy chair.

"Baby, I'll leave you to your business. I'm going to the pond."

"Sergeant, have you met my friend, Bob Simpkins?"

"Not formally." The men shook hands, then Simpkins left. Slat sat on a couch in the surprisingly spacious porch.

"I know you and I never met in the old days. You're too young. Baxter still there?"

"Yeah. He should be retiring soon."

"Stan Osinski?" She took a ball of yarn from a basket on the floor.

"He's still there. Stan's a detective."

"Leon Lovemore?"

"My boss."

"What do they call you?"

"Slat." He sat in awe of the gracious lady. He could answer her questions all day. He wondered why she had married someone like Billy.

"So what brings you here?"

"A few days off." Slat wanted that fact in the open if word got back to Pulaski about his being in Florida. "Since I'm down here, I thought I'd talk to you about a few things. I happen to be working on the murder of Tiny Watson and Stu Jackson."

Her deep-set eyes turned sad. "After all this time?"

"Yes."

"And you want to talk to me?"

"Yes. About what happened."

"A lot of tears happened. They were all my friends. I loved them all."

"Ma'am, I'd appreciate anything you could tell me."

"It all happened so fast. After the murders, Billy, Curly, and Sam Tyrone moved in to combine all the gambling interests."

So Ernie was right, Slat thought, with a sinking feeling in his heart. Sam was involved with the gambling. But not the murders—not Sam. He'd prove that to Ernie, too, before he was done.

"Then, at the funeral, May Jackson looked at me so strangely, as if she knew Billy had done it. I, too, felt that if Billy hadn't pulled the trigger, he was involved somehow. I was afraid even to talk with him about it." She pulled a tissue from a pocket and wiped her damp eyes.

Slat shifted in his seat.

"After that," she continued, "Billy and I fought constantly. Then there were the other women. We divorced. Billy sent lots of money; he was good that way. After our youngest graduated from college, I sent Billy a letter, telling him not to send me any more money."

"Where was Billy the night of the murders?"

"We were all at Curly's for a family get-together."

"Was Billy there the entire time?"

"I have my doubts. The men were playing cards in the basement for hours. They could have come and gone through the basement door without our knowing it upstairs."

"Who else was there?"

"Willie Patton, who died in prison, and Mountain Top."

So Mountain Top has an alibi, thought Slat. "How far was it from Curly's house to Watson's house?"

"Just across and a few houses down the alley."

Slat thought about Ernie's report. The paperwork never mentioned the close proximity of the two homes. Then he shrugged mentally; Slat himself had seen the addresses but their relative locations had never occurred to him.

"Was Sam Tyrone at the get-together?"

"I never saw him, unless he came and left by the basement door. There was no love lost, though, between him and Billy."

"Lillie, did you ever see Billy pay money to Sam Tyrone?"

"Don't know if I should answer that, even after all these years. I don't want to get Billy in trouble. He *is* the father of my children."

Well, Slat, you've got your answer on that one.

"Lillie, Sam Tyrone committed suicide over a week ago."

"Poor man." She set her knitting aside and rested her hands on her lap. "That's very sad, of course. But I'm not sorry." She picked the yarn up again.

Bob Simpkins walked in the back door. "Lillie. It's time for your medication and some rest." He set her walker next to her chair.

"Just another minute dear. Please." She turned to Slat. "Since the man's dead . . . Billy used to pay Sam regularly. Sam controlled the West Side. Everyone was afraid of him. Everyone hated him."

Slat stood abruptly. He had heard enough. "Lillie, was there ever another cop with Sam? Or did you ever see Billy pay another cop?"

"Yes."

"Who, Lillie?"

"I-I . . ." She was shaking, and her color looked bad. "I—let me think about this."

"Sergeant, that's enough," Bob said firmly. "She has a serious heart condition."

"I'm just leaving," Slat said.

"Why don't you come by tomorrow for lunch?" Lillie said.

"Thank you, ma'am. I'll be here."

* * *

Slat often imagined what mental wizardry he could accomplish if he could spend the day standing in the shower. His clearest thoughts occurred while the jets of water massaged his body. He planned his days in the shower, as its sizzle drowned out all external noise. The water even washed away the pangs of remorse when he thought of Sam Tyrone's guilt.

Slat had to ask Lillie about payoffs. He had to find out who the other cop was. Could Lovemore have been involved or anyone else on the force? he wondered. He'd also have to ask Lillie the names of everyone who had been at Curly's family affair. With their testimony and Lillie's, a grand-jury hearing no longer seemed so farfetched.

As Slat's cab drove into the trailer park, there was a commotion on the street in front of Lillie's trailer. An orange and white ambulance waited at the curb, alongside two marked Manatee County Sheriff's Department squads and two unmarked squads.

"Want me to wait?" the cab driver looked in the mirror at Slat reaching for his wallet.

"No, thanks," he said, handing over a ten-dollar bill.

"Keep the change."

Slat hurried from the cab and walked down the narrow street until he reached a marked squad. A uniformed officer was in the front seat, and

Bob Simpkins was sitting in the back. Slat knocked on the side window. "Bob. Bob. Sczlatski," he said.

Bob looked up, but before he could open his mouth, the uniformed officer jumped out of the squad. "Can I help you, sir?"

"I'm a police officer." Slat pulled his badge from his pants pocket.

"Sir, you can't talk to this man. You'll have to talk to the lieutenant in charge." The deputy sheriff pointed to a husky, darkly tanned, big-boned detective.

"What happened?" Slat asked.

"Ask the lieutenant." Again the uniformed officer pointed.

Slat interrupted the detective lieutenant, who was talking to a police photographer. He introduced himself, then asked, "Is Mrs. Boyd all right?"

The lieutenant took Slat's badge and ID card and looked at them carefully. "How'd you know her name?"

"I was questioning her last night about some homicides in Wisconsin."

"Then I want to talk to you. Come with me." He led Slat into the trailer and back into the master bedroom.

"Do you know that woman?"

Lillie was slumped in her wheelchair, right arm loosely dangling over the right side. Her head was hanging backwards over the same side. A gray powder burn showed around a small hole in the middle of her forehead.

"Yeah. That's Lillian Boyd."

"Do you know the man in the squad?"

"A friend of hers. Just met them yesterday."

"Why weren't we notified about your department conducting an investigation in our county?" The lieutenant directed Slat out of the bedroom.

"You see, I had a few days off. . . ."

"You conduct homicide investigations on your days off and out of state?" the lieutenant asked skeptically. "Come on, fella."

"Lieutenant, you and I need to talk."

"You bet we do."

"Peters," the lieutenant called to a detective, "get your business together. I'll meet you later, in the station."

* * *

While in the squad car heading for the Manatee County Sheriff's Department, the lieutenant introduced himself as Art Anton. "Now, tell me your story."

Slat explained the nature of the investigation.

"When did you say those homicides were?"

"Twenty years ago."

"We usually get into our homicides a little sooner here in Florida."

Slat tried to explain, but Anton interrupted. "Who is your supervisor and chief?"

Slat gave him both Chief Turski's and Lieutenant Lovemore's names. He hoped Anton would call the chief instead of Lovemore.

"Seems unlikely to me that your old investigation has anything to do with this homicide. But I've been around long enough not to overlook anything."

At the sheriff's department, Slat tagged along with Lieutenant Anton as he listened to his detectives. "Simpkins says that when he returned from his morning walk, he found her dead. Claims he locked the door behind him—a lifelong habit. He identified a few people he saw on his walk. And if needed, he'll take a polygraph."

"Run a background on him." Anton turned to Slat. "You know anything about him?"

"Nothing."

Slat followed Anton into his sun-lit office, where they were joined by another detective. "No forced entry, Lieutenant. She might have known the shooter and let 'em in."

"Guess our number-one suspect at this time is Simpkins." He turned to Slat. "What's your department's phone number?"

The lieutenant excused Slat from his office while he made the phone call. A few minutes later he called Slat back into his office.

"Your lieutenant was off today. Your chief backed you up."

22

"IT'S 'HEROES TO HARASSERS' on this second-page headline," said Stan Osinski, in his usual chair at Ski's.

Ski, behind the bar, turned the big thirty-six-inch television screen to the evening news while his customers traded various newspapers around the barroom.

"The assholes want a federal investigation into violations of civil rights by the Pulaski Police Department." Homer had his legs resting on a chair.

"What smells?" Jenny asked, wrinkling her noise.

"Homer," Stan said. "He's the only guy I know with vocal cords in his asshole."

"Pig!" Dawn got up in disgust and walked to the jukebox.

"The NAACP is in on the act," Jenny said, reaching for the beer pitcher. "They say they have years of documented abuses of blacks."

"Years?" Stan asked. "But Braun hasn't been here that long. Although with those dirty bandages on his foot and head, he looks like he's a veteran of World War One." Stan raised his shot glass in a toast to his partner, Odell, sitting across the table.

"This article says that the ACLU is looking into possible police violation of the right of gays to congregate in the park," Jenny said. "The attorney for the MRA questions the judgment of the department in placing two new detectives on a homicide investigation. He stated that during the investigation, one of the female detectives had asked if all the alibi witnesses for a potential suspect were homosexuals, intimating an investigation based on sexual preference."

"Did you really ask the fruit if they were fruits, Jenny?" Homer asked.

"Think what a wonderful world it would be if we had no Homers," Stan said.

"Gay, Homer. Gay! And shut up!" Jenny answered. "I'd rather have a hundred gay friends than one bigot like you."

Odell laughed. "That comparison is an insult to gays."

"Fuck you all," Homer said. "You have to burn some tail feathers during an investigation. At least you solved the homicide. Why can't everyone be grateful and leave you two alone?"

"I shouldn't have asked the question," Jenny admitted. "As soon as I said it, I knew I was wrong." She looked at Slat's empty chair. He was out of town, but no one sat there anyway. She was glad he wasn't there.

She still felt embarrassed and humiliated about the other night. She didn't know whether she should apologize to Slat, yell at him, or just pretend that the kiss had never happened—as if that were possible. Sure, she had been lonely that night, but she felt lonely tonight and every other night, too. She sighed. Slat was probably right. Even though what she felt for him was more than lust, losers and lovers don't mix.

* * *

Though deep in thought, Dawn had heard some of the banter. She slid her chair farther under the table, to hide her exposed thighs from Homer's leering. Ski's was no longer foreign to her. In fact, she had begun to feel at home there. She understood the language, both spoken and unspoken.

Although the rest of the crew teased Homer, she believed they held some feelings of fondness for the jerk. They had worked with him long enough to have shared stories and danger. She, on the other hand, felt no such affection for Homer and doubted she ever would. Homer was a product of his environment and as stuck in his stereotypes as a dump truck mired in mud. She drained her beer as thoughts of Homer reminded her of Chief Turski, Archie Dunn, and Billy Boyd . . . of love, prejudice, and hate.

If Martin Turski, a white man, had difficulty fighting the bigoted monster, Pulaski, she wondered how on earth had a black man like Billy Boyd fought Pulaski and succeeded?

The beer, her second, relaxed her. She enjoyed the buzz of the alcohol and the warmth of the evening's companionship, a feeling that had been unknown to her all of her life. The camaraderie had begun with Jenny, then extended to the others. She liked the feeling, but she was still afraid of it and terrified of being hurt.

She reached again for the pitcher. Jenny put her hand out and stopped her. "We should eat first," she suggested. "Let's go next door to Mama's."

Dawn nodded and followed Jenny outside. "I don't believe all this shit coming down," she said as the bright westerly sun slapped their eyes after leaving the dim interior of the tavern.

"That's the business," Jenny said. "Don't let it get to you. Nobody cares, really. Look at Slat—that man has solved more cases and made more felony arrests than anybody on this department—ever. He never gets credit for that. He always gets shit on. He says just to ride out the criticism. Slat says. . . . ."

While Jenny rambled on about Slat, Dawn's thoughts returned to Billy. She had never met a black man in Pulaski who interested her. They all had seemed so unreliable, so cocksure of themselves and with no good reason. Billy was in a class by himself. She was tempted to verbalize her curiosity and find out everything Jenny knew about him. Then she reconsidered. She didn't want her interest in Billy to make it around the station. While she was pretty sure Jenny wouldn't betray a confidence, there was no guarantee. But Dawn had come to a decision. She was going to create the opportunity to find out everything she wanted to know.

* * *

Steve Merriman sat in the front row and waited for the court proceedings to begin. He looked around, disappointed. The room was not as large as he had expected. He sat in a wooden pew, which reminded him of being in church, and he did not like that. The judge's chair and bench and the jury box and railings were dark wood. These pleased him. They seemed imposing and dignified. The high windows, separated by beige walls, were covered with venetian blinds. As time passed, they cast striped shadows across the room.

The sharp and relentless ache in Steve's heart was surpassed only by the rage he felt, thinking about his boy being fucked up the ass and suffocated by the pervert. Steve hadn't been able to eat for days, although beer and whiskey went down pretty easily. Every night he sat on the living-room couch and drank until the booze quieted his fury and put him to sleep.

His wife, Margaret, did not come to the courthouse with him. He was grateful for that. If it hadn't been for her and her precious church, David would still be alive.

"If David had spent more time with me, he'd have learned to take care of himself, like I did at his age," he would bark at her when she accused him of drinking too much. "But no, you wanted him hanging around the church, with all those fags."

Margaret's eyes were dulled and darkened by sorrow. Yelling at her made him feel guilty, but he couldn't help it. He had to lash out at someone.

Steve had felt a grim satisfaction when the cops nabbed the perverted son of a bitch, and he hoped that Hamlin would fry in the electric chair. He fantasized about asking the judge if he could pull the switch.

Today, he sat as close as he could to the front of the courtroom, then glared at the skinny, pimply faced pervert in a jail uniform. Sometimes he sneered at the little bastard's attorney—a tall blond fag in an expensive suit and shoes. He'd like to feel his hands around both men's necks.

Merriman felt proprietary about the trial of his son's murderer. He knew it was being covered by television and newspaper reporters, and that infuriated him. He felt strongly that David's memory should have a little privacy, for Chrissakes. He peered at an old, gray- haired lady with a handkerchief over her face across the center aisle. He wondered who she was. If she was a curiosity seeker, he'd like to throw her out. He envisioned himself walking up to her during a recess and demanding to know why she was there. If he didn't like her reason, he'd march her to the elevators.

He stood as the judge walked in. Then everybody sat down except the pervert and fag attorney, who approached the bench. The district attorney joined them. Steve had such high hopes for the DA, he ended up being disappointed with everything the man did and said. Steve couldn't believe that such a jerk had gotten through law school. The two attorneys argued about bond money. Then the judge said, "No bond" in a firm voice and that he'd hear motions next week.

Steve rejoiced in the pervert's disappointment as the bailiff grabbed Hamlin by the arm. His face soaking with tears, he turned and looked at the old lady, who began to sob.

Steve turned on the woman. "Stop crying, you bitch! Your boy's still alive!" Unable to contain his anger, he jumped up and screamed, "I hope you fry, you little bastard!" He ran into the area before the bench and reached for Hamlin. Two deputies surged forward and pulled him away.

"He killed my boy!" Steve wailed, and began sobbing in his hands as the bailiffs led him from the courtroom.

23

Is Lillie Boyd's murder connected to my investigation? The thought nagged at Slat during his flight back to Milwaukee. She had never had the chance to tell him about the other police officer with Sam Tyrone or about the other guests at Curly's house. If Slat was ever going to find out, he would have to learn more about Pulaski's gambling.

In the seat in front of him, Slat overheard a child say, "Is Daddy down there?"

"Yes, honey." The seated next to the child said. "And when we get off the plane, he'll be there to take us home."

At the mention of the child's father, Slat's thoughts moved to Sam Tyrone. He had come to the orphanage every Saturday, to take Slat bowling or to a Braves game, or just out for pizza. Before the Monkarians had taken him in, he spent Thanksgiving and Christmas with Sam and his wife. Sam had always been there. Slat tried to accept that his surrogate father was dishonest, but he just couldn't—or wouldn't. Not now. Not yet, with the grief still so fresh. Maybe someday it would sink in, he thought.

He forced his concentration elsewhere, to Mountain Top, who had been in Curly's basement the night of the murders. Slat knew he would have to get a statement from the big man. He'd put pressure on Mountain Top and the Boyd organization. Maybe something would break.

As soon as the plane landed, Slat took his carry-on luggage to the taxi stand and went right to the police station, where Stan briefed him on all routine activity. Then Slat arranged to have dinner at Mama's with Stan and his partner. Whatever Slat needed to know about the black community, Odell could tell him.

Detective Odell Fowler had been born and raised on the South Side of Chicago, attended the University of Illinois, Circle Campus, and married a Pulaski girl. He came home with her and never left. Because Odell was not a homeboy, he had experienced some difficulty making his way into the Pulaski black community. Although many whites assumed that all blacks are brothers—blood, at all times—Odell had proved the hard way that that simply wasn't so.

His wife had gone into private practice as a social worker, and Odell tested at the top of the list for the Pulaski Police Department. Six years later, after some excellent arrests, he ended up in the Detective Bureau, when Stan Osinski's Polish partner retired. They worked well together and were the only married members of the squad.

Odell had been a detective for only five years, but because Stan was so experienced, he had picked up a wealth of information, techniques, and short cuts. He showed the savvy of a twenty-year veteran.

* * *

Slat met Stan and Odell in a back booth. They were already giving their attention to the day's special, sauerkraut and kielbasa. Slat signaled to Mama to bring him the same.

"What do you guys know about illegal gambling in the black community?" he asked.

"There's a lot of it," Odell responded. "Of course we don't have much to do with it. If there's a complaint, patrol usually handles it."

Stan waggled a finger at Odell's face. Odell brushed a strand of sauerkraut off his chin.

"Even today, I don't know if there's an official policy about it," he continued. "When I started in patrol, no one ever told me to pursue or overlook gambling arrests. But every function I've ever gone to, police or otherwise, ended up with illegal gambling. I've seen command officers, patrolmen, and politicians—black and white—involved in almost every type of illegal gambling. If that doesn't tell me and every other cop what the unwritten policy is around here, I don't know what does."

"Odell," Stan said, laughing, "you sound as if you have to justify your actions." He set down his knife and fork and turned serious. "I'll tell you, Sarge, I was born and raised in Pulaski. During my lifetime, gambling has been legal here. Same thing in my dad's era. I don't give a shit what the State of Wisconsin says in its books. Hell, when I was an altar boy, I learned how to play pinochle in the rectory from a priest! We laid bets. Our parishes survive with gambling money, and I don't mean pennies from bingo. And if you'll check the city liquor licenses, you'll see that a priest from each parish holds a license."

"You guys are getting the wrong idea," Slat said. "I wasn't trying to put either of you on the spot."

"Oh, we know that, Sarge," Odell said.

"Yeah," Stan seconded.

"I just want to know what's happening on the West Side," he explained.

Odell thought for a moment. "Okay, there are five major houses there—plus maybe two or three small ones. I'm not sure."

"When we finish eating, we'll hit the bricks, and you can show me," Slat said.

* * *

Thirty minutes later, the three officers were traveling down Dodge Avenue. Odell slowed the squad and pointed at a green and white bungalow. Slat knew by its design that it was a Sears-Roebuck house, ordered from Chicago in the thirties and shipped via railcar—windows, rugs, even dining-room chandelier—for assembling in Pulaski. "That place belongs to a guy named Shorty. I don't know his last name. Actually, he rents the entire house. He runs the gambling and is known as the *houseman.*"

Slat filed the address in his brain: 6221 Dodge. "Who does he rent from?"

"Billy Boyd," Odell answered. "Four blocks west of here, on Emerson, is another house. I don't remember who the houseman is, but he rents from Billy, too."

"And the other three?" Slat asked.

"They all rent from Billy—or, more accurately, they rent from the Sunshine Property Management Corporation."

"Housemen usually operate the gambling in the basement," Odell explained as he turned toward Emerson Avenue. "We know one man who operates out of his garage and another, on Leland Street, who operates out of a basement or second floor, I'm not sure which."

"All but one are three-story houses," Stan added. "Each houseman lives in his house, and supposedly he rents out the remaining rooms."

"So each houseman is like a franchise," Odell said. "He makes his money off gambling and rent, but he pays rent for the entire house."

"Very clever," Slat said.

"Yeah," Stan agreed. "There's the potential of making very good money. But I've heard that each houseman pays hundreds a week to Billy for renting the house. That way Billy's revenue is washed as legitimate rental income."

"I heard on the street yesterday that Billy gave Pitford two more houses, plus the one he already runs."

Stan looked at his partner in admiration. "No shit."

"Nope," Odell said. "I don't know what the deal is, but Pitford has a bigger piece of the pie now."

"What if they don't pay Billy?" Slat asked.

"They have to pay him to operate," Odell said. "I suppose he would try to put them out of business by evicting them. But it works just like one big happy family—all peace, no war."

"Anything else, like drugs or prostitution or stolen goods?" Slat asked.

"Not with the gamblers," Odell told him. "This isn't like a mafia thing, where one outfit controls all illegal activities. That shit goes on, but it's with the punks, the gangs."

"Those gamblers are regular people like us," Stan said. "They're family men. Some make a living at gambling. Some make a part- time job of it."

"The gangs don't fool with Billy, and he don't fool with the gangs," Odell continued. "A couple of gang leaders would like to take over Billy's operation someday, but they won't mess with Billy or Mountain Top."

"So Billy has his hands out of it. He's legally clean," Slat said.

"Yeah, just like the archbishop's clean." They chuckled over Odell's joke about illegal church gambling.

Is it really a joke? Slat thought. He was raised in Milwaukee County, and all his life he knew gambling was illegal. In his recruit- school law classes, a lecture on gambling was followed by a lively discussion about victimless crimes and morality. The young recruits reasoned that if gambling is against the law, it should be enforced. *We took an oath to enforce the laws of the State of Wisconsin,* they had said. When the idealistic recruits hit the streets in various cities, however, their partners told them to forget that bullshit they had learned in school. There was one rule: If you think about arresting somebody for gambling, you better tell your priest about it at confession.

"How long has it been working like this?" Slat asked. "The rental system, I mean?"

"Long as I've been here," Odell said.

"Fifteen, maybe twenty years," Stan guessed. "Billy went into the property management business, and alleged—mind you I say alleged— gambling payoffs to the police ended."

"Just like that?" Slat asked.

"Just like that," Odell confirmed, snapping his fingers. "Can you imagine a cop taking a bribe during the civil-rights movement? Every activist was digging for complaints against the police. If you were on the take, and I was a gambling boss, I'd tell you I wasn't paying you shit. If you came down on my game, I'd holler about the gambling that was going on unchallenged in the white clubs and churches. Can you imagine what would have happened then? So now time has passed. We're busy with drugs and gang wars and worse shit. Guys like Billy get rich and richer, and the cops can't do a fucking thing about it."

* * *

"Son of a bitch!" Tony Tattaglia was fuming. "What else did the archbishop say?"

"He simply said to wait, that he'll let us know."

"Wait? Wait?"

Tony's sedan was parked about a hundred feet from where Father Julius had pulled his car into a cemetery on the north side of the city. Tony had been in a foul mood ever since the Hamlin kid was arrested for murder. He was well aware that some errant priests used a procurer, but more often they worked alone; being a pedophile is not a secret easily or comfortably shared, and Tony couldn't imagine that Hamlin would go to jail without squawking if Father Julius had been involved. But the kid was taking the rap solo. And that meant that either the priest had Hamlin intimidated with the wrath of God or was innocent of involvement.

Going after Julius had felt rewarding to Tony only while the innocence of children was at stake. He did not like the idea of keeping track of a cleric whose only sin was alcoholism or chasing women.

He was tired of this assignment and sick of spending time with Patrick. The man had had a stick up his butt in the seminary, and the intervening years hadn't loosened him up any.

"Tony, somebody has to do it." Daley's eyes darted back and forth to see if anyone in the cemetery parking lot heard Tony's language. "Relax. So it takes a few more days. Big deal."

"An errant priest," Tony grumbled. "I'm used to handling major problems —hostage negotiations, war-crime intervention. That Polack I work for has it in for me. Pulaski is my penance."

"Why are you so angry with Monsignor Popodowski?" Father Daley wanted to know.

"Because Popodowski could insist that Archbishop Coughlin see me. And I would think that you, as his financial secretary, could ask him to see me." He sank low in his seat. He knew he was sulking, but he didn't care. "Why the hell did they put a Polack in charge of the Vatican's Intelligence Unit? Most of the agents are Italian, for Chrissakes. The only Polack is Popodowski, and he's the boss. Doesn't make sense."

"It makes sense to me," Patrick sniffed. "He's a monsignor."

"In this country it may make sense, but not in Rome."

"Regardless, somebody has to handle these errants."

"That's not the point. The son of a bitch doesn't like Italians."

"Please watch your language." Father Daley rolled up his car window. People climbing out of other cars were within earshot.

"Whose burial is this?" Tony asked. "There are as many blacks as whites."

"I don't know, but Father Julius is down there in the middle of them. The deceased must be Catholic."

Father Daley released his seat belt, then shifted his position to face his tall friend. "You must be mistaken about Monsignor Popodowski. You are privileged to be working out of the Vatican and handling Church assignment! Count your blessings!"

"You're right, of course." Tony chuckled. He had endured more than enough of Patrick's self-righteous prattle and decided to have some fun.

"Did I say something funny?" the priest asked.

"Would you like to hear why Popodowski sent me on this assignment?"

"Well, sure." Patrick's eyes lit up.

"I was part of an entourage from Rome, headed by Popodowski. We were trying to determine the extent of Communist influence in the IRA. It was of such concern to the Vatican that Popodowski came along, though he seldom leaves Rome. I had my own room in the Belfast safe house. I brought a woman in through a side entrance."

"Really, Tony. I don't care for any of your stories about female conquests."

"I don't remember her name," Tony continued. "But I'll never forget her beautiful, taut, nude body."

"I don't get your point," Father Daley said coldly.

"You will." A charming smile graced his handsome features. "The only light was from the moon, which shone through the sheer curtains. I was kissing the back of her neck. . . ."

"Tony, I don't want to hear this!"

"I thought you wanted to know why Popodowski shits on me."

"Finish your story, then. But it better make a point."

"As I was saying before you interrupted me, I was kissing the back of her neck. Did I say we were nude?"

"Yes. Please get to the point."

"We were nude, and my hands were cupping her breasts." The color rose from Patrick's neck to his cheeks. Tony felt a little guilty but managed to overcome it.

"You don't have to be overly descriptive."

"Remember what they told us in class? That celibacy is a mystery not to be explained by argument? Ridiculous. Nothing in the Bible or any other writings require celibacy. The pope better wake up to the fact that his army of priests is depleting. I'd be a priest today if it weren't for that vow."

"Celibacy is a choice we make," Patrick said hotly. "I'm proud that we priests can devote our minds and bodies to Christ. Celibacy wasn't your problem, Tony. I don't think you could commit yourself to any relationship, be it marriage or the priesthood. Don't blame the pope if you're a tomcat."

Tony wanted to throttle the man, but he kept his temper under control and even managed a smile. "You know me too well, Patty," he said lightly. "Well, back to my story."

"I thought you had made your point."

"There was a single light bulb hanging from the ceiling. Suddenly it burst on. My Irish lass grabs the sheet and pulls it up under her chin, leaving me exposed, kneeling in the bed, with my engorged penis in my hand."

"I've had enough of this!"

"So guess who is standing there with his hand on the light switch? Popodowski. And you know what he said to me?"

"I can't imagine."

"This Polack says, 'I hope she isn't Catholic.' Then he leaves the room and slams the door. Of course, my dick had lost its enthusiasm."

Patrick sat with his mouth agape.

"So I looked down at the girl, blushing and peeking out from under the sheet, and asked her if she was Catholic. But before she could answer, the door flew open again. Popodowski. He shouts, 'I'll see you in my room as soon as possible!' and then he slams the door again."

"You're disgusting."

"He has tried to have me fired several times since then, but I still have friends. Popodowski gets his revenge with the assignments." Making me put up with you, Patrick, you supercilious shit, in Pulaski. Tony sighed, lay his head back, and closed his eyes.

24

AFTER SPENDING MOST OF THE DAY WITH STAN AND ODELL, Slat had called Maybelline Jackson before the shift ended and made plans to meet her the next morning for Lillie's funeral. The Boyd children had arranged for their mother's body to be brought back to Pulaski for burial in the Boyd family plot.

Slat picked May up, and together they attended the small funeral service at the Tabernacle Baptist Church, then rode in the short cortege to the cemetery. After a brief prayer service, they strolled back to Slat's car and stood in the parking lot, talking about the wounds of time. As the conversation slowed, they glanced around and realized they were the last to leave.

After one final look at the burial site, they got into the car, and Slat drove slowly toward the cemetery gates. A car pulled into the cemetery and passed him. The driver, who didn't notice Slat, was Archie Dunn. Slat took his foot off the gas pedal and watched Archie in the rear view mirror park near Lillie's grave..

"Somebody's a little late," May said.

"Yeah," Slat agreed. "I guess he is."

* * *

Archie left his car and walked slowly through the cemetery, each step bringing him back through the years to his happy high school days. He stopped within a few feet of Lillie's grave and shook his head slowly. "I haven't seen you in so many years," he whispered. "I can still picture you, though—blond, sixteen, and so pretty—like an angel, really. I never . . ." Archie took a handkerchief from his back pocket and wiped his eyes, then, embarrassed, looked around to make sure he was alone. "I never forgot you, Lillie. I still have our prom pictures. I'm sorry I never looked for you after you left Billy."

Archie stepped closer to the grave. "I'm so sorry. I thought about finding you and making up for lost time, but the years kept going by, and I . . ." He pulled a folded eight-by-ten photograph from his suit pocket. "Here, you can have this now." He let it drop onto the grave, where it drifted alongside the casket.

"My life is crap, Lillie. It's been crap since you broke up with me."

He wept freely until the wave of grief passed. Then he turned and walked across the cemetery to another grave. The cold marble slab read Archibald Dunn, Senior. Archie felt a sharp pain in his chest, as if his father's bony fingers were reaching up through the dirt and grass and squeezing Archie's heart. His father's unsympathetic voice echoed in his ears. He covered his ears with his hands, but nothing blocked the harsh sound.

Blonds and niggers, Son. Never trust a blonde; more than likely she'll run off with a nigger. You know that now, don't you, boy? You were a fool to care about Lillie. She never loved you. Your dick wasn't big enough for her, was it, kid? Well, don't worry. All women are alike. Ya put a flag over their head, and they all look the same.

"No-o-o-o . . ." Archie wailed, and tears streamed down his face. "She did love me! If you hadn't been such a bastard, I could have had her back. Well, now you're gone, Ma's gone, your fucking tavern's gone, and Lillie's gone—and I'm still trying to keep all those assholes you warned me about from screwing up your precious Pulaski." Archie wiped his face. "I always tried to make you proud of me," he wailed. "Well, you should be real proud of me now. I've done everything you told me to. And now I've got nothing. Do you hear me? Nothing! I oughta piss on your grave!"

* * *

"You say nothing about me, under penalty of eternal hell!" the priest whispered into Jack Hamlin's ear.

The Roman collar, like a police badge, eliminated much of the bureaucracy inside county buildings. He had simply told the corrections officer that Hamlin had requested his own priest, rather than the jail chaplain, for confession. Now he sat in a metal chair, close to Hamlin, alongside a single table in the small, grim holding cell.

"The Church has provided you with an attorney, but under penalty of hell you must never mention my name to him. Do you understand, Jack?"

"Yes, Father." Jack brushed the tears and mucous from his face as he sat hunched, miserable and shaking. "But I don't want to go to jail."

"Of course not, Jack. Just trust the Church and the Lord. We'll see that you are taken care of. Now get on your knees, and I'll hear your confession."

* * *

Cheri Duncan settled into the front row in the courtroom, where the reporters customarily sat. As usual she was alone. Cheri wished she was with the Milwaukee Journal or even the *Milwaukee Sentinel* instead of the small-town daily. Well, she thought, at least she was assigned to cover the Merriman murder case.

Cheri saw Dawn and Jenny walk into the court and sit two rows behind her. She couldn't understand why they weren't more friendly toward her. They seemed as guarded as the male cops. Why did they act like the men?

She had planned to do a feature story on them; she'd never heard of a team of two real-life female detectives. But her editor said that it was only temporary—they'd be split up soon.

I'll keep trying, Cheri thought, and went back to sit with the detectives.

"Hi, girls," she chirped, sliding in beside Jenny. "What do you think is going to happen with this case?"

"Don't know," Jenny said.

"Me, neither," Dawn said.

Then they both ignored her.

* * *

The two men standing before the judge were arguing in whispers. Even from his front-row seat Steve Merriman couldn't hear what they were saying, so he leaned forward over the railing. He noticed the gaze of the judge following him. He still couldn't hear, so he walked back to the third row, to sit with the detectives who had busted the murdering pervert. As he moved back, he narrowed his eyes at the gray-haired lady–Hamlin's mother. She was as much at fault as her kid for David's death.

He sat next to the blond. "What's going on?"

"Hamlin's lawyer is trying to get the confession suppressed," Jenny whispered.

"What does that mean?"

"Trying to get the confession thrown out."

"Why?" Steve raised his voice.

"He says it's tainted."

The judge looked over at Jenny and Steve Merriman talking. A white-shirted bailiff placed a warning forefinger across his lips.

"I'll tell you later. Got to hear this," Jenny whispered.

"If the court pleases . . ."

At last Hamlin's attorney spoke up as he turned and looked directly at the women. "The police had focused their investigation on my client Jack Hamlin when they ordered him into the station for questioning. Except for fingerprints on the motel room door, the state has not provided any corroborating evidence to establish probable cause. Jack Hamlin was an employee of the motel. It is only reasonable to expect his fingerprints to be found in his place of employment.

"If police investigators had checked other doors at the Sunshine Motel, they probably would have found my client's fingerprints on most.

"Furthermore, Your Honor, when you listen to the tapes of the interrogation, you will hear my client crying loudly when his rights were eventually read to him. He couldn't possibly have heard them."

The idea that the confession might be nullified so shocked Steve Merriman, he could not concentrate on the district attorney's rebuttal. He vaguely heard the judge's statement about rendering a decision the following week. Then two bailiffs took Hamlin out a side door.

Merriman sat numbly as the courtroom emptied. Why, he wondered, hadn't the district attorney called any witnesses? He jumped up and hurried into the hallway, where he found the two detectives about to get into an elevator. He bumped into the closing doors and managed to ride down with the women.

"What just happened in there?" he demanded angrily.

"The defense is trying to suppress the confession," Jenny explained. "It's upsetting, of course, but we can be hopeful that . . . .
"

"What do you mean? My kid was killed by that little pervert! He told you two! When are they going to send him to the chair?"

"It's a little more complicated than that, Mr. Merriman," the dark detective told him.

"It ain't complicated to me, lady. My kid's dead. That pervert did it, and he's going to pay. That seems pretty straightforward."

"Mr. Merriman," Jenny sympathized, leaving the elevator and the building, "that's not the way the system works. There are formalities, procedures of the law."

Steve was enraged. "That pervert's attorney was making a lot of noise. He wouldn't be making that noise if he wasn't trying to get the pervert off."

"That's right, Mr. Merriman," Jenny concurred. "And that's the man's job. Everyone has the right to a competent defense."

Now he was feeling scared. "Is there a chance that Hamlin'll get off?" They were walking down the cement steps of the courthouse.

"Mr. Merriman, if the court . . . " Dawn began.

"You mean the judge?" Merriman interrupted.

"Yes. If the judge suppresses . . . "

"What do you mean 'suppresses'? Christ! 'Suppresses, tainted'- -doesn't anybody talk English around here?"

"If the judge doesn't let the confession into the trial, then we have no case," Jenny answered.

"What does that mean?"

"That means," Dawn said, lacking patience, "that Hamlin gets off. Goes free. Walks."

Steve Merriman stood with his mouth open. Hot tears burned behind his eyes, and he turned away so the women wouldn't see his shame.

"We're sorry, Mr. Merriman," Jenny said gently. "We'll do all we can to get him convicted."

"I'll talk to Archie Dunn," Merriman said. "He helped with the funeral arrangements. He's a decent sort. He'll give me a hand."

* * *

"Mr. Dunn! Over here!"

Archie heard Steve Merriman's voice from a side booth in the Clark Restaurant.

"Be right with you, Steve," Archie called, then walked to the bar.

"Archie's here, Chester," the bartender said to a man at the far end of the long bar.

The beefy fellow hurried over to Archie and pumped his hand warmly. "Glad to see you, Archie! Sit down and have a beer with me."

"Thanks, Chester, but I'm meeting someone. Next time, all right?"

"Sure, Arch. Lunch is on the house for you and your guest."

"Thanks."

"But first . . ."

"Sure, Chester. What is it?"

"As president of the Tavern Keepers' Association, I've been getting complaints about the local cops. They're stopping customers as they leave the taverns and arresting them for drunk driving. Borderline cases, you understand."

"Of course," Archie responded.

"Sure, some guys have a few too many. But in the old days, the cops always took 'em home." He laughed. "Hell, sometimes they'd get 'em up the stairs and into bed."

Archie laughed with him.

"Jeez, we're losing business, Archie."

"I'll take care of it, Chester."

"Knew you would, Archie." Chester reached for Archie's hand and grasped it warmly. "We all count on you."

Turski is stepping into my domain now, Archie thought as he grabbed a couple of beers from the bar. The Tavern Keepers' Association had gotten Archie elected. Part of his ward covered the downtown area, where most of Pulaski's taverns were located. Something would have to be done. He knew that Gordy Mac Bell, head of the Tactical Unit night shift, had a hair up his ass when it came to DUI charges. He made a mental note to complain about the hyperactive shit.

Archie greeted Merriman, then led him to a back booth and set a beer in front of him. "I know things are difficult, Steve, and the Parish Council wants you to know we're here for you and Margaret. At a meeting last night, I—well, we decided that this check for five hundred might defray some of your recent expenses."

Steve rubbed his cheeks and blubbered. "Archie, you been so good to me."

"Forget it," Archie said, then watched Steve throw the entire draft beer down his throat.

"Another," Archie called to the waitress.

"No," Steve said. "I can't."

"Don't worry. It's my tab."

After a few beers and two corned beef sandwiches, Steve was spewing hatred against all women who raise boys to be sissies.

"I agree that a father should have the dominant say in raising a boy," Archie said, then shuddered involuntarily as he remembered the burn of his father's belt across his backside.

"That Hamlin better fry for killing my kid," Steve growled as he banged his empty glass on the tabletop.

"He'll fry," Archie said.

"Sometimes you hear about slick lawyers getting these punks off."

"Well, if it was my son and the killer got off, I'd shoot him myself." Archie peered at Merriman over the edge of his beer mug. "I really would."

25

SLAT WANTED TO KNOW MORE ABOUT BILLY BOYD'S FIVE GAMBLING HOUSES. He had felt embarrassed while Odell and Stan explained West Side gambling to him. Like every other cop, he had paid little attention to it. The only gamblers he knew were men or women brought in because of some other offense. He knew many of Pulaski's black citizens and was already acquainted with three of the housemen Odell had mentioned; but Slat had no idea that these three men worked for Billy.

Slat decided that after a light dinner of pilaf at Mama's, where he ate when too lazy to fix something at his apartment. After dinner he would drive by the five houses and see what he could see. He glanced at the public phone by the restaurant's doorway and wondered if he should bring Theresa along. He had talked to her earlier that day, and she had hinted broadly about their going out. *Am I hot to date Theresa,* he wondered, *or am I running away from Jenny?* Either way, Slat decided, Theresa was a good kid and a lot of fun. He fished a quarter out of his pocket, wiped his month with one of Mama's napkins, then headed for the telephone.

Theresa sounded husky, as if he had wakened her from a nap. Her voice sounded seductive when she was sleepy.

"Want to go for a ride?"

"Sure, baby. How do I dress? What do you wear to a ride?"

He laughed. "You look great in anything. How about jeans? Nothing fancy—there are a few places I have to go and see, like from the car."

"You've lost me, Sczlatski."

"Like a stakeout, a surveillance."

"Ohhh," she drawled. "Not dinner and dancing. How exciting. Like 'Hill Street Blues'?"

"No, more like 'Barney Miller.'"

He was met with a long pause.. "When?"

"Half hour?"

"Meet you in front."

"You're a good sport, babe. I'll take you to a nice place some other time."

Slat didn't check out a detective car because everybody recognized them. He didn't want it known he was working, because he didn't want to use more overtime hours. And there was a third reason: Theresa couldn't go with him in a police car.

As Slat approached the cream-colored four-flats of Dobson Street, he saw her—a large-breasted brunette in designer jeans and a light- blue denim shirt. He flipped his cigarette out the window. She was another one who complained about secondhand smoke, he remembered. He stopped his car at the curb in front of her, and reached over to push open the door. As she got in, her blue eyes sparkled, and her sensuous lips parted in a smile.

Oh, baby, Slat thought.

"You're not on duty?" she asked.

"No. This is a little extra I like to do." Slat drove slowly, waiting for dusk to darken into night.

"Bullshit, Sczlatski. If you want to give a little extra to a citizen, I'll show you how." Theresa's dimples deepened as she talked.

Slat smiled.

"Seriously, honey, do you ever think about a little extra like a commitment to someone?"

His gut seized up. "Sure, I think about it." Sam's squalid room flashed into his mind again. Loneliness . . . suicide . . . He forced them away. "I think about growing old alone, but I can't change my life- style or my job. Not now."

"I think you're just blaming it on your job," Theresa said. "I think the big bad wolf is afraid of making a commitment."

"I tried it once, and it didn't work. Maybe I'm afraid of trying again, of making myself and—uh, someone else unhappy."

"You're not getting any younger, Sczlatski."

"No, I'm not," he agreed.

"I'm not getting younger, either."

"Sure you are, baby. Pretty soon you'll be a teenager, and I'll have you out after curfew."

She laughed and punched him gently on the arm. "So where are we going?"

Slat was grateful that she had dropped the subject. "West Side."

"After dark?"

"You got it." Night had fallen, so Slat swung the car toward the targeted neighborhood. His first objective was the house at 6221 Dodge Avenue. He drove around the block and through the alley several times, looking for the best spot to park and watch. A few minutes later, he pulled over to the curb, between two cars under a street lamp.

"Don't you think somebody might call the police about our sitting out here in the car?"

"Because we're white in a black neighborhood?"

"I wasn't thinking of that." She kicked off her moccasins, leaned against the passenger door, and tucked her feet under her. "We may be considered suspicious, white or black."

"Come to think about it, I've been on many calls about suspicious blacks in white neighborhoods, but never the other way around."

They had been parked for about a minute before they saw the men coming and going at the side door.

"What are we looking for or at?" Theresa asked.

"A gambling establishment," Slat answered.

"How can you tell? The only thing I see are a few men standing around that corner, and some others going in that side door."

"I know it's a gambling place because I was told by someone who knows. Remember the names I had you check at the credit bureau? Well, they relate to that, and everything is connected to an old homicide case. Let's move to another place. I've seen what I want here."

"Is there gambling every night?"

"Yeah, but Friday is the busiest because it's payday. Saturday's big, too."

Slat pulled out into the heavy nighttime traffic and drove to 3902 Emerson, where he made a couple of passes before finding a parking spot.

"The gambling is in the garage beside the house," he explained. On the other side of the alley, opposite the garage, a kiddy park was strewn with beer cans, which reflected headlights from passing cars.

Slat and Theresa slid down in the seat, not to hide but to appear like any couple lounging in a parked car. He adjusted his outside mirror so he could see along the left side of his car and behind him. Then he adjusted the inside mirror so he could see out the rear window and toward the sidewalk. That way he'd be aware of what was happening around him. He wasn't expecting anything in particular; it was just a cautious habit.

From where they sat, they could view the inside of the garage whenever the door opened.

"I see guys going in the side door," Theresa told him.

"Yeah. That's the place."

The sound of laughter drifted toward them in the cool air.

"It looks crowded," she said.

"Yeah. Lot of cars in the neighborhood. But maybe it's this way all the time."

"Why is gambling such a big deal on the West Side?" she asked.

"Possibly they don't have any other place to go."

"If they're enjoying themselves, why bother them? What's so terrible about their playing cards?"

Slat didn't want to explain what he was really working on. "It's my job."

"I suppose it is." Theresa lapsed into a moody silence. She leaned her head against the side window and gazed outside.

Slat felt guilty now that he had brought her along. He decided to see another gambling house or two, then he'd take her for a drink somewhere and try to end the evening on a happier note. He turned the ignition and threw the car into gear.

* * *

It was funny, the man thought, how loud his footsteps sounded on the pavement—loud enough for Sczlatski to hear him coming. He told himself to calm down. The sergeant would never be able to hear him above the traffic noise and laughter from the garage. Besides, someone else was in the car with him, and probably they were talking. No, he assured himself, everything was going fine. No need to worry.

But he couldn't take any chances. Whoever was with Sczlatski would have to die, too.

He had followed the sergeant's car from Mama's to Dobson Street, to Dodge, and now Emerson Avenue. From the addresses. But in a few minutes and a couple of blasts from his shotgun, it would be all over. Sczlatski would be dead, and he could go home and get a good night's sleep.

The man adjusted his long trenchcoat, which flapped around his ankles in cadence with his footsteps. As he walked toward the right rear of Sczlatski's car, he casually unbuttoned the coat and grasped the pistol- grip stock of the .12-gauge shotgun, which swung from a leather strap tied to his right shoulder.

Suddenly Sczlatski's ignition turned over, and the car pulled away from the curb and disappeared down the street.

"Shit! Shit!" The man hurried back to his car.

26

"WHERE TO NOW?" THERESA ASKED.

"This next place is in a black business area, but a lot of university people hang out at a few of the rib joints. We shouldn't look out of place."

"Did you see what you wanted at the last place?"

"Sort of."

"What do you mean?" she asked.

"I got the lay of the land, so to speak, and it looked active."

"I'd say it was active." Theresa snapped her seat belt.

"But I was hoping to see one or two certain people."

"You mean Billy Boyd?"

He glanced at her in surprise.

"Just a good guess," she told him. "You asked me for credit checks on Boyd and his corporation, remember? And I know who he is."

"You? How?"

"He's one of our customers and comes in on occasion. He's handsome, I'll tell you that. And he always has sweet things to say." Her dimples were dancing.

"Like what?"

"Oh . . . let me see." Theresa was obviously enjoying herself. "Like, 'A woman as charming and lovely as you should not have to strain those beautiful fingers on a typewriter.' "

"The very soul of sincerity, I'm sure," Slat muttered as he backed into a parking place next to an alley entrance and in front of a printing store with a dark entryway.

"So you don't think I'm charming and lovely?" she challenged, only half teasing.

"Of course I do, baby." *And I had to bring her along, he thought wryly.* "Theresa, Boyd found out about my checking on him."

Her eyes flashed. "Well, I didn't tell him, if that's what you're driving at."

"Jesus, Theresa, relax, will ya? I just want to know how he found out."

"After I pull a file, I place it in the billing clerk's file basket, so the customers get charged. On a freebie, like yours, she writes police on the routing slip and passes it to the filing clerk."

"Who sees them?"

"The billing clerk, the filing clerk, and my boss—except the ones I check on for you. I give those to the file clerk and tell her not to log them, so no one knows."

Except you and the file clerk, Slat thought. He didn't mention that Archie Dunn learned Dawn had requested a credit check on him. He'd find out the clerk's name later; he didn't want to put Theresa in the position of ratting on a coworker. "Anyway," he said, ending the topic of Theresa's knowing Boyd, "I was hoping to connect him directly to one of these gambling houses." After some thought Slat added, "Let's keep this whole thing to ourselves."

"Yes, sir, Sergeant." Theresa saluted.

"The place is across the street on the second floor, over that paint store or in the basement—I don't know which. See those guys going between those two buildings?"

"Yeah."

"Well, the entrance is somewhere back there, but I'm not exactly sure where."

"It's way too dark to see," she said. "Besides, you're parked in a bad spot to see all the way down."

"Yeah. I'm going to stroll across the street, then down the alley behind the place."

"You mean you want me to wait?"

"Just for a few minutes. You'll be fine. Just lock yourself in with the windows rolled up."

As soon as he left the car, he lit a cigarette. He crossed Leland Avenue, walked half a block up the street, then crossed and doubled back on the opposite side. His destination was an alley that ran along the rear of the paint shop. He walked into the passageway as two men walked out, paying no attention to him. The constant drone of traffic, an occasional squealing of tires, a staccato shout, and the shrill laugh of a woman penetrated the dark alley.

He peered down the walkway between the paint store and the adjacent building. Suddenly two men approached from the front between the buildings and came toward him. To avoid them, Slat quickly crossed the alley into the darkness between two garages.

The pair entered a doorway alongside the building, and he couldn't tell where they went. He looked up. From this angle, it seemed that lights shone on the second floor, while the basement was dark. But he couldn't be sure. Suddenly, three more men entered the walkway from the street.

A hand landed on his shoulder. Slat's heart flipped. He jumped and grabbed for his weapon.

"Hey, man!" The angry voice tore through the night. "What the fuck are you doing on my property?"

Slat could hardly see the man in the darkness, only his white hair and eyes. "I'm just looking—uh—for a place to piss."

"Well, piss in the alley. I get enough motherfuckers pissing against my garage."

"I'm going, man," Slat said, and walked into and down the alley, and took deep breaths to slow down his heart rate. After a few feet, he turned and moved toward the passageway between the two buildings. If the side door was unlocked, he decided to step inside and listen to find out if the noise was coming from the basement or from the second floor.

Slat almost made it to the side door when he heard three loud explosions. *Whoom! Whoom! Whoom!* They were shotgun blasts, and they had come from the street.

Theresa! Adrenaline surged through his body as he ran through the remainder of the passageway, the buildings rising high on each side. He dashed into the street, causing a car to screech to a stop and its driver to scream obscenities. He looked toward his own car—a crowd of people were running toward it.

Slat panicked. He sprinted south on Dodge Avenue, and fear engulfed him when he pushed through the onlookers and saw the shattered windows of his car.

"My God! Theresa!" he cried, forcing himself to look inside the car. He saw the glass particles glittering in the streetlights' glow, strewn across the upholstery and floor. And the front seat was empty.

Slat straightened and looked around. People were converging on the scene from all directions. He heard distant sirens. What happened to Theresa? he wondered, frantic. Had the shooter taken her, and left a warning by blowing away his car?

"Slat! Slat!"

He turned to see Theresa running toward him from down the street. She slammed into him and threw her arms around his neck. "Oh, God!" she sobbed. "I thought something happened to you!"

He held her tightly and felt relief wash over him. "Where'd you go?"

"I saw the drugstore at the corner. I went to get a pack of Dentyne."

"Thank God you did."

She looked past him and stared at the car. "What's going on, Slat? Why would somebody do that?"

"I don't know. But I intend to find out."

* * *

An hour later, after a squad had taken Theresa home, Slat stood stiffly before Leon Lovemore's desk. The muscular, square-jawed, balding lieutenant glared up at him.

"Don't screw around with me, Sczlatski." The supervisor was furious, and Slat could see that he had a very tight rein on his temper. "You always go to drugstores on the West Side?"

"Lieutenant, my lady wanted a pack of gum."

"You were parked almost half a block from the drugstore," Lovemore shot back.

"There wasn't a closer spot."

"Sczlatski." The lieutenant leaned back in his chair. "Why do my instincts tell me that your feeding me a line of shit?"

"Lieutenant, you're misjudging me."

"Midnight, and I'm here instead of in bed."

"Sorry, sir." And he meant it.

"Patrol will write out an initial report on this. You make a supplemental to it, giving the time you parked there—and if you saw anybody or if you suspect anyone."

* * *

Steve Merriman's heart pushed at his rib cage as he stared at Judge Stern on the bench. For the past three days Merriman had sat in the courtroom from nine each morning until court was over.

During the two-hour lunch break, he would wander aimlessly around downtown Milwaukee and suck air deep into his lungs, hoping somehow to ease the pain caused by the loss of his son, the hostility toward Jack Hamlin, and the new hatred for Judge Stern.

At night he slept fitfully, not even bothering to get into bed. He and Margaret hadn't spoken in days. She apparently was content to have him sleep on the couch, where he pulled hanks of hair from his head and tried to exorcise the nightmares. When he did doze, he was haunted by dreams of walking into David's bedroom and finding Jack Hamlin. The pervert would be laughing at him, then the sniggering face would melt and be transformed into Judge Stern's.

Even in the courtroom, Steve's eyes would play tricks on him. He would see the judge floating in midair, his black robes billowing around him. Steve would have to blink hard before the judge returned to his chair.

A litany of logic repeated in his head: Jack Hamlin admitted he killed David. If you kill someone, you pay.

Now, Merriman slid along the wooden pew to sit directly behind the defendant and his attorney, then concentrated on his antagonism and narrowed his eyes. If he focused hard enough and stared long enough at the back of Hamlin's skull, he knew he could burn a hole through the little bastard's hair and flesh and into his brain and kill him.

"The State of Wisconsin versus Jack Hamlin," the bailiff called.

Merriman leaned forward and reached for his insurance under his windbreaker. That's how he thought of it, as insurance. It's what Archie would've done, he knew, fingering the trigger.

The attorneys and the judge exchanged some quiet words, then Stern cleared his throat and said, "The state has failed to prove. . . ."

Merriman felt the room tilt crazily, and he pressed his sweaty palms against the railing to keep himself from falling onto the floor.

"Motion sustained," the judge said, and struck his gavel on the bench.

Merriman looked up dumbly as the blond attorney, smiling hugely, slapped Hamlin on the back.

"My boy! My boy's free!" a woman's voice behind him sang out. Steve turned and saw the gray-haired woman hurry past him and toward the little pervert.

Merriman pulled out his gun and did what any self-respecting father would have done, then watched as the back of Jack Hamlin's head exploded. Merriman was surprised by how good he felt—jubilant, really—as he turned toward the judge and fired again.

Stern grabbed his chest, then tore open his black robe to stare down at the blossoming red stain on his white shirt.

Merriman looked around, his job done. People were running from the room and ducking under the benches. "Don't run away!" he shouted. "I'm not going to hurt anyone!"

The two women detectives stood stiffly facing him, their arms stretched out, weapons pointing toward him. As he gaped in amazement, short flames spewed from the barrels. He felt the impact of the bullets and fell back. "Don't you understand?" he said, gasping for breath. "It's only fair. If you kill someone, you pay. . . ."

27

DAWN WORRIED ABOUT HER SANITY. She couldn't understand why she felt no remorse after shooting Merriman. She had felt some reactions, but they were all associated with fear, and moments later her heart rate had returned to normal.

It had been different for Jenny. The two women were at the station until midnight the night before, completing paperwork. While Dawn quietly worked on her reports, Jenny muttered, "Animals. They're all animals," under her breath.

"Who's an animal?" Dawn had asked.

"Mac Bell. Braun," Jenny answered venomously, never raising her gaze. "They like this shit. They look for violence. Killing a father wouldn't bother them a bit. Maybe I'm not tough enough to be a cop."

Dawn turned in her chair and was surprised to see a tear roll down Jenny's nose and onto her report.

"All I have to do to get out is give Slat my badge and a little piece of paper with two words—I resign." She looked up. Her liquid eyes were filled with pain, and her face was blotchy. "Why don't I, Dawn? I see violence every day. Am I an animal, too?"

"Maybe it has something to do with Slat," Dawn suggested gently.

"Then I'm an idiot," Jenny said, and burst into tears.

Dawn got up and, after hesitating a moment, went to put her arms around her friend. She felt Jenny's shoulders heave.

"I should have been with him that night, not Theresa! She's not a cop! He could have been shotgunned in his car, and she couldn't have done anything about it."

Dawn tried desperately to think of something to say, but Jenny was right. Obviously Slat had been investigating something on the West Side, or he wouldn't have been there. Jenny had every right to feel hurt. Dawn fished in her pocket for a tissue and held it out.

Jenny took it, hiccuped, then blew her nose. "Why do I still care about him? The jerk." She blew again. "And he wouldn't fall. His body just kept taking the bullets."

Dawn was confused until she realized that Jenny was talking about Merriman again.

"We had no choice," Jenny added. "He'd fired at Hamlin before we pulled our weapons."

"That's right, Jenny. We had no choice."

Then Slat had come in and told them to take the next day off, that if he needed anything, he'd call.

That night, Dawn dreamt about the shooting. First, Archie Dunn shot and killed Hamlin and the judge—but the judge was Martin Turski. Then Father Julius was the murderer.

The phone woke her at four in the afternoon. It was Jenny, wanting to come over. They had talked some more about Merriman and Slat, spent the evening together, and felt emotionally fortified to come into work.

Now Dawn sat on the edge of her desk and listened as the sergeant, leaning over the counter at the bureau's entrance, argued with Cheri Duncan.

"No, you can't interview these women," he said flatly. "They've got work to do."

"How about you then, Sergeant?" she asked. "I just want the facts of the shooting from the police perspective."

"You were there. If you want a police report, then go see the Milwaukee police. The shooting was in their jurisdiction."

"It was a Pulaski case, Sergeant," Cheri pointed out.

"You're welcome to see Lieutenant Lovemore."

"By the way, weren't you off duty the night your car was shot up?" the reporter asked sweetly. "Or should I ask Lieutenant Lovemore about that, too?"

"Ask him whatever you like." Slat turned from the counter and walked toward the glass cage. "Come to my office," he told Jenny and Dawn as he passed their desks.

The women settled into the chairs opposite his desk. He sat down and studied their faces. "Father Julius has offered to counsel both of you."

"Don't put that priest on me!" Dawn said. "Shooting or no shooting."

Slat held up his hands. "Okay, okay. You don't have to."

"I'll let you know," Jenny said coldly. Then she stood. "If that's all, I have work to do."

* * *

Gordy Mac Bell swung his squad into a U-turn. Slat had called him on the radio and asked to meet him in front of Mama's Place.

Sergeant Gordon "Gordy" Mac Bell, sandy haired and freckle faced, was the only person of pure Scottish heritage on the Pulaski Police Department. He was also one of the few who didn't go out drinking after work—not that he hadn't in the past. He had the reputation of a wild man, craving booze and women every night, enjoying wine and lovemaking on the beach during the summer months.

On days off, he'd drive to a northern neighborhood of Milwaukee for dinner with his mother. He never drank when he was with her, but she knew he was a booze hound. "It was the drams what killed your fay-ther. May he rest in peace. Don' let it kill ye, laddie."

But the drinking and whoring didn't stop. And then came the big scare: a sore the size of a pencil eraser on his penis. When he urinated, he suffered a burning sensation. For three days, he took several showers, hoping the sore would go away. What was it? he agonized. Syphilis, herpes—or AIDS? Never in his life had he ever been so frightened, especially while waiting in the doctor's office.

"Drop your pants and bend over, mister," the doctor said as he grabbed a needle. "You've got gonorrhea."

At about that same time he met Priscilla, a nurse who worked from seven in the morning till three in the afternoon at St. Luke's Hospital. Usually he tried to bed a woman the first night they went out; but he wanted the disease to clear up, so he never made a move on Priscilla.

Gordy fell in love. He stopped drinking, smoking, and chasing skirts. He filled those voids by dating Priscilla and by running. She ran with him on weekends. For four years he ran to work, then after work he'd run five or six miles. Now he ran ten miles after work every day. As a result, Gordy, who stood six foot, three inches, was as thin as a rail.

He found running the same route after work boring, so he changed his path often. Sometimes he'd do silly things, such as run up outside stairways in the business district, across connecting rooftops, and back down to the alley. On one set of roofs, three stories above the street, was a seven-foot span that he would jump when he felt daring.

Occasionally on a Friday or Saturday night he went through the black West Side. Passersby would call out, "Go, man, go," and "Run, you motherfucker," or threaten, "Stop and it's your fucking ass."

His stamina had paid off more than once when he was on the job and chasing perpetrators. He attached a soft, one-pound weight bag to the left side of his gun belt to maintain balance while running. He never lost a perp.

His other love, besides Priscilla and running, was his job as a police officer. Gordy worked hard and after six years was promoted to sergeant. A year later, he was assigned from a regular patrol shift to the Tactical Unit, which handled special nighttime assignments—crowd control and tavern and street fights—and backed up Patrol Units.

On most nights eight to ten patrol officers worked on the Tactical Unit. All were hardworking men in their twenties and early thirties. If they weren't responding to a call, they looked for something to do. Sergeant Mac Bell and his unit had declared war on a particular enemy: the drunk driver, a potential killer. Pulaski, with its 107 liquor licenses, was fertile ground, especially at bar closing time around one. Homeward-bound drunks, the old-timers warned, drove from curb to curb.

As a supervising sergeant, Gordy didn't personally have to seek out arrests, but he did. This motivated his men. Each year the Tactical Unit increased the number of drunk driving arrests and convictions. The Pulaski Press reported that the local Tavern Keepers' Association was filing a claim of harassment against the police department, but Gordy didn't consider that to be his concern. That problem belonged to the chief and the politicians. All he wanted was to work, run, and make love to Priscilla. Besides, because of its excellent conviction rate, the unit was never criticized for sloppy enforcement.

* * *

Slat sat in a booth near a window at Mama's. As he waited for Gordy, he had a cup of coffee and a cigarette and thought about Jenny. He couldn't understand her coldness to him. Of course she was upset about shooting Merriman. The man's stricken widow, already grieving a son, was on every newscast and the front page of the Milwaukee and Pulaski newspapers—her thin shoulders hunched, her skeletal fingers clutching a handkerchief, as she thanked friends and strangers for their outpouring of love and sympathy. It was a damn shame.

But Slat suspected that Jenny was suffering from more than that because she was so damned aloof and angry. They'd worked together fine since the night at her apartment, so it wasn't that. He remembered the pleasant sensation of having her body pressed to his, the warm softness of her lips, the roundness of her buttocks under her jeans, the—then it came to him. Theresa! Jenny was angry about Theresa's being with him the night of the shooting. He groaned and rubbed his eyes with his fingers.

"Hey, old buddy!"

Slat looked up as Gordy slid into the booth. "Apple juice, Mama," he called toward the counter. "A large." He turned to Slat. Gordy waved the cigarette smoke away. "You ought to quit them. They're not healthy. They cause . . . .

"

"Okay! Everybody is on my ass about them." He reached into his shirt pocket and pulled the pack out. "I quit. Here, Mama, throw 'em out."

Gordy grinned. "What's up, man?"

"I need help on some old homicides, but our talk can't go past you and me."

"Got it, old buddy."

Slat explained about the old gambling murders as Gordy listened with interest.

"Hey, this sounds great. How can I help?"

"I need your men to roust up the black gambling houses."

"No problem-o." Gordy drained his glass of water and looked ready to shoot out of the restaurant. "I'm ready."

Slat laughed. "Hold it, Gordy. We have to do this right and legally."

"Oh, yeah, of course." Mama set down the juice, and he swigged that, too. "Tell me what you want done."

"I'll call you tomorrow and say that I've got complaints about some illegal gambling. I'll give you the addresses, and you and your men will hit each place. Bullshit your way in and break up the games, but don't arrest anyone. Just cite the statutes and say this is a warning, that patrons will be arrested the next time."

"The guys will like the change of pace."

We'll all love it, Slat thought, thinking of the pressure this would put on Billy and Mountain Top. He wanted results, and he wanted them now. Lillie's death had made it more serious.

28

MEMORANDUM
City of Pulaski

From: Alderman Archibald Dunn

To: Mayor and City Council

The Pulaski Police Department has recently been sued because of admitted civil-rights violations. I have learned that the police chief took no more disciplinary measure than a minor reprimand against the police officers involved.

It has been learned that a detective sergeant, off duty but on a stakeout with a non-police female in his vehicle, was allegedly involved in a shooting.

Fortunately no one was injured. If a citizen had been injured, the city would probably have been liable.

I urge each alderman to be cognizant of this apparent lack of good judgment within the ranks of the police department. Corrective measures requested of Chief Turski have apparently been ignored.

cc: Chief Turski

Chief Martin Turski tore the memo in half, then slowly, deliberately crinkled the piece of paper, rolled it into a ball, and dropped it in his wastebasket. He had always thought of himself as an intelligent man with high moral standards, but he didn't know how much more he could take of Archie Dunn. Violent thoughts about the alderman were beginning to consume him. Although the chief was careful not to let anyone else know it, he was anxious and infuriated for most of the day and nearly all of the night. His anger at Dunn had affected his sleep, his appetite, and his sex life. He and his wife rarely went out anymore, so fearful was he that he'd bump into Dunn at a restaurant or movie theater. I came here with such high hopes, Martin thought, despondent. He had watched his goals fall by the wayside because he was forced to waste time and energy ineffectually fending off Dunn's political attacks. His only defense was to throw away the memos. But, like ignored parking tickets, Martin Turski knew the reprimands would catch up with him sooner or later. At times he had felt so impotent in the face of Archie Dunn's attacks and solid support within Pulaski's old-boy political network, Turski had actually entertained thoughts of suicide. The spells always passed, but they never failed to frighten him. He thought about applying for a job elsewhere, or even leaving law enforcement altogether, but he never had the strength to pursue it. Instead he sat down, instructed his secretary over the intercom to hold all calls, then turned his chair and gazed sightlessly out the window.

* * *

"What did Popodowski say besides telling us to hurry up and see the archbishop?" Tony adjusted his tie as he and Patrick Daley hastened from the restaurant, where they'd had breakfast, to their car parked outside. Father Daley squeezed his bulk into the passenger seat. "Tony, you ask so many questions about my conversations with the monsignor. I don't like being a go-between. Why don't you talk to him yourself?"

"Because I can't stand the son of a bitch."

"Well, that's your problem, not mine." Patrick clucked his tongue. "Such talk." Tony adjusted his seat belt, then pointed the car toward Cousin's Center. "At least we'll find out now what we're supposed to be doing. Did you tell Popodowski that we can't find Julius?"

"No. I just said that his car is parked behind the rectory, but the sister said he isn't in."

"Why?"

Patrick shrugged. "I didn't have the heart to tell him that Vatican Superagent Tony Tattaglia lost a priest." Tony fell silent, taken aback by the nastiness of Patrick's reply. After a brief ride along the shore of Lake Michigan, Tony pulled into the long driveway.

"Cousin's Center. Finally." They drove along a winding driveway. Tony admired the magnificent grounds; the low modern buildings set against a backdrop of ancient religious buildings. The archbishop has it good, he thought, pulling the car into a parking place. A matronly woman responded to the doorbell. She tilted her head upward. "Come in, young man. Hello, Father Daley." The priest mumbled a greeting, then, with Tony at his heels, strode down a long corridor. He knocked. There was no answer, so Patrick opened the door and ushered Tony into an enormous, oak-paneled study. Tony looked around. They're always the same, he realized, with their floor-to-ceiling, musty smelling bookshelves, the identical books, the familiar artifacts and statues. A door across the room opened. In walked a drably dressed, heavy- set, distinguished-looking man with a pock-marked complexion. He wore the regalia.

"Father Daley, good morning. Mr. Tattaglia, it's good to see you so promptly."

"Archbishop Coughlin, Your Reverend," Tony said from between clenched jaws, "on matters that could cause a great deal of consternation to the Church, the Vatican acts promptly."

"Ah, well put. A brandy, Mr. Tattaglia?" The archbishop opened a cupboard. He smiled. "Christian Brothers, of course."

At ten in the morning? Tony thought, aghast. He sneaked a look at Patrick's face.

"Thank you, Your Reverend."

The archbishop handed a brandy to Tony and another to Father Daley, who held it as if it were nuclear. "Do you do this sort of thing often for the Church?"

He waited for the archbishop to be seated. "Not I, although, sadly, there are many, many priests in need of counseling and sometimes even supervision. Other agents usually handle that. Because I'm an attorney, I'm usually assigned to financial investigations and international legal matters." Tony raised his brandy to the archbishop. "Always something."

"Indeed," Coughlin agreed. "The matter we have to discuss is one of the most serious problems I have encountered since my ordination. I apologize for not giving you more explicit direction."

"Of course. Quite all right," Tony lied.

"Father Daley, as my financial secretary, has stayed on top of this matter." Tony, watching in amazement as Father Daley poured himself another brandy, wondered exactly what information Daley was on top of that he hadn't bothered to mention.

"Mr. Tattaglia," the archbishop continued, "I've been assured by the Vatican that we will have secrecy in this matter. Recently here in the United States the Church has had too much negative publicity regarding errant priests, with adults bringing criminal action against clerics who supposedly molested them decades ago, and complaints from parents regarding the transfer of errant priests to different parishes within the US. The media has been trying to track our errant transfers. Television networks are saying that the Church had spent twenty-five million dollars defending priests accused of pedophilia."

"Over what period of time?" Tony asked.

Coughlin waved away the question as if it had no relevance. "I don't recall. I don't know where they get such information. Many bishops are taking the position that we get these errants out of the country and to Latin America or Italy, where they can be treated, of course. My concern is that we get them away before local police jurisdictions press charges. Actually, most prosecutors would prefer to see the Church's errant matters resolved by the Church. I couldn't agree more. I trust you'll handle this matter promptly?"

Tony felt his hand tighten on the crystal snifter. "If I may be so bold, Your Reverend, I've been ready for days."

Coughlin pulled back his sleeve and glanced at his watch. "Well, I must go. A thousand things to do. Father Daley will keep you moving forward with this, Mr. Tattaglia. I hope to see you again before you return to Rome." They stood while the archbishop left the study.

* * *

"Capital punishment sucks." Odell Fowler wiped suds from his eyeglasses. "If I had to do life in prison, I'd kill myself. Like old Patrick Henry. Death is the easy way out. Don't these liberals know that?" With practiced skill the detectives shared newspapers around their table at Ski's Inn, shuffling the sections and pages between and around pitchers, mugs, popcorn bowls, and ashtrays.

"Public is synonymous with apathy." Stan Osinski finished his shot, then washed it down with a half mug of beer.

"Capital punishment is all right, if done properly," Homer Braun said. He stood. "First, you scare the unexpected shit out of the felons, just like they did to their victims. Then take five guys off death row and give each one a parachute, but only four of the parachutes open. The five know that, but they don't know which one is the dummy. So they all jump, suffering the same uncertainty about their fate that their victims endured. One of the assholes dies. The other four are joined by another one from death row the next week to go through the same routine. That, my friends, is justice served."

"Homer, you should get your head bandage changed." Odell turned the page of the newspaper he was reading. "Says here the judge was sent to intensive care."

"TV said he's still critical," Homer said, taking a seat.

"Some shit the girls went through," Odell said.

"This article says that the police should have anticipated a demented father in the courtroom. The editorial calls for a probe of the Pulaski Police Department policies. Jeez." Stan licked foam off his upper lip.

"Aw, fuck 'em," Homer grumbled. "Next week it'll be a different crisis. If you don't want to be criticized, work for a newspaper."

"Yeah," Odell said. "It used to be said that judges sat next to God. Not anymore. Now it's newspaper publishers."

"Hey, look who's here!" Homer shouted. "Miss Smith and Miss Wesson." Clusters of cops applauded and called out support as Jenny and Dawn made their way to their colleagues.

"Another pitcher," hollered Homer, pushing a chair away from the table with his good foot. The women sat down.

Stan leaned toward them and spoke in an avuncular tone. "I want to tell you kids something. We all understand that Steve Merriman was a victim, just like his son. But the second he pulled that weapon, he was no longer a victim; he was a criminal. You two did your job as police officers. Don't ever forget that." Stan stood and walked around the table to where Jenny was sitting.

"Now give Stan a big hug." Jenny jumped up and grabbed Stan around his neck. She began to cry.

"Let it out, kid." Stan hugged her against his barrel chest and patted her on the back until her sobs eased. "Now we can cry in our beer," he told her, and poured her a mug. Then he went to stand beside Dawn's chair. "Okay, kid, your turn." But Dawn's eyes were riveted on the table. No one spoke.

"Hey, kid," Stan said, "am I poison or something?" They all laughed. Sheepish, Dawn stood and, with tears in her eyes, and hugged the big bear.

"Who needs psychologists when we have Stan Osinski around?" Odell asked.

"Where's Slat?" Dawn didn't direct the question to anybody in particular.

"He left to meet Gordy."

* * *

At 10:30 that evening, Slat gave five addresses to Sergeant Gordy Mac Bell, who met his men in the south parking lot at St. Luke's Hospital. When he arrived, he found the eight members of his Tactical Unit standing outside their two-man squads, which were parked in a wagon-train circle.

"Okay, guys. Pay attention. We're going to take care of business, and we'll only need two vehicles. I'll take three in my car, and the rest go in squad forty-seven."

"What's up, Sarge?"

"Fellas, we are going to hit some black gambling joints."

"What?"

"I'll be dipped in shit," one of the cops said.

"I'll be damned!"

"I know you're surprised, but we've had verbal complaints against five places. We just go inside, warn them, and photograph them."

"Ain't no such thing as a gambling arrest," another said.

"That's for sure," one of the men said, and the others laughed.

"And no roughhouse," Gordy ordered. "Lock the other squads and let's go. Just follow my lead."

"And I almost didn't come to work tonight," said another as several car doors slammed.

* * *

It was not unusual to see squad cars in the West Side. When two of them pulled into a darkened parking lot next to a paint store, no one on the streets paid any attention. The cops quietly got out of their vehicles and followed Gordy single file a short distance from the parking lot, down an alley, and into a passageway between two brick buildings. He stuck his head into the unlocked door, then held up his hand. The train of officers stopped. Gordy listened. The loud talking came from the second floor. He motioned them forward, and they tiptoed to the second-floor landing, where he waited until his men had bunched up behind him. Then he tested the knob. It wasn't locked. Slowly he opened the door into a dense fog of tobacco smoke and a rush of body oder.. The officers rushed into the room. Thirty card players sat at four green, felt-topped tables. The gamblers sat like onyx stones. Only their eyes were in motion as the policemen walked to each table, then picked up the cards. They did not touch the money. At Gordy's direction, one officer started flashing a thirty-five millimeter camera at each table. The camera was a psychological weapon used in tavern and street fights. Half the time it had no film, but the flashing tended to break up fights and served to move people from the scene.

"What's going on?" asked one participant, breaking the stunned silence.

"Halloween," said another gambler, referring to the uniforms.

"Who the fuck invited them?" one cigar-chomping gambler demanded.

"I got to go," another said, rising. Gordy jumped onto an empty chair, which extended his height above the low-hanging lamps. His face couldn't be seen in the shadows. Silence reigned. All eyes looked upward.

"Gentlemen," Gordy began in a reasonable tone, "I am here to speak about the law we tend to lean against on occasions. I'm asking each of you—"

"This motherfucker's crazy," one of the gamblers said.

"Quiet, please," the sergeant requested. "This is a warning. I am asking each of you to stop gambling."

"Ain't nobody going nowhere, man!" someone challenged. "We's staying." Silence. Gordy jumped to the floor, then walked to the speaker, who was the same height as Gordy but sixty pounds heavier. They stood nose to nose. "Listen, you—if anybody except the tenant is left in this room in one minute, you'll all be arrested!" The gamblers shoveled the money off the tables and into their pockets and left.

"Pig motherfuckers," one mumbled.

"Honky fuck head," another said.

"Now, now, gentlemen," Gordy said. "Go in peace and be grateful that I've stopped you from sinning." One man remained. "I want to know what's happening," he demanded. "There's going to be some shit flying somewhere."

"Are you the houseman?" Gordy asked. The man nodded.

"Have a good night," Gordy said as his men marched out behind the gamblers. He stopped at the door. "One more thing. Next time—and that will be soon—you all will be arrested."

* * *

As the Tactical Unit squads were heading for Dodge Street, Slat followed. He wondered who the houseman would telephone first about the indignity he had just endured. He glanced in his rearview mirror and noticed that a car was following him. Visions of shattered glass from the shotgun blast played before his eyes. Slat knew where Gordy was headed, so he could turn down a side street and catch up with the unit later. If the car stayed on his tail, then Slat would know he was the target. If the car continued after Gordy instead, then the driver might be some jerk looking for the excitement of another gambling raid. Slat looked for a convenient place to turn right, then changed his mind, deciding he was being paranoid. Besides, who knew what might go wrong in one of these gambling houses. It made more sense to follow Gordy.

29

TWO MARKED SQUADS DROVE HALFWAY DOWN THE ALLEY, then parked on two garage aprons a few doors away from their destination. The gambling establishment the Tactical Unit was interested in was the second house from the corner. The officers quietly followed Gordy to the corner of the garage behind 4819 Foster Street.

He peeked around the garage corner, then ran lightly across the yard to the rear of the house. He peered around the corner of the building toward its side entrance, located in a passageway lit only by a small bulb above the door. No one was in sight, so he motioned his men to move from the garage to the back wall of the house.

"Wait here while I check the door," he told them, then removed his hat and held his hand over his breast badge so nothing would reflect off it. He quietly walked into the passageway. Before he reached the side entrance, he noticed a small glass window about a foot square in the door. That was not good; the houseman might have a lookout stationed there.

Suddenly two men turned from the front sidewalk and started down the passageway toward Gordy. He backed unseen around the corner of the house and listened, heart pounding, as the men knocked. The door opened, and the men greeted one another.

How do we get through that door? he wondered. He peered around the building's edge and watched as yet another man knocked and was admitted.

He went back to report to his unit. "The door's locked," he told them. "We'll have to wait until the next patron comes, then I'll sprint to the door. You guys follow me."

Not thirty seconds later, two laughing men came down the passageway from the front sidewalk. One knocked on the door as Gordy edged around the corner. As the second man stepped into the doorway, Gordy dashed forward. He reached the door and pushed it open. Before the surprised doorman could speak, the officer at Gordy's heels had the man by the throat.

"Keep your mouth shut, asshole," the officer whispered through clenched teeth.

The two gamblers who had entered just before Gordy reached the bottom of the right-angled, basement stairway. The air was dank and musty. Gordy and his unit quietly trailed down the dimly lit steps. Above, pipes running along the ceiling dripped on them. The two laughing men opened a door and entered the noisy gaming room. Gordy followed.

A bar was to the left. A large table, encircled by about thirty men, was to the right. A big man with gold teeth and a Hawaiian shirt was raking money from marked circles on the green-felt tabletop.

Gordy and his men casually followed the two laughing patrons into the room.

"What the fuck, man?" The bartender, the first to notice the cops, raged at the two patrons. They were dumbfounded when they turned and saw the police behind them.

"Leroy, what the fuck you bring them in here for?" the man with the rake demanded.

"Not me, man! They ain't with me! No fucking way."

"What do you want, man?" the houseman asked angrily.

"Can we play with you guys?" Gordy inquired.

"Say what?" the houseman said.

Sixty eyes stared at Gordy as he pointed to his officer with the camera, signaling him to start flashing.

"What the fuck's going on?" the houseman asked.

"Gentlemen." Gordy spoke to the nervous patrons, most of whom were eyeing the room's only door, which was blocked by a uniformed policeman. The gamblers didn't know how many more policemen waited beyond the doorway. "Gentlemen, and I mean all of you." Gordy pointed to every man. "We got fifty calls from fifty wives, all saying that they want their husbands home, that their man is spending all his money gambling. So I want all of you to go out this doorway and head on home. Move over, men, and give them room." The officers positioned themselves along the bar and watched the disgruntled patrons leave.

Gordy looked at the houseman and bartender. "You have a good evening?"

The houseman was so angry, he was nearly jumping up and down. "What kind of shit is this, man? I take care of business. Why are you fucking me over?"

A wall phone behind the bartender rang once, twice, three times. Everyone looked at it, but no one made a move.

"Answer your phone!" Gordy ordered.

The bartender did as he was told. "Yeah," he said grimly into the mouthpiece. "You're too fucking late. They're already here." Then he slammed the phone against the wall. The impact jolted a decorative mirror, which dangled precariously on its hook, then fell into the sink.

"Temper, temper," Gordy said. "You'd better find a new line of work."

With that, the police left.

* * *

Slat watched the Tactical Unit leave the Foster Street address. Then he followed as they headed for Dodge Avenue. He glanced repeatedly in his rearview mirror but didn't see a car following him.

Within a few minutes, the Tactical Unit left the Dodge Avenue house. No game was going on there. More than likely the first two houses had warned the third. The same was true for the Emerson and Asbury addresses. Satisfied that the mission was a success, Slat followed the two squads to the south parking lot at St. Luke's Hospital where he thanked the officers. He watched as they went to their own squad cars.

Slat stood beside Gordy. "How do you think it went?" he asked.

"Hey, no problem," Gordy said. "In fact, it was kind of fun."

Gordy swatted at the cigarette smoke. "I thought you quit."

"Yeah, yeah," Slat said with an edge of irritation. "Then I started again."

Gordy got a call on the radio. He leaned into the squad to answer.

"Sergeant Mac Bell, call Lieutenant Lovemore at his home," it squawked.

"Ten-four." He straightened and grinned crookedly at Slat. "Hear that?"

"Yeah. Lovemore must have gotten some calls. He's going to ask you what was going on. Just tell him you got the beefs from me and honored my request to give out warnings."

"Got you, Slat. If you need us again, let me know."

"Thanks, Gordy. But now I just sit back and wait for Billy Boyd and Mountain Top to get in touch with me."

* * *

A man wearing a rolled-up ski mask was parked between two cars in the hospital parking lot. He waited, watching and fingering the pistol grip of his sawed-off shotgun. When he saw Slat's and the marked squad's headlights go on, he immediately started the ignition of his own car. He had followed Slat all night and didn't want to lose sight of him now.

Slat drove to the exit, and the marked squad followed. The man in the mask was third in line. Slat turned right and entered the roadway, but heavy traffic prevented the squad from making a left turn. There was no room for the man to go around the squad and follow Slat. Fuming, he thought the officer was being needlessly cautious and missing perfectly good opportunities to cut across the street, but honking at a copper to get the lead out was never a good idea. The man in the mask watched in frustration as Slat's car disappeared down the darkened streets of Pulaski.

* * *

That night and early the next morning, Slat neither answered his home phone nor his beeper. He had deliberately left his beeper's receiver on so the batteries would run down. He didn't want to spend the night listening to Lieutenant Lovemore. Listening to him during the day was, he believed, bad enough. Slat fell asleep and dreamed of Lillie Boyd and Sam Tyrone lost on a moonscape.

Slat arrived at his office an hour early after stopping at the firehouse for a cup of coffee. Confident that Lieutenant Lovemore wouldn't be in this early, Slat knew he would have time to get his daily assignments set up before the shit hit the fan.

He found a sheet of paper taped to the glass window facing his desk. It read, Sergeant Sczlatski. Wait for me. I'll be in at 8:30. Lieutenant Leon Lovemore.

By 8:25 Slat had reviewed all reports and organized his assignments for his crew. At 8:29 Slat put his pen aside, pushed back his chair, and folded his arms across his chest. He looked up at the wall clock and watched the second hand twirl. At ten seconds to 8:30, he heard footsteps in the hallway. Five seconds later he saw the shiny, balding head and square jaws of Lovemore hurry along the counter to the swinging gate. The lieutenant slapped the gate open. As the second and minute hand hit 8:30, he heard, "Sergeant, where the fuck have you been?"

"Me?" Slat asked.

"Who the fuck else is in this room? Don't give me your shit, Sczlatski! Where were you all night? I beeped you."

Slat pointed at the batteries sitting in the charger. "Dead. Check for yourself."

Lovemore flexed and unflexed his hands. "Ach! Forget it! My phone didn't stop ringing last night. I got a call from every alderman on the West Side, from the NAACP and the ACLU, not to mention a couple of attorneys. They all want to know why some black card-players were being harassed. A few of the calmer callers simply wanted to know how many white homes were walked into last night. And churches, Sczlatski. They want to know if the Catholic Church was visited by police officers. How the fuck do I explain that to them, Sczlatski?"

Slat shrugged. "My informant mentioned only a few places on the West Side. If you know of any others violating the law, give me the orders, Lieutenant. I'll close them and the churches. . . .
"

"Cut the shit, Sczlatski. I want a report on my desk explaining what your informant told you and your—shall we say logic?—for the action you took."

"Right away, sir."

"Don't get sarcastic with me, Sczlatski. And don't you dare say shit to the press."

"But, Lieutenant, I thought you wanted me to handle the press on matters concerning my shift."

"Not this time, Sergeant. You'll fuck that up, too." He threw up his hands. "I don't even know what the fuck I'm going to tell them."

* * *

As Jenny followed Odell, Stan, and Dawn into the Detective Bureau, Lieutenant Lovemore brushed past them on his way out. He nearly knocked her over. "Excuse me, Lieutenant," she muttered sarcastically.

Slat was standing between the rows of desks as the four officers walked through the gate.

"Sarge, you missed a roll-call training session with patrol," Stan said.

He was probably on the phone with Theresa, Jenny thought.

"I had a meeting with the lieutenant," Slat explained.

"The subject was AIDS," Stan told him. "This AIDS stuff is scary."

"Yeah," Odell agreed. "I'm glad I'm married. I don't have to use a condom."

"Me, neither," Stan said.

The female detectives looked at each other.

"A quick meeting here, everybody," Slat said. "The judge is going to recover, thanks to Dawn and Jenny. If you two hadn't stopped Merriman, he might have gotten a few more slugs into the judge. With Merriman and Hamlin dead, we can put this case behind us and move on. It's been suggested to me that I split you two ladies up. For the life of me, I can't imagine why."

"Thank God." Stan swung his bull frame back to his desk. "When's Duffy coming back from fishing? He's missed all the fun, with Homer shooting himself, and Jenny and Dawn playing Cagney and Lacey . . . "

The phone interrupted Stan. Slat answered. A moment later he said, "We've got a homicide. Centennial Park. A young boy."

"Oh, shit!" Stan said.

"Son of a bitch! Doesn't it ever stop?" Jenny wailed. She couldn't handle much more. She looked at her friends. She saw hollowness in Dawn's face, the bitterness in the eyes of Stan and Odell. And, as Slat's gaze met her own, Jenny knew that she probably looked the worst of all of them.

"Osinski," Slat said, "you and Fowler have this one."

30

SLAT HAD NOT MADE THE ASSIGNMENT LIGHTLY. There was no way he would give a homicide to Dawn and Jenny, not with their emotions running so high. Stan and Odell were the logical choice.

Stan Osinski had been a detective for nine years after spending ten years in uniform. Before he became a cop, he'd worked in the steelyard at the Poole Tractor Company, alongside his brothers, father, uncles, and cousins. His grandfather had put in his time in the Poole yard, too, beginning in 1919, when he immigrated from Poland.

The yard was hard labor, loading and unloading steel parts and crates. The heavy work developed a family of what some might consider grotesque giants. Stan was one of those guys with muscles on his muscles.

He had been married to Mary for twenty-four years. He owned his row house, which he bought from his former employer. He bought a new four-door Chevrolet every five years, and he was the first one to leave Ski's Inn after his three shots and beers.

"Hey, if I'm such a dumb Polack, how come I'm not as fucked up as you guys?" he'd ask. He was right. Stan was anything but dumb. He was sensitive and tough.

Few people knew that he held a degree in botany from the University of Wisconsin. If anyone asked him about it, he'd say, "What the fuck's the matter with you, asshole? Me, spend time with all them fucking punks talking like they know everything? Bullshit."

But it wasn't bullshit when you saw Stan's backyard and greenhouse. He loved plants. "Plants are like women," he once confided in Slat. "Treat 'em well, and they'll reward you with fragrance and beauty."

Slat understood his brother Pole, but he'd never try to explain him. Stanley Osinski was his own man. He complained about every racial and ethnic group, calling them assholes, but he'd still battle the odds for them to make sure justice was served.

Osinski was the solid workhorse of the crew. The job stress and victims' pain washed off him. On tough assignments, he let the iron mask of emotionlessness clamp shut. Slat, marveling at how Stan held it inside, had asked, "Hey, Bro, how do you handle the shit?"

"Cartoons, kid." *Kid* was a word he used affectionately when no one else was within earshot. "Every Saturday morning I watch the cartoons on TV. Then I'm okay for the rest of the week."

"Come on," Slat drawled, laughing.

"Okay, okay," he admitted. "With me, kid, it's mass every Sunday. It helps. To me, this job is like climbing a ladder with a weight on my back. Each rung is next Sunday's mass. It's a tough climb, but when I grab the next rung, it gives me the strength to reach for another."

"What's at the top of the ladder?" Slat asked.

"Retirement."

Slat chuckled. "I thought you were going to say heaven."

"Maybe it's the same thing," Stan remarked, shrugging.

* * *

Now, Osinski and Fowler, another workhorse, parked their detective car next to two marked squads in a small parking lot at Centennial Park. They walked a short dirt path through some trees and bushes and out into a little meadow centered by a tiny pond. Swans glided on the water, blending, Stan noticed, with the beauty of the park's lush botanic background.

They approached a group of officers staring into a depression a few yards from the pond. The beauty was destroyed. When Stan looked down at the dead boy, his iron mask clamped shut.

MEMORANDUM
City of Pulaski

From: Alderman A. Dunn

To: Mayor and City Council

The shootings in Judge Stern's courtroom again reflect the inadequate management of our police department.

It has come to my attention that Steve Merriman had spent several days in court staring at the judge. The police should have taken preventive measures.

I request that the City Council reevaluate the present administration of the police department.

cc: Chief Turski

Dawn and Jenny spent the day handling burglary follow-ups. It was an easy schedule, without mental challenges, which left Dawn free to think about the Merriman homicide. She wanted to believe a second person had been present during the murder, but she didn't want to mention it to Jenny. The truth was, Dawn wanted Hamlin's accomplice to be Archie Dunn, and she knew that was ridiculous. She tried to distinguish between valid suspicion—that Hamlin had not acted alone—and her fantasy of seeing the alderman get what she thought he deserved for giving the chief such a rough time.

Now, at four o'clock, as Jenny and she were getting ready to check out of the bureau, Dawn glanced over at Fowler and Osinski, both grim faced and somber. The murder victim, they had told her, was a twelve-year- old boy, raped and suffocated.

Dawn leaned over toward Jenny. "Between you and me," she whispered, "I'm glad we didn't get that homicide."

"Yeah," Jenny agreed. "One a month is enough, especially when it's a kid."

"Do you ever wonder about Raymond Tee?" Dawn asked quietly.

"That was one of those leads that goes nowhere, I guess," Jenny replied. "We staked out his place, but then the Hamlin lead developed and ended the case."

"Jenny, I've listened to that confession tape a half-dozen times, and I don't think Hamlin acted alone."

"That kid was so scared, I don't think he was capable of hiding anything, Dawn, especially someone who could share the rap."

Dawn opened the front door to leave. "See you guys," she called. As the door was shutting behind her, she heard a partial sentence from Stan that echoed behind her: ". . . funeral at St. George's."

Dawn spun around and walked back into the bureau. "Was he an altar boy at St. George's?"

"Yeah." Stan looked up, both index fingers hanging over his keyboard. "But so are seventy-five percent of the Catholic boys in this city."

"Which means about fifty percent of the boys in this city," Odell added. He never stopped typing. "Why?"

Dawn hesitated. There couldn't be a connection. The number of altar boys was too high for it to be a meaningful coincidence. "Oh, nothing," she said at last, and decided to head for Ski's Inn, to wash this Merriman homicide from her brain.

* * *

Mountain Top angrily paced in front of Billy Boyd's desk, and the vibration from his size-sixteen footsteps came up through the legs of his boss's chair.

"The brothers said they won't be able to make this week's payments, boss, because the police closed them down."

"Calm down, man," Billy said irritably. "Soft Sound is on his way. And Popper's out calming the housemen down now. We'll discount their payments by one or two days. That'll keep them happy."

Billy, wearing a white, open-collar sport shirt and white casual slacks, turned his back to his desk and stared out the window of his office at the Sunshine Management Corporation. It was a Saturday afternoon. Usually he spent his weekends boating on Lake Michigan, playing tennis on his private courts, or just reading the newspaper. Seldom was he in his office, and he was not happy about it.

"I should have pounded the piss out of that motherfucker Slat-ski when he stopped me the other day."

"And we'd have been arrested. No, we'll figure something else—or Soft Sound will. Whatever we do has to be legal and politically advantageous." Billy swung his chair around to face his bodyguard.

"Is that possible?" Mountain Top asked, smiling.

Billy laughed appreciatively.

"If your way doesn't work, Boss, let me know. My way will."

"No, we want everyone quiet about this. Too much noise by some of the aldermen will attract notice from the local papers. Fuck this civil- rights bullshit. We don't need publicity."

A knock sounded on the outer office door. "That must be Soft now," Mountain Top said, and went to open the door.

A small woman of about forty stood in the doorway. "Is Mr. Boyd in?" she asked timidly.

"He's busy," Mountain Top said. "Can you come back later?"

"Please, Mountain Top," she said tearfully.

"Just a minute." The big man turned. "Boss, Dicey Taylor's widow's here. Wants to talk to you."

"Of course," Billy called back.

Mrs. Taylor followed Mountain Top inside. "Mr. Boyd, Billy, sir, I don't know where to turn for help in this city. Everybody says see Billy."

"What can I do for you?"

"My boy, Kenny. He's almost thirteen. He's missing. Almost three days now." She worked hard not to cry.

"You go to the police?" Mountain Top asked, bringing her a chair.

"Yes, day before yesterday. They made out a missing person report. Called him a runaway."

"Well, you did what you're supposed to do," Billy said.

"But it's been three days." She began sobbing. "He's all I got left, the only child Dicey and I had. He's no runaway. Kenny's a good boy!"

"I'm sure the police will find him." Billy glanced at Mountain Top.

"But I don't see them looking. They ain't talked to his friends or teachers or nothin'."

Billy rose from behind his desk, walked over to Mrs. Taylor, and helped her from her chair. "I'll see what I can do. I'll talk to the police myself."

"Everybody says see Billy. Oh, thank you. Thank you."

Billy passed Mrs. Taylor to Mountain Top's care, and the man ushered her from the office as the small attorney came quickly through the door.

"That's right, that's right," he screeched, his pronounced Adam's apple bobbing. "Billy's your man." He sat down in her vacated chair. "I've been making calls, calming folks down. I've asked the NAACP and the four black aldermen to my house this evening for cocktails."

"Who called the aldermen?" Billy asked.

"For chrissakes, Billy, when something like this happens, word gets around." Soft Sound put his hands on his skinny knees and leaned forward. "You talking about a few hundred people who had their evening fucked over."

"Man, you got to take care of business so nothing gets in the paper," Billy said.

"The media is something I can't guarantee. But let's not worry about that. Let's think about business."

"Yeah, man," Mountain Top said, coming back in and dropping his hulking frame onto the office couch.

"Let's stop this shit about gambling raids. Tonight I'll request that the West Side aldermen and a rep from the NAACP meet with the mayor and the police chief," Soft Sound said. "Then we'll demand an immediate meeting, or there'll be some civil rights demonstrating—marching or some shit like that. Honkies shiver when you mention that civil rights shit."

"What about the ACLU?" Billy asked.

"We don't want 'em. They stir up too much shit."

The phone rang. "I thought nobody'd bother us here," Billy said in disgust. There was no secretary today, so he picked up the phone. "Hello?"

"Billy. Sergeant Sczlatski here."

"What do you want?"

"Mountain Top. I want a statement from Mountain Top about the old murders. And since his Boss and lawyer are both there, I thought it'd be a good time to call. You know, get everybody's okay."

"Wait a minute." Billy pushed the hold button. "It's that motherfucker Slat-ski. Wants to talk to Mountain Top about the old shootings."

"How did he know I was here?" Mountain Top asked.

Billy shrugged.

"That motherfucker wants to know what I was doing that night," Mountain Top complained.

"Well, where were you?" Soft Sound asked.

Mountain Top looked at Billy.

"Tell the man," Billy said.

"I was playing cards in Curly's basement with Curly, Billy, and Lincoln," Mountain Top said.

"Any witnesses?" Soft Sound asked.

"The women and kids was upstairs."

"Then why haven't you told the police?" Soft Sound asked.

Mountain Top folded his arms across his chest and pouted. "No one asked me back then, and I don't want somebody fucking around me now."

"I see where Slat-ski's coming from," Soft Sound said, nodding slowly. "Those places you gave Pitford weren't hit. Slat-ski's trying to communicate with you."

"You lost me, man," Mountain Top said.

"Give me the phone," Soft Sound screeched, reaching out. "Sergeant Slat-ski, this is Sanford G. Washington, representing Sylvester Eugene Jefferson. What do you want with my client?"

Billy grinned at Mountain Top. Sylvester, he thought. Mountain Top's mama used to call him that when she was mad. And he'd come running on the double.

Soft Sound listened for a moment, then asked, "How about now? We'll be at your office in thirty minutes."

After Soft Sound hung up, Mountain Top said, "Hey, man, I don't- -"

"We're going to talk to him. Maybe that's all he wants. Talk to him, and maybe he'll back off from the gambling. You know the uniformed sergeant didn't dream up the raids on his own."

"You think that outsider chief of police put them all up to this?" Mountain Top asked.

"I doubt it. At least I hope he isn't that dumb. If the new chief's starting shit on gambling, he'll have the black community climbing up his ass, plus the whites and the archbishop. My bet is it's Slat-ski squeezing you on the shootings. We'll give him what he wants but still follow through with the political angle."

Soft Sound stood up and gestured to Mountain Top. "C'mon boy. We're gonna see Slat-ski."

* * *

The pitcher of beer the detectives soaked up at Ski's didn't help. Stan and Homer talked about the Milwaukee Brewers, then gazed off, pretending they were listening to the TV or each other. Then one would say something, and the other might or might not answer. They didn't expect much from the evening because they came from different worlds, talked about different things, and carried on two different conversations. The next day they'd swear they had a hell of a good time.

"Hungry?" Homer asked. "We're going to Mama's. Come on, Dawn." While trying to walk with a cane, Homer bumped into Stan.

"No, I'm tired," Dawn said. "See you guys tomorrow."

But she didn't go home. Instead, unable to get the Merriman case off her mind, she went back to the Detective Bureau. When she was concentrating on the Hamlin confession, she wasn't thinking about Billy Boyd. She'd never been in love, and she'd never been so attracted to any man before. She wished she weren't so inexperienced. She wanted to understand what was happening to her and what to do about it. All she knew was that she couldn't sleep, didn't have an appetite, and a warmth spread across her lower abdomen whenever she thought about the man.

The homicide folder was in the Case Closed files. Merriman, David. Homicide. Cleared. Closed. It had not yet been sent to the original in the Records Bureau. Dawn sifted through the reports until she learned that nothing new had been added since Jenny and she had last made an entry. Then she recalled the homicide Odell and Stan had been assigned— an altar boy, raped and suffocated. Hamlin was not alone, she thought.

Thirty minutes later, Dawn was driving into Milwaukee. If anyone found out she was conducting an investigation, a stakeout, in Milwaukee without notifying the Milwaukee police district station, she'd be in big trouble.

Raymond Tee was the only lead not followed to its ultimate conclusion. She fantasized that she would find Tee, who would lead her to Archie Dunn.

* * *

For two nights and on her own time, Dawn stared at the apartment of Raymond Tee. She saw nothing. *Maybe I'm being foolish,* she thought. *The stakeout could go on for weeks. The man could be on vacation or away on a business trip.*

That day at work her friends wondered why she hadn't been at Ski's the night before. She couldn't tell them she was working on a case but didn't like lying to them, either.

For the first two nights, she sat alone in the car for long, dark hours and tried to sort out her feelings about Billy Boyd. Why did a man who was old enough to be her father have such an effect on her? Her life was complex enough. She craved peace of mind and simplicity, then wondered if she'd ever find those in Pulaski.

During the third night, she knew she had to try something different. She considered coming by for an hour every other day, then realized that she didn't have that type of patience. She needed help.

* * *

Mountain Top's statement provided Slat with another lead. Nobody else mentioned to him that Curly's stepson, Lincoln Pitford, had been playing cards that night. Strange . . . he thought, unless Pitford entered and left early and the people upstairs didn't see him.

Slat checked the Records Bureau and learned that Pitford had been arrested for battery to a prostitute on three different occasions back in the sixties. He'd had numerous arrests for drunk and disorderly since then.

Slat returned to his glass cage and made a phone call to Ernie Pope. Elinor answered and said that her husband was probably somewhere at the police station.

Slat looked up at the sound of raised voices. "Elinor, I see him now, arguing with Stan. Thanks." Slat said.

"Osinski," Ernie was saying, "you're full of shit. The Brewers should have kept Gorman Thomas a couple more years. He gave the team flavor and excitement in those days."

"The Brewers had to think of potential!" Stan stood back a couple of feet and studied Ernie's face. "You know, you little shit, you look like a hermit with that half-ass beard."

"Potential, my ass."

"Ernie, got a minute?" Slat called from his office doorway.

"A minute?" Ernie responded. "I got a week if you want to go fishing."

After Ernie came into the office, Slat told him what he had learned from Mountain Top. The older man rubbed his chin, and the corners of his mouth turned down. "I didn't know Pitford was playing cards that night. But there was no reason to consider Pitford as a suspect. He'd have had no motive.

Back then he was a pimp. No, I still think Sam Tyrone was the trigger man. But they ain't going to tell you that."

After some small talk and another invitation to go fishing, Ernie left. Slat, feeling dissatisfied, made a phone call. "Theresa, I got another name for you to check: Lincoln Pitford."

She made it short and sweet. "Sure, Slat. I'll drop it off at the station on my way home from work."

After hanging up, Slat stared at the phone. He had expected her to say it would be under her pillow tonight.

31

FATHER PATRICK DALEY TORE THE STRAY PIECE OF THREAD from his ancient Notre Dame sweater and dropped it on the thickly carpeted floor of the archbishop's study. Tony, wondering whatever happened to his own letter sweater from Loyola football, thought Patty looked like a Christmas- tree ornament, with the blue and gold sweater, red pug nose, and bright blue eyes.

"You've got to be on the up-and-up with me from now on, Patrick. Otherwise we can't work together."

"I understand," the priest said. "And now that the archbishop has given me the nod, I'll tell you everything I know."

"I'm listening," Tony said, still fuming. "Start with how long you've known Father Julius."

"We've been friends through the years. During the past five or so years, I've noticed a slow deterioration in Julius' judgment. Regardless, lately the archbishop and I have suspected a somewhat intimate involvement with young male parishioners."

"What evidence do you have?" Tony asked.

"We believe he uses his middle name, Raymond, and the last name of Tee on his days off—to get away from things, so to speak. Priests have been known to have other quarters, secret ones, such as summer cottages on lakes. Well, my source said that the police are looking for a Raymond Tee in the Merriman murder investigation."

"Do the police suspect that Father Julius is Tee?" Tony asked.

"We're not sure."

Tony pointed toward where the brandy was kept, and Patty nodded his go-ahead. The agent poured two glasses. "Has he received any psychological help?" he asked, handing a snifter to Patty.

"Not to my knowledge, but I have suggested it. The police must be closing in on him—maybe that's why Julius disappeared. Maybe the heat was on. We have to get to him first."

"We have to get him the hell out of the country," Tony said grimly. "Shit. Where is he?"

"The police will want to know where he is."

"I'll take care of that. Why do you think the police are getting close?"

"One moment." Father Daley rang the archbishop's secretary. Moments later the woman escorted a middle-aged man with reddish hair, graying at the temples, into the study. Patty introduced him as Archie Dunn. "Mr. Dunn's positions as president of St. Michael's parish council and city alderman give him excellent insight into the current concerns of the city police department. He's the source I told you about."

While shaking hands with Tony, Archie said, "I just received word that a boy from St. George's parish was murdered. The police are not releasing any details to the public."

"My God!" Father Daley sank into his chair and cradled his head in his hands.

"Raped? Suffocated? Like the boy from St. Michael's?" Tony asked.

"Please!" Father Daley stood suddenly. "Please, Tony, do something! If there's the slightest possibility that Father Julius is involved . . . My God! My God!"

"We'll take care of matters, Father." Tony didn't use Father Daley's boyhood nickname in front of Archie. He was infuriated that, after the archbishop's and Patrick's procrastination, another boy was dead and the priest was urging haste.

Archie had seated himself on a couch near their chairs. "We believe Father Julius has an automobile registered to Raymond Tee at an address in Milwaukee. It appears that on his days off he dresses like, uh, a civilian, and goes to the apartment of Raymond Tee."

"Mr. Dunn, how did you get this information?" Tony asked.

"As a former police officer and a city official, I'm privy to certain information. I read the case file on the Merriman murder and learned that Sergeant Sczlatski's detectives had a lead on Raymond Tee. They gave up on it after the case was closed, but I felt I should continue to investigate. I've been watching the Tee apartment, hoping to see Father Julius. I wasn't alone—one of Sczlatski's detectives was also watching the apartment."

Dunn shook his head mournfully. "I'd hate to think of Father Julius being a . . . pedophile. I had, in fact, planned to confront him with it. But for the past two days I haven't been able to find him."

Tony wondered if Dunn knew that they, too, had been looking in vain for Father Julius.

"And, of course, I pay close attention to matters affecting the parish, especially since Father Daley told me he suspected psychological problems with Father Julius. Any questionable behavior would be embarrassing for the church."

"Is the police case still closed on the Merriman murder?" Tony asked.

"Yes, at least officially. I'm trying to find out why the Tee apartment is being watched. And I plan to put a stop it," he added.

Tony stood and walked over to the credenza, where he freshened his brandy. He held the bottle up to Patty, who quickly shook his head no. Tony realized that the priest had concealed his snifter around the far side of his chair, out of sight of Alderman Dunn.

"The police are not releasing details on the second homicide to the public," Archie continued.

"If the police are watching the Tee apartment, then they suspect something," Tony said. "Case closed or not."

* * *

"Dawn, my office," Slat said after handing out the morning assignments.

She followed the sergeant into the glass cage and sat down at his request. "Dawn, I just got an anonymous complaint on your staking out a location in Milwaukee." Slat remained standing, hands on the back of his desk chair.

"What? I don't believe this! I never told a soul. I was off duty. My own time. Nothing wrong with that." Her fists were dug into her hips, legs spread, her short skirt tugging against her thighs.

"Relax, Dawn. Just tell me about it."

She dropped her hands to her sides. "I've been trying to get a line on Raymond Tee. But it's as if he doesn't exist except with motor vehicle."

"Dawn, the chief is getting too much heat from too many sources. He doesn't need any more. Now, let it go. Hear me?"

"Sergeant, I have the highest respect for Chief Turski." She stopped and cleared her throat. "And I want to do what's right."

"That's it."

"But listen to Hamlin's confession tape! Please!" She looked directly into his eyes.

Slat looked at her for a long moment. "All right. Bring it in."

Slat tried listening to the short tape in his office; but he was constantly interrupted, so he decided to listen to it at home. It was almost quitting time anyway.

As he was leaving, Cheri Duncan walked into the bureau. "Lieutenant Lovemore sent me here on my daily merry-go-round, Sergeant."

"And I'm going off duty."

"So the merry-go-round spins faster. The St. George murder case? . . ."

Slat turned and looked at Stan.

"Aw, Slat," the older man groaned, "I'll talk to the New York Times, USA Today, even the National Inquirer, but don't make me talk to the Pulaski Pisser."

"The Pulaski what?" Cheri asked.

"Piss rag," Stan answered.

"I'll talk to her," Odell offered.

"Just the basics, men," Slat said as he left.

* * *

At home, Slat grabbed an Augsburger beer from the refrigerator before reclining in his lounge chair. He reached his shirt pocket and took out a pack of cigarettes, stared at them a moment, then took out a cigarette and lit it. After listening to the tape several times, he understood exactly where

Dawn was coming from. Slat had his doubts now, too. The last "we" did it. Why did Jack Hamlin say "we" after the kid was dead?

Other thoughts flashed through his mind. Stan told him that the Centennial Park victim was a copycat of the Merriman homicide. Stan had used the term copycat because Hamlin was dead. Dawn could be right, and the only lead left was Raymond Tee.

He dialed her phone number. No answer. He dialed Ski's Inn and asked Ski for Dawn.

"She's here. I'll get her."

"No, tell her to meet me at Mama's in a half hour."

* * *

They were sitting at Mama's counter. Slat took a bite of his cheeseburger, chewed a few moments while Dawn waited anxiously, then swiveled on his stool toward her. "Tell me everything you know about Tee."

She explained what little there was, then expressed her amazement that someone knew she was watching the apartment. "I swear I never told anybody. Nobody could have known I was a Pulaski cop."

"All right, I'll call Jenny and tell her to meet us at the station. We'll stake out Tee's apartment again."

Dawn took hold of his wrist. "Thank you, Sergeant," she said with great feeling.

* * *

After meeting Jenny in the Detective Bureau and after some discussion about the stakeout, Slat said, "No way will we enter illegally." He was looking at the two women sitting on the other side of his cluttered desk.

"'We'?" Dawn questioned.

"Yes. I'm not letting you two go alone. We aren't supposed to do it anyway. So if something goes wrong, I can take the heat; I'm used to it." Slat remembered his gambling adventure and the expected fallout from it. "I almost forgot. I've got this other thing I have to finish."

"How long will it take you?" Jenny asked.

"Till about eleven."

The women looked at him, and he felt the heat of their accusatory gaze. All three of them knew that if Jenny and Dawn had been men, he never would have offered to go with them.

"Yeah," he said, resigned and embarrassed. "You two go ahead. If any problems develop, call me. Otherwise I may or may not stop by. Meanwhile, keep quiet about this."

* * *

By 7:30 that night, the two detectives had assumed their stakeout location around the corner from the yellow-brick Milwaukee apartment building. It was on a corner, with the front facing Twenty- seventh Street, which was zoned for business. This two-block area, however, included a few residential buildings.

The women had parked so they could see the garage and rear entrance of Tee's apartment. They couldn't see the front, but that didn't matter. If Tee went in the front door, they'd see a light go on in his apartment windows.

"You know I'm really half-Polish." Dawn said with no preamble.

"Well," Jenny said, "I never knew a black person with a Polish name."

"Yeah, it throws a lot of people. My dad was Polish, born here in Pulaski. He and his dad owned the building at Florence and Webster, the one with the hardware store. We lived on the second floor."

"I didn't know."

"My mom was Jamaican, and she met my dad in London. He was stationed there during the Korean War." She shook her head. "Can you imagine that?"

"You grew up in Pulaski?"

"Yeah. I hated it. People called my dad a nigger lover. He was a tough guy who argued and fought back. He worked at Poole Tractor and never took shit from anyone. It was different with my mom. The neighborhood women and merchants treated my mother so badly, she never went out of the house."

"Sounds like he did more fighting here than in the war."

"You know, that's true. My poor mother didn't know how to fight. She just faded and died of misery in her sleep when I was fifteen."

Jenny reached out and put a hand on her partner's shoulder. "I'm sorry."

"Yeah. Me, too."

"Any brothers or sisters?"

For the first time in her life Dawn felt something different, a warm swelling in her chest, a good connection. Except for her sister, she'd never talked to anyone like this before. "A sister. Satin. Five years younger. She's at U of Wisconsin."

"No brothers?"

"No, although my dad wanted one. To help him fight, I think. But Satin and I were pretty tough. You think I'm mean, wait till you meet her."

"Your dad still alive?"

"Not anymore. After Mom died, I took care of him and Satin. Everyday after work he'd sit in his chair, drink beer, and stare out the window at the city we all hated."

"Hated?"

"I can't tell you how many times I was called a nigger-polack. Everyday while working I see someone, grown now, who called me a name or beat me up in the school yard. They don't remember me—or else they're too embarrassed to admit who they are. But my feelings haven't changed. I still hate them for destroying my family."

Jenny pushed her seat back farther and slid lower on the cushion.

"Anyway," Dawn continued, "I wasn't around much, what with going to college in Milwaukee. And I liked my studies, so life got a little better."

"When I first saw you, I thought you were Latino."

"I'm not surprised." Dawn laughed. "People have mistaken me for Italian, Spanish, and Greek. But I'm proud of what I am. I readily admit I'm Polish-Afro-American."

"I never heard of that combination before."

"Me, neither. But it's the wave of the future."

"You never mentioned what happened to your dad."

Dawn hesitated. She had never trusted anyone with this information before. "He shot himself."

"God, I'm sorry," Jenny said. "Listen, Dawn, it's none of my business. . . . I don't want to pry."

"I don't mind. I mean . . . "

"But I'm your partner—in every way. What we talk about in the squad stays here. I promise you that."

In the dimness of the car's interior, Dawn saw the intensity of Jenny's expression. "You know, I never cried when my dad died. I didn't grieve, I just hated, like he hated." Dawn felt her chest heaving again. Her voice was a raw, constricted croak. "And then I sold the building. I stood outside it, in the pouring rain, and swore I'd be back." She cleared her throat. "I think I went a little nuts, even. I yelled up and down the street, 'I'll be back one day, Pulaski! And I'll make you pay for the misery you caused my family!"

And from deep, deep inside, the anguish welled up and gushed over, expressed in a moan that grew to a wail. The sound and the emotion filled the squad as Jenny held her partner tightly and whispered soft sympathy in her ear.

After a few moments, Dawn straightened up, took a mirror out of her purse and looked at herself.

"You're sure you're all right?" Jenny asked.

Dawn nodded.

"Because we can come back tomorrow."

"No, no. I'm fine. Let's do it."

About forty-five minutes had passed since Dawn had calmed down. As Jenny looked at her companion now, Dawn seemed transformed, even prettier, with the edge gone.

"I'll take a walk around the front and down the alley," Jenny said. "I'll make sure his car isn't parked on Twenty-seventh."

She was glad to get out of the car and stretch her legs. After watching Dawn, Jenny wanted to do some serious thinking, too, about quitting the force. If she and Slat couldn't have a relationship, she'd get out of town. She didn't want to be around for any happy announcement about Slat and Theresa's engagement. No way.

And yet how close could they be? Jenny wondered. Slat was always socializing at Ski's and eating at Mama's, and he never brought Theresa around.

It still won't work, she decided, walking back toward the squad. *Slat's a loser, and I'm a loser, and there's nothing worse than two losers trying to make a relationship.*

* * *

At about 10:45, after a couple hours of idle conversation, Jenny stretched, arching her back. "Look's like another wasted night."

"Maybe not," Dawn said. "More headlights." They both slid farther down in their seats.

"The car's turning into the alley."

They leaned forward, straining to see how far the car drove.

"Is that Tee's car?" Jenny asked.

Dawn picked up her binoculars. "Looks like it, but I'm not sure."

"No, it's going past the garage."

"I'm sure there were two people inside, anyway."

The car's taillight shrank into the distant darkness.

The women lapsed into sullen silence. After ten minutes, Jenny gasped. "Look! The kitchen window! A light flickered."

Dawn sat upright. "A flashlight! That sneaky bastard, he won't put the lights on!"

"Probably doesn't want the neighbors to know he's home," Jenny said.

"Probably tiptoeing around," Dawn added. She flashed a grin. "Well, my dear, shall we meet Raymond Tee?"

"Maybe we should wait for Slat," Jenny said.

"You've got to be kidding! The guy might not stay long. I don't want to lose him."

"But . . . "

"I'm going alone, then. I don't need any man baby-sitting for me." Dawn opened her door.

"All right." Jenny climbed out. "We'll have to cover both entrances. You take the back. If I get in the front, I'll let you in the back right away. If he runs out the back, march him back through the apartment to the front door."

They blended into the night.

* * *

The vestibule door to the four-flat was unlocked. She couldn't believe her luck when the inside vestibule door was unlocked, too. The stairwell to the second floor was dark, and she had forgotten her flashlight. She couldn't find a light switch. She knew she was losing time and had to hurry—Dawn would be at Tee's back door soon.

The old, wooden stairs under the carpet runner creaked as she started feeling her way up to the second-floor landing. When she got there, she felt for her weapon, holstered under her left armpit under her sweatshirt. She breathed a little easier as she reached for Tee's doorknob. She listened a moment and heard a slight noise in the apartment. A slight flash of light slid under the door.

Breath held, she turned the doorknob. Tee's apartment door was ajar. Her heart slammed against her chest as she eased the door open.

32

JENNY OPENED THE DOOR A FEW INCHES, just enough to slide her hand along the inside edge of the molding. Reaching the area of the lock plunger, she felt a slight sliver of wood. Whoever was in the apartment had jimmied the door. It must not be Tee but a burglar. Her pulse slammed in her head and perspiration ran down her face.

Jenny extracted her detective special from its holster. Then, with her left hand, she reached in and felt for the light switch.

She bumped the switch and accidentally illuminated the living room before she had time to plot her strategy. She burst inside with her weapon in both hands and shouted, "Freeze! Police!"

Startled, a tall man with dark, curly hair and black clothing stood erect. He held a Magna-lite in one hand and some papers in the other. He let the sheets flutter to the floor.

"Drop the light! Put your hands on top of your head." Her sentences came out in gasps.

The man complied.

Despite her anxiety, Jenny focused on his handsome face and mesmerizing eyes. She eased toward the corridor that led to the kitchen. His mocking eyes followed her. She turned the hallway light on, never letting her gaze leave him. Then she backed away and said, "Move into the kitchen."

The man moved. When he reached the center of the kitchen, Jenny ordered him to stop, then she turned on the overhead fluorescent lights. The white walls and floors reflected a blaze of light. She looked around, blinking. All the cabinet drawers and doors were open and empty, except for some glasses and liquor bottles in one of the cabinets.

"Sit down," Jenny said, motioning to a small kitchen table with four chairs around it.

The man reached with both hands to pull out a chair.

"No! Use your left hand. Keep your right hand on your head."

The man cooperated, then sat down. As his eyes examined her body, she felt embarrassed. Her heart pounded, and she felt disoriented. When she looked away from his eyes to his smiling mouth, her dizziness passed.

Jenny stepped sideways to the kitchen door, where she separated the white kitchen curtains and peered out the window. She couldn't see beyond her own reflection. She unlatched and opened the door to the moonlit porch. Dawn wasn't there.

"Dawn?" she whispered.

No answer.

She looked back at the smiling man, who now had his hands on the tabletop. He should have been frightened, but no fear showed in his eyes. She held the gun and the power, but for some reason, she felt terrified, as if he were in control.

"You are, without question, the most beautiful police officer I have ever met. I'm delighted you caught me."

"Who are you?" Jenny asked, pushing her weapon forward.

"Please, madam, hold that gun steady. My name is Tony. What is yours?"

Jenny glanced out the back door. "Dawn," she called.

"Please sit down and give me your weapon," Tony invited. "If you have an associate, then she is my prisoner."

"What do you mean?" Jenny demanded. Her heartbeat throbbed in her temples. She felt as if she were caught in a nightmare.

Suddenly, a man appeared in the back doorway, grasping one of Dawn's arms. She had a three-inch-wide strip of white tape across her mouth and the muzzle of an automatic pistol touching her jawbone. Her frightened eyes appealed to Jenny.

"Now, miss," Tony continued, "place your weapon on the table."

Jenny had been taught that giving up her weapon was discretionary only as a last resort. Chances were that if she surrendered her weapon, she and Dawn would be shot. Many cops had said they'd rather die with their weapons up than their hands up. She looked at Dawn, then back to the man who held her. He wore an open-collar black shirt. Around his tan neck was a gold chain with a tiny gold crucifix. She stared at the cross.

Tony stood slowly and raised his hands. "In my right front pocket is my identification badge," he explained. "We are private investigators."

Then, slowly, he reached in with his forefinger and thumb to withdraw a badge case. He flipped it open to display an unusual gold shield with a cross of red stone. Jenny couldn't make out the words, nor had she ever seen anything like the case, which was lined in red velvet. But she didn't feel she had a choice. She wouldn't put Dawn's well-being in jeopardy. Slowly, she set her weapon on the kitchen table.

Tony picked it up and slipped it into his back pocket. "Sit down, please," he said, then he nodded to his colleague, who tore the tape off Dawn's mouth.

"Asshole! That hurt!" Dawn shouted.

"Please," Tony said quietly. "If you can't be quiet, we'll have to tape you up again."

Dawn, in a fury, sat down hard across from Tony and folded her arms across her chest.

"My dear ladies, may I inquire what you're doing here?"

"You're in serious trouble," Jenny warned. "You've kidnapped two police officers, plus committed assault with a weapon, and burglary of this apartment."

"My apology," Tony said, inclining his head. The confidence never left his eyes. "May I see your search warrant for entering this apartment?"

"I saw the door jimmied open . . . "

"In the dark? At this time of night? And I'm not so sure either of you is a police officer. May I see your identifications?"

The women placed their badges and ID cards on the table.

Tony picked up Jenny's and studied it. "Beautiful picture," he remarked. "Incidentally, where is Pulaski?"

"A suburb," Jenny said.

"A suburb of Milwaukee? Well, well. You are in Milwaukee, you know. Then this other beautiful police officer must be from the Milwaukee's police department." He smiled knowingly, his ivory white teeth contrasting with his tan skin.

He pushed Jenny's identification across the table to her, then picked up Dawn's. "Dawn," he said warmly. "What a charming name! It befits your fresh beauty."

"Fuck off!" Dawn snarled.

Tony laughed. "I didn't know the Dawn could be so stormy. Mazurski. Polish. How interesting. Married?"

"None of your fucking business, asshole!"

"It's hard to believe that two such beautiful women are detectives. Actresses, maybe, or models, that I could understand." He clucked his tongue. "But here you both are, in the middle of the night, entering a Milwaukee apartment, without a warrant, without an accompanying Milwaukee police officer."

Jenny started to relax. This man was no burglar. He knew procedure—and was aware that she was in violation of it. "Who are you investigating for?" she asked.

"I will ask the questions." He stood and withdrew Jenny's weapon from his back pocket. "If you ladies would please get up?"

They stood.

"Now take off your clothes."

"Bullshit!" Dawn said.

"Except your underwear," he conceded. "Please, ladies, we're not going to harm you. We're only interested in a little time. You'll have to get dressed before you chase us."

As Jenny angrily yanked down the zipper of her jeans, her eyes were on Tony, and his were on her. She peeled off her sweatshirt, then stood, embarrassed, in her lacy blue bra, matching French-cut underpants, and her holster.

Dawn slipped off her jeans, then balked. "I don't wear a bra."

"Then you can stop there," Tony said. "Now follow that man."

They entered a tiny bedroom, which had a small cot, a chair, and bureau. Nothing hung on the beige walls. Jenny began to tremble.

"Into the closet, please," Tony said.

Dawn and Jenny entered the empty cubicle, and the door shut behind them. They heard the sound of the bureau being pushed along the wooden floor and shoved in front of the door.

"My evening's fantasy will be wishing I was in the closet with you two," Tony said through the door. "Good night, now."

Dawn and Jenny waited for a few seconds. The sound of breaking glass rang out.

"What the hell is he doing?" Jenny whispered in the dark.

Before Dawn answered, three gunshot blasts woke the night.

Jenny cringed at the sound. "They'll have to get out of here quick after that!"

"So will we!" Dawn cried out, and the two women began pushing at the closet door.

* * *

Slat was sipping coffee at Mama's, waiting for Gordy and thinking about what he had heard from Odell: Apparently there had been a meeting with Lieutenant Lovemore, the chief, and a few black aldermen about the gambling warnings. Lovemore hadn't said anything to Slat about it, so the chief must have backed him.

"You spend too much time thinking, Slat," Mama said as she refilled his cup.

Slat also learned that Billy's gambling dens had gone back into operation Tuesday night, though business was slow. Lincoln Pitford, however, seemed to be doing better-than-normal business.

"Hi, Slat."

Slat looked up. "Theresa!"

"I took a chance you'd be here." She sat next to him, minus her usual smile. "Slat, I got something to say. I-I'm afraid we can't see each other anymore."

"What?"

Mama, put a cup of coffee in front of Theresa, beamed at her, then hustled away.

"Yeah. I've been thinking. After that shooting, I was terrified. But you hardly seemed fazed by it. A normal guy—I mean not a cop—would still be shaking. You worry me because danger doesn't frighten you. But the next time you may not be so lucky. I want a normal guy with a boring job."

"Theresa . . ."

"Let me finish. I can't take the chance. I really care about you. But I know you'd never give up your badge for me."

"C'mon, Theresa, we've had a lot of laughs, haven't we?"

"Sure, but I'm ready for something more. I've thought about this and nothing else since the shooting. My mind can't be changed."

Theresa stood just as Gordy walked in the door.

"Bye, Slat. Feel free to call me at work whenever you need a credit check."

She turned and left. As he watched her retreating back, Slat felt strangely relieved but didn't know why.

"Gordy," Mama said, "you're a bag of bones. I should fatten you up."

"Then bring on the food," Gordy challenged, and slid into the booth to face Slat. He didn't order anything particular, they all knew whatever Mama's special of the day was it would be good.

"Bring something for me, too, Mama," Slat called.

"Hey, buddy, what's up?" Gordy asked eagerly.

Slat laughed. "Don't you ever want to stay out of trouble?" he asked.

"Heck, no! I need a high level of mental stimulation to keep my heart pumping. It's the running, you know—it raises my expectations from life."

Amused, Slat looked fondly at Gordy. "Then I'll make you very happy. Tonight give Pitford a warning. Take a couple men with you and talk to him. Tell him to close down his three places. No show. Just a warning."

"That'll be easy. But when are we going to make arrests? I see the other places are already back in business."

"Yeah, I know. Trust me. Pitford is Billy's stepcousin. He may be a missing witness to those old shootings and know about the payoffs I told you about. If Pitford doesn't close down, we'll make arrests—I want him to see Billy's places staying open. We'll get him good and pissed off, and then maybe Pitford will try to get even with Billy by talking."

* * *

After they pushed the door slightly open, Jenny was struck by the strong odor of bourbon. As she and Dawn ran to the kitchen to retrieve their clothes, they heard tires screeching below, and flashing blue lights reflected up to the ceiling and walls.

Chunks of plaster across the floor prompted Jenny to look at the ceiling—three bullet holes. Four half-empty whiskey glasses and a bottle of Scotch sat on the kitchen table alongside the women's badges, ID cards, and handguns. A bottle of bourbon lay broken on the floor, and its contents were spilled on their clothes.

The kitchen door slammed open, and two uniformed Milwaukee officers burst in with weapons. "Holy shit," said the first officer when he saw Jenny, half-nude with a shoulder holster.

Tony Attalla had bought himself some time.

33

DAWN WAS SITTING NEXT TO JENNY IN FRONT OF SLAT'S DESK. "I was totally humiliated standing there in my panties, Sarge. I'd like to get my hands on that son of a bitch."

Slat put the women's badges in his desk drawer. "Understand that this suspension is just a formality while the matter is under investigation. You still get paid, and I believe the whole thing went down exactly as you described it. I know neither one of you'd touch straight whiskey."

"Glad it wasn't beer then," Jenny said, managing a wan smile. She shuddered. "It was more than embarrassing. I didn't know if we were going to be raped, killed, or what."

"How about meeting me at Mama's for lunch? I have to sort this out and see what's happening. All I know is that the chief is getting more heat."

"I'm sure," Dawn said. "Please tell him I regret any problems."

"I hope the press isn't on his ass," Jenny said. "I can't handle any of their perfection bullshit."

Slat stood. "Go on, now. Just relax. I'll see you at lunch."

After Dawn and Jenny left, Slat, seeing Lieutenant Lovemore step into the Detective Bureau, watched to see if his boss would walk the distance to Slat's glass cage. He did not.

"Sczlatski!" Lovemore hollered from the counter. "The chief wants us in his office. Now!"

Once again, Slat and Leon Lovemore strode down the long hallway, past several administrative offices, toward Chief Turski's office.

"Sczlatski, if I die a middle-aged man, it'll be because of you and your crew. You'd better pray to whatever spirit or tavern sign you worship that if this city ever decides to promote a black man to chief of police, it won't be me. I swear I'll get even with you for all the shit you pushed me into."

Slat stifled a grin. "You talking about me?"

"Who the fuck else is in this hallway?"

"I'm in the hallway, Lieutenant," Mary Lou said behind them.

"Oh, I-I'm sorry, Mary Lou. I didn't. . . ." Lovemore stammered.

"You're excused, Lieutenant," Mary Lou said, her eyes twinkling.

Slat grinned. "Really, Lieutenant, you should watch your language."

A few steps beyond Mary Lou's earshot, Lovemore growled, "See what I mean, Sczlatski? You're always leading me into shit!"

The chief's secretary waved the two big men into Martin Turski's office, where they found him sunken into his overstuffed chair. Slat thought the chief's cheeks seemed sunken, and his face looked thinner.

"Sit down, gentlemen." The chief gestured with a knobby knuckle toward the chairs. "Tell me everything you know about the incident."

"First of all, Chief, I haven't gotten a call from the press," Lovemore said.

"Neither have I," Martin said. "Just the mayor and an alderman," he added wryly.

"The detectives, with my approval, were following up on the Merriman homicide," Slat said.

"I thought that case was solved," the chief said.

"It was, but the young boy from St. George who was murdered with a similar MO. Back when we were questioning Jack Hamlin, he implied that another person was in the room, possibly another offender. The Tee lead had never been resolved, so the officers went to find him." Slat repeated what Dawn and Jenny had told him.

"Do you believe them, Sergeant?" the chief asked.

"Yes, sir. I know those two."

"I guess we all know what the media could make out of this. Now perhaps I can shed some light on this situation. Listen to this." The chief played an audiotape. . . .

"Chief, my name is Tony. For obvious reasons, I'll not give you my last name. Last night my friend Ray and I dated a couple of your officers. Ray invited us all to his place. We all had a few drinks, partied a little. Ray had too much to drink. He grabbed one of the girl's guns and fired into the ceiling. I got scared and ran out. Ray followed. So I hope this call explains what happened."

The tape ended. The chief hit the Eject button and flipped the tape to Slat.

"I got the message, Chief," Lovemore said in disgust. "This explanation is much more credible and suitable for the time being."

"Yes," the chief agreed. "But the detectives tested clean for alcohol consumption. Zero. So cancel their suspension."

Slat nodded, satisfied.

"Use Tony's explanation," the chief said. "Let the women hear the tape. And, Sergeant, get to the bottom of this. Obviously something is very wrong."

* * *

Slat had an hour before meeting the women at Mama's. In spite of a downpour, he left the station and drove to Centennial Park. On the way he stopped at a 7-Eleven and bought a pack of cigarettes. He parked in the corner of one of the small parking lots, lit up, inhaled, enjoyed the warmth spreading across his chest, then coughed horribly. He tried another drag but didn't hold it in for so long.

Because of the rain, he decided not to walk around. He noticed a car parked behind him at the opposite corner of the parking lot, but he didn't pay much attention.

He had to piece this thing together. He pulled a small notebook from his pocket and wrote: Mayor and an alderman called the chief this morning about Dawn and Jenny. How did they know so quickly? Who is Tony? Why the burglary of Tee's apartment? Why were Dawn and Jenny set up?

He tried to stay focused on the problem, but his mind kept going back to Sam Tyrone's suicide, then his mind flashed to the chief, who seemed tired and distant. *No,* he thought, *Turski's got a wife, a nice home. He wouldn't. . .* . Next Slat thought about Theresa's breaking off their relationship. It hadn't been much of a relationship, he admitted. He'd felt no deep commitment toward her, aside from enjoying her company and lovemaking and liking her looks.

Then there was Jenny. Unlike Theresa, Jenny understood the danger that came with the job. She wouldn't walk away from a relationship because of the job's risks. Maybe for some other reason, though. It was hard to know what Jenny would do, what with the stress she was under now.

He thought about Sam again. Painful as it was, Slat accepted the fact that his idol had been on the take. Sam had been wrong. Slat had tried to excuse it with loneliness and had even tried to shoulder some of the blame for Sam's solitary existence. Slat rolled his window down and threw the burning cigarette butt onto the wet asphalt and listened to the dying sizzle.

But damn it! Sam sure as hell hadn't been a murderer, and Slat would prove it.

* * *

The man fondled the shotgun on the seat next to him as he watched Slat's car. Although it was raining, the sky was light gray, and it would be impossible to approach Slat without being seen. The man tugged the collar of his trench coat closed and watched as his breath fogged over the windshield.

* * *

As Slat walked into Mama's and headed for the phone, he waved at Dawn and Jenny, who were sitting at a table. He held up one finger, and they nodded.

Jenny watched him. He made a call, spoke for a few minutes, then hung up and stared at the telephone. "Look at him," she whispered, moving her lips as little as possible. "Something must be the matter."

Dawn didn't even bother to turn around and look. "Too much work," she said. "It's this shitty job."

After a few moments, Jenny left the table and walked over to him and put a hand on his arm. "Are you okay?" she asked.

"I, um . . ." Slat patted her hand.

Her hand tingled where he touched her.

She looked up into his eyes. "Please, Slat. Is there something I can do?" She wanted to hold him, to soothe away his worries. She wanted to love him. "I know I haven't been very warm lately, but . . ."

He interrupted her. "I have to talk to you. To both of you. Come on, let's go to the table."

As they sat down, Mama brought Slat a cup of black coffee. Then he told the detectives about Tony's call to the chief.

"Somebody set you two up, and we have to figure out why. I just talked to Osinski about the homicide of the boy from St. George. Stan just told me he got an anonymous tip that the victim was seen going into the park with Father Julius."

Both women stared open-mouthed at Slat.

"Father Julius!" Jenny erupted.

He nodded grimly. "That's not all. Besides being an altar boy, the kid was also active in the paper drive at St. George. Get this: Hamlin picked up the papers at each school."

"Hamlin's dead," Dawn said, "but Julius and Archie Dunn are very much alive, and both were connected to the paper drive."

"Stan and Bill have been trying to locate Father Julius all day," Slat continued, "but he hasn't been around. His car's parked behind the rectory, which doesn't make sense because his car goes where he goes, unless he's jogging." He shook off his thoughts as vigorously as a hound shakes off water. "I'm sure he's okay. Nothing to do with this case. I'm sure."

"Ha," Dawn mumbled.

Slat and Jenny looked at her.

"He's just a man," Dawn said, shrugging.

"We have to find him," Slat said.

* * *

"Good afternoon, Sister. I'm Detective Herschel, and this is Detective Mazurski."

"Come in." The housekeeper at St. Michael's church rectory, bent with osteoporosis, looked up with bright blue eyes at Dawn. "Your name is familiar. Of course, most Polish names around here are familiar. . . ."

"I was a student here," Dawn said as the woman led them into a neat sitting room next to the entryway. "Sister, we understand Father Julius has been . . . incommunicado. People are concerned about his well- being."

"I can't remember a time when he's been gone so long," the nun said. "It's very unlike him."

"So there are times when he leaves without saying where he's going?" Jenny asked.

"Oh, yes," the nun said, then trilled a laugh. "There are few people to whom a priest must report his actions."

"May we have a photograph of him?" Dawn asked.

"Oh, I'm sorry, dear. Father Daley, from the archdiocese, called earlier and said we are not to let anyone in Father Julius's room or release any information about him. I must obey the good father."

"We understand. Thank you, Sister."

* * *

"This stinks," Dawn said as they got into their squad.

"It'll be an interesting confrontation—the police and the archdiocese," Jenny remarked.

They drove down the alley behind the rectory and saw Father Julius's dark blue Chevy Caprice in its stall.

Jenny looked at the dashboard clock. "We'd better meet Slat."

* * *

The waiting room outside Soft Sound's law office was too much like a doctor's office, Lincoln Pitford thought uncomfortably, with its cushioned chairs and round coffee table stacked with old magazines.

Lincoln shifted in his chair. Although he hadn't spoken with Billy Boyd for years, they used the same attorney. Soft Sound was the best fixer in town, and he kept the peace between the step-cousins. Soft Sound had said repeatedly that Billy would be glad to offer any help he could. Lincoln snorted, and a scowl sharpened his bearded hatchet face. He wouldn't go to that over-inflated, arrogant nigger for the time of day.

Lincoln Pitford had lived most of his life on the West Side of Pulaski. After he was born in Mississippi, his mother, Edna, took him and escaped that southern jungle to another one, up north. Lincoln didn't know his real father because his mother said he didn't want to know.

When they arrived in Pulaski, she was befriended by Bertha Boyd, an unwed mother with a son named Billy, who was about the same age as Lincoln. Bertha worked as a housekeeper at the Allerton's mansion in an upper-class neighborhood in Pulaski..

Bertha's brother, Curly, who shared a small bungalow with her and helped with expenses. When Bertha got pregnant, Curly chased her boyfriend out of town, then helped her through her pregnancy. When Billy was born, it was Curly who first held him. From that special day, Curly treated his nephew like his own child.

Bertha let Edna and Lincoln live in a basement cubicle in her home, and Curly eventually married Edna. Lincoln was only three at the time, and he looked upon Curly as his real father. Curly, however, considered the boy to be nothing more than another man's bastard.

Lincoln knew his stepfather favored Billy, and because of that favoritism, Lincoln despised Billy. Even now he wanted to kill the man who made his life miserable and was the reason behind a life of accepting secondhand shit.

Lincoln had never forgiven his stepfather for giving one hundred percent of the gambling business to Billy. Even though Lincoln himself had opted to control the West Side's prostitution, he thought Curly should have left half the gambling business to him, too. Now Billy was rolling in money, and Lincoln was subsisting on Billy's leftovers.

Worse, the cops were telling him to close down his three houses. He'd heard that Billy had been warned the week before, but he was still operating. Lincoln's fingernails dug into the palm of his hand.

"Come on in. Come on in, Lincoln," Soft Sound screeched.

Lincoln stood and went into the man's office.

"I didn't mean to keep you waiting," the attorney said, ushering Lincoln to a chair. "I was making some calls on your behalf. I wanted something concrete to tell you. Sit down."

He'd been in this office before. He had never seen so many books on so many shelves. He wondered if the skinny little lawyer read any of them. "I heard Billy was . . ."

"Warned. Warned," Soft Sound interrupted. "And now he's in business. Billy's taking a chance. We got some political things working. Now I can't tell you what to do. It seems that maybe the police chief or somebody is just trying to keep things looking straight by just giving out warnings. I don't know for sure. But things are up in the air, and many people are nervous. I'll tell you that Billy, after being warned, has gone ahead and reopened and nothing has happened. I'm not telling you to try that, and I'm not telling you not to try it. Hear? I'm just outlining what's happening, my man. You have to make your own decision."

"Then I'm opening up," Lincoln said angrily. "Fuck 'em. If Billy can get away with it, so can I."

"Your decision, man, your decision. Understand? Not mine. Not mine."

"Yeah, Soft Sound, I hear ya. I'll be open tomorrow."

34

MEMORANDUM
City of Pulaski

From: Alderman A. Dunn To: Mayor

It has come to my attention and other citizens' that detectives Herschel and Mazurski were drinking, partying, and partially dressed at a party and fired their service weapons in the kitchen of an apartment in Milwaukee.

Needless to say if such behavior is not corrected by the police chief, it should fall within the scope of the mayor's office.

The activities of these two detectives have been previously brought to your attention.

I'm sure the City Council will want to hear an explanation from you and Chief Turski.

cc: City Council Chief Turski

MEMORANDUM
City Of Pulaski

From: Alderman A. Dunn

To: Mayor and City Council

Re: Police harassment

My phone---and, I'm sure, many of yours as well---has been ringing with complaints about the police department harassing black citizens playing friendly family card games in their homes.

Such discriminatory action reflects the continual mismanagement of our police department.

Again I urge the City Council to convene a special session to discuss this matter.

cc: Chief Turski.

Slat parked his recently purchased five-hundred-dollar beater where he could observe the side door of Pitford's three-story, gray-frame house and an adjoining alley. The games were played in the basement. As the evening progressed, men entered the side door. Obviously, Slat thought, grinning in the dark, Pitford had not heeded the warning. An informant of Odell Fowler's told him about Pitford's reopening the night before and the gambling activity.

"Much money floating?" Odell had asked.

"Not much. A small crowd because of the warnings," the informant said. It had been casual conversation but enough for Slat to obtain a search warrant. He had the form typed and ready, except for the date and the final paragraph. Slat hoped that after tonight's raid, Pitford would be so angry about his being singled out that he'd vent his rage at Billy. And the sergeant also hoped that Pitford's spewing would include relevant information about the assassinations and payoffs. At about eleven o'clock, Slat stepped out of his car, pulled a baseball cap low over his forehead, folded his jacket collar up, and walked down the alley alongside Pitford's house. He could see the basement lights on, but he couldn't see through the window because of the venetian blinds. Nor could he make out any words—just a murmur of voices. He quickly stepped onto the sidewalk, then dropped to his hands and knees. With an ear close to the window he heard, "I raise you two."

"You got it. I call and raise you two more." With those statements, Slat finished the last paragraph in the affidavit for the search warrant.

* * *

An hour later, Slat met Gordy in the St. Luke's Hospital parking lot.

"I've only got five men tonight," Gordy said. "Two guys were injured in a tavern fight about dinnertime."

"So I heard. But you and I make seven. I'll get us a driver." Gordy nodded . That was enough, and the officers plotted their strategy. At 1:40 in the morning, a plain brown van stopped in the alley by Pitford's side entrance. The van's doors opened, and seven men exited the vehicle. The first in line found the house door unlocked, so the sledgehammer was put back into the van. Two blocks away, another police van was waiting for a radio call to come to pick up prisoners. The Tactical Unit and Slat quickly entered and quietly filed down the small dark stairway into the low-ceilinged basement. The dingy room had one large table with five seated players, and several men were standing around the table and watching. Six more men were at the bar. Lincoln Pitford, behind the bar, was the first to see the police.

"Pitford! I've got a search warrant here!" Slat announced as the uniformed men started collecting dice, cards, and money from the tables. "You're all under arrest for gambling."

"You motherfuckers got no right fucking me over!" Pitford hollered as he ran around the bar. "Get them! Get them motherfuckers!" A melee ensued. The gamblers weren't out to injure the police; they just wanted to escape. As they fled toward the exit, however, they pushed and shoved at the few policemen in their way. Slat was in the midst of the crowd, which was pushing against the direction he was struggling toward. He wanted to grab Pitford and shut him up. Gordy, struggling with a big man trying to get by him, heard the *snap* of his portable radio antenna. Now he had no way to call for backups or for the prisoner van. One patron jumped up and grasped on to the water pipes along the ceiling in an effort to swing himself up and over the brawlers. Unable to bear his weight, the pipes burst, and water gushed everywhere, soaking everyone. Slat made his way toward Pitford, who was still raging at his friends to fight back; but two patrons shoved Slat back against a wall. Another pushed him to the floor, which was already under an inch of water. Gordy was on his knees, trying to hold on to two patrons, but another man was trying to pull Gordy backwards by his neck. Slat surged forward around some of the fallen gamblers and knocked his friend's attacker into the water. Slat looked up. Pitford was about ten feet from him, swinging a small metal tackle box—probably filled with cash, Slat thought. Only one person stood between them. Slat rose quickly as Pitford shoved the man hard into Slat, and both the patron and Slat crashed to the floor on top of several writhing opponents. Slat got to his feet and looked for Pitford but couldn't see him in the chaos. The sergeant ran to the doorway, which was jammed with officers and gamblers. He saw Pitford in the crowded hallway, elbowing his way past two patrons scrambling for freedom. Slat lunged forward over one man's shoulders and grabbed Pitford's Afro.

"Let go, you motherfucker!" Pitford shouted, his head jerking back. One of the men between Pitford and Slat slipped and fell back toward Slat, which allowed Pitford to spin around and slam Slat in the head with the metal box. After glancing off Slat's head, the box hit the man between the two adversaries. The fellow lost his balance and grabbed Slat, and they both tumbled to the floor. Slat, suffering bursts of pain and flashes of light from the impact of the tackle box, managed to push himself over the grasping customer and dive for Pitford's feet. He clutched the man's ankles and tripped him. Three bettors jumped over Pitford, Slat, and the prone patron. One stepped on Slat's arm, loosening his hold on the house-man. Pitford sat upright, twisted, and swung the box again, this time hitting Slat across the shoulder. Slat grabbed at the water-slick box but missed.

"Billy put you up to this!" Lincoln shrieked, a man possessed as he leaped to his feet and ran up the stairs. "He set me up!"

The sergeant struggled to stand, took off after Pitford, and caught him four steps from the top of the narrow staircase. He grabbed Pitford's belt and yanked him back down the stairs. Pitford fell on top of Slat as they both tumbled back onto the floor, Pitford on top. He turned and, straddling Slat, swung the metal box back and forth, hitting Slat on the arm as he held his hands up to ward off the blows.

"You let that motherfucker Billy stay open! He set me up!" Pitford jumped off Slat, turned, and started back up the narrow staircase. Slat got up, pounded up the staircase, and raced out the side door. He caught on to the back of Pitford's shirt collar and swung him around, then slugged him in the face with his right fist. Pitford flew backward and landed hard on the sidewalk. The metal box broke open, sending coins and bills everywhere. Slat stooped to reach for Pitford when the side door banged open and hit Slat from behind. He stumbled forward, giving Pitford the seconds he needed to get to his feet and pull a knife. Slat put up his hands for protection, and the blade punctured his left palm. Slat looked at the knife stuck in his hand, then looked at Pitford. Pitford froze. "Hey, man, I didn't. . . . It's Billy's fault. That motherfucker caused this!" He let go of the knife, turned, and disappeared into the night. Clutching his bloody left hand and grimacing in pain, Slat put his back against the building, then slid down to sit on the sidewalk. In a few moments, the officers came outside. Each was holding on to one or two prisoners.

"Slat's hurt!" one of the officers hollered.

"The radio ain't working," Gordy said. "Use what you can to bandage his hand. I'm going to get help."

* * *

Slat was sitting on the edge of an emergency room gurney at St. Luke's Hospital when the draw curtain parted.

"How bad is it?" Chief Turski asked.

"Went through the palm. No fingers gone. Hurts like a son of a bitch, though." Slat smiled at his round-faced nurse. "The people here are the greatest."

"Gambling raid, I understand?"

"Yes. Made a few arrests."

"Good work." The chief sat on a chair next to Slat. "You had a warrant?"

"Yeah." Slat looked into the chief's weary eyes, eyes that said something Slat couldn't read. "I guess you've been getting some heat about my gambling warnings, sir."

"Don't worry about it, Sergeant. If I can't take the heat and all that, I better get out of the kitchen, so they say."

Slat noticed that the chief's pug nose pointed higher when he smiled. "Is it that easy, sir?" Martin Turski said nothing. They both watched the artwork of the skillful nurse securing the bandage. Slat sensed the pressure the chief had to be enduring.

"Why haven't you told Lovemore or me to lay off the gambling?"

"I would never tell a police officer to disregard any laws."

"But you could have advised us to—uh—re-evaluate our priorities until policies are written or understandings are reached with the community."

"The policy is written," the chief replied. "It's called the Wisconsin State Statutes. Backing off because of political pressure would be cowardly. You issued warnings. That was more than satisfactory. You have a job to do. Do it. Understand, Sergeant?"

"I understand, sir."

"Take as much time off as you need, Sergeant."

"Thank you, sir." Turski turned to the nurse. "Take good care of this young man."

"I'll do my best," she said, blushing. Slat stared after the chief as he walked between the draw curtains. The last time he had seen Turski, the man was sitting down, and Slat had noticed that his face was thinner. Now, with the chief standing, Slat saw that Turski had lost a significant amount of weight. He sighed, then looked at his hand. "At least this'll heal."

"Of course it will," the nurse said crisply. "The doctor left a packet of pain pills to get you through the night and a prescription for tomorrow."

"Thanks."

"You're all set to go home," she said, and bustled away to another case. Before Slat slid off the gurney, the drapes parted, and Jenny peeked in. "How're you doing?"

Jenny, here, with no hysteria, no bitching about the danger, he thought, comparing her again to Theresa. "To tell you the truth, I'm a little dizzy."

"Put your head between your knees." She stepped closer to him and placed her hand on his arm, her body touching his knees.

"You've got to take it slow."

"I'm okay," he responded. As he slid off the gurney he reached to her for support, then his hands slid down her arms to her elbows. He wanted to pull her to him. He started to, but she resisted him gently. "Come on,

Sarge," she said indulgently, "some people are waiting to see you." Slat followed her into the waiting room, where he was greeted by Gordy, Dawn, Homer, Odell, and Stan.

"What the hell? You're out of bed!" Stan teased.

"Boss, the flower shop was closed," Homer apologized.

"Ski called and said the back door to the tavern would be open for us," Odell said.

"He's coming with me!" said a booming voice. "I'll take him home. You all get some sleep. You have a lot of work in a few hours." They all turned to see square-jawed, Lieutenant Leon Lovemore in the doorway.

"Come on, Sczlatski. Nobody stabs one of my staff and gets away with it. I got people looking for Pitford now. I'll need all of you in the morning to relieve them." The crew parted like the Red Sea for the lieutenant to come through and take Slat's arm. "Let's clear out of here before the press arrives."

* * *

While driving Slat home, Lovemore said, "The way you go about things drives me crazy, Sergeant, but maybe something will turn up on those old homicides you've been working on. You working on any new ideas?" Slat, still surprised by the lieutenant's kindness, said, "Yeah, I think Pitford may know something about Billy Boyd and Mountain Top and the payoffs. If we can find Pitford before he hurts somebody else, I think he'll talk."

"If they did it," Lovemore said.

"I'm sure they know something. They were the only ones with a motive."

"Untrue. But we have to find Pitford anyway."

"Why the sudden change about, you know, the old homicides?" Slat asked.

"Those murders occurred the first year I was a detective. If you were here back then, you'd be convinced Willy Patton was the killer. He had a real good gambling den operating, and one of those gamblers forced him out of business. He's the other one with a motive. Also, Patton was on bond for armed robbery. So whatever else they had, it seemed to fit." Lovemore parked in front of Slat's apartment, then continued, "I still think Patton is guilty, but now you've raised the issue in the black community that must be dealt with, and that is illegal gambling—or rather the equality of illegal gambling in the black and white communities."

"Lieutenant, you make it too heavy."

"Ha! Too fucking much schooling. That's a social problem we'll let the community work out. Our job is to apprehend the person who stabbed you. And I am curious now whether or not Patton was involved in the assassinations. After we find Lincoln, I'm sure he'll want to talk."

* * *

Officer Barnard Baxter enjoyed an occasional switch to the midnight shift. When he was younger, he had enjoyed the tavern fights, the family battles, and the gang wars. Now he preferred the relative quiet of the midnight shift, like tonight. The tired, overweight, twenty-five-year veteran of the force was happy as long as he was off the streets. Fortunately, the shift lieutenant willingly put Baxter on the desk because he didn't want the overly cynical pessimist mentally contaminating the young officers on the street. Baxter heard some rumbling from the back room. The young Turks from the Tactical Unit were making more DWI arrests. He couldn't understand this younger breed of cops, arresting honest citizens and wasting the taxpayers' money. *In my day,* he thought, *I knew most drunks and their wives and kids, so I'd take 'em home.* Baxter dialed the radio to his favorite station, which played instrumental versions of hits from the fifties. He dimmed the lights, lounged back in his chair, and nodded off while listening to "Harbor Lights." His languor was abruptly disoriented by a screeching noise. "I demand! I demand to see the po-leece chief!"

35

SOFT SOUND WASHINGTON PEERED THROUGH HORN-RIMMED GLASSES over the edge of the police counter.

"For chrissake, Soft Sound, what the–?" Baxter caught himself before uttering an obscenity. An angry crowd of black men and women had entered the lobby behind the attorney. Baxter glanced at his watch. He had been asleep for a half hour.

"How many white folks you got arrested?" a very tall black woman demanded.

"That's right! That's right!" Soft Sound said. "I want to know what the charges are, and I want to see the po-leece chief!"

Baxter looked around for help. Behind him in the glass- enclosed dispatch/radio room, he saw Sergeant Gordy Mac Bell and Lieutenant Leon Lovemore.

Lovemore walked into the desk area. "Has the chief come in yet? And get the rest of those lights on, Baxter!"

"Oh, no. Yes, sir. Yes, sir," Baxter said, not knowing if the chief had been in or not.

"Leon Lovemore! We demand an explanation. The brothers are being persecuted!" The irate black citizens pushed up against Soft Sound as more entered the front lobby and compacted the crowd.

"Yeah! Right on!" several in the crowd cried out.

"Now, Counselor, what can I do for you?" Lovemore asked mildly.

"Several black brothers have been arrested for playing cards in one of their homes."

"Soft Sound," Lovemore said with elaborate patience, "they've been arrested, so you'll have to do your thing in court. We'll let them out on their own recognizance."

"I want answers now!"

"You aren't getting any answers now," the lieutenant said firmly. "We've got an officer injured, and we're looking for his assailant."

"You call yourself a brother, Leon?" someone in the back challenged.

"Please, everybody. Tomorrow morning we'll be thinking with clearer heads. I promise you all . . ."

The flash of a camera cut Lieutenant Lovemore short. A photographer and reporter Cheri Duncan entered the lobby. The media had been tipped.

"You're violating our civil rights," Soft Sound screeched.

Baxter bellowed, "Everyone clear the lobby before I call in some men to clear it!"

"What about these gambling arrests, Lieutenant?" Duncan asked.

"I'll give a press conference in the morning at nine o'clock."

"I have a deadline tonight, Lieutenant Runaround Lovemore."

"Can you wait a couple of hours?" Lovemore asked.

"Sorry," she said with mock sweetness, "but there seems to be plenty of people in this crowd who'll talk to me." The crowd followed her out the front door. "Be prepared to respond to questions about the boy from St. George, also," she called over her shoulder.

"Shit!" Lovemore shouted after the crowd had left. "The fucking press. And, Baxter, your ass is mud for sleeping."

* * *

It began raining as Lincoln ran between houses and through backyards. He had to find a place to stop, so he could catch his breath and think. He ran mindlessly from the sounds of sirens and suddenly found himself on the banks of the creek that angled through the city and emptied into Lake Michigan. He sprinted along the creek side until he came to the protection of a bridge, where he rested on a concrete slab. His face and beard were soaked from rain. He had to plan. He had to think.

He knew he'd have to hide elsewhere, and he had to get a weapon. He kept a sawed-off shotgun under the front seat of his car, which was parked down the street from his home. He was glad he hadn't parked in his garage; he'd left it out, planning to drive to his girlfriend's house. Now he couldn't risk going back to his house or hers. But he might be able to get to his car, especially on a night like this.

Lincoln watched as the rainwater gushed down the banks. The bridge protected him from the torrential onslaught, just as it protected him from the police onslaught that engulfed the West Side.

The creek began to rise as it raced toward the lake. It reminded him of when Billy and he were kids, and they'd occasionally ride a small raft to the lake on the way to work.

"To the Allerton and Smith mansions," he said aloud. The estates were next door to each other. When the boys' work was done, they would play in the wooded backyards and ravines or walk down to the private beaches. Sometimes they'd hide in the woods and watch the Allerton sisters swimming in their pool. Billy and he weren't allowed in the pool, even if no one else was using it.

A loud clap of thunder tore him from his memories. He had to hurry and get his gun. He left the security of the bridge to take routes through alleys and yards, shortcuts he hadn't taken since he was a kid. The neighborhoods were the same. Yards and structures didn't change in black areas, except to get a little more run-down with every passing year.

At last Lincoln stood in the darkness across the street from his house. He spotted a detective car parked around the corner, but because of the angle of their vision, the coppers would not be able to see his car on the street a few houses down.

He shivered as he hurried between the houses toward the street. His eyes darted left to right. He crossed a front lawn, sidestepped between two parked cars and into the street, then ducked low and crossed to the passenger side of his car. He knew he had to work fast because of the car's interior lights. The shotgun would be on the front seat. He always carried the sawed-off shotgun because gang members and punks knew he carried a lot of cash.

He unlocked the car door, opened it, and grabbed the shotgun, which was wrapped in a long trench coat.

"Police! Hold it there!"

Fright electrified Lincoln. He turned his head to see an overweight, uniformed officer lumbering toward him in the downpour. The man's raincoat hung open. He held a flashlight in his left hand and was raising a portable radio in his right.

Fool, thought Lincoln as he raised his shotgun.

Whoom! . The blast from the shotgun was loud.

The officer, flashlight, and radio flew backward. The message was never transmitted.

Lincoln ran toward the direction whence he came. Out of the corner of his eye, he saw the detective car racing from the alley toward the source of the explosion. With the shotgun wrapped in his trench coat, Lincoln sprinted through the backyards, alleys, and playgrounds of his youth to that dry, secure spot under the cement bridge. For fifteen minutes he sprawled on the concrete, catching his breath. Then he shrugged on his trench coat and began to walk along the slippery creek bank toward Lake Michigan.

* * *

Lieutenant Leon Lovemore reported to Chief Turski in the hospital emergency room, where the ambulance had brought the shot-gunned officer.

"How's Baxter?" The weary lieutenant's voice had lost most of its rich fullness.

"He's on the table," the chief answered. "The doctors say it's too soon to tell what'll be. He took several slugs." He shook his head in disgust. "What a night . . . have you called everyone in?"

"Everyone except the officers out of town on vacation and one with a leg injury. They refused overtime; they just want Pitford's ass for shooting one of our own." Lovemore bent closer to his boss's ear. "Chief, I was so pissed off at Baxter for sleeping on desk duty that I had his supervisor put him on the street to wake him up."

"No guilt trips on this job," the chief said. "You call them as you see them, then live with your decision. It's one of the frustrations of being a supervisor."

"I know you're right."

"But some calls are easier than others, eh, Lieutenant?"

"Yes, sir. Another thing, Chief: the press was at the station interviewing people about the raid at Pitford's."

"There's not much we can do about that now, Leon."

"No." *They'll crucify you tomorrow morning,* he thought. "You, uh, look a little tired, Chief. Maybe you'd like to get some rest? I'll handle things tonight. It'll help me relieve my guilt."

"I-I thank you. Maybe I'll put my feet up in my office. Keep me posted."

* * *

The ER waiting room bustled with activity. The officer with a broken leg rolled into the room, in a wheelchair pushed by his wife.

"I want to do what I can, Lieutenant," the man said.

"Thanks, Micky. We've already got officers everywhere," Lovemore said. "Teams of detectives are running down his friends. Patrol is doing his haunts. It's just a matter of time. They can use your help in the station."

* * *

Five minutes after Slat got home, the phone rang, and he was told about Baxter's being shot. Slat knew he wouldn't be able to sleep, so he went back to work. He could have chosen to work with a team of detectives, but he could think and analyze better alone. He drove up and down the alleys in the neighborhood of the shooting and passed several squad cars. The heavy downpour hindered visibility and made driving a nightmare. Pitford could walk within ten feet of the car and not be seen.

Slat turned up the radio's volume because of the thunder. His ears were assaulted by the incessant loud voice traffic from patrol units who were stopping everyone and everything that moved.

Where is Pitford? Slat wondered. Why would he shoot a cop? Something other than the gambling raid must have set him off, Slat decided. Had his mind snapped from the pressure Slat put on him?

"All supervisors call the station," the radio dispatcher requested.

Slat drove to a gas station a half block from a creek bridge. He showed his badge, and the attendant, glad to see a cop at that time of night, invited him to use the private phone.

All the telephone lines were busy, so he walked to the window and stared at a marked squad stopping a car on top of the bridge.

Slat tried the police station again and got through. "Sergeant, be advised that Pitford called Billy Boyd and threatened to kill him."

"When?"

"About twenty minutes ago."

Slat dashed through the rain to his car. He didn't drive out of the gas station immediately. Instead, he stared at the bridge through the slanting downpour. The flashing blue lights of the squad car on the bridge were dancing off the raindrops.

So Pitford's anger had to do with Billy Boyd, not with the police. Not with the criminal justice system, but another system. If Pitford wanted Billy dead, he'd have to get to the Boyd mansion. Pitford never got his car, but he could have gotten another or stolen one—but he probably would have been stopped by patrol. It was about three miles across most of the city from Pitford's house to Boyd's estate. Pitford would have to walk through residential areas, a large business district, then into the area of wealthy homes with no back alleys.

Except when the lightning flashed, which was every three to five seconds, the torrential rains created a dark screen in which to travel.

After the marked squad pulled away, Slat drove his vehicle to the top of the bridge and looked out along the fast-flowing, roaring creek. Half of his life he'd lived in this area, but he'd never paid much attention to this creek, which flowed from the western edge of the county to Lake Michigan. Only a narrow line of the creek bank had not been washed away or flooded by the rising water. No, Slat thought, only a desperate fool would try to walk the creek bank in this storm. But then Lincoln Pitford was a desperate fool. Slat continued watching from the apex of the bridge.

If Pitford did walk the banks, he might make it close to the lake near Boyd's mansion. The creek twisted through the entire city. A bridge was situated about every three or four city blocks.

Slat took his binoculars from the glove box and looked up the creek at both banks. Even during lightning blasts, he couldn't see all the way to the next bridge because of the intensity of the rain. Slat drove the three blocks to that concrete span and used the binoculars again, then went on to the next bridge and repeated the process. Never was he able to see the next overpass.

Several times, because of the different direction of the lightning flashes, shadows moved and danced along the creek's banks. He wasn't sure what the shadows were, so, hopeful of being able to distinguish the animate from the inanimate, he'd keep working his binoculars and wait for the next lightning bolt.

As time passed, patrol units stopped fewer cars. There had been no calls for supervisors to contact the station, and that meant two things: there was no change in the status of Officer Baxter, and no tips had been received about Pitford's whereabouts.

Slat was on the last bridge, about two city blocks from Lake Michigan, viewing with the binoculars. Visibility in both directions was hampered by trees and foliage that thickened near the lake. His left hand throbbed from holding the binoculars. The nurse had given him a small envelope with three pain pills. He swallowed one dry.

He had checked three miles of roaring creek banks. *No way,* he thought, *could a man or animal have made it.*

36

"You sit tight,Boss," said Mountain Top. After Pitford had threatened Billy's life, Mountain Top used the next hour to call in eight armed security guards and position them around the mansion. "He won't get in here."

Billy pointed to one of Mountain Top's guards walking down the stairway. "What's he doing in my suit?"

"He's bait. We're going to drive around the West Side and this neighborhood in your Caddy to see if we can draw Pitford out."

Billy nodded, as he paced across the white rug with a gold border. "Soft Sound called from the police station. He's pissed. Says the media are all over the place. Says he can't stop the press now."

"Will the publicity hurt business much?"

"Soft Sound says only for a while. But that's not our problem right now. Man, we got to get to Pitford before he gets to me."

"Don't worry." Before Mountain Top left the room, he stopped and turned. "Boss, you remember Dicey Taylor's widow? She stopped me a couple times. Her boy's still missing. Did you call . . . ?"

"Yeah, I called the Youth Bureau. They said they got all kinds of missing kids. And hers has run away twice before."

"Yeah, but only overnight."

""'What the fuck am I supposed to do? " Billy's voice rose.

* * *

The saturated path along the creek was getting hazardous. Old memories told Lincoln he had to hurry. If this rain continued, no ground would remain. If he slipped into the creek —which was now like a small river—the current would carry him into the huge, crashing waves of storm- thrashed Lake Michigan. He plunged and struggled his way through the rain- soaked night to the shoreline.

Lincoln knew he had to travel about a half mile north along the beach, then up a wooden stairway to either the Allerton property or the adjoining Smith property, where his mother and he had worked years before. The waves pounded the short bluffs. He couldn't walk the beaches like he did as a youngster —they did not exist. Now, because of the rising creek, he couldn't return the way he came. He had no option but to climb the cliff side. Fortunately, it wasn't a steep grade.

Two trees were lying along the eroding slope, their tops pointing down toward the water. Using the belt from his trench coat, Lincoln strapped the shotgun to his back, then discarded the cumbersome garment.

Using the slippery branches of the fallen trees, he pulled himself up the slope. Several times he lost his footing but was able to grab exposed roots and steady himself. After he reached the top of the bluff, he leaned on his elbows, his hands holding his forehead as he gasped for air.

He recalled that he'd have to pass through four or five lakeside yards to reach the mansion. When Lincoln worked at the Smith estate, the two boys had roamed these wooded backyards. In those days he knew every bush and tree. Now, as he struggled through the yards, he encountered no fences separating the backyards—only thickets of bushes.

Finally, exhausted and with numb legs, he arrived at the back of Billy Boyd's mansion and sank down on a stone garden bench. He looked ahead at a dozen dumly lit windows. He couldn't see inside; the draperies were drawn. The mansion looked the same, except the backyard pool was enclosed in what appeared to be a glass greenhouse.

"Scraps," he muttered. "Gives me scraps. I should have had half, half the good houses. Then he sets me up to get busted, gets rid of me. Keeps it all. Motherfucker."

He looked around. Several cars were lined up in the driveway, and Lincoln guessed that Billy was home. I have to find a way to get to him, he thought. And he desperately wanted shelter from the rain. He was soaked to the bones, and seeing the magnificent home, where his step-cousin no doubt sat warm and dry, infuriated Lincoln all the more.

He remembered there being a shed in the back of the Smith property next door. The Smith and Allerton properties were connected by a trellis gate behind the house, near the pool. Lincoln passed through and found the shed. It was the same old structure with worn gray planks. There was no padlock in the hasp.

He went inside. Lightning flashes bounced through the dirty, cracked windows to illuminate a garden tractor, lawn sweeper, rakes, and other yard tools. Filthy rags hung from a rafter. He grabbed one and wiped his wet face and beard, then dried his weapon.

The shotgun reminded him of his two years in the army. He had served in 'Nam, while Billy stayed home. Curly had pulled strings, claiming that Billy was his mother's sole support. Billy made good money those years Lincoln sweated in a jungle and ate rations out of cans. Thinking back now on that iniquity, his anger and sense of purpose continued to grow and fester.

Lincoln looked out the window. No lights were on in the Smith house. Years before, the family always left a lamp burning in the kitchen. The dark, four-story mansion loomed weirdly in the ominous weather. He remembered the attic, where he played as a youth, just as he had played in this old shed.

As the wind increased, the shed shuddered. Lincoln, fearful that it would collapse on him, opened the door, and a strong gust pulled it from his grasp. Holding on to his weapon, the man sprinted toward the rear of the mansion. His feet sank in the soft sod and slipped on the slick grass. He picked himself up ran toward a stand of wind-whipped bushes halfway between the house and shed, rounded the right side of the foliage, then increased his speed.

Twice he slid to his knees before gaining the rickety back stairs to the screened porch. He pushed through the broken screen door and, chest heaving, trudged across the porch to the kitchen door. It was locked and too solid and heavy to break in. Frustrated to the point of tears, he suddenly remembered a side entrance to the basement. He left the porch and walked around the outside of the house.

An old, stone stairway led down to a covered five-foot-high basement door. It, too, was locked. He leaned his forehead against it for a moment, wondering if anything in the world ever worked in his favor. He set down his shotgun and vented his fury, pounding his fists against the heavy wood door and screaming unintelligibly with rage. Finally, drained and weakened, he sat on a stone step and rested, his head cradled in his hands.

Then he remembered: Whenever the butler or cook wasn't home to let his mother and him in through the kitchen, they entered through this door by means of a hidden skeleton key. He felt along the edge of a stone protruding an inch on the left side of the entrance and found the key, still there after all those years. Lincoln believed this was a good omen.

After several finger-wrenching tries, the rusted key slowly released the lock plunger. The door still wouldn't open. He heaved with his shoulder, and it gave way.

The basement was dark, but thankfully dry. He didn't know what to expect—if anyone was home, if they had guns or attack dogs. Clutter was everywhere, primarily old lawn furniture and paraphernalia for the swimming pool. He shut the door behind him and listened. He heard nothing beyond the storm. He drew the damp, musty air into his nostrils—no animal smells.

The invasive lightning flashes penetrated the Windows guided him to the old, wooden stairway. Thunder penetrated the house and covered the noise he made. At the top of the stairs the door opened into the kitchen. Pots sat on a countertop. Towels hung from the side of the sink. Lincoln grabbed a towel and dried his face and beard as he opened the refrigerator. It was half full, but with condiments and other non- perishables. He couldn't judge from the contents if people lived there; he was nonetheless very grateful no one appeared to be home.

After drying his shotgun with another kitchen towel, he went to the second floor, then the third. He walked down a long, carpeted hallway and picked out a bedroom whose windows faced Billy's mansion.

The room had the three curtainless floor-to-ceiling windows. The furniture was shrouded in white sheets. Lincoln peeled off his clothing and hung it over a chair. Using a sheet that covered a bureau, he dried himself while looking out the window at the Boyd mansion. He watched as a car pulled into the driveway. Lincoln recognized the vehicle as a police car. The driver jumped out of the car and rang the front doorbell.

After the detective was admitted, Lincoln's eyes traveled up the side of the house. There, only one window—on the landing between the first and second floor—was not covered. He could see through it, into Billy's front hallway and partway into the living room. He knew his weapon would not be accurate at this distance. With a rifle, though, he could easily kill Billy when he walked into view.

Lincoln lifted the sheet off the nightstand and found a decorative candle in a small brass holder with some wooden kithen matches on the side of the holder.. He lit the candle, then walked downstairs to the first floor, into a large oak-paneled room. An ornate antique pool table with fringed leather pockets stood in the center of the floor. Lincoln remembered it well from his youth—he had never seen anything so fancy in his West-Side neighborhood. So the Smiths probably still lived here.

On the back wall was a glass-fronted upright cabinet, which held several shotguns and rifles. He smashed the glass paneled door, took out a thirty-thirty rifle with a scope, and leaned it against the wall. In the drawer below he found some ammunition and several smaller guns. He helped himself to a four-inch thirty-eight caliber handgun and a box of shells. He opened the handgun cylinder and loaded it with a sense of purpose and satisfaction.

With the handgun in his right hand and the rifle in his left, he walked to the kitchen and scouted the refrigerator for beer. There was none. There were too many cabinets in the old kitchen for him to waste time looking for liquor. He remembered that Mr. Smith had a special cabinet in the dining room where he kept bottles of booze. Lincoln walked through the house and helped himself to a fifth of John Powers Irish whisky from the mahogany breakfront. He stuffed the bottle under his arm, then hurried back upstairs.

37

AS SLAT PARKED ON THE LAST BRIDGE, headlights appeared in his rear-view mirror, then the car passed him. It was the squad Gordy MacBell usually drove. Slat smiled when he heard quick double taps on his radio receiver; it was Gordy's habit to tap his radio mike button as a way of waving hello over the radio.

Slat followed Gordy to the long, rain-splattered driveway of the Boyd mansion. The brick-and-stone canopy could cover five car lengths. Considering the intensity of this storm, the protection from the elements was a real asset.

Gordy and Slat, raincoats whipping around their legs, exited their cars and hurried up the stairs to the front door, where two giant men with shotguns stood guard.

"We're here to talk to Mr. Boyd," Gordy said, and the men stepped aside.

Slat followed Gordy into a massive foyer. Another guard led them to the kitchen, where Billy was sitting at a table, eating a bowl of granola. Popper, Billy's bodyguard, sat beside him, sipping coffee. The two of them were dwarfed in the spacious kitchen, with the highly polished wooden cabinets reaching the top of the ten-foot walls. Butcher-block counters and an array of copper pots, pans, and mixing bowls added warmth to the utilitarian room, with its restaurant-size appliances.

"Sit down." Boyd pointed to the empty chairs on the other side of the table. "Coffee?" He indicated the percolator.

Popper rose and started to leave.

"You can stay, pop," Billy said.

"Not me, Boss." He looked with his ping-pong eyes at Slat. "Those two motherfuckers what started all this fucking shit. I don't want no fucking thing to do with them motherfuckers." He left the room.

Billy shrugged. "My man's right, you know. If gambling were stopped at the Catholic churches or white clubs, both would continue to operate without any problem. No white man would lose his job as a result. But when you stop gambling on the West Side, you put black men out of work. You see, white folks would lose a pastime, while black folks would lose a living." Billy wiped his mouth. "Now what the fuck do you two want?"

Gordy began, "Hey, man, we all got a problem here. We want Pitford before he gets to you. The Tactical Unit is all over this neighborhood. We'll get him."

"Yeah," Billy said. "Well, you could have saved yourself a trip. Lovemore just called with the same information."

Gordy turned to leave. "Just wanted to extend the courtesy of letting you know. I'll be in the area if you need me."

"Catch you later," Slat said to Gordy. "I'll stick around awhile."

After Gordy left, Billy and Slat sat quietly for a few seconds. "Coffee, man?" Billy repeated.

"Thanks." Slat helped himself.

"What'd you start that hassle on us for?" Billy asked. His voice had lost its edge.

"I'll be straight," Slat began. "I don't give a damn about the gambling. It's against the law, but . . . "

"You wouldn't last two months on the job if you keep this shit up," Billy interrupted. "And it won't be us blacks that shit on you, man. It'll be your honky brothers."

"You know that's not what I want. I want whoever killed those two gamblers and whoever killed your first wife."

Billy leapt out of his chair. "I'm going to tell you something, Cop! That woman was the mother of my kids. I've listened to their cries and seen their heartbreak over her death. A couple of them blame me. They say it's because of I'm living large."

He sat back down, and Slat could see Billy make a concerted effort to calm himself.

"I've hired a detective agency in Florida to work on her death. I keep calling those cops down there, and I keep talking to a Lieutenant Anton." Billy said. "He released the man she was living with. I want to find out who did that to her. Best as I can tell, her death had nothing to do with anything around here in Pulaski. She'd been gone a long time. You're looking at the wrong people."

"As for Lillie, I really don't know." Slat swallowed some coffee and never took his eyes off Billy. "But I think you know something about those old gamblers."

Billy threw down his napkin. "Fuck you, man! I don't know who did it! None of my people did it!"

"What about Pitford?"

"Pitford was playing cards with the rest of us."

"But he left early."

"Listen! If he left early, I can't remember. If he did it, I don't know anything. He never told me shit. And why the fuck didn't you motherfuckers work on this shit right after it happened?"

"Because I think somebody got paid off! What do you think, Billy?"

"I think I'm not saying another thing without talking to my lawyer."

Slat shrugged. "Have it your way."

"Fucking right, man."

"Good coffee," Slat said after draining the cup.

"Lots of good things around black folks, if you wasn't so prejudiced."

"Listen, Billy. If I'm wrong, I'll apologize. But I've got a job to do." He stood to leave.

"Fuck your job."

"Tell me: What do you think Pitford will do? You know him. Is he serious about getting you?"

"Fucking right, man. Didn't he hit that cop?" Billy stood also. "I'll walk you out."

As Billy walked alongside Slat to the front door, the sergeant asked, "Why do you think Pitford'll try to get at you here?"

"Because Lincoln knows the house and the neighborhood."

"How?"

"Oh, you wonder because he's black, right, Slat-ski? How would a black boy know a rich, white man's turf? How else? He worked next door, polishing shit, just like I did as a kid. I made it into your white neighborhood. I stepped into what most of you honkeys dream of having, but I'm still a nigger to you all."

"I don't think it'd do me any good to argue with you, Billy. You're going to believe whatever you want to about me."

"Another thing—a black kid, about twelve, the Taylor boy. He's been missing a few days, and no cops do shit about it. But white kids missing, everybody looks."

"That's not true, Billy," Slat said. "What's the kid's name?"

"I don't know his first name. Taylor's the last name."

"I'll check into it. If you need me, I'll be in the neighborhood."

"I'll never need you, Slat-ski," Billy said as Slat ducked into the wind.

The storm seemed worse as the angle of the rain violated the protection of the large canopy. Slat started down the steps toward his squad, only to see that it was blocked by another vehicle. One of the two guards watching the door said, "I'll get the keys and move the Caddy."

"Don't bother," Slat told him. "I'll wait awhile."

He walked to the downwind edge of the canopy and looked around. When he'd driven in, he thought he'd seen a light on in a third-floor window next door. Now the light was off. Because of the lightning flashes, however, it was difficult to be sure of anything.

"Who lives next door?" Slat asked the security guard.

"No one now. It's one of our accounts. The old lady who lived there's in a hospital or nursing home."

Slat turned his raincoat collar up and hurried down the long driveway. He wanted to check out that house, but he didn't want to fight his way through the thick stretch of drenched bushes separating the properties. Instead, he decided to walk out Boyd's driveway to the street, then up the next driveway to the darkened Victorian. Despite the rain, he felt good walking in it.

Halfway down the driveway, Slat saw a pair of telescoping headlight beams coming toward him. He stepped onto the lawn to let the car pass. It was Gordy, who stopped the squad and hollered out the window, "Geez, man, get out of the rain."

Slat didn't have to be convinced. Gordy looked pale. "What's the matter?"

"Came back to tell you. Baxter didn't make it."

"Shit." Slat turned toward the passenger window. "It's murder now. Let's go next door. The house is supposed to be empty, but I caught sight of a light."

Gordy backed the squad car out of the driveway and into the street. Then he drove into the next driveway, up to the Smiths' stone canopy.

"On the West Side, you sometimes find twenty people cramped inside some small, six-room house," Gordy said. "Here's a wasted twenty- some-room house, empty. It ain't right."

"Nothing's right." Slat wiped his bandaged hand.

"I've got some fresh bandages in the trunk."

"Later. Thanks." He looked up at the huge Victorian. "Okay, Gordy, let's see who's home."

38

BILLY WALKED THROUGH THE KITCHEN AND INTO THE DINING ROOM, to re-join his guest. "They're gone now," he told her.

"I'm not embarrassed I'm here," Dawn said. "I just felt it best not to have to explain myself, what with everything else going on tonight."

Billy smiled. "I understand, baby."

"Don't call me that," she said. "I don't like it. I came here on official business."

"Right, and hid your car in the garage," he said with a knowing smile. "Looking for a guy who shot a cop. You happened to be in the neighborhood . . ."

"And thought you'd be nice enough to give me a cup of tea to warm my bones while I'm out in a hurricane trying to save your butt."

He took her arm and led her back into the kitchen. "So you didn't know that Lincoln Pitford is my step-cousin and that he leases property from me?"

Surprised, Dawn stopped and looked at him. "Why, no! I've been working homicides and some burglaries."

Billy studied her closely, then burst out laughing. "You know, I actually believe you." He ushered her to the table and introduced her to Popper. "Go find Missy for me, man. Have her find Officer Mazurski some of my daughter's clothes to change into."

The bodyguard jumped up and left the room.

Billy pulled up a chair next to Dawn and took her hand. It was slender and elegant. The rounded fingernails reminded him of translucent shells on the beach at Longboat Key. "If you're really interested in saving my butt," he said, "you can spend some time here, let me get to know you better." His fingers trailed up her arm, across her shoulder, and came to rest on the back of her neck. "Because if I don't get you out of my mind, Detective Mazurski, I'm going to die from lack of sleep."

He pulled her toward him, and she did not resist.

* * *

The man waiting for Slat knew that the sergeant would eventually come to Boyd's mansion. He backed his car into a driveway across the street and watched patiently for the sergeant. After a while, when he saw Slat illuminated by the lightning and walking alone toward the road, the man reached for the shotgun laying next to him on the seat.

Suddenly a marked squad pulled in, picked Slat up, then drove into the next driveway. At first the shooter was disappointed, but then he realized how to turn the situation to his advantage. Tonight was the night; he was sure of it. He got out of his car and crossed the street. The rain stung his face, and the wind tore at his long trench coat as he walked toward the Victorian mansion.

* * *

"How the hell are we going to get in there if nobody's home?" Gordy asked as they arrived at the front door. He pressed himself against the front door in a futile attempt to hide from the rain gusts.

"Don't worry. We'll get in." Slat wiped the water off his face with a soaking handkerchief.

"Without a search warrant?" Gordy's eyes were wide.

Slat didn't answer. He walked up and down the L-shaped porch with Gordy at his heels.

"You know, Slat, we need a search warrant, even if we know the bad-ass is in the house."

Slat tried the front door. It was locked. His plastic ID card wouldn't trip the bolt lock. "Gordy, I'm going to bust the window and go in."

"Why not ring the fucking bell?"

Slat grinned. "Because no one lives here. You can take off if you want. This'll be my call."

"Oh, shit!" Gordy moaned. "No, I'm behind you, old buddy."

Once inside, they shook the rain off as best they could, then padded through the large, thickly carpeted living room toward the foyer. Gordy pulled out his flashlight and played its funnel of light until he found a staircase. In another direction, Slat saw a thin strip of light coming from under a door.

"Let's check the room with the light," Slat whispered.

They drew their weapons. Gordy followed Slat. After reaching the doorway, Gordy stood with pistol at ready on the right side, and Slat assumed his position on the left. Because Gordy was in uniform, he'd enter first. When Slat nodded, the men spun into the room.

It was empty. They looked around. An open gun cabinet with an empty holding spot caught their eyes. The drawer for handguns and ammunition was open.

"Hey, man," Gordy whispered, "I think we got something."

"Your radio?" Slat kept his eyes on the open door to the hallway.

Gordy reached for his radio holster. "Oh, shit, I forgot it."

Slat pointed to a telephone on the desk.

Gordy picked it up. "Disconnected. I'll use the car radio." He cautiously headed for the hallway. "Be right back."

"I'll meet you at this end of the third-floor hallway."

"Be careful, man." Gordy disappeared into the darkness.

* * *

Gordy stepped out through the open window and onto the canopied porch. After he straightened, he noticed a person in a long trench coat walking up the driveway. Realizing it could be Pitford, Gordy quickly descended the stairway into the swirling rain and moved toward the man. But suddenly the stranger turned and began to run toward the street.

Gordy stopped and glanced at the squad car, then at the fellow running down the driveway. He was already about one hundred feet away.

A run, Gordy thought, elated, and shed his raincoat. Every day he ran for fun, for the sheer love of the sport; but he seldom ran on the job after someone who desperately wanted to escape. He started off. If it's Pitford, what a great challenge! he thought.

As Gordy's long legs pumped under him, the raindrops slapped his face. Exhilaration! Ahead, the man slipped and fell to the pavement. The distance had closed to only seventy-five feet. How unfair it was, Gordy realized, to compete against someone who had fallen. So he slowed into a standing jog until the man rose and began running again. Gordy breathed the dampened air deep into his lungs as he continued the chase.

Gordy was gaining. The challenged man was now about fifty feet ahead of him. Gordy's legs and breath obeyed the rhythm set by his arms. He watched the man reach the square brick gateposts, then round the side of one of the posts, to move out of Gordy's vision.

Gordy calculated the turn: He'd increase his speed now, then decrease it slightly during the slippery turn. He slowed his long stride slightly as he ran into the turn, took a wide step, pivoted, and started to pour on the power when he saw the man had fallen yet a second time. Again, gamely, Gordy slowed.

A flash of lightning brought an instant's horrible clarity to the young man when he saw the stranger raise and level a shotgun.

"No!" Gordy cried, but the word had hardly been uttered when a yellow flash mixed with the pale lightning.

He couldn't distinguish the thunderbolt from the shotgun blast as the impact knocked him back and down. Strangely, as he lay there with the rain beating on his face, he simultaneously kept running—now in his bright nylon suit and Addidas shoes—with hundreds of others dressed similarly, all jogging toward a long, yellow-taped finish line somewhere in the distance. . . .

* * *

Slat waited for Gordy at the top of the stairs leading to the third floor. He could see down the hall toward a thin line of light under one of the doors. Because of the missing weapons, he'd be totally out of procedure if he tried to enter without a backup.

Slat was half sitting on the third step from the top. His right arm rested on the top step, gun in hand...waiting. He wanted a cigarette. His bandage began unwrapping. He took the wet handkerchief out of his pocket and, as best he could, reinforced the wrapping. He was a tough cop, but this darkened, massive house had him spooked.

Where is Gordy? he wondered.

The cracking thunder drowned the possibility of hearing any sounds, so he decided to crawl down the hallway toward the light in the hopes of hearing something. The thickness of the carpet made it easy on his hands and knees.

* * *

Lincoln set his rifle and handgun on the bed. He placed the liquor bottle on top of the bureau against the wall, between the head of the bed and the wall by the window. As he walked past the window, he caught a glance of Billy and a woman in the hallway. He grabbed the weapon and sighted it on his step-cousin, but Billy moved out of view.

Lincoln moved the rifle's scope until he had the woman in the cross hairs. "Must be one of his bitches," he murmured. "It'll hurt him if I take her out."

He found it impossible to hold the scope steady on the woman's head or back, so he dragged a small-upholstered chair from a corner of the room to the window, to use as a prop to steady the rifle. Again he looked through the sight, but Billy and the woman were gone.

At that moment, Billy's white Cadillac stopped partly under the driveway canopy. The front door of the house opened, and Billy, bent low under an umbrella, hurried down the steps and to the waiting limousine.

"That son of a bitch belongs to me now!" Lincoln muttered. He crouched on one knee and sighted the scope as Billy slid into the Caddy's back seat. So I kill him inside the car. No problem, Lincoln thought.

But having to penetrate two pieces of glass might deflect the bullet enough to miss. He tried to raise the bedroom window, but it was stuck. Desperate, he smashed the glass with the stock of the rifle. Oblivious to the gush of wind, he aligned the cross hairs on the image in the center of the car window, then squeezed the trigger.

* * *

While crawling down the dark hallway, Slat hearing a different noise between the thunderclaps, raised himself on his knees. Then he felt a gush of wind from under the door and recognized the reverberating crack of a rifle. The shot came from the room with the light.

Weapon in hand, Slat pushed the door open against a greater force of wind. In the dancing candlelight, he saw a naked man turn toward him with a rifle in his hands.

"Drop it, Pitford!" Slat shouted.

Pitford recognized him immediately. "Man, I didn't mean to hurt you or that other cop. It's that fucking Billy—he made me crazy."

"The other cop is dead, Pitford. Now drop your weapon!"

"Oh, no, man . . ." He raised the rifle barrel toward Slat. "I got nothin' to lose now, killin' one cop or two. I got to get outta here."

Slat's gun belched flame. Pitford's arms flung outward as a hole burst in the middle of his chest and his weapon flew into a corner. He fell backward onto the floor.

Slat lowered his gun and took a deep, shuddering breath. He tried to shake the sound of drums from his ears. Then something hard and heavy slammed against the back of his head, and he dropped to the floor.

* * *

He must have been unconscious for only a few seconds, because the candle was still flickering; but it seemed as if hours had past. Slat raised his aching head from the floor and saw the bottom of a long trench coat.

"On your feet, Slat."

The voice was familiar. Slat tried but couldn't stand up. He made it to a sitting position and leaned back against the bed. The unshaven retiree with the pointed chin kicked Slat's handgun into a corner.

The answer came to him now. Everything fit. He looked up. Slat had never looked into that end of a shotgun. "It was you *and* Sam taking the gambling payoffs, wasn't it, Ernie? And Pitford, Boyd, and Mountain Top knew it."

"You got it, Slat. If you hadn't started all this investigating, I'd have been okay. But your pressure on the niggers might make them talk."

"Did Boyd and the others know you wasted Jackson and Watson?" Slat asked.

"No one but Sam knew I killed those gamblers. He just wanted to scare them. He was chicken shit, Slat, but because he was an accessory he had to keep his mouth shut about my wasting them. Then, a few weeks ago, I was afraid Tyrone would fold. He came and told me the attorney general's investigators wanted to talk to him. He was getting older, and his life sucked. People like to clear their conscience when they're facing death and have nothing to lose."

A moan drifted up from the other side of the bed.

"Ernie, Pitford needs medical attention."

"Fuck him." Ernie pointed the gun over Slat's head toward the other side of the bed. "As I was saying, Sam had been drinking too much the past year. I couldn't trust him. So I put him away. You guys made it out as a suicide, like I knew you would. You're a dumb, fucking Polack— you know that, Slat?" Ernie chuckled. "Ain't you going to ask me how I wasted Sam?"

"Fuck you, Ernie," Slat said, rubbing the back of his head. "I don't give a shit how you did it."

"But I got to tell you how good I am. I went to see Sam, and I got the drop on him. He was sitting on the bed. I shot him in the temple with a gun

I borrowed from him years ago. Then I placed the weapon in his hand and shot it into the mattress, so he'd get the powder burns on his hand. Pretty slick, huh?"

"Yeah, Ernie, you're a fucking genius. So Boyd, Pitford, and Mountain Top paid you and Sam off."

"Yeah, for a while. Then they told Sam and me to get fucked. Nothing we could do about it. If they talk about the payoffs because of the pressure you've been putting on them, I might lose my pension. Nobody can place me at the murders. But I got to protect my reputation and my pension. I got to think about my kids and Elinor."

"What about Lillie Boyd?"

Ernie's face fell. "Aw, yeah, Lillie. I almost forgot about her. She knew about the payoffs. Hell, half the time she gave us the envelopes because Billy was out. She never said anything, not even to Elinor. They knew each other from school. You told me you were looking for whoever was at Curly's house that night? Well, Lillie was there, and I knew you were going to Florida. You and I almost took the same flight."

Slat touched the back of his head, then looked at the blood on his hand. He had to stall for time, and he felt lucky that Ernie felt like bragging. "You sure had me fooled, Ernie. You wanted me to believe it was Sam."

"Yeah, and I wanted you to think the whole thing had died with him, too. But you wouldn't quit. So now I got to waste you. I tried to get you sooner, but you've been one lucky son of a bitch. I almost got you in your car....

" He laughed. "—and blew the shit out of it, huh?"

Slat rubbed his head again. He wouldn't take a hit without a fight. He remembered seeing a handgun on the bed—Pitford's. He could jump onto the bed and grab the gun as he rolled over to the other side, where Pitford was.

"I got a backup coming, Ernie. You won't make it out of here."

"No problem. I took out Gordy in the driveway."

"You fucking prick!" Slat hollered as he raised himself to his feet, ready to hurl himself backward onto the bed.

Ernie lifted his shotgun, and Slat leaped back.

Whoom! Whoom! The deafening blasts filled the room.

Slat catapulted himself onto the mattress in that instant, and the shot missed him. Slat misjudged his grab for the pistol and landed weaponless on the floor next to Pitford. As he scrambled back to reach for the weapon, he saw Ernie falling onto the floor.

A black giant with a shotgun in his hands filled the doorway.

Slat stared, not believing he was still alive. "Thanks, man," he rasped to Mountain Top.

"Don't thank me, motherfucker. Next time you smell shit, look in your own backyard."

39

THE TWO MEN RELAXED IN LEATHERETTE COMFORT in Father Daley's adorned study. Father Daley, with his blue eyes and ruddy complexion, dressed in his Roman collar, blended with the decor. Tony Tattaglia, tall, dark, wearing a sweat shirt and jeans, offset the environment. They were nursing brandies when the phone rang. Patrick answered, and as he listened his expression darkened, and he adjusted himself slightly in his chair.

Seeing nothing but trouble in the priest's face, Tony gripped his heavy glass tightly. After what seemed like an eternity, Father Daley replaced the phone on its cradle.

"That was Archie Dunn," the priest reported. "According to the alderman, the murdered altar boy from St. George was last seen going into the park with Father Julius." He finished his brandy in one gulp. "My God! What a tragedy."

"Let me get us some bourbon," Tony said.

Father Julius has to be caught before he does it again, Tony thought. Otherwise the Church will be embarrassed, and Monsignor Popodowski, citing malfeasance, will blame the second death on me.

"I've been trying to delay Sczlatski," he told Patrick. "He isn't far behind us, though. Do the police have a warrant for Julius's arrest?"

"No. I'd hear about it before it was typed up."

"Then Sczlatski's still not sure what he has."

"What are we going to do?" Father Daley accepted a glass of bourbon from the agent.

"Find Julius before Sczlatski does. I've got men watching the Tee apartment. I've hired a private investigative agency, and they're checking every parking lot in Milwaukee county for the car registered to Tee. I've also got men watching St. Michael's rectory." Tony drained his glass of bourbon. "I'd like to see every file you have on John Julius. I've got to study him, get into his head, and begin to think like him. Then we'll catch him."

* * *

Slat arrived late for work the following day. His throbbing headache kept the same tempo as the pain in his stabbed hand. He knew he could have taken the day off—or even the week off—but too many things were happening, too many shootings and murders. The chief was on the firing line, with politicians, black community leaders, and the press all taking aim. Even the local schools' Parent-Teacher associations were clamoring about the murder of the boy from St. George.

In the midst of the chaos, at least he had learned definitively that Sam had not murdered Tiny Watson and Stu Jackson. Now Sam would rest in peace, and Slat would enjoy some peace of mind in that department. He couldn't condone that his mentor had accepted payoffs, but he knew he'd eventually forgive Sam for that. It would serve no purpose to write any reports implicating Sam in the gambling payoffs, and no one would be the wiser. **

Dawn and Jenny were waiting in the Detective Bureau to talk to him about Father Julius. Slat asked them to hold off any further investigation involving the Church until after he had talked to them. Johnny Ninkovich, the evidence technician, had called and said he'd be in to see Slat with something important.

Slat looked out his cage window and saw Cheri Duncan talking to Odell Fowler at the counter.

"Get rid of her, Odell," Slat muttered to himself. Then he remembered something Billy Boyd had said, so he grabbed his phone and dialed the Youth Bureau's supervisor's extension.

"Smitty," he said, "you got a Taylor kid missing. Don't know his first name."

"Just a minute."

Slat could hear Smitty flipping through papers.

"Kenneth Taylor."

"I guess."

"Missing a week now."

"Isn't that a long time?"

"Yeah," Smitty confirmed. "Most just stay out overnight. But this is the third time for this kid. He's just a runaway. We can't do much about it. We probably got a dozen runaways right now."

"Many black kids?"

"I don't know."

"Can you put some extra time in on this one?"

There was a momentary silence. "Slat. Where the fuck am I supposed to get the people? Do you have anything over there to indicate that he's more than a runaway?"

"No," Slat admitted.

"Well, we'll do what we can. . . ."

Johnny Ninkovich burst into the Detective Bureau and hurried into the glass cage. He was nearly dancing with impatience, so Slat ended the conversation with Smitty with a quick thank-you.

"What's up, Nink?"

"Slat, there are a few things from Ernie Pope's wallet that might interest you. First, these." He took a couple of checks from the wallet and placed them in front of Slat. "They're from his part-time job at the archdiocese. If they get caught up as evidence, Elinor'll have a long time waiting for them, and God knows she probably needs them now. So I made Photostats of them."

"Thanks, Nink. I'll take them to her."

"But here's the thing I called about." Ninkovich opened the wallet in front of Slat and pulled out the inner lining of the billfold, to expose a secret compartment. "The dicks must have missed this." A folded and worn photograph fell onto the desk.

Slat carefully unfolded the three-by-five photo. Along with the line down the center caused by the fold, other lines were twisted in a puzzle-cut arrangement. In spite of these, the photo was clear enough to see two people: a man bending over from within a public-bathroom toilet stall and reaching for the penis of a young boy. The boy's face couldn't be seen, but the man's could. It was, however, too small and worn to be recognized.

Slat looked up. "Nink, blow it up and don't tell anyone. Let me know as soon as it's done."

"Sure, Slat. It'll take some work. See that sign on the wall? It's small, but with a mag glass it reads No Books Allowed in the Washroom."

"The library?" Slat asked.

"That's what I think," Nink said.

After Nink left, and before Slat could leave the office, his phone rang. He listened for a moment. After placing the receiver on its cradle, he stood and slowly, numbly walked into the bureau. "That was the hospital," Slat said.

Stan and Odell looked up, their hands still poised over their keyboards. Dawn and Jenny looked up. Tension tightened their features.

"Gordy lost his right leg."

After a crash of silence, Stan slammed his iron fist against his desk top. "Shit! Shit! Shit!"

Odell Fowler put his face in his hands.

Jenny turned her face away.

Dawn walked to the window and stared out at Pulaski.

Cheri took notes.

"Jenny, Dawn, let's get out of here," Slat said, and they brushed past Cheri at the counter.

* * *

After the three cops entered the squad car, Slat asked, "You ladies ever been to Cousin's Center?"

The women shook their heads.

"I never talked to an archbishop before," Jenny said from the passenger seat.

"I've never talked to one, either," Dawn said from the back seat.

"Makes three of us," Slat said. "We have to find out where Father Julius is. If they don't know at St. Mike's, then the archdiocese should know."

Jenny smiled wanly. "What do you wear to a meeting with an archbishop?"

"Who gives a fuck?" Dawn muttered.

As they rode in silence, Slat glimpsed Dawn through the rearview mirror, staring out the window. She seemed lost in her own thoughts. He looked over at Jenny and smiled.

"Has your girlfriend recovered from the shooting of your car?" she asked, a slight edge to her voice.

"Theresa? She's not my girlfriend—at least not anymore. She dropped me liked a hot potato after the shooting. Got scared, I guess. But there was no real relationship to begin with."

"That's too bad," Jenny said, and turned her face away from Slat toward the door window.

He thought he saw part of a smile before she turned her head. He felt encouraged. He decided to continue the conversation another time soon, when they were alone.

Slat turned into the driveway and parked the car in the lot behind the archbishop's office. Everyone got out, and Dawn and Jenny walked side by side ahead of Slat. Jenny had slacks on. Dawn wore a skirt Slat thought might be a little short. Their hips swung in unison.

Slat opened the door for Dawn and Jenny to pass through, then he entered behind them. Suddenly Dawn stopped, and Slat collided with Jenny, knocking her sideways against a man apparently intending to exit through the same doorway. They all spilled out of the building.

"You son of a bitch!" Dawn pushed at the man's chest.

"That's the bastard!" Jenny shouted as she moved forward.

Dumbfounded, Slat grabbed Dawn's upper arms from behind as she swung her fist at the man.

"You motherfucker, I'll kill you!" Dawn resisted Slat so he wrapped his arms around her.

"Slat, he's the one who set us up!" Jenny was advancing toward the man, stabbing a finger at his face.

Slat let loose with his right arm and grabbed Jenny, then Dawn burst free.

"Dawn!" Slat shouted. "Jenny, back off!"

"Well, Jenny and Dawn, how nice to see you again," Tony said, smiling graciously as he grabbed Dawn, spun her around, and eased her toward Slat. "We had such a lovely evening together."

"Fuck you!" Dawn hollered.

As Slat held on to Dawn, he felt her heaving chest. "That's enough!" he said emphatically into her ear.

Tony's eyes shifted to Slat. "You must be Sergeant Sczlatski. I'm Tony Tattaglia," he said as he edged around the threesome.

"I imagine we'll meet again," Slat said. It wasn't a question.

Tony grinned. "My pleasure if we do. Good day, ladies." He walked into the parking lot.

"I guess the church is involved," Slat said.

Slat kept a hand on each woman as they watched Tony enter a Lincoln. "You two wait for me in the squad car."

Dawn and Jenny stalked off toward the squad. Slat reached into his pocket to assure himself that he had the squad car key.

Slat entered the archbishop's reception area. "I want to see the archbishop," Slat said to the secretary.

"You can't have had an appointment. He isn't scheduled in today," said a large-jowled priest who was standing in an office doorway.

"Never mind, I'll call back."

Back in the car, Slat told the women what had happened. "Why didn't you make an appointment?" Jenny asked.

"I don't need one. I learned what I needed to know. They're looking for Father Julius, and your pal Tony Tattaglia is involved in the search. Because he tried to discredit you, my guess is he wants to locate Julius before we do. And you know what that means, don't you?"

"What?" the women asked in unison.

"We're going to find him first."

MEMORANDUM
City of Pulaski

From: Alderman A. Dunn

To: Mayor and City Council

Re: Request for special session

The police problems in Pulaski have not only reached the local media but also the national networks.

Over the past few days our black citizens have encountered continual harassment from our police department. As a consequence, we have had two police officers shot--one fatally and the other on permanent disability--- and another stabbed. Two citizens have been killed, and another has been injured.

There should no longer be any question in the minds of the City Council members as to the extent of mismanagement by the police chief.

I urge the mayor to call for a special session of the City Council to assess the management of the police department.

cc: Chief Turski

With damp eyes, Ellen watched the short man with the craggy face read the memo. He was breathing deeply, trying to quell his anxiety.

"Political astuteness has always been my weakest link, Ellen," he said to his secretary. "My generation in Chicago took pride in standing up to politicians. I didn't know there was any such political Pirhanas here in Wisconsin. I'm losing control. I've always been in control."

"You can ride this out, sir. But to be in top form you need your rest. These past few mornings you've been here when I open the office, and I can tell you've been here most of the night."

"Yes," he admitted, "I have had trouble sleeping. Might as well do something constructive."

"Please go home now and get some rest."

He seemed not to hear her.

"I should probably try to be more flexible, see if I can go along with what Dunn suggests." He took another look at the memo.

"Chief, the officers involved were doing what they believed was right. And they were right—they were trying to do a good job for you. Politicians come and go. They have enough trouble keeping their own necks off the chopping block. Don't bend your principles for them. Archie Dunn wants to control you. Think of your officers and staff. Think of your wife and children. We'll all stand behind you through all this."

"Thank you, Ellen."

* * *

"Sergeant, we're waiting," Dawn said as she stuck her head into his glass cage.

"One more minute." Between phone calls, Slat was prioritizing a pile of assignments. When he, Dawn, and Jenny had been driving back from Cousin's Center, he plotted a strategy. First, they'd need to locate a photograph of Father Julius, to be certain the priest and Raymond Tee were the same person. Then they'd meet at Mama's, where it was relatively quiet, and they could figure out what to do next.

Slat was on the phone with Lovemore when he saw Cheri Duncan enter the bureau. He watched as she spoke with Dawn and Jenny. All three women smiled, laughed, and turned to look at him. He felt his skin flush. Dawn and Jenny looked away, but Cheri kept her appreciative gaze on him. She was, he hated to admit to himself, extremely attractive.

Lovemore had Slat on hold when the sergeant suddenly remembered that Father Julius's picture had occasionally appeared in the Pulaski Press. Tired of holding for the lieutenant, he hung the phone up and stood.

Jenny walked into his office. "Slat, Cheri Duncan wants to talk to you about the recent shootings."

The phone rang, and he shrugged helplessly. "Excuse me, please," he said, and she nodded.

"Yes, sir," was all Slat said before hanging up the phone. "Jenny, I've got to go. I need a favor from you."

"Sure."

"Take Cheri out to lunch and try to get a photo of Father Julius. Don't tell her what's happening. If her antennae go up and she starts asking too many questions, then drop it."

"Okay, but she sure wants to talk to you." She paused. "How's your hand today?"

"Much better, thanks. I have to go. The chief wants to see me immediately."

40

SLAT HURRIED DOWN THE LONG HALL to the chief's office, where the secretary met him.

"Oh, Slat!" Ellen said. "He looks terrible. He stayed in his office all night, and I don't think he slept at all." She lowered her voice confidentially. "He hasn't dictated anything to me in days. Most of the time he just stares out the window."

He put a reassuring hand on her arm. "I'll see what I can do, Ellen. Thanks for telling me."

Inside, Martin stood without saying a word of greeting and lifted his suitcoat from the clothes tree. Slat noticed the man's hands were shaking. The chief's shoulder holster was empty.

"Sergeant, I need a ride."

"Yes, sir. My car?"

"Please."

"Uh, sir, your weapon."

But the chief continued toward the doorway without responding. He led the way out through one of the building's side doors. The chief's clothing was much too large for him—clownish, almost. Slat realized that Martin Turski was wasting away.

"I'll wait here for you while you get your car."

Two minutes later, Slat picked up the chief.

"Head for Milwaukee and make sure we aren't being followed," Martin said. Then the chief remained silent.

Slat drove on side streets until they arrived in Milwaukee. "Where to now, sir?"

The chief seemed to shake himself out of deep thoughts. "Wha– ? Oh! West on Oklahoma Avenue. I'll tell you when we get there."

"Chief, is there something I can help you with?"

After a minute of silence, the chief spoke sadly. "I have trouble trusting people in this city. I feel like a total stranger here. Of course I trust my wife, but she doesn't understand the working environment you and I operate in, Sergeant. God knows, I don't, either. Slat, for some reason I've always felt that I could trust you."

"Thank you, sir."

"I've been unable to sleep and have had an extremely high level of anxiety lately. The pressures keep accumulating. I've even been passing up my speaking engagements. Well, I hope you'll keep this all in confidence?"

"Of course, sir."

"I'm seeing a psychiatrist. I realized I need some help to minimize this anxiety. B-but I'm sure it's all temporary."

Slat knew that several of the politicians wanted an insider for chief, one born and raised in Pulaski, someone they all knew well and could control.

They couldn't control this chief, and his progressive management style was a mystery to them, so now they'd do anything to oust him. "I understand, sir."

"Good." The chief pointed to a parking lot ahead of them. "Pick me up here in an hour."

* * *

An hour later, during the drive back to Pulaski, the chief seemed more relaxed.

"Chief," Slat ventured, "I want to ask you a question that has to do with an investigation we're conducting. It may sound as if I'm prying into your business, but I promise you I'm not."

"Fire away, Sergeant."

"You said the mayor and an alderman called you about the incident in Milwaukee involving Herschel and Mazurski. Who was the alderman?"

"Dunn. Dunn calls me more than all the other aldermen put together."

"Did they say where they got the information?"

"Sources. That's all they'd say."

Dunn, Slat realized, had to be connected to Tattaglia and the Church. Of course Dunn had been involved in church activities at St. Michael's for years.

"Sergeant, would you bring me back here next week at this time?"

"Of course, sir."

* * *

After dropping the chief off at the police station, Slat drove straight to St. Luke's Hospital. He chain smoked two cigarettes before he got on the elevator and felt the urge for a third as he walked down the hall to Gordy's room.

"Hi, Slat." Gordy smiled from his hospital bed. "You know, with my being here at St. Luke's so often, seeing Priscilla while she's working, the visiting injured cops and making ER runs, I thought a couple of times, I should rent a room here."

"But not this way, old buddy," Slat said. He made a concerted effort not to look at the flat place on the bed where Gordy's leg should have been.

"What the fuck, man? You play the cards dealt to you."

Slat glanced around the private room full of green plants, floral bouquets, and get-well cards. He looked for a place to sit. Both chairs were full of recently delivered plants waiting to be appropriately placed in the room.

"Priscilla'll be here soon to clean this shit up." Gordy slid over slightly and patted the bed. "Here, sit."

Slat carefully took a small space next to his friend.

"You know," Gordy continued, "God gave us two legs and two arms so if we lost one, we'd still have the other."

"Yeah." Slat felt very uncomfortable. He knew that Gordy's clown routine was bullshit and didn't know what to say.

"Thank God Ernie didn't blow my dick off, huh, Slat? Hey, I got a smile out of you on that one."

"Gordy." Slat cleared his throat. "You holding up all right?"

"Sure! Hey, you know who came to see me?" He didn't wait for an answer. "Mountain Top. I open my eyes this morning after a nap, and that behemoth is standing in the doorway . . . scared the shit out of me."

"Yeah, he sure is big," Slat said. "Saved my ass."

"Yeah, well, Mountain Top said to me, 'How you doing man?' I said, 'Fine, and thanks for taking Ernie out and saving Slat.' He said, 'No problem, man.' I said, 'I don't know how else to thank you, man, except maybe you can have those dozen red roses by the window,' and he says, 'I don't want no motherfucking roses.'"

Gordy and Slat both laughed, then suddenly Gordy's laughter turned to sobs, and as he cried he turned his head away from Slat toward the window.

"I won't be able to run anymore, Slat," Gordy sobbed, his chest heaving. "What am I gonna do? I got no leg."

Slat looked at the closed door, then he looked back at Gordy on the bed. He placed his hand on Gordy's shoulder, and his friend turned suddenly and leaned into Slat's chest. Awkwardly, Slat held Gordy and patted his shoulder.

"It's th-the risks of the job, we all knew that," Gordy hiccuped. "Didn't we, Slat?"

"Yeah, we knew, Gordy."

"What am I going to do, Slat?"

Slat could feel the swelling behind his eyes. He gritted his teeth and fought against bursting into tears himself. "Gordy, you got to stand back and check your options. Yeah, you lost your leg, but you kept your life. You got a wife and a mother who love you, and you got more friends than anyone I know."

"You're right," Gordy said. "I got people who love me. My mother and Priscilla need me, right, Slat?"

"Yeah, man, and that means a lot. I got nothing—no mother, no wife. To have someone like them, I'd give . . . .
"

"A leg, would you give a leg?" Gordy asked bitterly, then fell back onto the pillow. "Oh, God, Slat. I'm sorry. I didn't mean to say that." He grabbed Slat's hand with both of his and, sobbing, held on tightly. "I'm so sorry, buddy. That wasn't fair." Gordy let go of Slat, then wiped his eyes with the edge of the bedsheet and forced a smile.

"You ever meet my mother, you'd love her, Slat."

"Yeah, Gordy, I know I would."

"She's from the Old Country, you know."

They sat in awkward silence.

"Okay, you guys, party's over." A robust nurse burst through the door.

"Hey, Slat, you know Linda. Great nurse."

"Yeah. Hi, Linda."

"Slat, you have to go for a while. I gotta take this guy's vitals."

"Linda, Slat and me had some laughs. He had me laughing so hard tears come to my eyes. Right, Slat?"

"Right, old buddy." Slat stood and headed for the door. "Catch you later."

Slat made it to the parking lot, where he let his jaw relax and his eyes dampen.

* * *

Cheri Duncan, a graduate of Northwestern University's Medill School of Journalism, was frustrated that she hadn't landed a job with a big city newspaper. Two months before, she was hired by the Pulaski Press and was so embarrassed that she hadn't been back to Chicago to see any of her friends. Cheri had grown up on the affluent North Shore and was used to having things go her way.

Exuding the confidence of a woman who's good-looking and bright and knows it, she expected to waltz into a brilliant career in journalism— perhaps even television broadcasting. The process of job interviewing presented her life's first setback, and although she accepted the position in Pulaski, she did not embrace it.

She decided that if she encountered any of her old acquaintances, she'd say she turned down an offer from the Plain Dealer in Cleveland because she wanted to start at the grass roots and experience the depths of ethnicity and diversity offered by the Milwaukee area. Her girlfriends would accept that explanation.

Now these two Cagney and Lacey bumpkins wanted to take her to lunch. She didn't want to go to lunch with them; she wanted to go with Mr. Blue Eyes in the glass cage. She wanted the source—not his messengers.

Cheri didn't want to waste time. She had to write some good, exclusive articles. She had to stay ahead of the Milwaukee Journal reporter assigned to Pulaski. If the Journal recognized her abilities, she could get a job with that paper, then on to the New York Times.

Jenny and Dawn took Cheri to Mama's Place for lunch. The restaurant had no atmosphere, no wine list. One seated oneself. The booths were full—a few cops, hard hats, secretaries, blue collars, men and women. A few dark foreigners waited on people. *A greasy spoon,* she sniffed, *and we have to wait for a table.*

After being seated, they made small talk over lunch. Cheri patiently waited for the detectives to show their hand. This was no act of friendship or sisterhood; they had to have an agenda.

"Cheri," Dawn asked, "are you going to cover the police department's awards dinner next month?"

"I don't know yet. Probably. What's it about?"

"It's an annual event when the chief and mayor give various awards to the police and citizens who have distinguished themselves," Dawn said. "Jenny and I are helping to set it up this year."

Cheri, noticing Jenny's eyes flash toward Dawn, became wary.

"Maybe you can help us," Dawn continued smoothly. "There's a surprise planned. Father Julius may be recognized for his volunteer work. We need his photograph but don't want to alert him that something's in the works. We can't go to the rectory. How about doing us a favor and getting us a photo? We'll owe you one."

"Sure, if we have any."

The business seemed to have been transacted, because the detectives took their final sips of soda, then got ready to leave. Cheri quickly finished her water with a lemon wedge, then followed her companions to the cash register, where Jenny paid the bill.

"I'll drop any photos off on my way home after work," Cheri offered.

After bidding good-bye to the reporter, Jenny and Dawn drove off in their squad car.

* * *

"That was outright lying, Dawn!" Jenny said. "She'll never trust us once she finds out the truth."

"What do I care? That fancy-ass bitch will never survive in this shit jungle anyway. Besides, with this other kid missing, we've got no time to waste."

* * *

The first question Slat intended to ask the librarian was when the library was built. Before he entered the front door, he noticed the words Dedicated in 1962 inscribed in a large stone next to the entrance.

He walked directly into the men's room for a look around. The tiny octagonal floor tiles were worn. Stone walls bore scars from repeated sandblasting to erase years of graffiti. The toilet doors were gone. Two washbasins were situated under a long mirror.

He took his Magna-light from his pocket and pointed the beam close to the mirror. The light shone through and revealed wood grain. All right, he thought, it's a two-way mirror, and the back has been boarded up with plywood.

He positioned himself with his back to the mirror. Yes, it was definitely the same washroom as the one in the photograph. Slat left the room and walked across the lobby to the office marked Library Director— Mrs. Little. The door was open, but Slat still knocked. "Mrs. Little?" he called.

"Come in," the middle-aged matron responded.

"I'm. . . .

"

"You're Sergeant Casimir Sczlatski. I've read about you occasionally in the Pulaski Press. Please come in and sit down."

Slat sat on a wooden captain's chair. "Mrs. Little, I'm curious about there being a two-way mirror in the men's room."

She blushed. "Oh, that. Well, thank goodness we haven't had any complaints in years about the safety of our children in the public facilities. Several little boys had been . . . " Mrs. Little's blush deepened. "But of course if you think it's necessary to reopen . . . .

"

"No, that's not it," he quickly cut in. "We found an old photograph taken from behind the mirror, and it wasn't dated. I'm trying to pinpoint when it was . . . .

"

"It'd have to have been before nineteen seventy-five. That was when my predecessor had it sealed."

"Nineteen seventy-five," he murmured. "Thank you."

"Any time, Sergeant."

* * *

"Gumpa! Gumpa!" The two-year-old twins piped as they splashed Billy Boyd while he sat in the shallow, specially designed toddler section of his pool.

Colorful beach balls, rafts, an inflated alligator, and a Donald Duck head on a minutiae surrounded them as Billy kept them within arm's reach.

"Don't hurt your grandpa," his daughter-in-law, Tristin, said from her lounge chair.

Billy loved playing with his grandchildren, but this day his mind wandered, thinking about the desirable Officer Mazurski. She was too young for a serious relationship with him—but what the hell, he'd sure like to get the girl in bed. Also, maybe he could develop her into an inside track into police department information.

Billy wanted to see her again but decided the next move was hers.

"Up you go," he said, lifting one of the plump twins into the air, then back into the water, while the other giggling toddler grabbed at his arm and shrieked, "Me, too!"

Missy, his housekeeper, called to him. "Billy, the policewoman is here. She wants to talk to you."

*

Dawn was feeling a little better. However, still guilt-ridden, that horrible night she had fled Billy's house after a security guard had found Gorgy with a shotgun-shattered leg . The violence next door in the darkened mansion hadn't helped matters. She believed none of it would have happened if she hadn't been in the kitchen, kissing Billy.

*

As Dawn walked through the doorway, Billy started to get up, but his heel slipped on the bottom of the pool, and he fell back. Both grandchildren jumped on him, screaming "Gumpa! Gumpa!"

Billy sat up, trying to wipe the water from his eyes, and wrestled with the toddlers. Taking one in each arm, he stood in the shin- deep water and looked up. It was the first time he saw Dawn smile.

"These are my grandbabies," he said proudly, then went on to introduce their mother to Dawn.

After the two women acknowledged each other, Tristin said brightly, "Nap time for you two little sausages. If you'll excuse us?"

"Of course," Dawn said.

The room became very quiet when Billy and Dawn were alone. "What beautiful children," she said.

"They are the loves of my life," he replied, searching her face for some indication of her purpose. "I try to talk Tristin into coming by here more often." He put his terrycloth robe on. "I wish I had spent time with my own children when they were that age." He pulled out a wrought- iron chair from a patio set. "Coffee, tea, Miss Mazurski?" he said, trying to act a little formal.

"No, thank you," she said, sitting. "Nothing to drink."

Billy sat across the breakfast table from her. "I wanted to call you."

"'Why? you have some information for me?" she asked.

"No, I just wanted to talk." He had wanted to invite her out for dinner, but he could not admit that.

"I'd be happy to talk." She ended the sentence abruptly, and they sat in silence for a few moments.

Billy cleared his throat. "I don't know why you're here," he said lamely.

"The reason I came by is confidential." She seemed to speak with difficulty. "And the people I talk to tell me you can be trusted."

"Who?"

She smiled, and his world became bright. " I don't tell on people I talk to."

He chuckled, hoping for another smile from her. "You're all right."

She looked away for a moment. "First, I want you to know I'm very grateful to your employee for saving the sergeant's life."

Billy nodded acknowledgment.

"Needless to say, the files on Jackson, Watson, and, um, Lillie Boyd are closed. Second, I, um, need some help. I'm working on the David Merriman homicide—you know, the one that happened in your motel? You're familiar with it, aren't you?"

"Not really." He knew all about the case but didn't want to tell her. He'd use any excuse to prolong her stay.

Dawn explained the case to Billy, including her suspicion of Father Julius's involvement and having seen Tony Tattaglia at the apartment and at Cousin's Center.

"Why was Tony Tattaglia trashing the Tee apartment?" she concluded. "And why was he at the archdiocese?"

Billy whistled low. "Accusing a Catholic priest in this city of homicide is . . . ."

"And it's just a gut feeling. But cops know these things."

Billy saw the tension in her face and wanted to make it go away. Her pleading eyes melted him. "Okay, baby, relax. Let's work this thing out. Tell me more about this Tattaglia."

After Dawn had told Billy what little she knew, he walked her to the front door.

"Maybe you can do me a favor?" Billy said. "A twelve-year-old black boy. His father's dead. His mother came to me. He's been missing over a week and . . . ."

"Over a week?" Dawn stopped and faced Billy.

"At least. Name's Taylor. Forgot the first name."

"I'll get right on it."

* * *

While Jenny was typing reports in the bureau, Dawn went directly to the Youth Bureau. "Smitty, what about the missing Taylor boy?"

"For chrissake!" Smitty exploded. He stood up from the file- cluttered desk and ripped his cigar from his mouth. "What the fuck's with you dicks? Slat already called me about that kid."

"He's been missing over a week."

"So big fucking deal. Like you dicks ain't got homicides over a week old?" Smitty riffled through his files. "Here! If you're so interested, handle the fucking case yourself."

Dawn grabbed the file and left without another word.

Thirty minutes later, she marched into Lieutenant Lovemore's office.

He looked up, surprised. "What can I do for you, Detective?"

"I found out something about the missing Taylor boy."

"Who? How old?"

"Twelve."

"What's Slat got you doing with juveniles?"

"Slat doesn't know anything about this. The boy's mother went to Billy Boyd for help because your Youth Bureau hasn't done shit."

"Just a minute, young lady!"

"You just a minute! He's been missing for over a week. I talked to his mother and his pastor. He was very active at his church, and he headed his church's paper drive. He worked with Jack Hamlin, the Merriman boy, and that boy from St. George who was murdered." She stopped to catch her breath.

"Sit down," Lovemore said as he picked up his phone. "Slat, you get Smitty, and I want to see both of you in my office on the double."

41

THREE HOURS AFTER DAWN HAD GONE, Billy still sat at his poolside. His heart ached. He felt old, bereft, just as he had felt when he lost Lillie.

A call from Mountain Top, subdued his pain. "Boss, I can't find anything current on Tony Tattaglia. Credit bureaus have nothing. The computer came up with an Anthony Tattaglia from Chicago, who graduated from a high school called Quigley—boys who want to be priests go there. He studied to be a priest in Mundelein, Illinois, then dropped out and went to Loyola Law School in Chicago. He graduated, but he ain't listed with any law associations. On paper this guy disappeared about ten or so years ago. I'm checking further. I got some sources in Washington, DC. If he ain't from here, he might be from out of the country. And I got people at Cousin's Center watching him."

"Good, Top. Keep on it."

"Hey, Boss, I know it's your business, but the priest being a pervert... hey, man, I don't know. It don't involve us."

"Stay with it, Top."

Dawn wanted to be the one to solve the case and make the arrest. Billy wanted to help her—and eventually himself. He knew from their visit the other night that, like him, she wanted to beat the system. Dawn and he wanted the same things from different sides of the wall.

She would keep him posted about the police investigation. He'd keep her posted on Mountain Top's investigation.

* * *

When Dawn and Jenny arrived back at the smoke-filled Detective Bureau, the room was abuzz with activity. The day shift was there with the evening shift, the Narcotics Task Force, and the Burglary Task Force. Lieutenant Lovemore was standing with Slat in front of the glass cage.

Lovemore raised his deep voice above the noise. "Stan, close the door. I don't want any reporters walking in here."

"Lieutenant?" Dawn said. "I don't think it's fair for me to have to inhale all this smoke."

"All right," Lovemore responded. "Put the smokes out until later."

Dawn didn't pay attention to the grumbling from the men.

Lovemore, however, did respond. "Shut up!" he yelled, then he walked to the center of the room and looked around. "Some of you'll be assigned to grade schools for Stranger Danger talks. And I don't want any goddam lip. Days off are cancelled until further notice.

"We've had two homicides of young boys, and a third is missing. Parents are threatening to pull their kids out of school. The pressure is on, and I want you to feel it. I'm taking half from Narcotics, half from Burglary, and half out of the Detective Bureau and temporarily transferring you to the Youth Bureau until that kid is found."

After Lovemore left the room, the unit sergeants distributed the assignments. Meanwhile, Slat weaved his way to Jenny and Dawn and told them to wait in his office.

After Slat assigned some of the detectives to the Youth Bureau, he joined the women in the glass cage.

"You sending us to youth?" Jenny asked.

"No."

"You're going to get some bitching from the guys if we aren't sent to Youth," Jenny said.

"Forget it. Get out of here and show Father Julius's picture to Raymond Tee's neighbors and landlord." Slat wiped sweat from his forehead while they stood looking at him. "So go!"

The partners hurried from the room.

* * *

At Tee's apartment building, they found a couple at home on the first floor. The man and woman didn't recognize the photo of Father Julius because they'd never seen Mr. Tee during the day or up close.

No one else in the building was home, so the women drove to see the landlord in suburban Brown Deer. Jenny, impatient, tailgated cars. Dawn said nothing about it; she, too, was anxious.

They rang the doorbell at the landlord's home, but no one answered.

"We can't just leave," Jenny said after they walked around the house. "We have to find someone."

Dawn pointed behind Jenny. "There's a lady in that yard next door."

They walked over to the cyclone fence. An elderly woman in a large-brimmed straw hat came to meet them.

"Ma'am, we're police officers," Jenny said. "We're trying to locate Mr. Marshall."

"I hope it's nothing serious." The woman pulled off heavy gardening gloves. "They're good friends of ours. Such a wonderful couple."

"No, nothing serious," Jenny said. "We have to talk to him about a tenant in his building in Milwaukee."

"Well, you'll have to wait. They left yesterday for Hawaii. Their pastor needed someone to accompany him on the trip. Paid for by the church. They'll be back in a week."

"I see," Dawn said. "Which church?"

"The Catholic church down the street."

Jenny and Dawn exchanged quick glances. The same thought passed through both their minds—a Church conspiracy to take the Marshalls thousands of miles away.

* * *

In the chief's office, Alderman Archie Dunn shouted in anger. "How in God's name can the police department justify the number of police personnel it already has?"

The mayor and Dunn had called on Martin Turski at Dunn's request. Archie pointed at the chief, who had sunk into the padding of his chair. "Chief, your department requested my committee's approval to hire what you call....

" Archie looked at the paper in his hand, "–a victim-witness advocate. Which is the last thing this city needs. Naturally, my committee voted it down. Why the hell do you persist with bullshit like this?"

"Mr. Dunn," the haggard chief asked, "why the violent disapproval?"

Archie's face reddened. "Because you want additional manpower and money, but you're not properly using what you already have."

"What do you mean?" The chief's voice took on an edge, and his fists clenched. "My people are overworked, primarily because we're shorthanded."

Archie Dunn leaned back and smirked. "Yesterday, your two female officers were in Brown Deer, still working on a cleared case. The Merriman murder has been solved. Now let it go!"

The chief shook his head. "That's police business. We don't need your interference."

Dunn looked to the mayor. "And what do you have to say about this?"

"I'm going to confer with the city attorney," he replied, "to put a stop to this nonsense. Police overtime is much too high."

"You're setting poor standards of management, Turski," Archie added.

The chief looked with disgust at the politicians. "No matter what I say or do, it won't make any difference with you two. Your minds are made up and closed." He stood. "Please leave my office."

* * *

Cheri Duncan, waiting in the outer office for an interview with Chief Turski, heard every word. The chief's secretary had left her desk momentarily, so Cheri got up and moved closer to Turski's door and listened.

Suddenly, the door flew open, and the mayor and Alderman Dunn charged past her. They did not look happy.

Earlier that day, at the newspaper office, she'd mentioned the annual awards dinner to the religion editor. He called St. Michael's and learned that Father Julius was on an extended vacation, but no one knew for exactly how long. The editor had asked when he was expected to resume Church responsibilities. According to the date St. Michael's secretary had told him, it was possible that Father Julius might still be out of town on the evening of the awards dinner. If Dawn and Jenny were still investigating the Merriman murder and if they had lied about the reason for needing a photo of Father Julius, then something very strange was going on.

Cheri decided not to interview the chief. Instead she returned to her office, called the police station, and asked for the officer in charge of special community events. "Lieutenant," she said after introducing herself, "I'll be covering the awards event. Is there any information you'd like to tell me in advance?"

"Not much to tell. I'll have a complete list together of recipients for you by tomorrow."

"I heard a rumor that Father Julius will be recognized for outstanding volunteerism."

"Don't print that. I don't have any clerics on the list."

After completing that conversation, Cheri knew something strange was happening. Her heart started beating fast. If she could uncover an irregularity and follow it through, her scoop could be her ticket out of Pulaski. After deciding to read the entire Merriman case, she drove back to the police station.

* * *

"The supervisor approved your getting the Merriman report because the case is closed," a woman in a wheelchair told Cheri, "but if you want the entire report copied, I can't have it ready until tomorrow."

"May I read it here?"

"Sure." The clerk wheeled around to retrieve the file. On the back strap of her chair was a sign that read: Don't Make Your Lack of Planning My Emergency.

Cheri spent an hour reading the report. Finally she found the loose end she was trained to look for. Jack Hamlin had implied there was another person. Dawn and Jenny were still working on the case after they trumped up a phony story to get a photo of Father Julius. There was, Cheri knew, a story there.

Why hadn't they gotten a photo from the rectory? she wondered. Obviously, they didn't want the church to know they were on the priest's trail.

* * *

Tony sat in Father Daley's study poring through files on Father Julius's background. So far the records offered no clue as to the clergyman's whereabouts.

Father Julius's credentials were exemplary. His civic involvements had earned him many awards and letters of commendation. He played golf with parishioners at least twice a week at the city golf course in Centennial

Park. He jogged in Centennial Park at least once a day. He had competed in marathons.

Tony read the file again. Father Julius's crowded schedule gave little time for him to assume another identity. Could the police and the archdiocese be wrong? Tony wondered. Maybe Father Julius was too active, too involved in his work. Maybe the stress had gotten to him, and he'd slipped over the edge.

Frustrated, Tony shoved the pile of papers on the giant desk as far as his arm could reach. He stood and stretched, arching his back, then walked to the window and stared out at the Center's property. Young high school students in gray sweatpants and T-shirts were jogging across the grounds. Tony envied their exercising in the sunshine. He missed the activities he'd built into his daily schedule at the Vatican like swimming in the indoor pool. But he had no access to a pool here in Pulaski.

The archbishop's personal secretary had taken a call from Monsignor Popodowski at the Vatican an hour before. He left a message that his agent, Tattaglia, was needed for another assignment and to make every effort to wrap up the present mission immediately. The delay caused by Father Julius's disappearance and Tony's inability to locate the man would probably prompt Monsignor Popodowski to seek his termination. Tony threw his pencil across the room.

He sighed, then forced himself back to the desk and Father Julius's files. Again he looked for habits, patterns, and routines that the priest might not change, no matter where he was hiding. Tony suddenly got an idea: jogging—Julius jogged every day. Runners rarely gave up running, and, unlike swimming, it was a sport that could be enjoyed anywhere.

What about this Centennial Park? Tony thought. Before he had a chance to ring for Father Daley, that man burst into the study.

"Tony! The archbishop is extremely upset. He just got a call from Archie Dunn. The police are conducting a massive search for another twelve-year-old boy who's missing."

"Oh, no," Tony groaned. "Which parish?"

"He's not Catholic. The boy's colored. Attends public school. From a Baptist church, thank God. I mean this could be unrelated to Julius and our problems. But the boy was active in the same paper-drive program that our schools took part in. Totally unrelated, I'm sure. Regardless, the archbishop wants more help."

"More help?" Tony asked.

"Yes, he wants me to contact the Vatican embassy for . . . .
"

"Patty," Tony interrupted, visualizing Monsignor Popodowski's ranting and raving if he heard of this request. "It'll take too long to get help that way. I'll just hire more local people."

"Do whatever you think best. But you'd better find Julius fast!" Father Daley turned on his heels and, robes flying, slammed the study door as he left.

The door reopened immediately, however, and the archbishop's secretary walked in. "Mr. Tattaglia, a reporter from the Pulaski Press has been trying to reach the archbishop. The archbishop said to refer the call to you." He held out a note.

"Thank you." Tony took the slip of paper, then went into his temporary office next to the study and returned the call. "Miss Duncan, I'm Tony Tattaglia, public-information secretary for the archdiocese. May I help you?"

"Yes, thank you. I want to do a feature story on Father Julius but I'm unable to locate him. His parish says he's on vacation, but no one seems to know if he's in town or not."

"Let me check our files." Tony's grin switched to a frown as he pressed the hold button. "Son of a bitch!" he said aloud. "Now the press. They must suspect something. Think, Tattaglia, think!"

But it was difficult to organize his thoughts into some cogent action. The archbishop was demanding more help, the monsignor was impatient, Sergeant Sczlatski was applying pressure, and now inquiries were coming room the press. He counted ten deep breaths, then pressed the hold button again. "St. Michael's . . . let me see. Oh, yes. Father Julius is on a short retreat in Winona, Minnesota, then he was going to visit friends in St. Paul."

"Ah," the woman said. "Well, there's no deadline on this piece. I'll just wait for him to come back. "

"He's expected soon," Tony lied. "Is there anything we here at the archdiocese can help you with?"

"No, thank you."

"If he calls in, I'll let him know that you'd like to talk to him."

He hung up the phone then walked to the window. "God, I need some luck. Sczlatski needs facts, but the press only needs a rumor."

42

CHERI DUNCAN SLOWLY WALKED UP THE STEPS into the police station, not sure what to do next. The news editor had kept her busy with one mundane city meeting after another. The only interesting part of her assignments was reading police reports.

She couldn't understand why the detectives might waste time on a solved case, especially when politicians objected to it. And why would a couple of politicians be concerned about two detectives following up any case in Milwaukee? After reading endless police reports, she knew that detectives had to follow-up on many cases in the city of Milwaukee.

After entering the Detective Bureau, she asked Stan Osinski if he had anything new on the murdered boy from St. George.

"Nothing," the older, white-haired detective said.

"I'd like to meet the sergeant sitting back there in the office."

"Sarge!" Stan bellowed, and Cheri winced.

Slat looked up as Stan pointed toward her. She watched as he stood and beckoned her to his office. The invitation was reluctant, but she noticed his blue eyes sweep her body and make a quick and positive appraisal. She smiled.

"I'm sorry, Miss Duncan. I haven't meant to put you off." He held a chair for her. "I've been busy, at least lately. . . .
"

"Sergeant, please," she interrupted. "I'm beginning to understand. You don't have to make excuses. Please—call me Cheri, and I'll call you Slat, like everybody else does."

"Fine. But it's not just my being busy. I give my detectives plenty of leash." He paused. "They can all talk to the press. If it's about the boy. . . .
"

"It's not, and I don't think any of your staff can help me with the Father Julius investigation." She knew by the look in his eyes, she had captured his full attention.

"What makes you think there's an investigation of Father Julius?" he asked.

He seemed to be stalling when he tapped a cigarette out of his pack, lit it, and took a long drag.

"Cheri, there's really nothing to talk about, and I really am busy, with so many things going down right now."

Changing your tune, eh, Slat? she thought. "I guess I could pursue this some other way." She stood.

"Wait a minute."

She sat down and fought back a smile.

"We'll get together—another time."

"We can get together anytime you want." As she crossed her legs, Slat's eyes glanced down. "Like you, I'm on duty twenty-four hours a day. You just tell me when and where."

"How about tomorrow?"

"How about tonight? Tomorrow may be too late."

"Okay. Five o'clock back here. The next shift will be in then, and I'll have time."

"Good. See you." She smiled as she stood turning slowly, so he could admire the sleek lines of her body before she left his office. At the far end of the bureau, before going out the door, she flipped her thick chestnut hair back over her shoulder and gave him one last smile.

* * *

Despite the woman's nonstop legs and come-hither voice, Slat forgot about her. He finished telling his relief sergeant about the day's activities and was looking forward to going home for a hot shower and a cold beer. Although days off had been canceled because of the missing boy, the shifts changed every eight hours, and some detectives continued to work overtime.

At shift change, the relief sergeant glanced up and said, "I hope that piss rag reporter's here to see you and not me."

It was then that he remembered. Slat walked to the counter and decided to stall for time. He wanted to give Jenny and Dawn a few more hours to find Julius. "You know, Cheri, I'm bushed. I've got to go home and take a shower. Could we put this off until tomorrow morning?"

The woman laughed. "No way, Slat. You said five o'clock. Your place or mine?"

"What do you mean?"

"Do we go to your shower or mine?"

"My place—and my shower," he said, and felt his face flaming.

Once on the road, Slat followed her car to her apartment parking lot, where she left her maroon BMW and got into his beater.

"Is this your car or the city's?" Cheri asked as she adjusted the passenger seat.

"Mine."

"Good. I'd hate to think the city was that broke."

He laughed in spite of himself. "I have a hard time keeping a new car in shape."

After he pulled out of the lot, Cheri said, "The reason we're meeting, as I remember, is to discuss Father Julius—unless you've got something else in mind."

* * *

Slat had not planned to have company. The Milwaukee newspaper was strewn across the sofa, yesterday's socks were draped over the television, and the crusty cardboard tray from last night's microwave dinner sat on the floor, next to a can of iced tea. The draperies were closed, and the place smelled a little musty.

Cheri looked around in disbelief. "Totally macho, a little rustic," she said kindly. "The furniture belongs in a mountain cabin somewhere."

"Bingo," he told her. "After my divorce, the only furniture that was left for me was from our summer cabin."

"You sure have a clean place—relatively speaking—for a single man."

"I've got a housekeeper who's the best." Slat went into the bedroom to change. He kept the door slightly ajar, so they could continue the conversation.

"No permanent guest?" she asked.

"No. My rule is, I don't keep my clothes in your closet, and you don't keep yours in mine."

"I read that somewhere."

"Me, too. I'm not much of a host, so help yourself to a beer."

"Thanks, but I'll wait."

"For what?"

"Dinner. I know you'll try to put me off, but I'm going to hang in here until the bitter end."

"Excuse me. I have to take a shower."

"Don't let me stop you."

Her voice sounded close—too close. He glanced up to find her leaning on the bedroom door jamb. He was in his briefs, and she was smiling at him.

"You're going to have a problem with that bandaged hand, Sergeant. I can wash any parts you can't reach."

"I can manage." He escaped into the bathroom.

After getting the shower water adjusted to a comfortable temperature, he looked out of the shower and, feeling somewhat foolish, eyed the lock button on the bathroom door. *No, she wouldn't dare,* he thought. *I'll hurry, and we'll get out of here.*

After doing a turn under the spray head, he heard the shower door slide open. He wiped the water from his eyes and saw her leaning her forehead against the edge of the glass door. She wasn't smiling, and her eyes held a most appealing look.

Oh, Christ, he thought as his gaze slowly absorbed the beauty of her young, nude body.

He watched his hand move forward, uncontrolled, toward the protruding nipple. *No, not a reporter,* he told himself. *What am I getting into? She's too young. I'll owe her big time.* He watched his fingers trace the outline of her firm, round breast. His breath was shallow and fast, and he stepped closer as if moving through a dream. His fingers traced up the gentle curve of her neck and over her chin to her mouth, where they stopped.

Beads of water bounced off his shoulders and through the air, onto her face and hair.

His fingers traced her lips, then trailed across her cheek and over her ear to the back of her head, where he grabbed her by the hair. Slowly, he guided her under the curtain of water.

* * *

The Tower House Restaurant boasted plush, maroon draperies, Oriental rugs, and an unbeatable collection of Tony Bennett and Englebert Humperdink compact discs. The Rotary Club met there for lunch on Tuesdays, and the Kiwanis Club booked the banquet room for breakfast meetings on Thursdays. It was also where seventeen-year-olds from middle-class families dined with their dates on prom night. By widespread acknowledgment, it was the nicest place in downtown Pulaski.

Cheri ordered a Manhattan, and Slat had a beer.

"I don't have a housekeeper," she said, "but after dinner, when I go home to shower, maybe you'd like to come along and see how clean *my* apartment is."

"Thanks, but....

" Slat watched her over the brim of his beer glass.

"You don't know what you'll be missing," she teased, then looked deep into his eyes until he glanced away. "Then I'll change the subject, since the sergeant is getting embarrassed. Let's discuss the missing Father Julius and the investigation of Raymond Tee by Herschel and Mazurski. And perhaps you can enlighten me as to why the mayor and aldermen are getting on Turski's ass about it."

Slat was flabbergasted. He had underestimated this young woman. He reached inside his blazer pocket for his cigarettes. "I don't know....

"

"Don't give me the runaround," she interrupted. Her eyes became hard. "I already have enough to write a why-this, why-that story." Then her voice softened. "Slat, please trust me. We can work this out by cooperating. I'll respect anything off-the-record."

He signaled the waiter for another round of drinks. What choice had she given him? He feel tightness in his stomach—too much pressure over these cases. The press created another dimension, one he didn't need. He'd have to trust her, at least with what she already knew. "Off the record?"

"Yes. But it's got to be exclusive—no other reporter."

"Okay." He explained that they needed to talk to Father Julius because he may have been one of the last persons to see the boy from St. George alive. He didn't mention the paper-drive link with the missing boy because she hadn't. Maybe she was holding that back.

"Remember, we just want to talk to Father Julius about the boy and who else he may have seen in the park that morning. Develop more witnesses." He left it at that and asked how long she'd been living in Pulaski.

"You forgot about Raymond Tee."

He'd hoped she'd forgotten about Tee. "Where'd you hear about him?"

"I overheard some politicians arguing with the chief about Dawn and Jenny looking for him. It connects, Slat, especially since it's tied into the Merriman case and Hamlin's statement. It sure sounds as if another person was involved. Strange case."

Christ, he thought, *she knows more than I do.* Slat hadn't known about the chief's being confronted by politicians. His stomachache became intense. "Who were the politicians?"

"The mayor. The other was the tall, redheaded guy."

"Archie Dunn." *Stall, Slat!* he told himself. "We don't know if there's any connection. Tee is wanted for questioning because his car was seen in the motel parking lot about the time of the first murder." He hoped that would satisfy her.

"Tee was seen at the motel, but the case is closed."

"We want to be sure Hamlin was alone. You know, no loose ends."

She narrowed her eyes at him. "You're hedging, Slat."

He held out his palms. "That's it. You'll have to trust me, like I'm trusting you."

"Why lie about the photos of Father Julius?"

Slat wished Dawn hadn't told Cheri that story. "We need photos to help find him. We didn't want to alert the press or anyone else, not even the Church. We don't want people to jump to conclusions. Now, you understand that everything I told you is off the record?" He looked around for the waiter. Her glass was empty.

"Of course, Sergeant," she assured him. "You didn't see me take any notes, did you? Now to my apartment."

"Cheri, I'll drop you at home. That was a lot of fun tonight, but you should avoid old men."

* * *

My mission success rate is about ninety-five percent, Tony Tattaglia reminded himself while driving from Cousin's Center to Pulaski. He had never solved any of the problems in Northern Ireland, but he hadn't been sent there to stop that war. The Vatican wanted to direct the Irish Republican Army toward nonviolence and away from Marxism. The world would never know how often intervention from the Vatican dissuaded the IRA from taking lives. So, he decided, he could take credit for Vatican successes in Northern Ireland.

Tony, like other Vatican agents, was given assignments of international importance and, depending upon schedules, minor missions, also. Delivering Father Julius to Rome should have been completed in a day. Whether

Father Julius was Raymond Tee, and whether Raymond Tee was a murderer, wasn't at issue. Tony wasn't sent to solve a murder; he was sent to escort Father Julius to Italy.

"Damn it! I've got to find you, Julius!" Tony interrupted his thoughts as he pulled into the parish parking lot, next to Father Julius's car.

A nun let Tony in the rear kitchen entrance, then led him to Father Julius's suite, which included a large bedroom with a corner balcony overlooking the parish flower garden and a spacious upstairs study with oak walls and oak bookshelves on two walls. The other two walls were covered with photos, plaques, and trophies.

Tony scanned the shelves. He saw volumes on theology, world religions, adolescent psychology, deviant behavior, and marriage counseling. There was a collection of Father Andrew Greeley's novels and Jim Fixx's two books on running.

John Julius's diplomas—a doctorate in theology and a master's degree in behavioral science—were proudly displayed near Man of the Year awards from civic organizations. Trophies for golf and running were scattered throughout the study.

As the nun watched quietly, Tony sifted through Father Julius's orderly desk drawers and found the usual pens, clips, rubber bands, Post- its, and papers.

The bureau drawers and the closet revealed nothing about any habits or preferences that might deviate from the norm. Nor was there anything hinting to his whereabouts.

Tony decided to leave. "Thank you, Sister. I'll let myself out." As Tony opened the front door, a United Parcel deliveryman in a brown uniform was reaching for the doorbell.

"Package for Father Julius," the fellow said.

"Thank you." Tony took the small package back upstairs. The return label read Samuels Sports Store. He opened the package and found a royal blue, red, and black Gor-tex running outfit. He set the garments on the bed and again looked into the closet. He counted four running suits.

As Tony prepared to leave, he noticed two unlabeled videotape cassettes on one of the bookshelves. Because they had been standing up like books and between volumes, Tony had not noticed them earlier. Using Father Julius's VCR and television, he played the beginning of both tapes. They were recordings of Father Julius before two different civic groups. He left with the cassettes . . . and a plan to delay Sczlatski and the press.

43

"SLAT,"STAN OSINSKI CALLED as the sergeant entered the Detective Bureau. "You've a message to call Father Julius at a Holiday Inn in St. Paul."

At his desk, Slat dialed the number. "Extension one-twenty-one, please," he requested.

A few seconds later, he heard the priest's voice.

"Father Julius, this is Slat. I'm sorry to bother you, but we've had some serious problems. A boy from St. George has been murdered."

"Slat, I'm so sorry. I heard about it from Archbishop Coughlin. How can I help? I knew that boy from St. George. He was involved in interchurch activities. I saw him for a few moments in the park on the day he was murdered."

"Was he alone?"

"Yes. I feel so awful for the families."

"Father, are you familiar with a boy from Calvary Baptist, Kenneth Taylor? He was active in the citywide paper drive."

"No, the name doesn't sound familiar."

"A black boy. He's missing."

"Sorry. I can't place him."

"When will you be back?"

"Day after tomorrow. As soon as I get settled, I'll be in to see you."

"Thank you, Father. I'd appreciate that."

Slat sat back in his chair and thought about the conversation. The priest had readily admitted seeing the boy. *Maybe we're all wrong about Father Julius,* Slat thought. *I sure hope we are.*

* * *

Tony impatiently waited in Father Daley's study for the call from St. Paul. The actor Tony had brought up from Chicago had watched the videotapes of Father Julius and within a few minutes was able to imitate the priest's voice.

Tony put the fellow on a plane to St. Paul, where he took a taxi to a Holiday Inn and placed long-distance phone calls to Pulaski—to Slat and then to Cheri Duncan. The ruse was brilliant, Tony thought. It bought him the time he needed. Now, with both the press and the police believing the priest to be in Minnesota, Tony felt confident he could beat Sczlatski and that reporter to Julius.

The phone rang and the actor reported a successful completion of his assignment. Now Tony went to Samuels Sports Shop, where Father Julius had bought his last running suit.

The window display had a male and female mannequin in jogging outfits. On display inside the store were athletic shoes, socks, wrist and ankle weights, and running and tennis outfits.

"You look like a runner, young man, so I bet you know what you want," said a casually dressed middle-aged man.

Tony laughed. "Guilty as charged. I'm Father Tattaglia, and I'm in town for a few days. Going to stay at St. Michael's."

"Welcome to Pulaski. I'm Elliot Samuels. Call me Sam."

"I forgot my running outfit and shoes, Sam. Can you get me outfitted?"

"Sure." He looked Tony over. "Large, tall?"

"Yep. So where do people run around here?"

"Centennial Park, mostly, on the bike paths, which wind around the golf course, through the woods, and along the creek. Very peaceful and away from the traffic fumes."

"I'd like to try that." Tony picked out a nylon running suit from the rack, then tried on a pair of size twelve Nikes.

"Ask Father Julius to show you around the park. He runs every day in Centennial."

"I don't know if I'll meet him. I heard he's planned a trip out of town."

"Well, he's in town now," Sam said, tallying the order on a calculator. "He called me a short time ago and thanked me for a suit I sent to him."

"Today?" Tony was afraid he sounded too surprised. "These shoes are perfect."

"Glad you're pleased. Want a sweatband?"

"Nah." Tony paid for his purchases. On the way out the door, he casually asked, "So what time do you guys run in the morning?"

"Six sharp. I don't know where Father Julius starts, because I come from home. I suppose he starts from the rectory."

"Great. And what about the evenings?"

"Occasionally I see him around eight. Neither of us is too regular in the evenings."

"Thanks." Tony let the front door he'd been holding slip from his hands.

He went back to St. Michael's rectory and found Father Julius's room the same, except the running suit that had come earlier was now hanging in the closet. The nun who had let Tony in claimed not to have seen Father Julius today. But the agent knew that the priest had been there.

Tony called the private detective agency and was upset to learn that it had arranged for only one surveillance unit, watching the front door of the rectory. He told them to double up surveillance.

* * *

Dawn wanted to move forward with Billy Boyd, but she didn't have the time. She was proud that her commitment to her job overpowered her personal life. She had always wanted a man and envied the women who had one. But now, even while being so intrigued with Billy, she knew what she must do: concentrate on her job.

She knew that her decision was a good one. She felt confident that he would wait for her. His interest in her would never cool, just as her desire for him was burning as hot as before. From the moment of their first kiss, she felt settled with him, as if this was the man she'd been waiting for all these years.

Every day after work, Dawn drove through the neighborhood and alleys around St. Michael's and looked for Father Julius. She always made certain that his car was behind the rectory. Then she'd cruise the environs of Calvary Baptist and searched for the missing Taylor boy. She checked inside garages and stood on tiptoes to shine her flashlight into dumpsters, looking for a corpse she hoped she would not find.

Earlier that day, Slat had told her about Julius's phone call from St. Paul. She didn't believe the priest was there. She wouldn't trust a murder suspect or Tony Tattaglia. So, not altering her established routine, she drove for what seemed like the hundredth time behind the rectory and parked in the stall next to Father Julius's car. It was in the same spot, and she could see the penny she placed in the right rear tire tread. As she started to execute her turn to back out, she stopped abruptly. Something was different.

She got out of her squad and looked through Julius's car windows. An empty plastic clothesbag lay on the back seat. This morning a running suit had been in the bag hanging on the hook by the left rear passenger door.

Dawn tried all the doors. They were locked. Somebody with keys had taken the running suit. It had to be Julius, and if he had taken his suit, then he was going for a run.

Dawn knocked on the kitchen door. The nun told her that Father Julius had not returned.

Dawn had run in the park often, and on some occasions she'd seen Father Julius there. That's probably where she'd find him, she decided.

* * *

Chief Martin Turski didn't have to go to the mayor's office. He could say he was too busy. He could ignore the mayor's request until His Honor was forced to come to the police station. Martin always felt more secure in his own office than elsewhere, but he had respect for the mayor's status.

Before Archie Dunn built up a head of political steam, the mayor used to come by alone to see Martin, to praise the chief and his people for their good work. "Be sure to pass along my compliments," the mayor would say. Nowadays, Martin was summoned to the mayor's office, usually for criticism and threats.

It was easier to walk the two blocks to City Hall than to take the squad. As he strode down the street toward City Hall, Martin felt his anxiety begin to overwhelm him. He felt faint, and his stomach ached. He had always thought of himself as a tough man, in control and directing the actions of those around him. But now he wanted to turn and run. He felt weak and ineffectual, a midget among giants. He tried to stabilize himself as he walked into the mayor's office.

"The mayor will see you now, Chief," a foggy image in front of him said.

Martin hesitantly stepped into the spacious, trophy- adorned, political museum of an office.

"Sit down, Martin." The mayor walked behind him and closed the door.

Martin saw another image in front of the mayor's second- floor corner window. He blinked. Why was he having difficulty seeing?

"Please, Martin, have a seat," the mayor said again.

Whenever others remained standing, Martin didn't like to sit. The standing person usually had control in an adversarial situation.

"Please, Chief." The mayor indicated one of the overstuffed chairs.

Martin lowered his squat body into the chair. *I shouldn't sit,* he thought, beginning to panic. *That person by the window is standing. He may take advantage of me.*

Martin's eyes narrowed suspiciously as the mayor walked around his desk to his chair. *I should have brought one of my people with me,* he thought, frantic. *To protect me.*

As the person at the window began to turn, Martin squeezed his left elbow into his body, so he could feel the hardness of his weapon, his security. It wasn't there! he realized with a shock. Where was it? Then he remembered: he had left it in his office! Now he had nothing—no backup, no weapon.

Halfway into his turn, the silhouetted person at the window moved into a shaft of sunlight that highlighted his red hair. *Of course Dunn would be here, the chief thought.* He blinked again. Did he see two horns growing from the top of the alderman's head?

Archie Dunn walked from the window and sat in a corner chair, from which he could see the mayor and the chief. He folded his hands across his belt and nodded solemnly toward the mayor.

"Martin," the mayor began, "I wish you'd confided in me about any problems you're having." He leaned forward, heavy arms on his desk.

Martin exploded. "I tell you continually in the committees and by memo about the shortages and problems!"

"That's not what I mean, Martin," the mayor said meaningfully, then glanced at Archie for encouragement. "I mean your personal problems."

Martin's square frame sank deeper into the chair. He wished he could take the arms of the chair and wrap them around himself.

"We know you're seeing Dr. Pepperdine."

"That's my business!" Martin shouted.

"Yes! Yes!" the mayor agreed. "I understand, and of course we want to help. It's been obvious that recent events have been overwhelming you."

"Chief Turski," Archie said, "why didn't you come to me? To either of us? We'd help you if you'd let us."

Martin's anxiety disappeared, and in its place a cold calm enveloped his body. He felt utter hatred as he turned his eyes to Archie Dunn. He squinted until the horns vanished from the man's head.

"And exactly what would you have done, Dunn?" Martin carefully enunciated each word.

"We probably would have suggested a vacation. Maybe some administrative help from another department head."

"The fire chief," the mayor put in.

"Chief," Archie said, rising and walking toward Martin.

As the alderman approached, again, a cold wave of anxiety washed over Martin. He knew he should defend himself. Again his elbow pressed against his side.

"The mayor is calling for a special executive session of the City Council the day after tomorrow. At that time we'll discuss your health. We all must consider the safety and welfare of the city. A person in your position must be emotionally stable." Archie rubbed his hands together. "Well, I've said what I needed to say. Good day, gentlemen." He turned and left the room.

Martin felt relieved. The enemy had backed off, retreated. Martin had won.

44

MOUNTAIN TOP PICKED UP THE TINY CELLULAR PHONE in his massive right hand and called Billy while steering left-handed.

"Figured it out, boss. My sources say that Tony Tattaglia works out of the Vatican's legal department. The Vatican wouldn't have sent one of their lawyers here to find an unknown person like this Raymond Tee, so your cop friend must be right—they must want that priest."

"You'd better talk to Tattaglia," Billy said. "Tell him that maybe he should leave town. We'll find the priest."

"Yeah, Boss."

"Dawn's given me a photo of Father Julius. Hand out copies of it to all your people. Tell them to find the man and bring him to me."

Mountain Top had no idea where to find the priest. He didn't know much about priests or religion. His world had to do with private investigation. If the priest was involved with a wife in a divorce action, then Mountain Top would know what to do.

His starting point was Tony Tattaglia, who, at the moment, was at Cousin's Center. The big man positioned three of his units at Cousin's, ready to tail Tattaglia. They had already placed a tracking bug in the agent's rental car. Mountain Top would talk to the Vatican lawyer, but not in the Catholic domain. That province was strange, foreign to him. He wanted Tattaglia on his own turf—the street.

Five minutes after he talked to Billy, Mountain Top received a message on his radio. "Top, target southbound on Sheridan Road, entering Pulaski."

"Stay on him," Mountain Top responded.

The Surveillance Unit kept Mountain Top posted. "Turning into Centennial Park."

"Amen."

"Top," one of the men called on the radio, "he's parked in the center parking lot and is getting out of the car in a running suit."

"Let him run. It's too light to do anything now. He'll come back to his car. Intercept him then."

* * *

Cyclists and runners shared four hundred acres of park with ten miles of winding, crisscrossing paths. Tony started at a slow jog, and after a short distance he realized that a person could run all day in Centennial Park and never intersect the path of a particular runner. Instead of following the recommended arrows, he made right and left turns when the paths crossed.

After a half-hour, Tony slowed to a walk. He was not in the best of shape. He decided he could bump into Father Julius whether he ran or walked.

Tony must have passed a hundred people on this pleasant summer evening: men, women, boys, girls, senior citizens, blacks, whites, Latinos, and Orientals. They wore colorful running suits or T-shirts with sweat pants or leggings. The few bicyclists seemed frustrated by the legion of runners and walkers who slowed them down.

Whenever Tony arrived at a path crossing, he'd look both ways for a silver-haired runner. He walked along a path that twisted between high bushes, then up a slight grade for fifty feet, to where it turned and ran parallel to Sheridan Road for about two city blocks. He pivoted into the turn. A block ahead of him, he saw a silver-haired man wearing a black and white outfit. Tony started running again and soon noticed the man was pulling away. Tony increased his speed and gained on the man. Several times the fellow would vanish from sight around a corner.

That son of a bitch is in good shape, Tony thought, panting. After a mile, though, Tony had reduced the distance to about fifty feet. His late hours and too much bourbon with Patty Daley were taking their toll.

As he got closer, he was sure the man ahead was Father Julius. It had to be Father Julius. He wanted it to be Father Julius.

Tony was sucking wind. When he started running, passing runners had nodded. Women smiled, and he smiled back. Now, with only twenty feet separating him from his quarry, Tony didn't have the energy to smile. He wiped the sweat from his forehead before it flowed into his eyes. He regretted not buying a sweatband.

Fifteen feet . . . He wiped his stinging eyes again and prayed that he'd get a second wind.

Then he saw her. She was wearing a pink and blue running outfit. Her ponytail flowed out behind her. Dawn Mazurski. The golden- skinned detective was on the same path, running toward Father Julius and him.

Tony didn't want Dawn to recognize him. He didn't want her to connect his being in the park with the search for Father Julius. He slowed and watched her look at the silver-haired man, then pass him. Tony, finding himself at a crossing, quickly turned off that path. If Dawn didn't react to the silver-haired man, then it wasn't Father Julius.

Because Dawn was there, Tony had to assume that Sczlatski was counting on Father Julius's running in the park the next morning. He decided to go back to Cousin's Center, stretch out, and rest up for the exertion that would be required the next day. It was getting too dark to run now anyway.

He trudged down the path toward his car and passed through a small wooded area. A black man walked into the woods toward him, then stopped abruptly, threateningly.

Tony reached inside his jacket, then realized he had left his weapon in the car. Before he could do anything else, he was staring into the business end of a machine pistol. Two giants materialized from out of the darkness and grabbed him.

"What's going on?" Tony demanded, struggling.

"Shut your fucking mouth before I stick my foot in it," one of the assailants said.

The two Goliaths and the man with the machine pistol walked him about one hundred yards into the woods. Tony had thought that he was in a populous city park. The woods, however, may as well have been in northern Manitoba.

"What can I do for you gentlemen?" Tony asked without a quiver in his voice. Instead, his stomach quivered.

"Shut the fuck up, asshole," the man with the weapon growled.

They stood there silently. His captors held his forearms with viselike grips, and the third man kept the muzzle aimed at Tony's head. It was obvious they were waiting for somebody else to arrive.

A long minute later, Tony heard the crunching of dried leaves and twigs, and another man came into view, the largest Tony had ever seen.

"Tattaglia?" the monster thundered.

Tony kept his mouth shut. He'd test them. The hold on his arms tightened, and he winced in pain.

"Hey. Asshole. I don't want to hear my fucking echo."

"I'm Tattaglia. Who are you?" His trained voice hid his fear.

A fifth man, carrying an oversized camp chair, entered the area and set the chair down. The monster sat, lit a large cigar, blew some smoke in Tony's direction, then said, "I'm tired motherfucker, and I'm in a hurry. I don't like castoff dago priests. And I don't like people fucking over Pulaski priests."

"So what do you want with me?" Tony asked. He could no longer see any part of the chair.

"Asshole." The monster blew a smoke ring. "The fact that you work for the pope don't cut shit with me. I want to know why you want this priest."

Who are these people? Tony wondered. *How do they know who I work for? This guy wants information, but why?*

As Tony watched, the monster raised three fingers, and the men holding him released their grasp and walked off to the side. Suddenly the machine pistol spurted several rounds into the ground inches from Tony's toes.

Tony jumped. "Wait! Wait!"

What price were these thugs willing to extract to find out why he was after Father Julius? Who would be crazy enough to pay that price, just to protect a perverted priest?

"Hey! I value my life! What do you want to know?"

"Fuck your life, man!" the monster shouted. "Nobody would miss your fucking ass, 'cause nobody but that Catholic bishop knows who you really are, and he ain't going to tell. Now why do you want that priest?"

The two giants grabbed him and squeezed his arms, causing sharp bolts of pain to shoot down to his fingertips. Then his arms went numb. Tony flexed and curled his hands.

"I'm an investigator hired by a special-interest group to find the priest."

"What group? The Church?"

"Yes."

"You're a fucking liar. You work for the Vatican. What do you want this priest for?"

"He's having psychological problems."

"You mean he killed some kids?"

"We don't know that."

"Do you know where the priest is?"

"If I did, I'd take him to the archbishop. That's my job. Then I'd leave Pulaski. But I don't know where he is."

"What the fuck would the bishop do with him?"

Tony thought out his answer carefully. "Probably hear his confession before turning him over to the police. And the bishop would probably want assurances there would be no bad publicity for the Church."

"Man, you are full of shit," the monster said.

Again the Goliaths squeezed numbness into his stinging arms.

"I'm going to let your ass walk, motherfucker, but you got to know this is my turf. Get the fuck out of this city and this state. If you so much as shit in this city, I'll snuff your motherfucking asshole out."

The monster and his thugs vanished.

This is almost as bad as Lebanon, he thought. Sczlatski, the press, and now a monster, all wanting to get to Father Julius before him. "Julius!" he shouted up between the trees. "Where the fuck are you?"

45

"JENNY. PHONE!" SKI HOLLERED FROM THE BAR.

She had arrived early this evening, before any of her friends. Slat said that he wanted to talk to her privately, that he'd pick her up and they'd go for a ride. Jenny wore a new pair of jeans and a new, wide- necked purple pullover. It was a little special, just for Slat. She hoped he'd notice.

For two hours, her mind had been racing. Had she screwed up on the job? Was she being transferred? Did he want to talk to her about a new assignment? Did he want to discuss something personal?

She took the phone from Ski. "Herschel here."

"Jenny, this is Dawn. I got some information. Father Julius's jogging outfit is gone from his car, but the car's still locked and parked in the same spot. On a hunch, I just ran in the park. I didn't see Father Julius, but I saw that asshole from the archdiocese. He was running, too, and my guess is that the church can't find Julius but that he's in town and jogging. We'd better be in the park in the morning. Can you tell Slat for me?"

"Sure. Are you coming to Ski's tonight?"

"No. I've got some personal business to take care of. I'll see you at Centennial tomorrow. Main parking lot, just before sunup."

Jenny waited at the bar. As soon as Slat came through the door, she stood and met him. They left immediately.

On the ride, Jenny then told him about her conversation with Dawn.

"Father Julius couldn't have made it back from Minnesota already," he said, frowning. "Tattaglia must have pulled a fast one on us. I'll call some of the crew tonight and get them in early, and I'll get a few from patrol."

"Most of them'll be at Ski's tonight," Jenny said.

"Yeah." Slat smiled. "That always makes it easy for me to find them."

Slat drove to the north beach and parked in the lot. Jenny's heart pounded. *Why did he bring me here?* she wondered. She was afraid to look at him, afraid to speak. Nor did Slat say anything. She looked out the window and watched the few couples who walked out to the moonlit water. All were holding hands or had their arms slung around each other's waist.

"Come on," Slat said abruptly, and opened his car door.

They walked side-by-side in the sand toward the water's edge. "Nice sweater," he said.

"Thanks."

"New?"

"Yeah."

"I like it."

"Thanks."

They strolled without speaking. His bringing her to the beach meant they would have a personal talk, and Jenny felt buoyed and bubbly. A feeling of expectancy hung large and bright in the air. She forced herself not to fill the silence.

"How about some straight talk, kid?" he asked at last.

"I'm not a kid, Slat," she said quietly. She stopped and kicked off her shoes.

"No, you're not. I try to see you as a subordinate, a coworker." Slat looked toward her. "But it's tough, Jenny. I want to make love to you."

Jenny's breath caught.

"Sometimes I say to myself, tell Jenny how you feel. Make love to her. At other times I'm positive that it can't work out, and deep inside I'm afraid to love you. You know, I'm worried that I'll screw up our friendship and ruin our working together. I've seen it happen over and over."

They walked on, and the waves lapped over her feet. She felt confused. Had he brought her here to make her miserable? She looked away, hiding the buildup of hurt and tears. "Slat, why are you telling me this? If you don't think we can have something going outside work, why even bring it up?"

"I don't know."

"Why don't you know?" she asked bitterly. "You always seem to have the answers."

"Maybe I was hoping *you* could tell *me.*"

Jenny looked up at him in the moonlight. Suddenly he seemed so . . . mortal. She nearly laughed at the idea. "Slat, I have dreamed about our quitting the force and going off somewhere. But I know you'd regret quitting. I'd feel the same way. I love my job." She thought a moment. "And to tell you the truth, I don't think I would give up my work for you."

"Yeah," he whispered. "And you see, Jenny, one of the things I love about you is that you're as serious about the job as I am. I've learned that I can't care about anyone who doesn't understand what being a cop is like. I hate to bring up Theresa at a time like this, but she saw my work as a form of insanity. Well, maybe it is. I could never get serious about her because of that."

She stopped walking and turned toward him. Her face was wet. "What about love, Slat? Do you love me?"

"Jenny, I feel something, but I'm afraid to say love."

"I'm sorry I brought it up. That was silly of me." Again she felt unreasoning anger. She turned and began walking quickly up toward the parking lot.

He caught up with her. "I don't know what I feel. Maybe it's lust—although I don't think it's that simple. I don't just want to go to bed with you." He chuckled. "Although, to be honest, I've never felt such a strong attraction for anyone before. But I want to be with you all the time."

Jenny stopped and looked up into his eyes. "I. . . .
"

He grabbed her and pulled her into his arms. She yielded her mouth to his and, curling her fingers into the hair on the back of his head, reveled in the warm strength of his body.

Beep. Beep. Beep. Slat's pager sounded, and they both laughed.

"You see?" he asked, bending his lips to the curve of her throat. "No woman but a cop would laugh at that."

"Your fucking beeper will always be a part of your life," she said.

"Our lives," he corrected. "Until we're too old. Come on, let's go." He took her hand and led her back to the car.

* * *

"Billy? You out there?" His housekeeper called into to the pool area.

"Yes, Missy. Come on out."

"That police lady is here to see you."

"Thank you. Show her out here." He hurried to the wall light switch and turned on the pool's underwater lights. The soft aqua glow offered tender illumination.

He watched the doorway. Dawn's elegant silhouette glided across the family room, then into the doorway. He got up to meet her.

"I hope I'm not interrupting. . . .
" She hesitated, allowing her eyes to adjust.

"Not at all. In fact, I'm glad you're here. I was indulging in self-pity and needed to be distracted. Please." He held a chair for her. "Please sit down."

He looked into her glistening dark eyes. Her face was so soft, so young, so beautiful. He felt the urge to crush her tightly against his chest.

"I suspect that Father Julius is in the city, and that he'll be running in the park tomorrow morning," she began.

"I'll be there."

"So will the police. You don't have to come."

"I want to help. You helped me get some action on Kenny Taylor. Now I'll do what I can for you. I'll have some people in the park to make sure the priest doesn't get away."

"That would be great." She smiled, and Billy felt a great weight lift from him.

They sat for a few moments, reveling in each other's presence. Dawn shifted in her seat, and Billy saw uncertainty in her eyes. Afraid she was about to leave, he reached out and put his hand on her arm. "Don't go," he said. "How about a drink? You're not on duty."

She took a deep breath, then exhaled slowly. "I wasn't planning to go," she admitted. "And I didn't come here to tell you about Father Julius. The truth is. . . .
"

"Let it go, girl."

She raised her chin and spoke almost defiantly. "The truth is I wanted to see you again. I want to know what's happening with us."

Her look held a challenge. All softness and youth were gone from her face. Billy thought about this girl-woman sitting next to him. He was overwhelmingly attracted to her beauty and grace. He admired her tenacity and straightforwardness. But what else was there, rippling under the surface? Her anger was almost palpable. Was she angry with him, he wondered, for some imagined slight? *I'm too old to get involved with a neurotic woman. My life is complicated enough. I want a simple woman.*

Billy studied her. As the seconds passed, he watched her rebellious look change to fear. "Tell me about yourself," he said at last.

"What do you want to know?"

"Tell me why you are so angry."

She gasped. "What makes you say that?"

He shrugged benignly. "Your frown, your squinting eyes, your voice."

She dropped her gaze. "You're making fun of me."

"I'm not! The other day when you saw my grandbabies, your face, your eyes were bright and soft. And your smile was so happy! I say that's the real you, the Dawn you should be."

She looked up, and again her face held warmth and gentleness. "I certainly had a different image of the big, bad Billy Boyd before I saw him splashing in the pool with those two little dumplings."

They both laughed, and the tension melted away, to be replaced by a feeling of closeness.

"Tell me about the anger," he coaxed.

Her smile faded, and suddenly her eyes glittered with tears.

"Let it go, girl, let it go."

Suddenly Dawn burst into tears. Body-wracking, heart-rending sobs came from her soul as she lowered her face onto Billy's hands. Her tears wet his palms and flowed between his fingers.

"I hate. I hate everyday." She looked up at him, tears running down her face. "I hate Pulaski. I hate people like Archie Dunn and the heartless politicians who care about nothing but themselves. And I hate so many white people."

He pulled out a handkerchief and offered it to her. She took it gratefully and blew her nose.

"Nothing's fair," she whimpered. "I can't stop hating. And it hurts. It hurts inside my chest."

"That's okay."

"It's *not* okay." She kept sobbing. "But I don't know how to get rid of it. When I killed that white man in court, I felt nothing—no remorse, no guilt, nothing." She cried louder.

"That's okay, honey. You're okay." Over her shoulder he saw Missy standing in the door. She pointed at herself, then at Dawn. He shook his head no, then grabbed a towel off a chair and handed it to the young woman.

Her sobs diminished. After drying her face, she asked, "How do *you* do it? Don't *you* hate? You had to suffer what I suffered. You were beat up and called a nigger, weren't you?"

He nodded.

"And you were shut out."

"Yeah, baby." He took her hands again.

"How did you survive it?"

"Lots of ways. When I was a kid, I was in a street gang. We fought the Irish gang and the Polish gang. I got satisfaction by punching in white faces."

"That's what I'd like to do sometimes," Dawn admitted.

"After that, I stayed on the West Side. I made my money in gambling and real estate—all in the 'hood. I assisted black aldermen to get elected. I helped build recreation centers and playgrounds for black kids and donated money for other projects—all in the 'hood. I didn't tough it out in the white world, like you did. Guess I'm not as tough as you, girl."

She chuckled humorlessly. "Right. I'm real tough." She blew her nose again. "But the white people respect you."

"They respect my money and political influence," he corrected. "Otherwise I'm still a nigger. A man said, it's none of my business what they think about me, so fuck 'em. It don't bother me. Don't let it bother you."

"But you don't live in the neighborhood. You live in this wealthy white neighborhood."

"Baby, I get the same satisfaction out of living in their face as I did from punching them in the head when I was a kid. But mostly I'm showing my grandchildren that just because they're black doesn't mean they can't succeed in the white world."

She smiled at the mention of his grandchildren.

"Hey, that's better." He covered her hands with his. "Think of the beautiful people who don't care about color. Think of the Now, as your generation calls it. Let the pain go. Beat the bastards, baby, not because you hate them but because you want to be the best you can be, and that's better than anything they can offer. The hate hurts *you,* girl, not them."

She flipped her hands over his and squeezed them. "Thank you, Billy." She took a deep breath. "You made me feel better."

"Anything for you."

"I better go now."

He stood and pulled her chair back, though she was clear of it. It was an excuse to get close to her. She turned and came into his arms. Their eyes spoke as he slowly guided her nonresisting body to him and tasted the sweetness of her soft lips. Her body responded.

Missy cleared her throat from the doorway. "Billy. The phone. Mountain Top says he's got to talk."

"I have to go anyway," Dawn whispered.

"Please stay."

"I'm sorry." She blew her nose again. "I have to be up very early tomorrow."

* * *

The next morning, as the thin, predawn light filtered through the trees bordering the center parking lot at Centennial Park, Tony bent from the bench seat in the back of the van to tie his Nikes. He winced, his arms still sore from the attack on him the night before. Next he attached a small electronic receiver to his waistband, then fed the wire up to his ear. The device was set to a special frequency used by the investigating firm recommended to him by the archdiocese. Now he could hear the two dozen investigators, who were in the park in running gear and outfitted with two-way radios.

Tony knew he had to find Father Julius before Sczlatski and the press got to him. And before the black behemoth got to Tony himself. He still hadn't puzzled out the interest that monster had in the cleric.

He had attended to all details pertaining to his quest. At each of the six parking lots, he had stationed a tan, windowless van with a driver. Wherever Father Julius was brought out of the park, a vehicle would be ready to take him to the Vatican airplane. The pilot was prepared for takeoff, and Patty was already on board—he had to go to Rome for the deposition.

At six o'clock sharp, Tony started running on the morning dew.

* * *

After learning from Billy that the police were going to stake out the park in the morning, Mountain Top put ten men in gray sweatpants and hooded sweatshirts on the running trails. He also arranged to have one vehicle in all six parking lots.

Mountain Top and Billy parked in the center lot in Billy's Lincoln Continental. Mountain Top lit a cigar, and the men settled in against the leather upholstery for their vigil.

"Sometimes I can't figure you out, Boss. Wasting all this money on this priest. There's plenty of cops and private dicks hired by the Church. One of them'll get him." Mountain Top looked at Billy, but the man did not respond. He stared out through the windshield, where the first rays of sunlight shone on the tiny streamlets of condensation. "Known you for over thirty years, Boss," Mountain continued, "and believe me—it won't work. The woman's a cop."

Billy blinked. "I hear what you're saying. The cop. Dawn. Well, I can use her. You know, find out what's happening at the police station . . . ."

"She's still bad news, man."

"Anyway, I want her to know that I'm helping her. The other thing is Dicey Taylor's widow. The priest might know where her kid is. That's why we got to get to him first. We don't read him no rights. If he took Kenny, you know he'll tell us."

"Yeah, man. Now Joli Taylor is something for you."

"I know. I called her last night, after I talked to you. She came over for a few hours. I never noticed before what a fine-looking woman she is. I told her to meet us here."

* * *

At six o'clock, a half-dozen police officers in running suits began jogging down separate paths. The day before, Dawn had located a series of trails that crossed the width of the park in a figure-eight pattern. Because most joggers ran the length of the park, she figured her odds of seeing more runners would be better if she ran the figure eight.

She felt an extra surge of adrenaline and hardly noticed her legs moving. She smiled. All was right in her life. She was on her way to destroy a cornerstone of the city she hated. Father Julius represented not only Pulaski but the Catholic Church as well. She would have preferred bringing down Archie Dunn, but Father Julius would do for now. She also relished a wonderful new feeling, which must be love—love for Billy Boyd.

46

THROUGHOUT THE YEARS HE RAN TO CLEAR HIS MIND, to resolve problems, and to relieve mental anguish and sexual tension. While running, he was John Raymond Julius, not Father Julius, even here in Centennial Park. After about twenty minutes, the endorphins would kick in, and his breathing and legs would find a compatible rhythm. At that point, it was as if he were free of all worldly concerns and restrictions. Running gave him a peace and joy that prayer never offered.

Lately, though, no matter how often or how far he ran, his problem kept pace with him. He needed to unload his troubles, but he knew no one could help him. In fact, his parishioners and acquaintances would be shocked to learn that he was a human being just like they were, with faults and challenges. Even his family put him on a pedestal.

Oh, he'd tried to talk to his old friend Father Daley, but Patrick's counsel was always the same: prayer. The advice was delivered with a trace of condescension, which left Julius feeling discouraged and more than a little embarrassed. Evidently Father Daley had his ducks all in a row, he thought.

I've prayed so much. I want someone to help me, to hold me, to tell me they love me. I want someone to talk to.

He knew the power of prayer, but he wanted what his parishioners had: someone there in the same room, in the next room, just to look at, just to know they're there. *Should I leave the priesthood? Should I return to teaching? Should I find a relationship?* But that idea was as terrifying as it was tantalizing.

A few days before, because he had been so upset about the desires that threatened to overpower him, he began crying in his room. And every time he gained his composure, he started crying again. He couldn't leave his room; he couldn't answer his phone. His only solution was to sneak out the back door and run. He had extended his morning run northward, into Milwaukee, before he realized where he was; but he felt good, he kept running.

"I'm running away!" he shouted to an elderly lady pushing a grocery cart. "I'm running away! And it feels good."

He arrived at the Milwaukee County Fairgrounds in the western suburb of Wauwautosa. He felt exhilarated, but also so exhausted, he stayed at a motel near Blue Mound and Mayfair roads for several days. During that hiatus, he ran through the Milwaukee County Fairgrounds. On another day he ran to the veterans cemetery off National Avenue and prayed with and talked to some older veterans who were walking among the thousands of white crosses, paying last respects to their buddies who had been laid to rest. Because the men didn't know he was a priest, they talked openly about the war and the care they'd received at the VA hospital. They treated him like one of their own, and it felt good to him.

He knew he'd be missed and would have a lot of explaining to do after he got back to the rectory in Pulaski. Still, he took his time. He had to make a difficult decision about his future and deserved to work through his frustrations in his own way, at his own pace. He never rushed his parishioners through problem solving, and he promised to treat himself with at least the same respect.

The day before, in the late afternoon, he felt rejuvenated and settled in his mind. Ready to return to reality, he took a taxicab to the rear of the rectory. He retrieved the fresh running suit from his car, went up to his room, examined the new outfit from Samuels Sports Store, then decided to wear the suit he had hanging in the car. He changed, then left the rectory by the back door and decided to walk awhile instead of running. He walked by a youth sports complex, and stopped to watch a couple Little League games. Then, he went to a motel downtown, chose a movie from their cable box, and stayed the evening.

Now, this morning, he decided to jog his usual route in the park. While running, he would mentally formulate his letter to the archbishop. He hoped he wouldn't see anyone he knew; he didn't want his concentration distracted. If he did, he'd pretend he hadn't seen them and keep running.

* * *

It was still very early, but already there was a lot of activity in Centennial Park. Every thirty seconds a runner was either coming toward Tony or passing him at a path intersection. Whenever the agent jogged through a patch of woods, the low morning sun was blocked, and he was enveloped in darkness, hoping one of those monsters from last night would not jump out at him.

Tony jogged rather than ran. He wanted to conserve his energy for a burst of speed if needed. As he made his way through a thicket, he spotted Jenny about fifty feet ahead of him. *What is she doing here? he wondered, feeling a cold rush of panic.* He fervently hoped that she was exercising for her own enjoyment, on her own time, and that Sczlatski did not know what Tony himself suspected.

After she ran out of sight, Tony turned right and angled toward one of the parking areas. The path curved along the edge of a lot that contained about a dozen cars. As he passed the widely spaced vehicles, he glanced toward each one. The front seat of a sedan in a far corner was shadowed, because someone was sitting in it. At the other end of the lot was one of his vans. In the corner nearest his path he saw a late-model luxury car with two black men in the front seat and a woman in the back.

"Son of a bitch!" Tony fumed. "Sczlatski and that monster are here." Everyone knew what he knew: Father Julius would be running this morning. He prayed that the black behemoth hadn't noticed him.

Tony heard a panting voice in his earpiece. "Twenty-one to the leader." Leader meant Tony and all his personnel. "Subject fitting description—in a black and white nylon running suit—running north on the path. Along lake bluff—about the center of the park."

Tony knew he was parallel to that location, and if he ran fast across the park, he might be able to intercept Father Julius. He turned and sprinted east, past tennis courts and toward Lake Michigan.

The radio blared again. "Leader!" the person reported, excited. "A female runner passed me. She's carrying a police radio. Suspect has increased his speed—with the female in pursuit. They're— fast," the voice panted.

Tony knew it would be a disaster for the Church if Jenny or Dawn got to Julius first. Monsignor Popodowski would probably ship Tony to Siberia. He put on a burst of speed and topped a grade in the middle of a patch of high shrubbery. Ahead, the path ended in a T at the route that followed the top of the lake bluff. A flash ran from Tony's right to his left at the intersection of the asphalt paths as a runner pounded by in the blaze of the rising sun. . . . Then another flash as a second runner flew by in pursuit. Tony took off after them.

When his eyes adjusted to the white light, he saw the golden- skinned Dawn running behind a man with silver hair. It had to be Father Julius. Dawn had recognized him and brought a portable radio to her lips. Tony knew more police would be coming.

Suddenly, another runner pivoted off from an adjoining path. He was one of Tony's men.

* * *

Cheri Duncan had been in such a hurry, she hadn't even brushed her teeth. Instead she grabbed a pack of Dentyne with her camera on her way out the door.

She had never been particularly interested in listening to calls on the portable police radio scanner her news editor had given her. This past week, however, she'd paid attention to Dawn's and Jenny's whereabouts. This morning, when she'd gotten up to use the bathroom, she heard Jenny on the portable scanner signing off at Centennial Park. Cheri looked at her digital clock: It read 5:59. *But Jenny doesn't start work until 7:45,* she thought. Something was going on.

Cheri threw on clothes and sped to the park. Suddenly, she heard Dawn on the radio. "He's running toward the center parking lot."

* * *

As Tony watched, Father Julius turned off the trail and jogged into a meadow. He had given way to two black men running side-by-side down the path toward him. Dawn, Tony, and some others behind Tony followed the priest, and when Tony risked a quick glance over his shoulder, he saw that the two black runners had turned around and were entering the meadow.

Now two more joggers were approaching from Tony's left, from a path coming out of a patch of woods. He recognized them as his colleagues. Passing them, however, was Jenny.

The Vatican agent increased his speed, but he couldn't gain on Dawn or Father Julius. They ran into an opening between two stretches of woods and disappeared into the foliage. Tony's men on the left, and Jenny and two black men on the right, were at their heels. After ten yards, they ran in a cluster, with Father Julius in front, closely followed by Dawn. Tony was close enough to the others to hear their panting and grunting.

They burst into the sunlight beyond the edge of the trees. One of the smaller parking lots was about one hundred feet ahead of them. Tony suffered a sharp pain of anxiety in his chest as the group neared the van. *Christ,* he thought. *Don't tell me I'm going to have a heart attack now.*

He craned his neck to locate the vehicle. The driver, Dominick, was backing it up toward the edge of the parking lot. The vehicle's rear doors were wide open. Two cars suddenly sped into the area and screeched to a stop with smoking rubber. A man jumped out of the car to the right of Dominick's van, and two of Tony's agents jumped out of another car. Other men leaped out of a dark sedan that was already parked nearby. *Who the fuck are they?* he wondered.

Father Julius stumbled momentarily, and his head swung from side to side as a late-model BMW sped into the lot and squealed to a stop. All avenues were blocked. When a tall woman jumped out and began snapping photographs, Father Julius stopped dead, as if he finally realized that something was terribly wrong.

He began to run again, heading in the direction of the van, which was straight ahead, fifty feet from him, and backing onto the grass. All the runners behind Julius converged on it. Tony's agents ran up from the parking lot to throw body blocks at the other runners. Meanwhile, another of Tony's allies, who had been running with the pack, hurled himself in a rolling body block that toppled the two black runners.

Tony looked up. Success was only twenty feet ahead. He reached forward and, stretching his body to its full length, grabbed for Dawn's bouncing ponytail. Its ends tickled his fingertips; but when he made a fist, he came up empty. He reached again and, loosing an angry sound from deep in his throat, lunged forward and was successful. He yanked hard and pulled her to his right.

Dawn's head whipped back, and she screamed as she fell and rolled. Tony used the last reserve of his strength. He put his hands on Father Julius's shoulder blades and shoved the priest into the back of the van. The cleric crashed into the bumper and collapsed, his legs dangling outside.

"Go, Dom! Go!" Tony screamed as he catapulted himself into the back of the van beside his quarry and with one hand hauled a struggling Father Julius inside.

At that moment, Jenny clutched a handful of material from the priest's running suit and used it for leverage to jump onto the back of the van.

"Jenny!" Tony shouted. "You ever spend a summer at a camp near Iron Mountain, Michigan?"

"You asshole!" she snarled. "Why?"

"I've missed you." He tried to loosen her grip from Father Julius's jogging suit. "You were my first—in the lake."

Distracted, she looked at Tony.

"Sorry, Jenny!" He pushed her in the face with his hand.

She toppled backwards out of the van as it accelerated across the lot and toward the exit.

* * *

"Catch that motherfucker!" Billy shouted.

Mountain Top stomped on his gas pedal. He didn't see another van racing diagonally across the lot until the collision jolted them.

"Motherfucker!" Mountain Top shouted, slowing to check his steering ability. Though the side of the Lincoln Continental was half- shredded, the car still worked.

* * *

As Cheri reloaded her camera, she watched Dawn grab Jenny, who was clutching the side of her face. Slat's squad pulled up, and he and Dawn helped Jenny into the back seat. When Dawn jumped into the front seat with the sergeant, Cheri slid in next to Jenny. She knew no one would take the time to make her get out.

"What'd you bring her for?" Slat shouted over the wail of his siren and tires as he raced around Mountain Top's careening Lincoln.

"They didn't!" Cheri yelled back. "I jumped in for the ride, Sergeant."

"As soon as I can I'm dropping you off!" Slat shouted, spinning the steering wheel back and forth. "Keep the van in sight!"

"Hurry!" Dawn shouted. "They're pulling out of the lot."

"We'll catch them!" Slat swerved to the left side of the road around two cars. "He's got to stop for red lights!"

"What do you call that?" Jenny asked. "He went straight through that light!"

"And what the hell are Mountain Top and Billy Boyd doing behind me?" Slat said, looking in his rearview mirror.

Cheri took note as Dawn stared past her, out the back window.

"Was it Julius for sure?" Slat shouted as he sounded his siren and nosed his way through a busy intersection. Slat had caught up to within a few feet from the rear of the van.

"For sure!" shouted Dawn.

Again Cheri watched Dawn turn to look apprehensively out the rear window.

"Use the radio!" Jenny cried out.

Dawn grabbed the mike. "Two-ten is in pursuit of a beige van, north on Interstate Ninety-four! Notify the Sheriff's department!"

"Ten-nine, you're coming in choppy," the radio dispatcher said.

"Damn radio." Dawn tried again. "It's not working, Slat."

"I think they're heading for Mitchell!" he said as he pressed the accelerator to the floor, pulled up along the left side of the van, and sped side by side along the interstate.

After a few minutes of racing between and around cars, they were back a few feet behind the van when it turned onto the Mitchell International Airport entrance ramp.

Slat followed. His loose bandage tangled in the steering wheel. He tried to shake it loose, and Cheri leaned forward to help, but she was making matters worse. She became frightened as the car swerved. Slat's right knee was shaking, and the steering wheel was wet with blood and sweat from his palms.

Dawn leaned toward him. "Hold the wheel still!" she ordered Cheri, then quickly, expertly, freed the bandage from his hand.

The van turned off the main ramp and onto a utility road, which led to private hangars. Slat raced behind the van—bumper to bumper. He knew that as long as he stayed close to the van, that when it stopped, it would be a simple task to take control of Tattaglia and Julius.

The weaving van turned and skidded sideways between two hangars, kicking up dry dirt. Slat skidded sideways facing the opposite direction from the van. He momentarily lost sight of the van because of the dust cloud. Dawn shouted, "Turn around! Turn around!"

Slat threw the squad in reverse. In the diminished vision caused by the dust, he collided with the speeding Lincoln behind him. Cheri and Jenny were flung back, then forward. Jenny banged her scraped face on the back of the front seat, and Cheri's camera fell to the floor, causing both women to cry out.

"What the fuck's Mountain Top doing here?" Slat shouted as he jumped out of the squad. "Get outta the way!" he shouted through the dust at Billy who had stepped out of the Lincoln.

"You smashed my car, Slat-ski!" Billy railed.

It was useless to pursue the van. They were too late. Its passengers were beginning to board the jet.

Dawn left the squad car and ran to Billy, who grabbed her and set her aside. "I'm sorry baby, it won't work."

A woman hurried from the back of the Lincoln. She cried out, "Where's my boy? Billy, where's Kenny?" Then she turned and ran into Billy's arms, sobbing.

He held her tightly and made soothing sounds into her hair.

Dawn stared at the couple until Jenny left the squad car, took Dawn by the arm, and led her back to their vehicle.

Cheri scooped up her camera and snapped pictures: Father Daley, wearing his Notre Dame sweater, reaching from inside the doorway of the jet to help Father Julius aboard. Before the jet door swung shut, Cheri snapped a picture of a tall, handsome, smiling man blowing a kiss to them.

"Back to the car!" Slat shouted.

As Slat reached his car door, Mountain Top pulled up alongside.

"Hey, Slat-ski, was that motherfucker blowing that kiss to you?"

"Fuck you," Slat snarled.

"There's got to be a phone somewhere." Slat sped back the way they had come. "We have to stop that plane."

A Milwaukee County Sheriff's squad with lights flashing and siren blaring approached them. Slat stopped and jumped out. "Can you call the tower?" he asked. "We've got to stop that plane! A fugitive's getting away!"

The deputy contacted the tower as Cheri snapped pictures. "Pulaski Police want that last plane returned. They say a fugitive is on board."

"Stand by."

They waited. Thirty seconds ticked by slowly. Slat's hands flexed with fury and frustration. "Unit fifty-three, tell Pulaski we can't stop that plane. And if Pulaski knows who that plane belongs to, they'll understand why."

The deputy shrugged. "I guess we can't stop it. Sorry, Sergeant. Say, whose plane is it?"

"The Pope's," Slat answered, crestfallen. "Thanks, guy."

"Yeah. Sure. The Pope." The deputy shook his head, laughed, then drove off.

"Sometimes you just can't win," Jenny said, disgusted.

Mountain Top started up the dented, dusty Lincoln, then backed it up and pulled away.

The officers stood in stunned silence and, shading their eyes, looked at the sky until the jet was a small speck. Then, wordlessly, in disgust, they trudged back to the squad.

"I'm taking you to the hospital," Slat told Jenny.

"And while we're there, someone can look at your hand," she said, "and at Dawn's neck. That son of a bitch jerked her head back pretty bad."

47

CHIEF MARTIN TURSKI WAS OBLIVIOUS to the activity on the street. In his office, he held the memo in his knobby hand as he slowly rotated in his swivel chair. Around and around he turned, gazing at the plaques on the walls of his office, the certificates from the Chicago Police Academy, and the diplomas for various academic degrees. *So much hard work, studying for those degrees,* he thought. He looked at all the books on his shelves. If he hadn't read them cover to cover, he'd used them for reference purposes time and again. He stared at the mementos given to him by his wife, children, and close friends.

Then he read the memo again:

```
MEMORANDUM
City of Pulaski

From: Mayor To: City Council, Chief Turski

Re: Chief Turski's Performance Review

At 7:00 tonight, we will convene a special session of the
city council to discuss the administration of the police
department.

All aldermen, the city attorney, and the police chief are
directed to attend.
```

He placed the memo on his desktop and smoothed it out. "Maybe I should frame this with my other accomplishments," he said aloud, then stood and walked to the window. "How could an ex-cop from Chicago be so naive? How could I think that Wisconsin's politicians would be Little Leaguers compared to Chicago's? Wolves are wolves, wherever they're from."

Then he rose and went to sit in one of the chairs facing his desk. He was surprised that he could still see himself sitting behind his desk. "You're supposed to be so smart, Martin! What are your options?"

The Chief waited patiently for an answer, but none was forthcoming. After a few seconds, he asked again, "What are the alternatives? You've always been able to analyze and solve problems." He took a deep breath. "What do we do next?" he demanded.

He stood, walked around his desk, sat in his chair, and stared at the chair he'd just vacated. Tears flowed down his cheeks as he softly admitted, "I don't know. I just don't know."

* * *

While driving from the airport, Slat muttered to himself.

"What?" Jenny asked.

"Ach! Nothing! I'm just aggravated as all hell," he said. "Diplomatic immunity." He glanced at her. "How's your eye?"

"It's okay. I'm going to have quite a shiner, though. If I ever see that son of a bitch Tattaglia again, I'll kick him so hard in the balls he'll choke on them."

"I don't believe this whole thing," Dawn stared misty eyed out the car window.

"The archbishop's office promised he'd call back later today," Slat said. "And that's one phone conversation I don't want to miss. Let's take a late lunch."

"I get car sick when I write in the back of a moving car," Cheri said.

"Oh, shit." Slat had forgotten about her.

"It's all on the record now, Slat," Cheri said. "What excitement! This may be my ticket out of town."

"Give me that fucking thing!" Dawn reached across the back seat and grabbed for Cheri's camera. "You shouldn't even have been with us. This is police business, you bitch."

Slat waved Dawn back. "Forget it. It'll work itself out."

Cheri poised her pen to the notepad and looked pointedly at Dawn. "And tell me, Officer Mazurski, what was the name of that nice- looking man riding in the Lincoln?" she asked sweetly. "I saw the way you started toward him and the way you were looking at him."

"Fuck off!" Dawn said.

"Headquarters to Sergeant Sczlatski. Call the station," the radio blared.

Forgetting, Slat picked up the malfunctioning radio transmitter, then, in disgust, tossed it onto the seat and pulled into a service station, where he placed a call. He returned to the car a couple of minutes later.

"The missing Taylor boy was found by the police in New Orleans. He had run away. He's okay."

* * *

The *Pulaski Press* was an afternoon paper with a news deadline of eleven A.M. Cheri Duncan had submitted her exclusive, along with the photos, at 10 A.M. She also submitted the outline of a special front-page feature for the Sunday edition. The weekend report would detail the events of the chase. She'd have statements from all of the participants by then.

"Cheri, the boss wants to see you," one of the secretaries called to her across the maze of desks.

She walked with swaying hips to Mr. Baker's office and smugly smiled to herself. *Now come the accolades,* she thought. The news article was well written, and she had scooped the *Milwaukee Journal.*

"Yes, Mr. Baker?"

"Sit down, Cheri." The editor leaned back in his leather chair. "Did you verify sources in this article?"

"I did better than that, sir. I was there. I witnessed the action myself. And I've got photographs."

"Cheri, I've known Father Julius for years. I see no frontal face shots of him." He fanned the photos toward her on his desk.

Cheri's smile faded as she scooped up the photos. "In these two he's running to the van."

Mr. Baker pointed to them. "In this photo you can't tell if he's running to the van or past it. I certainly can't recognize him; this other person blocks part of Father Julius's face. And I don't recognize him here, either, in this partial side view."

"Regardless, I saw him, and so did the others."

"Cheri, I took the liberty of calling the archbishop. He told me that a delegation, including Father Daley and Father Julius, left by jet for a retreat in Rome. After the conference, Father Julius will take up a new parish. Maybe we can do a little article about the religious conference in Rome and a retrospective on Father Julius's time in Pulaski."

Cheri detected condescension in his voice, and she became angry. "Mr. Baker. Father Julius did not leave willingly. The police . . . .
"

"I called the police. The officers in the photo say they were jogging. Your photographs depict nothing more than a bunch of runners in nylon suits. I saw no *uniformed* police officers, which could give some credence to your story."

"The photo of the accident?"

"There is a police report on that collision. I called the owner, and he said it was an accident. He knew nothing about any priest or chase."

"The photos at the airport?" she asked, her voice rising.

"Three men getting on a plane, and a man waving a kiss good- bye. That hardly . . . .
"

"They're liars!" Her career, her plans, the New York Times— all were crumbling. "What about Sergeant Sczlatski?"

"He said he and his people have no comment about any investigations."

"I interviewed Sergeant Sczlatski about Father Julius."

Finally Mr. Baker looked interested. "May I see your notes?"

"Well, no. It was off the record."

"Please, Miss Duncan. Take the rest of the day off. You are obviously a little distraught. I'm sure you meant well. Use this as a learning experience, and someday you'll become a fine reporter for the *Press.* If you'll excuse me now, I have a lunch appointment with some friends and, incidentally, a new priest assigned to St. Michael's parish."

Cheri felt like screaming and clawing his eyes out, but she managed to sit quietly while Mr. Baker walked out of the office and joined three men waiting for him in the newsroom. The redheaded man, whom she remembered as Archie Dunn, smiled and patted Baker on the back. She recognized the other man, Regis O'Brien, the manager of the Pulaski Credit Bureau. They were with a priest. He didn't look much older than she.

* * *

Dawn sat sideways at her desk and stared out the window. She tried to blink the wetness out of her eyes. Pulaski had won again. She felt bitterly disappointed.

It was four o'clock. The archbishop had not returned Slat's call. The sergeant had called Cousin's Center again and was informed that the archbishop would call back when he received word from Rome that Father Julius had arrived safely. Disgusted, Slat gave the archbishop's secretary the phone number at Ski's Inn and walked out the door.

What the hell, Dawn thought. *Instead of sitting here and feeling miserable, I might as well join Slat at Ski's.* She gestured to Jenny, who nodded in compliance.

"I explained a little to Slat about you and Billy," Jenny whispered. "He said we should all forget about it."

"Thanks," Dawn said. "I wish it could be that easy."

* * *

Ten minutes later, Ski was setting a pitcher of ginger ale in front of the detectives. Admiring Jenny's eye, the bartender told her she looked nice in purple.

"Ginger ale?" Dawn asked.

"Shouldn't have beer on our breath if we end up seeing the archbishop," Slat said.

"Bring me a beer," Dawn said to Ski. "I don't give a shit what the archbishop thinks." Her mind kept picturing that woman in Billy's arms. *Why?* she wondered. *Why did he push me away?*

Slat reached to the next table, grabbed a newspaper, and divvied it up among the three of them. Over the next hour, while trading and sharing parts of the newspaper, Slat would glance at Jenny and smile, and she'd smile back.

The time ticked by. Every time the phone rang, Slat looked up. The three went to Mama's, then came back to Ski's to wait some more. Finally the bartender held the receiver in Slat's direction.

The sergeant held his hand up for quiet and got it. Very few people were in the bar at this time of day, and they all knew about his call to Coughlin.

Slat talked for a few seconds, then handed the receiver back to Ski and said something quietly to him. Ski nodded and handed Slat a pitcher of beer. Slowly, he walked to the table, pulled his chair out, and sat down.

"Well?" Jenny and Dawn asked in unison.

"The Vatican called the archbishop and reported there had been a traffic accident while Tony Tattaglia was driving from the airport to the Vatican. Father Julius was killed."

Dawn and Jenny sat erect.

"They'll fax us a death certificate."

48

SLAT, DAWN, AND JENNY lounged at their table even now, hours after getting the phone call from the archbishop.

"I feel as if I've been beaten with a stick," Jenny moaned.

"You look like you've been beaten," Dawn told her. "I feel like my heart's been ripped out."

Both women had their feet up on adjacent chairs in the dimly lit tavern, and their eyes were closed.

"Sam Tyrone's and Ernie Pope's deaths end the old assassination case," Slat said. "Father Julius's death solves the mystery of the accomplice in the Merriman and altar-boy homicides. But I still find it hard to believe that Father Julius was capable of pedophilia and murder."

Jenny sat up straight. "Excuse me for saying this, but I find it hard to believe that a killer gets away in a plane we aren't allowed to stop, then he conveniently dies in an auto accident on the streets of Rome, on his way to Vatican City. So now the Church is spared embarrassment. I don't believe this shit went down."

"You can't tell the good guys from the bad guys by who goes to mass on Sunday," Dawn said without opening her eyes.

"If I weren't so damn tired, I'd offer to drive you two home before you fall asleep here," Slat said.

No one spoke. Eventually Jenny refilled their mugs with the dark beer. "I'm going to stay here all night," Jenny announced. "I have to let these flakes floating around my head settle down. Ski can clean up the place without disturbing me."

"Me, too," Slat tipped his mug of Augie Dark and gazed at the ceiling. He fixed his eyes on one of the blades of the slow-moving fan. His eyes followed it around and around and around. He began to relax. He wanted to sleep... maybe wake up in a hundred years, with a long, white beard.

"It's all too much to swallow," Jenny said. "I knew Ernie and Sam, and in a million years I'd never expect either of them of dishonesty and especially murder in cold blood."

"But it all fits," Slat mused. "Ernie and Sam had been taking the payoffs together. Sam was a threat, so Ernie killed him. Ernie wanted Lillie dead because she could implicate him in the old payoffs."

Dawn pulled another chair closer to her and stretched her legs across it. "And Ernie didn't have to worry about Mountain Top or Billy. They'd never tell they were involved in bribing police officers in the old days."

Slat thought about Elinor Pope. She was religious, and he was hopeful her faith would pull her through this tough time. He'd thought Ernie had to have been kind of religious, too; after all, he'd worked part- time for the archdiocese.

Suddenly Slat sat up straight. He had forgotten about the paychecks from the archdiocese found in Ernie's wallet. He was supposed to have given them to Elinor. He reached into his inside jacket pocket and pulled out the two checks he'd taken from Ernie's wallet.

He'd never taken the time to look carefully at them because of all the complications since Ernie was killed. The first check was from the Archdiocese of Milwaukee, for security services, for eight hundred dollars. The dates matched the same two-week pay period as Ernie's last two weeks on the police force. "That's funny," he mused. "Ernie was working full- time as a cop. However, he had to put in a lot of part-time work at the archdiocese to make eight hundred bucks. I wonder how he managed."

The second was a payroll check for four hundred dollars, from the Milwaukee Archdiocese Maintenance Fund. This check was for the same two-week period. Slat's brows came together in confusion. Twelve hundred dollars for a two-week period while Ernie was working at the police department. Slat doubted if the archdiocese paid more than eight dollars an hour, and at that rate Ernie would have had to work seventy-three hours in extra part-time work a week. He looked at the signature on the face of both checks. Both had been signed by the same person.

"Slat!"

Slat hadn't heard Ninkovich, the evidence technician, approach. The women awoke from their lethargy.

"I did a ballistics on the slugs from the weapon that killed Sam Tyrone," the evidence technician said. "It was the same weapon that killed those two gamblers twenty years ago."

"Ties that case up for sure," Jenny said.

Ninkovich passed an eight-by-eleven-inch manila envelope to Slat. The sergeant undid the clasp, and out slid an enlargement of the folded photograph from Ernie's wallet. As it came to rest on the tabletop, Slat immediately recognized the man sitting on the toilet and grabbing at the penis of the young boy.

"Ugh!" Dawn said.

Jenny leaned over Slat's shoulder at the blowup. "That looks kind a like....

"

"Excuse me a minute." Slat stuffed the enlargement and checks back in the envelope as he walked to the phone at the end of the bar and made a call. "Stan, sorry to bother you at home. Who tipped you about Father Julius going into the park with the second homicide victim?"

He listened, nodding, then hung the phone up and asked Ski for the local telephone directory. He flipped the pages, found the number he was looking for, and dialed it.

"Sister, this is Sergeant Sczlatski from the police department. Could you tell me the name of the priests at the parish in the late sixties and early seventies?" Again he listened intently. "Thank you, Sister. You've been very helpful."

"Let's go, ladies!" Slat called from the bar.

Dawn and Jenny jumped and ran to catch up to him on his way out the door. They hadn't fully situated themselves inside the vehicle before he was spinning his tires out of the parking lot.

As they raced toward Cousin's Center, Slat explained the two phone calls to them. The women sat in shocked silence.

After arriving at the building housing the archbishop's office, they hurried inside. It was late evening; but if Archbishop Coughlin wasn't in his office, Slat decided he'd go to the man's residence. Fortunately his office door was open, and a light shone from within. There was no one to stop them, so they walked right in.

The archbishop was on the telephone. His eyes narrowed angrily at the intrusion.

Slat pulled the picture from its envelope and held it under the archbishop's nose. Coughlin's jaw went slack, and all color drained from his face. He awkwardly concluded his telephone conversation and hung up the receiver. With shaking hands he took the photo from Slat, then sank back in his chair and stared at the blowup.

"God in heaven!" he whispered, his chest heaving.

"You know what this means, of course," Slat said. "You've kidnapped the wrong man. Father Daley pointed all of us toward Father Julius, but Father Julius was innocent."

Slat stopped. His head was racing. He could feel the pulse beats battering his eardrums. "It all fits now. In the seventies a cop, Ernie Pope, was assigned to watch for pedophiles in the library bathroom. Ernie must have taken this photo of Father Daley. Instead of arresting him, Ernie blackmailed Father Daley into providing a plush-paying job at the archdiocese."

The archbishop's eyes were veiled now, secretive.

Slat raised his voice. "It was lucky for Father Daley that Steve Merriman killed the only witness against him. Poor Jack Hamlin. But how very convenient for the Church. But two witnesses remained–Ernie Pope and this photograph."

"Oh, my God." Dawn gasped. "Father Daley was the priest at St. Mike's when I was a kid there!"

"Yeah," Slat said, "I just found that out tonight. I also learned tonight that Father Daley tipped the police about Father Julius going into the park with the second murder victim. When Father Julius's impersonator called me from St. Paul, he said that he had seen the victim on the day he was found dead in the park." Slat looked in Coughlin's eyes. "But my detectives never released that tip from Father Daley. If the impersonator knew about Father Julius going into the park with the boy, then he had to have gotten his information from Father Daley. Isn't that right, Your Reverend?"

The cleric said nothing, but his eyes were hard.

"I don't think Father Julius went to St. Paul at all," Slat continued, "in spite of what your office told the police. His running suit was missing too soon for him to have gotten back. "I've heard stories about how the Church takes care of its own problems, for the so-called good of the Church. But I'd say the Church was guilty of obstruction of justice, wouldn't you, ladies?"

Dawn and Jenny agreed emphatically.

The archbishop's color started to return as he regained his composure, but the man said nothing to defend himself or to dispute Slat's claims.

"Father Daley probably killed both boys by accident," Slat allowed. "And when he figured our investigation would lead to him, he decided to frame his friend. Father Daley wanted us to think Julius was guilty, but he didn't want us to apprehend an innocent man. He wanted Tony Tattaglia to nab him, and unfortunately Daley got his wish. Of course, Tony must work for the Vatican—that's where the jet was registered."

Slat leaned forward against the archbishop's desk. "I'll show pictures of Father Daley to Raymond Tee's landlord, whom the Church conveniently sent on a trip to Hawaii. I'll bet Mr. Marshall identifies Father Daley as Raymond Tee. I'll bet he used archdiocese money for his escapades in that apartment."

"Oh, my God! All at one time!" The archbishop wiped his forehead with a lace handkerchief.

Slat dropped into the overstuffed chair. "'All,' Your Reverend?"

"Yes. I was talking to the Vatican when you barged in. Father Daley also died as a result of that automobile accident."

Slat felt nauseated. He turned to the women, who stood wide- eyed and bewildered. Then he turned back to the archbishop.

"Yes," Coughlin said angrily. "Father Daley died an hour ago from internal injuries."

Slat took the photo of Father Daley and shook it at the archbishop. "Your Reverend," he said between his teeth. "I don't believe you or the Vatican. You initially reported Father Julius's death because you thought he was guilty of rape and murder. Now, learning otherwise, you conveniently change your . . . .

"

"Sergeant Sczlatski! How dare you! Your charges are preposterous!" The archbishop stood. "I'll be reporting your behavior to your mayor. Now if you'll excuse me. The death certificates and autopsy reports will be sent to you from Rome."

49

ON THE DRIVE BACK TO PULASKI, Slat's mind was in a fog from the confrontation with the archbishop, and his eyes ached from the glare of the street lights and car headlights. Jenny, exhausted, sat with her feet tucked under her and her left arm stretched along the back on the seat. She lay her cheek on her upper arm. Dawn was stretched out on the back seat, her head against an armrest as she stared at the car ceiling.

Jenny broke the long silence. "I don't think those priests are dead."

"I don't believe it, either," Dawn said.

"You think the city is going to allow us to fly to Rome and conduct an investigation?" Slat asked. "We'll get death certificates, and then we'll close the case. The only loose ends will be in our minds."

"If we can't believe an archbishop, then who can we believe?" Jenny asked. "We'd never believe another person. There are some people we just have to believe in."

Jenny swung her feet to the floor and placed her hand over Slat's, which was resting on the seat. He gripped her hand and glanced at her. Their eyes met in warmth, affection, and—*love?* he wondered. *Maybe, just maybe Jenny and I. . . .*

"There's a powerful sub world out there that we know nothing about," Dawn told them. "We're not part of it, but it runs us. A system opposes ours, yet works with it. Or some shit like that."

"Do you know what you're talking about?" Jenny asked, then laughed.

"No," Dawn admitted. "But next week we'll be up to our asses in more cases, and we'll forget about this one. I hope I can forget about a lot of things."

The radio broke their conversation. "Sergeant Sczlatski, meet Detective Osinski by the beaver pond in the park! Immediately!"

* * *

A low cloud cover hid the moon and plunged the park into darkness. Slat pulled his vehicle alongside four marked squads and a detective car.

"Looks like a used-car lot," Jenny remarked. She looked back at Dawn, who was still stretched across the back seat. "Come on, Partner."

"Yeah, all right." Reluctantly, with a groan, Dawn hauled herself out of the car. "I just want to go home to bed for a month."

The threesome walked through the spectacular kaleidoscope of whirling red, white, and blue squad lights, which reflected off squad chrome and swept over trees, leaves, grass, and night-blooming flowers. The grassy path took them to an asphalt sidewalk, which led through a clump of high bushes and small trees. As they walked the trail, fingers of colored light flashed through the trees and bushes. Ahead, on the other side of the pond, flashlight beams moved about in a disembodied array.

Slat led Jenny and Dawn from the sidewalk and onto the grass, to the other side of the pond. Distance dimmed the squad lights. Frogs and crickets sang out. Once around the pond, the detectives moved into a sparsely wooded area, where an immense oak towered over the adjacent trees.

A man sat with his spine pressed against the mighty bole. His head lolled onto his chest. Slat squinted. A Saturday night drunk? The officers surrounding the man backed away as Slat and the women approached. As he gained the clear perspective of close proximity, he felt his gorge rise. A rivulet of dried blood from a bullet hole traced the furrowed cheek of Chief Martin Turski. Beside him, Jenny gasped and staggered.

Stan came up beside them. "Suicide," he said quietly. "Maybe an hour ago. Damned shame."

"God!" Slat stared up at the moonless sky, then looked at Stan. Pain was written across his face. No iron mask tonight.

"Please! God! No!" Jenny grabbed Slat's arm.

Dawn loosed a wail of grief from deep within her, then flung herself to the grass beside the chief. "No!" she keened. "No! Not you! Not you, too!"

Slat and Jenny picked Dawn up from the ground. They both held her. "The motherfuckers beat him!" she cried. "They beat him! Pulaski beat him!"

"Okay," Jenny crooned, trying to soothe her friend.

Her face streaked with tears and pummeled by sadness, Dawn looked at the others. "We can still win. Can't we, Jenny? Slat? We can beat them! Can't we?"

Slat brought Dawn tight against his right shoulder. Jenny turned her back to the grisly scene as Slat embraced her with his left arm. *The chief had somebody,* Slat thought. *He had a wife. He couldn't have been lonely. How—?*

Slat looked into Jenny's eyes, and as she leaned against him for comfort, he knew he'd never be lonely again. He held her tighter and mouthed the words, " I love you, Jenny." Her eyes filled with tears, and she rested her cheek against him.

He looked to see Lieutenant Lovemore and some night-shift detectives hurrying up the path toward them.

Quickly, Jenny reached up and wiped the tears from the face of the man she loved.

50

SLAT DIDN'T LIKE HIS NEW OFFICE across the hall from the Detective Bureau. Nor was he crazy about wearing a suit and tie every day, but that order had come from the chief.

"Lieutenant Sczlatski," the soft voice in the intercom spoke. The chief ordered that all subordinates address their superiors by rank. "A Mr. Tattaglia is here without an appointment. He insists on seeing you."

Slat was shocked. He never imagined he'd see Tattaglia again. "That's all right, Maureen. Send him in."

"Yes, sir. Don't forget you have a meeting with the chief in twenty minutes."

Thirty seconds later the secretary directed Tony into Slat's office. Slat stood, jaw set firm, hands on hips, and eyes narrowed.

Neither spoke. Then Tony smiled. "Are you angry?"

"What purpose would that serve?" Slat asked. Actually, he felt no anger or any dislike. Tattaglia was surprisingly ingratiating, in fact. So the man beat him out on that investigation. *Maybe Tattaglia was the better man and deserved to win—and all that macho crap,* he thought. "Sit down. What's it been? Two months?"

The men sat down. "Actually closer to three. They've sent me to Chicago. Problem with a Catholic-newspaper editor. Thought I'd stop in here and say hello."

"A long trip just to say hello, Mr. Tattaglia. Sure you don't have some unfinished business here?"

"No, but I felt I owed you something. I wanted to let you know what happened—closure and all that."

Slat cracked a smile and let go of his tension. He sat on the edge of his desk and extended his hand for a handshake. "I guess there might be a couple of things we might talk about."

Tony looked around. "Can we get out of here? Cup of coffee, maybe?"

Slat hit the intercom button. "Maureen, tell the chief I had an emergency and can't make the meeting."

Slat and Tony slid into a rear booth in the no-smoking section at Mama's.

Tony picked up a small tabletop sign listing the daily specials. He chuckled. "What's an Italian restaurant doing serving kielbasa?"

"Mama has an international appreciation of good food," Slat explained. "Try it. My treat."

Tony winced. "Too early in the day for me. Thanks, though."

After Mama served them both coffee, Slat sat back and smiled. "Well, Tattaglia, my boss is going to be pissed because I didn't show up for a very important meeting about bullshit."

"Bullshit's the name of the game. You like your new job?"

"Nah. Too much paperwork. Not enough time for the street." Slat blew on the steaming mug. "But since I'm missing a meeting, I'd better come back to the office with something to show. Enough small talk, Tattaglia. You came to see me."

"I just wanted you to know that things righted themselves. You know, justice prevailed."

"Come off it. I know Father Julius and Father Daley didn't die." He snorted in derision. "The Church and its lies."

"No bullshit, Slat, really. The Church is having a lot of problems here in the States. If we hadn't intervened and if your law enforcement had worked, you'd have had an endless, costly trial and possibly even lost the indictment. The Church's way, there's no doubt that justice was served."

"What happened to them?" Slat asked.

"Julius is happy. He was thinking of leaving the priesthood to go into education when we picked him up. Now he's teaching philosophy at a university in Europe and has a new perspective on life. You did him an enormous service by discovering his innocence and reporting it to Archbishop Coughlin. Otherwise, John would not be enjoying such a fine assignment. Father Daley, however, is confined for life—not as in your legal system life, which means fourteen years—but for life at a secluded monastery in Italy. Again, thanks to you, the right man is in confinement and kept away from children. And at no cost to your taxpayers."

"You're saying the end justifies the means?"

"Think about it," Tony said.

They both did in silence for several moments while Mama refilled their coffee mugs.

"What about that lovely detective Dawn Mazurski?" Tony asked. "How's she doing?"

"Sadly, she's in the hospital. I'm not sure whether or not she'll be able to return to work. Her sister, Satin, is a tough lawyer and is suing the city for a disability pension."

"That's tough. I'm sorry to hear that. Injured on the job?"

"Yeah. Mortally wounded, you could say."

Tony shook his head. "I thought I'd see Archie Dunn while I was in town. But his phone number's been disconnected, and I couldn't track him down at Poole."

Slat smiled. "No, Dunn had a problem and was let go."

"But Dunn was the parish problem solver." He held up his mug for a refill.

"Not this time. He figured he'd be getting the police chief's job after Turski died." Mama brought more coffee. "We all dreaded that. He had the vote of all five commissioners. The only other applicant was Leon Lovemore, who was my lieutenant."

"So what happened?"

"The strangest damned thing." Slat chuckled. "Some bird-watchers were at the cemetery one morning, snapping photos of birds, and one of them captured our illustrious alderman pissing on his father's grave."

"No!" Tony barked a laugh.

"It's the truth. A reporter named Cheri Duncan heard about it and tracked down the bird-watchers. She plastered the photo on the front page of our *Pulaski Press* —funny, we've always called it a piss rag—and Dunn was all washed up. He left town in the dead of night. No one knows where he is."

"So Lovemore was appointed?"

"Yep. All five votes. He's a pain in the ass, but we manage."

Tony brought up his mug, then set it down again after it got halfway to his mouth. Slat turned in the booth and looked behind him to see Jenny walking through the doorway and to their booth.

Tony tried to stand, but the table and booth seating prevented it.

"Remember this guy?" Slat asked, making room for her.

Her eyes narrowed. "You! The man I would most like to kick in the balls."

"Ow, that hurt," Tony said, dropping his hands to his lap. "How've you been?"

Jenny didn't respond.

"She's a detective sergeant now. Got my old job."

"Congratulations," Tony said.

"And we're getting married in six weeks."

"Again, my congratulations." After a moment of uncomfortable silence, he stood. "I really must be going. Maybe I'll see you again someday."

"Take care, guy." Slat responded to Tony's hand.

"I wish you all the best," Tony said to Jenny, but she didn't extend her hand.

"By the way, lover boy," she said. "That summer camp? You couldn't swim worth a shit, either."

THE END

About the Author

Author Bill Redding knows the territory.

Redding spent 31 years in law enforcement, 20 years with the Evanston Il, Police Dept. serving in all divisions. He retired from that department over ethical differences.

Next he became Chief of Police of Belvedere Illinois. After five years working with one of the most backward departments in Illinois, he was asked to leave because of a drug investigation involving a public official.

After the Belvedere fiasco, he became Chief of Police in South Milwaukee, Wisconsin. He left after five years because of illegal gambling issues with the Archdiocese of Milwaukee.

After those trying years he says, "I finally found solace in my family, the only place where I could find honesty."

Bill Redding now lives with his wife Ann in Florida.

CPSIA information can be obtained at www.ICGtesting.com
235301LV00001B/188/P

9 781600 191022